DESPERATE MEASURES

For Yvonne Bice

Thanks for reading my Book

Michael Heebe

DESPERATE MEASURES

A STORY OF
BETRAYAL,
TREACHERY &
ADVENTURE

MICHAEL HEEB

To order additional copies of this book, contact:
Xlibris Corporation
1-888-795-4274
www.Xlibris.com
Orders@Xlibris.com
68741

ACKNOWLEDGMENT

The authors of most literary works have received assistance from family members and friends. This novel is no exception and I want to thank those who provided the encouragement and critical reviews that made *Desperate Measures* possible. First, and most important, I want to thank my wife Karen for her long-term dedication and continuing commitment to the project. Early on, my brother Ferdinand and his wife Joanne and my good friend Jody Delzell gave critical readings and insightful comments that helped me shape the story. I thank Sandra Birnhak for her guidance through the world of publishing and Rachael and Amanda Plattner, and Mary Fisher Design for their artistic contributions.

Michael Heeb

INTRODUCTION

Desperation can force you to take chances. Dangerous, reckless, life-threatening chances that could destroy you. Chances you wouldn't take if you had any alternative. Or, maybe, if you are properly prepared, and have a little luck, they could save you. But whatever the outcome, committing to take such chances can give you the courage to challenge the dangers you face. This is the lesson Annaliese is about to learn.

CHAPTER 1

"Open the door, Annaliese! Open the goddamn door, or I'll break it down."

She knew if he had to break it down her situation would be worse. But she hesitated—the banging and yelling got louder. "Open the goddamn door," he yelled with an increasingly angry tone.

It was Sunday night, and Phillip had been drinking all afternoon. He had seemed preoccupied. In his drunken state, he would be angry either way, so she opened the bathroom door and backed away.

"Please, Phillip, you're drunk. Don't hurt me."

He grabbed her by the hair on the back of her head and dragged her into the bedroom. Wearing only a bra and panties, Annaliese struggled to get her footing while holding his arm with one hand and hitting him with the other. Trying to get loose, she was yelling, "Let go, you're hurting me." But Phillip spun her around and backhanded her hard across the face, shouting, "You dumb bitch, put the goddamn shirts back!" She could taste the blood in her mouth and feel the sting on her cheek but wouldn't quit struggling, a defiant trait that had incited Phillip to greater violence in the past. As he held her by the back of her neck and pushed her toward the shirts, she saw her blood dripping onto his shirts.

Phillip was a fastidious dresser and had carefully laid out several shirts on the dresser in order to select one for an important morning board meeting. Needing to get into the dresser, she had moved his shirts to the bed. And now she was dripping blood on them.

"Holy shit, Annaliese," he screamed with his eyes bulging, "you've got blood on my fucking shirts!" He yanked her back from the bed.

"Get away! You're hurting me!"

Swinging wildly, she landed a solid punch to Phillip's throat. He stepped back wheezing, trying to breathe.

"You stupid bitch!" He grabbed her shoulder, spun her around, and hit her hard with a full fist to the left side of her face. She could hear the sound of his fist on her face as loud as she could feel it. It was a muffled thud, like hitting a hollow log with a sledgehammer. Phillip recoiled in pain. His fist chipped two of her teeth, and they sliced into his knuckles. Annaliese fell backward, moaning a long, low visceral sound as she saw the light dimming around her. The force of the blow catapulted her across the bed. She bounced upward—naked legs in the air, arms flailing—and landed on the floor on her head and shoulders with the full impact of her 170-pound body.

Phillip was surprised at how hard he had hit her. Annaliese was a big woman, almost six feet tall, and although of slight frame, she had gained considerable weight in the last several years, which made her look heavier than she actually was. But Phillip was bigger and stronger. He was six feet, four inches tall, and worked out frequently at the gym in his office building.

In the past, when Phillip lost his temper, he tried to avoid hitting Annaliese in the face. But not always. Instead, he punched her in the body or threw her down and kicked her. Given his stature in the community, he didn't want his wife to appear in public looking bruised. But this night his rage was uncontrollable. As drunk as he was, he realized he had crossed a line. His patience had grown shorter, and he no longer cared how hard he hit her. She just couldn't seem to do things the way he wanted, and he was going to have to do something drastic to fix the problem for good.

Annaliese was sprawled on the floor in a foggy state of half consciousness with blood flowing from her eyebrow and nose, a split on the side of her mouth, and a long gash on her left cheek. Dazed, she slowly opened her eyes to see the lamps and walls were pink and spinning in a slow psychedelic whirl. She squinted hard to squeeze the blood out of her eyes. Managing to sit up and lie back against the bedside table, she accidentally knocked the lamp over. Through the buzz in her ears and the throbbing, hammerlike pounding in her head, she was crying and lowly gurgling, "Oh, Joey, how do I handle this? How do I get my gun? What do I do?"

Phillip couldn't hear her gurgling because he was kicking her, over and over, and yelling, "You pig, you bitch, you're going to learn who's in charge of this goddamn house. I set the goddamn rules, and you are damn well going to do as I say, or else! Do you understand?" He turned, walked into the bathroom, yanked a towel off the rack, and threw it at her yelling, "Clean up the goddamn mess you're making on the floor."

As he threw the towel, he could see blood on it. His hand was bleeding. His knuckles were cut where they hit her teeth. "Damn it, Annaliese, look what you've done to my hand. I have important meetings tomorrow. This shit is going to stop. I'm not going to put up with this anymore."

With her head in a dizzy fog and her eyesight blurry, Annaliese sat on the edge of the bed to regain her balance. Blood dripped down her cheek, onto her bra and panties, and then the light-colored bedspread. Phillip came out of the bathroom yelling, "Get off the goddamn bed. You're getting blood on the covers. Dammit, can't you do anything right? I've had enough of this shit."

Then he kicked the bedroom door open and stormed off shaking his head and muttering he was going to fix the problem once and for all.

CHAPTER 2

It was Monday morning, and Phillip had left early to go into the city. Their home was about four miles southeast of tony Doylestown, in Bucks County, about an hour's drive to his office in downtown Philadelphia. He had recently been appointed executive vice president of Kuefer & Bach Investments, Inc., one of the largest investment firms in the East, and he had to prepare for his Monday morning executive board meeting.

Anna (only her aunt and husband called her by her full name, Annaliese) pretended to be sleeping to avoid contact with him. She had a terrible night, tossing and turning while trying to hold an ice bag to her face. When she heard him leave, she sat up and dragged herself to the bathroom, feeling deep pain in her left cheek and ribs. It was not an unusual feeling. Anna had felt the wrath of his anger many times but not quite like last night. She felt sure he had broken several of her ribs, but she could still breathe. In the past, no matter how badly hurt she was, she tried to avoid doctors who were bound to ask questions. And this morning would be the same.

What Anna saw in the mirror frightened her. Her jaw was puffed out with a wide reddish brown area where Phillip had hit her the hardest. Black-and-blue areas also formed around her cheeks, ears, and nose. Her eyes were sunken and bloody red. The broad dark lump on her forehead had a bluish tinge that caused her eyebrows to protrude outward and downward, giving her what she thought was a brutish look. But above all, she now had two chipped teeth that would ruin her smile. Not that she smiled much anymore.

Looking at her swollen, puffy face and the split on the side of her mouth, she agonized as she thought how pretty she used to be when she married Phillip six years ago. It was a storybook wedding to a handsome, successful executive. She was tall and lithesome, with long almost-blond hair, blue eyes, and high cheekbones. But, at twenty-four, Anna was overweight, had a battered body, and now a disfigured face that made her look much older. Several years ago, distraught over Phillip's abuse, she cut her hair short. She took some pleasure when he threw a fit. It made her feel that in some small way he still loved her. But as her self-esteem crumpled under Phillip's dictatorial tirades, she lost interest in her appearance. That was just another thing in the long list of things that irritated him.

Anna stood looking in the bathroom mirror for a long time, no tears, no emotion. Phillip's short temper and physical abuse had grown worse over the several years since her aunt had died. It had become impossible to live with him. She had to do something before he killed her. She was certain he was going to do it. He had said so. She intended to shoot him the next time he hit her, but last night she couldn't get to her gun in the closet. If she left it somewhere easily accessible, Phillip might find it and use it to kill her. Clearly, she needed another plan. Perhaps she should just shoot him when he came home. Maybe she should wait until he walked into the bedroom. But whatever she was going to do, it had to be soon. She needed to talk to Joey right away. He would know what to do.

Anna continued to gaze into the mirror, gently dabbing a wet washcloth on the streaks of blood around her nose and mouth, while trying to formulate a plan. She wanted to get away but was terrified with the prospect of trying to live alone, without money or a job. She felt trapped. She had no college degree, no job training, had never held a job, and didn't know how she could survive. She read a lot of books, but her only real training after high school was at the Cobbs Creek Culinary Institute. When they first married, Phillip encouraged her to take courses there because he thought it would be helpful when he entertained his business clients. And, indeed, she graduated as a gourmet cook.

A year ago, after a particularly nasty and violent night, Anna became hysterically distraught. Phillip had grabbed her by the back of the neck, and in her struggle to break loose, she hit him in the face with her elbow. She ran upstairs to get away, but he caught her, beat her, and threw her down the stairs. The next day, in a fit of desperation, she drove her silver blue Mercedes coupe out into the country with the intent to find a cliff and drive off it. That would really upset Phillip, she thought. Not over her, but over the car he had bought her several months earlier to make up for hurting her so badly she had to go to the emergency room. But Anna's plan changed when she saw a gun shop and decided to buy a gun to defend herself the next time Phillip tried to hurt her. That was when she met Joey.

Joey had a small gun shop in an old stand-alone building pressed against the side of a high cliff about twenty miles west of Philadelphia. When she saw his weather-beaten sign, she stopped. Since then, Joey had been teaching her how to shoot, how to handle different guns, and how to protect herself. She was a good student, and Joey had said she was gifted with superb eye-hand coordination.

Last night's violence was so damaging that Anna had applied as much makeup as possible to cover her wounds. She knew she looked overly made up and a bit garish with the heavy red lipstick, eye shadow, and pancake base, but she had no choice. She wanted to see Joey and didn't want him to overreact. She just wanted to look presentable and searched her closet for an appropriate outfit. Anna had a lot of nice things, mostly because Phillip often felt guilty after beating her up and would buy her something special. She selected dark charcoal gray slacks and a light gray tailored shirt.

Anna retrieved her snub-nosed .38 caliber, scandium-frame Smith & Wesson revolver from her hiding place in the closet, flipped open the cylinder, and checked to be sure it had chambered cartridges. She slipped the revolver, a box of range ammo, and two small illustrated books on guns into a large open-top black bag. The books fit nicely on the side and helped the bag maintain its shape. Anna liked this particular bag. It was rather plain, and it looked like an oversized purse. It had both short loop handles and a shoulder strap that carried the weight of the gun and extra ammunition. She could also carry her small black purse with the makeup kit in it.

As she painfully, slowly descended the stairs, Anna glanced out the high front windows. Her attention had been drawn to a black SUV parked on the road across the street from the stone wall in front of the property. It was a long way off and partially blocked from view by a tall pear tree, but she saw the silhouettes of two men in it. She had noticed the vehicle from her upstairs bedroom window and thought it was out of place, but then she dismissed the thought as she focused on selecting her outfit.

Now suddenly, she had the uncomfortable feeling the men were probably watching for her. *Why else would they be there? The houses in the area are situated on five- to ten-acre lots and not very close together. They are really being obvious! And Phillip said he was going to "fix this once and for all."*

Anna had been followed several times in the past few months, but the men had tried to remain inconspicuous. She assumed they were private detectives Phillip had hired to watch her. She eluded them by taking circuitous routes to where she was going, especially when she was going to see Joey. If she wasn't able to shake them, she went shopping somewhere until they left. But the men in the SUV out front were not being stealthy or secretive. They were just sitting there, boldly and in plain sight.

She had left her car parked in the circular drive in front of the house. It was one of the things she had done that irritated Phillip last night. He had told her to always use the garage. "That's what our garage is for," he had admonished her several times. When she was ready to leave, she stood on the front porch and briefly looked directly at the SUV, but nothing happened. She drove out of her driveway, watching for the SUV. If it followed her, she would drive through some of the congested neighborhoods in Philadelphia before heading west to the gun shop. Since Joey's place was in the country and there was little traffic, it would be difficult to lose someone once she left the city.

CHAPTER 3

Anna left the residential streets on the outskirts of Doylestown and turned onto York Road when she looked in her rearview mirror and saw the black SUV several cars behind her.

Oh my god! They are *following me! And they're not being subtle about it.*

She drove several blocks and sped up to pass a few cars. The black SUV did the same. She decided to test the situation. She turned onto Almshouse Road at Jamison and stomped on the accelerator. It was not a main road but not strictly residential either. She sped dangerously through the curves, desperate to gain distance on the SUV, but the SUV followed. She made a complete loop and headed back toward Doylestown where she had started. The black SUV was still there. It was a long way back, but it was still within sight. There was no longer any doubt the men in the SUV were following her, and they were good. Very good.

How come I can't get away from them? It's like they're following a beacon.

When Anna passed the interstate, she remembered Phillip's firm had memberships at the Huntingdon Valley Country Club. *There are a lot of intersecting roads on the other side of the club. Maybe I can lose them there. I'll drive through the club area and then into the city. That should do it.*

As Anna entered the north side of Philadelphia, she thought she lost the pursuers. But after a few blocks, she was frustrated to see they were still behind her. Farther back but still there. It was then she remembered her car was an unusual silver blue color and would stand out, even in heavy traffic. When the sun shone on it, the car reflected the light like a blue diamond. That was what she liked about it. But now, she realized, it was the beacon the men in the SUV were following. There was no way she could lose them. *Drive carefully, but don't go to Joey's place. I'll just go downtown and mingle with traffic and try to lose them. If I can't lose them, I'll go shopping. What if they really are trying to kill me? I'd better stay in public places.*

Driving in the eastern more industrial part of town, Anna found herself in an older inner-city business area near the waterfront. The SUV was still several blocks behind her. As she drove over a hill on a heavily trafficked road, she saw a block of small businesses and a women's dress shop on the right side of the road. Cars were parked on the street but not on that block. The block was marked for loading zones and had a bus stop with a bench just past the dress shop.

The dress shop will give me a good reason to be down here. From inside I can get a view of the street to see if they are still following me.

With the SUV out of sight beyond the hill, she quickly turned right at the next street. There was a small two-story parking garage behind the shops. Anna drove in, parked in the middle of the lower level, and watched for the two men who were following her. She hoped she had lost them. Cautiously, she walked around the corner while keeping an eye out for the black SUV. She could smell the damp salt air blowing in from the harbor and hear the mechanical hum of a busy industrial area. This was definitely an older neighborhood and she wondered why someone would open a women's shop in such a run-down area.

The shop was not particularly tidy and needed paint. Dressing rooms were off to the right side in the rear of the shop and the clothing racks were in the middle of the store. Anna could see a lot of the clothes were copies of high-end dresses and blouses. The counter had a thick cracked glass top, an old-style cash register, and was located at the very rear of the shop. It was definitely an older store. The clothing was permeated with the sweet smell of cheap perfume.

Anna picked out a shirt and casually walked to the front window, as if to inspect it in better light. Her intent was to see if the men were still following her. She looked up and down the street but couldn't really see very well. As an architectural feature, the front of the store was set back about four feet from the sidewalk with a brick wall on either side. The wall limited her view of the sidewalk to the right, and clothing displays were on a platform in front of the window. She stood looking intensely out the window and was startled when the clerk, a small Hispanic woman, approached her and in broken English said, "Good shirt. Like to try on?" Anna turned to say yes and saw the clerk's expression change when she saw her battered face.

"I just had surgery," Anna apologized. "I hope it's not too noticeable."

The clerk looked confused, and Anna pointed to her face and said, "Doctor! Doctor!"

"Oh yes, missus. You look very nice. The trying-on rooms, over here," and she began walking toward the dressing rooms.

Anna followed and tried on the shirt. She needed to spend some time in the store to determine if the coast was clear for her to leave. The shirt wasn't what she would normally wear, but it had possibilities. She might use it at Joey's shooting range. She decided to buy it and put back on her own light gray shirt.

CHAPTER 4

Anna heard the tinkle of the entrance doorbell and knew someone had just entered the store. Terrified, she pulled back the curtain slightly to see if it were the men following her. A heavyset woman with short dirty blond hair had came in. She was wearing an outfit similar to Anna's, a light gray blouse and dark-colored slacks.

The woman hurried to the counter. She also had a black open-top bag with a strap similar to but not exactly the same as Anna's. Anna's bag had small silver metal rings where the strap was attached to the bag. The woman scanned the store to see if there were other customers. Then she put her bag on the floor in front of the counter and asked the clerk if she could use the phone. She put her cell phone on the counter and explained that the battery had just died. She desperately needed to make a call. At first, the clerk had difficulty understanding what she wanted.

"Missus, no use phone," the clerk said while waving her hand across the older style rotary-dial phone.

"I'll pay for the call! And besides, it's local," the woman pleaded as she waved a ten-dollar bill at the clerk.

Then the woman suddenly turned and walked quickly to the door leaving her bag on the floor in front of the counter. Because the store was set back a few feet from the other stores, she had to open the door and step out into the entranceway to see around the brick wall to the right. As she was opening the door, Anna came out of the trying-on room and went to the counter. While focusing on the woman, Anna put the new shirt on the counter, inadvertently covering the cell phone, and placed her bag on the floor. The woman carefully peeked around the wall and scanned the sidewalk. She jumped back from the doorway and walked briskly toward the counter saying, "Oh shit. Oh shit." She was almost halfway to the counter when she looked up and saw Anna. She stopped dead in her tracks. She was visibly surprised and looked Anna up and down for a moment.

Then without taking her eyes off Anna, the woman abruptly grabbed her bag, threw the strap over her head and shoulder, and hurried out of the shop.

Anna looked down and panicked. In her haste, the woman had grabbed the wrong bag. Anna's gun and identification were in the bag. As the door was swinging back, she yelled to the woman to stop, but the woman was already out the door.

Anna grabbed the woman's bag and ran to the door. She could see the woman at the curb, readying to cross the street. While still in the entranceway, Anna yelled to the woman, "Hey, lady, you have the wrong bag. You have my bag," while holding up the other woman's bag.

The woman turned to see Anna standing in the doorway. She looked at the bag Anna was holding then down at the one strapped around her chest. She glanced back at Anna. Then she scanned the sidewalk toward the intersection. Her mouth opened. She looked terrified.

"Oh fuck," the woman yelled as she turned and sprinted into the street, just as a truck was coming down the hill at high speed. The hinge assembly of the door on the square-cab truck caught the woman under the left jaw and slammed her body with the cargo box behind the door. Her body was catapulted forward with her facial skin hanging on the hinge as the truck continued down the hill. Her body hit the sharp edges of the metal post of a large traffic sign, split partially in two, pivoted around the pole, continued forward, and hit the corner edge of the bus-stop bench. Her body came to rest about twenty-five feet down the sidewalk with her split torso and legs positioned in the same direction as her head. Blood was splattered on the bench, all over the sidewalk, and even on the brick walls of the stores.

The ghastly sight of the woman's mutilated body, with pools of blood draining over the curb, caused Anna to freeze. She felt faint. She thought she was going to fall. She pulled back into the store's entranceway to get her breath.

Anna leaned her shoulder on the wall and scanned the sidewalk. What she saw next caused her head to pound and the arteries in her neck to throb. Two men in suits were next to the body. One was squatting, rifling the woman's black bag. After only a few seconds of looking, with bystanders rushing toward the body, they backed away, quickly, toward the intersection, turned the corner, and disappeared.

Anna's mind was racing. She felt certain the two men were the same ones who had been following her. But then she wondered, *Why did that woman seem so terrified? Did she think those men were after her? They were the same ones who were following me, weren't they? Oh my god, it's all my fault. Why did I yell at her? What have I done?*

People were running to the scene from all directions and yelling to one another, "Did you see that? Oh Jesus! Damn, I can't believe it!" One woman was screaming uncontrollably. The gathering crowd was intently focused on the grisly scene. No one noticed Anna walking away, up the hill and around the corner. She walked slowly, aimlessly, for hours trying desperately to make sense out of what had happened but was unable to think clearly. The constant throbbing in her head kept her from thinking logically.

It was just past noon when she passed in front of a small electronics store and heard her name. She stopped and, in disbelief, watched pictures of the accident scene flickering on a large flat screen TV near the door. *Did I hear that right? Did the announcer say my name? Annaliese Mueller?* She entered the store and heard the announcer say her name again.

The news anchor said a horrible accident had claimed the life of Annaliese Mueller who lived near Doylestown in Bucks County. They showed Phillip at the scene and were speculating on why his wife stepped out onto the street in front of a passing truck. Bystanders claimed to have seen the entire accident and were describing it to the police. The camera focused on the truck driver who was terrified and claiming it wasn't his fault. He said it happened so fast. After hearing a thud, he looked in his rearview mirror and saw the body on the sidewalk. A woman interviewed at the scene said, "The traffic on this street is terrible. There should be a crosswalk or traffic light, but the city doesn't care about us in this part of town."

How did Phillip get there so quickly? Anna wondered. She left the electronics store, still in a daze. The pressure in her head and the constant thumping were worse.

I'm dead? Phillip identified the body as mine? They think I'm dead? She was totally confused at this turn of events. She stopped to rest at a small run-down park between two tall buildings. It had been the result of one of those minipark efforts local residents had built with government grants to upgrade the character of the neighborhood. As it often happens, the neighborhood organizers had only enough government funding to build it and no will to maintain it. Without a continuing flow of government money, their interest waned and maintenance declined.

Trash was strewn about the grounds of the small park and on the two dirty park benches. Instinctively, Anna brushed the food wrappers away and sat down, staring at the ground and thinking. She couldn't stop the words she heard on TV from ringing in her head. *The guy on TV said I'm dead! If I'm dead, then who am I? What do I do now?*

It was almost two o'clock, and for the first time Anna looked in the woman's bag. The bag she had just lost was approximately the same size and heavy, but this bag, she realized, was heavier. She pulled the handles apart and was startled to see a .40-caliber semiautomatic handgun and a box of cartridges. She immediately recognized it as a Glock. It was the 23C, a short-slide vented model with reduced recoil. It was light and perfect for women. This was the gun she liked best, but Joey thought a snub-nosed revolver was a better self-defense gun for her. It wasn't very accurate at a distance, but at close range in a fast-moving emergency, the snub-nosed revolver would be better. She wouldn't have to chamber a round, and the short barrel made it easier to maneuver. Almost foolproof.

Anna had used many types of pistols from various manufacturers at Joey's range and had become an expert marksman with all of them. Joey had said she was a natural sharpshooter, better than anyone he had ever seen. She had thought he was just trying to make her feel good, but again, her targets showed extraordinary proficiency.

She pressed the clip release, and it slid out smoothly. It was heavy, and she could see the fifteen-cartridge mark was filled. She pulled the slide back slightly to reveal a round in the chamber.

Sixteen rounds total. The woman must have really known her guns to have picked this one. The fact she had a fifteen-round magazine indicated to Anna the woman was dead serious about defending herself, probably from more than one person.

But who was this woman, she wondered, as she looked further into the bag. Under the gun were the woman's wallet, a cloth cosmetics pack, and a blue scarf. Standing on edge, to one side of the bag were two black books. They looked like accounting ledgers, but Anna was more interested in the wallet. The wallet showed the woman to be Tatianna M. Wolinski. It contained, at a quick glance, about twenty bills, most of them hundreds. There were credit cards and several IDs. She studied the woman's photo on the driver's license and wondered, *Could I pass as this person? She had short blondish hair.*

Anna felt terribly confused. Her head was still buzzing with the thought that the woman's death was all her fault. Mixed with her intense feelings of guilt was her growing anger over Phillip sending thugs after her. The bruises on her face where Phillip had hit her last night began to burn, and she cried. *Phillip saw the body and said it was me. Why did he do that?*

Anna's mouth felt dry. She was becoming thirsty. In her hurry to see Joey, she skipped breakfast and didn't have lunch. She'd had nothing to drink all day. She walked up a street dotted with small businesses, looking for a store. It was a particularly seedy business district. She was lost, but it didn't seem to matter. Her increasingly pervasive thought was to find something to drink.

Trudging up a slight hill was a bit tiring for Anna after walking all morning. As she reached the middle of the block, she heard a car screeching to a stop as it crossed the intersection behind her. The engine revved up, tires spun, blue smoke puffed out from under the tires, and the car backed up. Again there was screeching, but this time the car was accelerating forward, turning up her street, and approaching fast.

As the car got closer, she saw two men in it, and the front passenger-side window was opening. As the window lowered, a semiautomatic handgun barrel began to protrude. Within seconds she recognized it as a gun, and it was pointing at her. They were going to shoot her. Instinctively, she remembered her training and dropped to the sidewalk to lie as flat as she could, just like Joey had taught her. As she hit the sidewalk, she could hear the car going by and the loud report of rapid gunfire. Four deafening shots in succession. She heard the pings of the bullets hitting the brick wall and sidewalk and felt the chips of brick and concrete striking her legs and face. Joey had lectured her to always present the smallest possible profile if someone was shooting at her. She and Joey had played many shooting games at his range where she routinely had to protect herself at the sight of a gun pointed her way—but this was not a game.

The car passed, and the driver slammed on the brakes about one hundred feet away. Anna could see the smoke from the tires skidding across the pavement as the car screeched to a stop. She could hear the driver shouting, "You didn't get her, shithead. You didn't get her. Maroon is going to be fucking pissed off." The shooter yelled back at the driver, "Back up goddamn it! Back up and I'll get her!" Anna rose to one knee and pulled the Glock out of the bag. Bracing the gun with her left hand, she took aim at the shooter. She didn't have to check for the safety and knew the gun was already chambered. She only had to take aim and fire.

The car was backing up fast, and the shooter was leaning out the window trying to get her in his line of sight. As he turned backward to aim, Anna fired. Two separate shots. Quick but each well aimed, just as she had so often done at Joey's place. The shooter fell back into the car, and his gun dropped to the street, spinning around on the asphalt and sliding to the curb. The car continued approaching her, and the driver was swinging his arm over the seat to fire at her through the right rear window. But Anna fired first. Four rounds in sets of two. The glass shattered, some of it hitting the street. Some of it ricocheted off a nearby-parked car. The car slowed but continued its backward travel. As it rolled past her, she stood up to see the driver's head leaning against the driver's side window with blood splattered across it and the windshield. She stood frozen, watching the car slowly roll backward down the hill, glancing off a parked car, crossing the intersection, and continuing down the next block.

Anna didn't wait to see where the car stopped. She ran over to the curb and picked up the gun the shooter had dropped. With her hands shaking, she put both guns in her bag and quickly walked up the street and around the corner. She was in a total stupor. She felt sweat dripping down her neck and wiped it with the blue scarf in the bag only to discover the bright red color of blood.

Have I been shot and not know it? Anna was shaking as she wiped the side of her face again and realized her forehead, ear, and neck were bleeding but not too much. The chips of concrete must have nicked her. She thought it seemed just like one of Joey's special training sessions, except this time it wasn't, and she was bleeding.

Anna walked a short distance and stopped again, for only a moment, suddenly realizing, *Someone wants to kill Tatianna Wolinski, and they must think I'm her. Oh my god, I'm a little taller but have short blond hair, and I'm wearing a similar outfit. That's why those gunmen were trying to kill me! I've got to get out of these clothes.*

CHAPTER 5

As she continued walking, Anna spotted an army surplus store several blocks away. When she was about a half block from the store she almost panicked. A tall man with a mustache, a badge, and a rifle was standing in the shadows next to the door and looking in her direction. His left foot rested on a small wooden barrel and the rifle was lying across his left knee. She stopped dead in her tracks and stared intently for just a moment before realizing the man was a mannequin and the rifle a prop. She was shaking and breathing heavily.

Oh, god, I have to get a grip on myself and act naturally. But what kind of demented store owner would put that kind of thing outside a store. She stopped just inside the open door. It was dark and had the heavy, musty smell of canvas and old leather. Having come from the bright sunlight outside, her eyes had not yet adjusted to the darkness inside. As her eyes slowly accommodated to the dim light, she could see the aisles were close together with clothing stacked high and in disarray on dark wooden tables. Military uniforms and helmets were hanging from wires strung across the room. The floor had a mixture of dust and dirt around the edges of the tables as if it had been moved there by foot traffic.

A deep voice to her left said, "Come on in, missus." She turned and had to squint to see the clerk, a tall thin man with thick glasses and an unkempt beard. He was standing behind a counter display of knives and swords. Bending forward and leaning on the counter, the clerk said, "Guns are in the back." He gave her a small smile, lifted his arm, and pointed to the far rear corner of the shop, anticipating that was why she was there.

"Which aisle has the jeans?"

"Second aisle," the clerk said, pointing to his left.

The merchandise was anything but neat, but Anna soon found stacks of rumpled denim shirts and jeans. She picked through them until she found sizes she thought would fit. She changed into her new denim outfit in a small closet with a long mirror on one side. It had more dust on the floor than the aisles in the store and a dirty curtain that was her only means of privacy. Her new clothing smelled like an old canvas tarpaulin. After checking her new image in the mirror, she stuffed her slacks and shirt into Tatianna's bag, paid the clerk with some of the money in Tatianna's wallet, nodded to the clerk, and left the store.

About a block from the surplus store, Anna turned the corner and spotted a city trash barrel. It was full and covered with a layer of old newspapers. Some of the newspapers had spilled over onto the ground, and the breeze was blowing them around. Surveying the area around her, she saw only a heavyset young woman with disheveled dirty blond hair across the street looking in a store window. The woman was carrying a large black bag, similar to reusable grocery bags, stuffed with her belongings. With no one else in sight, Anna quickly lifted some of the newspapers and stuffed her slacks and shirt under them while still looking all around. She then began to walk toward an industrial neighborhood that appeared to be clear of pedestrians.

The two thugs who had tried to kill her had left her terrified. She walked slowly on the left side of the street thinking intensely about what to do. She stopped to wipe the tears running down her cheeks. She was scared and felt all alone. *Stop crying! I've got to get a grip on myself! This is no time to break down! Joey would expect more of me, but how would he handle this mess?*

She decided to cross the street and use the other sidewalk that was in the shade of a long building. When she glanced back down the street, looking for traffic, she saw the woman with the black bag walking in her direction wearing her shirt. *Oh no*, she thought. *I didn't think she saw me. She must have been watching my reflection in the store window.*

No sooner had Anna finished her thought than a tan-colored sedan slowly turned the corner and stopped. After a moment, it began to move forward again but slowly. It was a plain-looking car like the ones the police used. It had fat black tires and downscale wheels. She immediately thought the police must be searching the area neighborhoods looking for whoever shot the two thugs. She remembered Joey lecturing her if she was ever in a suspicious situation to just act naturally. Be as curious as anyone else. Don't back away.

Walking casually, she continued to cross the street, hoping to get around the next corner without arousing suspicion. She took only short glances to see if the tan car was indeed a cop car. The car proceeded forward slowly and pulled alongside the woman who looked at the men in the car and then turned and ran. A man in a suit jumped out of the passenger's side of the car waving a badge and tried to catch the woman. Then the driver, who was talking on a cell phone, snapped the phone shut and joined him. They were yelling for the woman to stop. Anna, now on the sidewalk on the other side of the street, about half a block away, froze and watched what was happening. The woman was surprisingly agile. She yelled back at the men to get away from her as she backtracked on the sidewalk toward an alley between two tall buildings while holding her bag close to her chest.

The first man out of the car was pointing a gun at the woman while calling her a bitch and telling her to stop. Suddenly there were two shots. The sound of the gunshots echoed between the buildings up and down the street. Anna watched in horror as the woman collapsed in an ungainly movement and hit the sidewalk face first with a thud.

Anna backed up against the wall of the building, hoping to get out of sight. There were no doorways or windows along the wall. Judging from the mechanical noise emanating from the other side of the wall, the building was some sort of manufacturing shop, and this was the back of the building. There was no place to hide. The corner of the building and the next side street were about 150 feet away.

As the shooter turned the limp body of the woman over, his partner noticed Anna's movement down the street. He stood up straight and stared at her. She could hear the shooter, who was now on one knee, cursing that the woman couldn't be Tatianna. He was saying, "What the fuck! This can't be her. There's nothing but junk in this bag. Why the hell did she run like that?"

His partner grabbed him by the shoulder and yelled, "Look down the street. Look at that woman, she has a black bag like the accountant is supposed to be carrying."

"Holy shit, that must be her. They must have switched shirts. Don't let her get away." Both men raced toward her. She turned and ran toward the corner. As she neared the corner, she felt chips of concrete hitting her on her right side just as she heard four rapidly fired shots ring out. She turned the corner, retrieved the Glock from the bag, and, using the corner of the wall to protect herself, reached around the corner. With only her right eye and gun hand exposed, she took aim at the men running toward her.

When they saw her arm with the pistol come around the corner, one of the men started yelling, "Look out, she's got a gun!" There was no place for them to find cover. There was only the long straight doorless and windowless wall of the factory building. They had no choice but to continue running toward her shooting in the hope of overwhelming her with firepower. It was the wrong strategy. Shooting straight while running was next to impossible, and Anna didn't back off. It would have taken enormous luck to hit the small target she presented. The two men, however, were maximum targets, and Anna took full advantage of their predicament.

With bullets ricocheting off the wall and sidewalk all about her, Anna took aim and fired twice. Quick but again well aimed. The man closer to her tumbled over the curb and into the street. The other man stopped running and tried to find protection by getting close to the wall. Anna fired twice more. He fell to the sidewalk. She dropped her arm but continued to peek around the corner to see if they would get up. They didn't. A lot of people were coming out of the businesses down the street. The onlookers were running toward the woman in the alley and then began to look at the two men sprawled on the ground. They didn't see Anna who had moved back away from the corner of the building. She put her gun, still hot and smoking, back in the bag, stood up, and walked slowly down the side street.

The pain Anna felt on the right side of her face was where a chip of concrete grazed her cheek in front of her ear. She used the blue scarf once again to wipe the blood away. The wound was slight, but it made Anna realize how lucky she had been. She was now certain someone was out to kill Tatianna and would stop at nothing.

Anna was in shock about her life–and–death dilemma. She was frightened more thugs would be sent to find her, feeling guilty over Tatianna's death, and in pain. Her chest hurt when she breathed, her face throbbed, and her throat felt parched. Hoping she would not be noticed in her denim outfit, she walked quickly to get out of that neighborhood.

After about an hour, Anna crossed the street when the sidewalk ended. She looked up to see water and large ships. She was at a commercial section of the harbor, somewhere she had never been. On the harbor side of the street, a dirt path, protected by a rusty chain–link fence with an open double–wide gate, led to a broken concrete pillar lying on its side under a tree. Tired, hot, and thirsty, she entered the fenced area and sat on the pillar. The tree provided shade and protected her from view from the street. Anna sat there terrified, shaking, thinking.

What am I going to do? Anna kept asking herself, over and over. But no answers surfaced. *If I go back, I'll go to jail, or Phillip will have me killed. I have to disappear. But how do I do it? How will I live?*

Moored at the docks in front of her were two large cargo ships and sandwiched between them a statuesque sailboat. The rusty iron ships looked decrepit and had no activity on them. The sailboat was bright and shiny. It was conspicuously out of place, she thought. She could see two men on the sailboat working at various tasks. They seemed to be in a hurry.

Anna sat for almost an hour, transfixed in a catatonic stare, trying to make sense of what had happened that morning. Looking straight ahead at the ships and the water but seeing nothing. She had to do something right away or those people who wanted to kill Tatianna would find and kill her. She began asking herself over and over, *How do I get out of this nightmare?*

While lamenting her situation, Anna slowly focused on a sign on the stern of the sailboat. It wasn't a big sign. It wasn't done professionally. It appeared to be a short plank of wood on which someone had painted "COOK WANTED." It had been there all along but hadn't registered with her.

Out loud, she uttered to herself, "I can cook!"

She studied the sign for a few minutes. If she were to ask for the job, she had to look like a cook. Her blue denim shirt looked right, but her expensive, one-and-a-half-carat diamond engagement ring and diamond-studded wedding band didn't. She removed the rings and put them in the bag. She forgot her Rolex watch.

CHAPTER 6

"Hello? Hello? Anyone there?" Anna cautiously called out.

"Yeah, what do you want?" Rick yelled back. He was wearing grease-stained shorts, deck shoes, no shirt, and was sweating heavily. As he approached the stern railing, he wiped his greasy hands on a dirty rag. Disgustingly, he used the same dirty rag to wipe the sweat from his face, leaving swipes of grease across his cheeks and nose.

Rick looked carefully at Anna who was standing on the dock below. With untidy hair, too much makeup, and a wide-eyed facial expression, Anna was not an attractive sight. He studied the bruises and cuts on her face and assumed she was an alcoholic bag lady looking for a handout.

"I don't have any money on me. You'll have to go elsewhere." He started to return to his task, but she didn't leave.

"I don't want a handout!" Anna called back pleasantly but authoritatively.

"No? Then what do you want?"

"Is the cook position still open?"

"Are you a cook?" Rick asked with a note of skepticism in his voice.

"Yes! I'm an excellent cook."

In the first few years of her marriage, Anna had prepared a lot of gourmet dinners for Phillip's business-related parties. Although he had stopped inviting clients and colleagues over for dinner a couple of years ago, Anna felt she could still cook for a few people on a boat. How hard could that be?

"Have you ever been a ship's cook before?"

"This will be my first time. I have a lot of training and experience in gourmet cooking though. I'm certain I will be more than equal to the task."

Rick's first impulse was to say no, but this woman's speech was impeccable even though it conflicted mightily with her looks. *What kind of ship's cook uses words like "equal to the task"?* he thought. He also detected a slight vulnerability in her speech. Her voice had a slight pleading tone that piqued his curiosity.

"Do you realize this vessel will be gone for a long time, and we will be at sea a lot of the time?"

"I guess so," she answered flatly. "After all, it's a boat."

Sensing that the woman thought his question was a bit dumb, he continued, "We ship out at midnight, tonight. Would that work?"

"Certainly!"

Certainly? Who do I know who would answer 'certainly'? This woman seems odd, but we need a cook real bad. I better let Bart know someone is interested in the cook's job.

"Wait there. I'll have to get the skipper."

Rick turned and disappeared into the main cabin.

"Bart! Bart!" Rick called down to the galley.

Bartholomew Maclachlan, captain of the vessel, was a strong-looking man, about forty years old, with light-colored hair and a pleasant disposition. He got his captain's license when he was twenty-two and had been commanding ships ever since.

"We might have a cook," Rick explained.

"Yeah? Great!"

"Yeah, but it's a woman! She's on the dock. Doesn't look like much but claims she's a really good cook. I think she was in a barroom brawl from the looks of her."

"We'd better take a look. We're gonna be in deep shit if we show up in Bermuda with no cook. Tell her to come aboard, and I'll get Eddie."

Anna made her way up the narrow gangplank and was immediately impressed with the fine wood finish on the deck and railings. The shiny bright brass work was beautiful. The teak deck was spotless, and the overall appearance was one of elegance.

Bart approached with Eddie.

"I'm Bart, captain of the vessel."

"And I'm Eddie, one of the crew."

Bart asked, "You've already met Rick, right?"

"Actually no. We spoke only briefly about the availability of the position, but we didn't exchange names. Pleased to meet you, Rick."

Rick nodded in agreement.

Bart continued, "And what is your name?"

Anna hesitated slightly. She didn't want to use her real name but hadn't thought about another one. She had to make a decision immediately, on the spot, no thinking about it, no waiting. She used the first name that occurred to her.

"I'm Tatianna Wolinski, captain. I'm pleased to meet you," Anna said as she offered her hand to shake hands with Bart. She surprised herself with her new name. *I guess that'll work, and I can use her identification.*

Bart noticed her hesitation but dismissed his "alert reaction" when he heard the name of Tati-somethingorother. "Tati . . . who?"

"Tati-ANNA. It's Polish."

Bart continued, "Do you drink?"

"A little."

"We don't want an alcoholic aboard. Our last cook lied to us. Turned out he couldn't cook worth a damn and was constantly getting drunk at sea. When we found him sloshed one night, Rick and Eddie here threw him overboard off the coast of the Bahamas. He had to swim like hell so the sharks wouldn't get him."

Tatianna (as Anna was now known) stepped back slightly. Her eyes opened wider. Oddly, both Eddie and Rick noted her facial expression didn't change, only her eyes.

"Just kidding. We didn't throw him overboard, even though we wanted to. We actually disembarked him in the Bahamas, and that left us without a cook before we came here. But the question remains, how much do you drink?"

"Well, as I said, I do drink but only occasionally. I like to have wine with dinner, if I can, but only if it's the appropriate wine for the cuisine."

Wow, Bart was thinking *She sounds a hell of a lot more sophisticated than our past cooks, but she looks like she just got out of a bar fight. Or maybe her boyfriend beat her up, and she's trying to get away. Whatever! I need a cook.*

Bart's thoughts flashed back to his childhood. Before his parents broke up, they used to fight a lot, and his mother got beaten up on occasion. But he was very young then, and those times seemed far away. He dismissed them and focused on the present situation. He had to have a cook.

"Have you been a cook on other boats?"

"Actually no! I've not prepared meals aboard a boat before. But I have a lot of experience preparing everything from everyday functional dinners to gourmet cuisine. I attended a culinary school and have prepared seven-course dinners for more than twenty people on many occasions. I developed the entire menu, including the appetizers, the main courses, the proper wines, and the desserts. The guests always seemed pleased and usually complimented me on both the presentation and cuisine."

Curiously, Rick asked, "How do you know what the proper wine is to serve with a dinner? I thought it was either red or white."

Bart glared at Rick. *What kind of stupid question is that to ask right now?*

"Well, besides having taken wine courses covering everything from vineyards to serving at the table, I routinely read some of the better wine magazines such as *Wine Spectator*. And they had an excellent course on wines at the culinary school."

"We've never had a problem with the menus or wine selection. Mrs. Pisani usually tells us what she wants us to serve for the dinner parties," Bart responded while thinking, *If I hire this woman and she can't handle the job, how the hell am I going to have dinners served for the Pisanis when we're in Bermuda?*

"How many guests do you anticipate for your special dinners?" Anna asked.

"The owners usually have two or three couples join them. Once we had eight couples on board, and that was a problem because of space."

After a pause, Bart thoughtfully added, "We've never had a female crew member before. You would be the only woman on the boat for long periods while we're at sea. Can you live with that?"

Tatianna glanced at Rick, then Eddie, and answered, "Yes!"

"We sail at midnight tonight. Can you be ready by then?"

"Yes! Certainly," Tatianna answered. "Do you have all the food aboard, or will you need me to pick some things up?"

"No! The larder is fully stocked. Go get your seabag. We don't expect to return to Philadelphia any time soon."

"Thank you," replied Tatianna. She asked if a store was nearby where she could purchase some basic incidentals.

Eddie pointed to his left. "There's a chandlery and a yachting supply store a few blocks away."

Tatianna waved slightly and disembarked the boat.

Bart motioned to Eddie and Rick to stay put.

Eddie was apprehensive. "Bart, we've never had a woman crew member before, and this one looks like a drunk. She never even cracked a smile. Women usually smile a lot."

"Look, guys," Bart admonished, "we really need a cook. Our last cook was a disaster. I don't know how this woman can be worse, even if she looks terrible. You're going to have to live with it."

"Eddie, don't you remember throwing some of the food overboard?" Rick interjected.

"I don't know if this woman is the best choice," Bart replied, "but I don't give a damn. Mr. Pisani is going to meet us in Bermuda with Mrs. Pisani and three couples, and we damn sure better have a cook when we get there. You know what it's like when Mrs. Pisani is aboard. We're sailing tonight, and I haven't been able to find a cook up to now. Do whatever is needed to make this work. You got that? It's your responsibility!"

Rick and Eddie agreed, each saying, "You got it, Captain."

"If she doesn't work out, we'll get rid of her in Bermuda, but it will have to be after the first few dinners for the guests."

Bart turned to Rick. "Set up the forward port, single-bunk cabin for her. It's next to a head and it's securable. Get her stuff put away ASAP. We have to leave at midnight if we're to have any chance of getting to Bermuda on time."

CHAPTER 7

Two blocks south of the sailboat mooring, Tatianna found a West Marine store where she bought a seabag and a pair of canvas boating shoes. But what she really needed were feminine products, a lot of makeup, and crew type clothes. She envisioned jeans and denim shirts, not the yachting clothes she was finding at West Marine. For the feminine products and makeup, she had to walk another three blocks to a modest drugstore. But still she didn't have the jeans and shirts she needed.

She finally found the chandlery, but all the clothing was for men. With no other choices, she bought men's jeans to hide the bruises on her legs and lightweight denim shirts.

"Missus, I don't recommend short-sleeved shirts or shorts because of your fair skin. The sun will burn you like toast."

"Thanks for your recommendation. Is there anything else you think could be helpful?"

"It can get cold in the evenings out on the ocean. You might need a jacket."

"Anything else?"

"Since you don't seem to be familiar with boating, I think you should have some scopolamine patches for seasickness. You gotta put them behind your ears right away. Also you should have some Dramamine tablets. Just in case."

"Thanks. I hadn't thought about seasickness."

Tatianna bought a copy of *Chapman Piloting & Seamanship* on the old man's recommendation and several smaller paperback sailing books. It didn't occur to her to buy some general reading books, having never experienced the long unoccupied periods of time sometimes encountered at sea.

The walk back to the boat was tiring. As she carried her new purchases, she was constantly looking around to be sure she wasn't being followed. The seabag itself was light, constructed of a water-resistant-type fabric. But even though it had a shoulder strap, it was difficult to carry loaded with the new clothes and books. She had to balance the seabag on one shoulder with the black bag containing the two guns and accounting ledgers on the other. She was thankful she had Tatianna's wallet. She could use the money to get away from Philadelphia before the killers found her again.

When she reached the sailboat, Eddie was working on some fittings on the stern and saw her approaching. "Where have you been?" he called out with a concerned voice. "We thought you got lost or changed your mind. Rick is waiting to help you get your gear secured."

Rick came on deck. "Let me help," he said as he started to grab her black bag.

But she pulled it back, turned, and handed him her seabag. "I can use some help with this one. It's heavier."

On entering the small cabin, Tatianna was immediately surprised by the narrow entry door and amazed at the extensive use of mahogany, other fine woods, and bright brass. The bedspread was the blue color of the sky in the late afternoon on a clear day. It was trimmed with dark-blue-and-red-striped piping. Across the upper middle of the cover was a red-embroidered silhouette of a twin-masted sailboat. In the middle of the cover was an embroidered white dove, about the same size as the sailboat. When she looked more closely, she could see the stern of the embroidered sailboat carried the word "DOVE." The emblems seemed to reflectively stand out under the focused beams of the bright, hooded brass lamps on the forward bulkhead. Especially the white dove. The only thing that seemed out of balance was the small white porcelain sink at the far end of the cabin. But it had a shiny brass faucet and handles which helped it blend in.

Looking again at the emblem of the dove on the bed cover she thought, *That must be the name of the boat! It's the DOVE! Why didn't I see it on the back of the boat when I was standing there talking to Rick? I better start paying closer attention to what's going on here.*

—

Tatianna was also surprised by the small size of the cabin. She noted that the lower part of the cabin was a lot smaller than the top. As she looked about, she could see the outside wall sloped upward and outward. *That must be the outside of the boat,* she thought when she saw the curved mahogany wall. *Where is there room to stow anything?* She was desperate to find a place to hide the guns and ammunition. No handles or drawer pulls were in sight. *This is going to be a problem.* But she would soon learn that the ship's carpenters were a crafty lot and had built into the bulkheads and bunk considerable storage space with ingenious hidden handles and cabinet door openers that wouldn't catch on clothing when the boat was pitching and rolling at sea.

Rick was going to help her stow her stuff, but the cabin was too crowded with two people in it so she refused his help and asked for a little privacy.

As he was leaving, Rick stopped at the doorway, turned back, and explained, "When you've got your stuff stowed, I'll show you the heads and the galley and give you a copy of our work schedule. We have a night lunch when we are under way so you won't have much time to come up to speed. Bart said I should help you learn the ropes."

Tatianna was anxious to hide the guns and ammunition. The door of a small but long compartment, built into the bulkhead behind the bunk, had been left slightly ajar. The interior of the compartment extended all the way to the hull. It seemed to be a good place to hide the guns. When she removed them from the bag, she discovered the gun she had picked up from the street was a .40-caliber Beretta. *What luck! It's the same caliber as the Glock.* She popped the Beretta's fifteen-round clip and reloaded it. Then she checked to see if it had a chambered round. It did. Since the Beretta was a double-auto action, she didn't need to set the safety. Tatianna then reloaded the Glock, made sure it had a chambered round, and put the guns and ammunition in the back of the small compartment. It was common practice to store guns without a chambered round. But Joey had taught her that if she felt danger was imminent to be sure to have a round in the chamber. That was one of the reasons he preferred she have a revolver for protection.

Tatianna placed a box of cotton balls, her cosmetics, and a box of tampons in front of the guns and closed the finely crafted door. She hoped if one of the crew were to open the small compartment, he would be deterred by the sight of the tampons and cosmetics and wouldn't dig deeper to find the guns.

If the door to the little compartment had not been left ajar, she realized, she probably wouldn't have noticed it. The door had no handle, only a spring-loaded latch that required pressure on one side to open it. Tatianna found two other similar compartments at the foot of the bunk and two drawers under the bunk. It became obvious why sailors used seabags. There was no place to store a suitcase.

Tatianna put away the few clothes she purchased at the chandlery, left the black bag on the bunk, and looked for Rick. He first showed her one of the heads and spent an inordinate amount of time explaining how the toilet worked.

"Rick, you seem really concerned about the proper operation of the toilet. Why is that?"

In a rather condescending tone Rick explained, "On a boat, the toilet is called the head. When guests are aboard, incorrect use of the head, usually by women, is generally the biggest problem we have in maintaining the boat. And I'm the one who has to fix it. So I like to make sure guests and new crew members fully understand how to operate it."

They then reviewed the galley. Tatianna was at first surprised by the highly organized storage of food and utensils. *This kitchen, or I guess they call it a galley, is nothing like my kitchen back home. The only way I'm going to know what's available is to read the list of food items tacked inside the cabinet doors. I really better pay close attention to where everything is stored.*

"It's too dark to show you the boat and rigging. If we get everything in order, on time, we will be departing the dock at midnight. You should have a night lunch ready for the crew. Night lunches are mandatory when we're under sail. And breakfast is served at 0700!"

"What's 0700?"

"We generally use a twenty-four-hour clock, so 0700 is 7:00 a.m."

Tatianna returned to her cabin, or cubbyhole as she was beginning to think of it, taking with her the list of provisions and a diagram of the galley storage cabinets. She sat on her bunk, shaking. *What have*

I done? How am I going to prepare a decent meal while bouncing around in the ocean? If I don't pull this off, I'm in deep trouble.

Suddenly, in a heart-thumping flash, Tatianna remembered she wouldn't be able to meet with Joey on Tuesday as they had planned. *What is he going to think when I don't show up? I guess he's going to learn one way or another that I'm dead. I can't call him. He would be the first to tell me that.*

Tatianna sat back on the bunk, expecting to lean against the curved, fine mahogany paneling covering the hull, but leaned on the black bag. Pulling it around to her lap, she knew she had to hide the accounting ledgers somewhere, perhaps under the clothes. As Tatianna removed the ledgers, she was surprised they were not as long or as heavy as she had thought. She had assumed they were legal size, but they were actually much shorter. Something else was under them. It was a black panel, cut to exactly fit the bottom of the bag.

The panel appeared to have been made from a thick sheet of plastic and had downturned sides that acted like legs to help it stand off the bottom of the bag. Tatianna wouldn't have noticed it except that the ledgers were smaller and lighter than she thought, and the bag still felt quite heavy. Under the panel she found money. Lots of money. Four neatly packaged stacks of one-hundred-dollar bills. A total of one hundred thousand dollars in cash sitting right next to her on the bed.

Oh god, help me! This is getting worse and worse! No wonder those thugs were trying to kill Tatianna. Look at all this money. Now what do I do?

She picked up the stacks of money, one by one, placing them on the blue bed cover. They were so neatly wrapped and crisp. She opened the bag wide and felt around for any loose bills. The bottom of the bag was covered by another hard cloth-covered panel that made the bottom of the bag lay flat. When Tatianna slid her fingers around the edge of the bottom panel, it moved. She pulled it up and found Tatianna's passport. The photo was terrible, but she thought she might be able to pass for the real Tatianna. That is, unless an inspector looked very closely. Maybe she could smudge the photo a little.

Tatianna slid her hand back under the panel to see if anything else was hidden and was amazed to find a thin small black bankbook off to the side. The cover was embossed with a gold crest and the words

"CENTRAL CARIBBEAN BANK, CAYMAN ISLANDS." She was breathing heavily. Her head had not stopped throbbing all day, but now it was positively explosive, and she could feel her heart pounding in her chest. *Oh god, what have I gotten myself into? There's more money!*

Against her own will, her hands opened the bankbook. A yellow note was stuck on the first page with an account number, a special identification number, and a password. Under the note, taped to the page, was a thin long-necked brass key with the letters CCBCI and some numbers impressed into the round head—a safe-deposit box key. It was as if Tatianna hadn't had time to memorize the bank account numbers or password. The only entry on the first page showed a total of 257,000 dollars.

She stared at the book in disbelief. Tatianna must have been skimming the money and transferring it to the offshore bank. *She had 359,000 dollars, and it wasn't hers. And those killers wanted it back. And they think I'm Tatianna!*

Sitting on the bunk, Tatianna began to think hard about the events in the women's dress shop that morning—the happenstance of the similar outfits and what she actually saw when she looked around the edge of the entrance to the shop. After the real Tatianna had been hit by the truck, two men in suits had looked at the body, inspected the black bag, and then disappeared. But as Tatianna sat thinking, she remembered two casually dressed younger men farther down the street were also running toward the body. At the time she had assumed they were curious bystanders.

The better-dressed men must have been the ones following me and thought I got killed. After the accident, they must have called Phillip. That's how he got to the scene so quickly. The two casually dressed men must have been following Tatianna. They were after the money and would kill to get it!

These accounting ledgers may be even more important than the money. They may be looking for the books and not even know about the money she was skimming. It could be really dangerous to get caught with the books, either by the gang or the cops. But what do I do with them?

Tatianna couldn't stand it anymore and started to cry again, her tears falling on the open pages of the ledgers. Wiping her eyes, she tried to stop crying and scolded herself, *I've got to be tough. No more crying! No more emotions! If they find me, I'm dead and that's that! And if Phillip finds me, I'm dead too! I've got to make this cook job work. I don't have a choice.*

Tatianna thought about how Joey had taught her to protect herself in dangerous situations. If threatened with physical harm, with a knife or gun, she should use deadly force to protect herself. Immediately. No hesitation. He also trained her to pick up a weapon and use it, any kind, without thinking about it. "Hesitation will give your opponent the opportunity to take your weapon and use it on you. And hesitation gives the impression of weakness!"

Tatianna promised herself, *My main objective is survival. At least the thugs will be looking for the real Tatianna and not me. But wait, I am Tatianna now, so they'll be looking for me!*

Tatianna sat thinking about what to do with the ledgers and where she could hide all the money. Pulling the under-the-bunk drawers out, she discovered a lot of room between the sides of the drawers and the framework for the bunk. With considerable maneuvering, Tatianna was able to pull the drawers out without marring the fine mahogany paneling of the bulkhead. The only way to get them all the way out was to lie on the bunk and reach down to the drawers. When she succeeded, she thought it was the perfect solution to her problem.

Tatianna's effort paid off. There was enough space between the drawers and the bunk framework to hide the stacks of bills and accounting ledgers. She maneuvered the drawers back into the bunk frame and tried opening and closing the drawers several times to be sure they shut securely.

Tatianna's cabin began to feel stuffy. Bart had turned off the air conditioner while servicing the generator. Looking up, Tatianna saw a porthole above her bed. She got up on her knees and opened the polished brass porthole cover to get some fresh air, but there was very little. She decided to go up on the main deck before preparing the night lunch.

CHAPTER 8

Bart was not in a good mood. He had been given a deadline to meet the Pisanis in Bermuda. He was trying hard to be on time but already seemed to be running late.

Bart barked at Eddie, "Where the hell is Bo? He was supposed to be back by 1800! If he holds us up, I'm going to kick his ass!"

"He's always late, you know that. He'll be here."

"Yeah, but we could use some help in getting this goddamn boat ready."

No sooner had Bart finished his last sentence than they heard Bo yelling from ashore, "Ahoy there, you guys ready to sail?"

"Where the hell have you been? You're four hours late. Get your ass up here and help."

Dieter Boarman went by the name of Bo. He was a big fellow, thirty-one years old, six feet one inch tall, college educated, with long black hair in a ponytail, and an attitude of superiority. He knew he had an attitude but felt he could get away with it because of his size and the fact that he was the best sailor on the boat, not including Bart, of course, but at least better than everyone else. Smarter too. He commanded respect from the other crew members, one way or another. If he couldn't intimidate them with the implicit threat of force, he used his intellect.

Bo was used to Bart's raving when he was angry, and it didn't seem to bother him. He was always respectful to Bart, whose demeanor was generally pleasant. Bart's greatest asset was his ability to remain calm and collected during treacherous sailing conditions. He also worked well with the owners and guests. Although he only had a high school education, Bart had been sailing since he was a kid, and Bo had a high respect for his capabilities as a sailor and captain of big yachts.

Bo also knew how to sail big yachts. He had, after all, recently crewed on a 180-foot, three-masted, top-sailed, gaff-rigged schooner. He had sailed on other charter sailboats too, and he had crewed on several ocean sailboat races. Having been sailing since high school and been the captain of his college sailing team, he knew how to trim the sails for maximum performance. But the *DOVE* wasn't designed for speed. She was designed for comfort and seaworthiness.

Bo was telling Bart about his shore time. "Sorry I was late, but I met a great-looking woman whose father has a fifty-two-foot Hatteras, and they invited me to have dinner aboard the yacht. Her father offered to let me take the Hatteras out with his daughter the next time I'm in port. I just couldn't get loose any earlier." When he needed to, Bo could demonstrate a lot of class, and the woman's father took a liking to him.

Just then, Tatianna came on deck, looked at the four men, and turned to go stand at the railing, out of the way. She needed to get some fresh air but didn't want to have a conversation with the crew.

"Who's the big bitch?" Bo asked, deliberately loud enough that Tatianna could hear him.

Tatianna turned and tilted her head slightly so she could see Bo out of the corner of her eye. No one bothered to introduce them, and she couldn't determine if he was crudely trying to be humorous or deliberately denigrating her. Finally, Rick offered, "That's Tatianna, the new cook."

Bo laughed, "Bart, I knew you were hard up to find us a cook, but did you have to beat her up to get her on board?" Then he turned toward Tatianna and said, "Hey, Tati, get me a cup of coffee. If we're going to be up for a while readying the boat, I need some caffeine!"

Tatianna had heard everything Bo said, but she still didn't know who he was. No one had bothered to tell her Bo's name. She turned, looked at him for a moment, and asked, "Are you a member of the crew?"

Bo laughed and answered, "You're goddamn right about that. They couldn't sail this boat without me."

He's pretty much right, Bart was thinking.

It generally took six sailors to handle the *DOVE*, but Bart only had five including the new cook. He had been trying to hire one or two more crew members but was unsuccessful. If Bo hadn't returned, Bart would have been forced to delay departure until he could get at least one more deckhand. If that happened, Mr. Pisani would have a fit. Bart really didn't mind the limited crew. Overall, it was less hassle.

Tatianna went below to begin preparing the night lunch and brew a pot of coffee. She balked at the thought of being treated like a servant and wasn't going to take a cup to that overbearing crew member. She had enough of that with Phillip. *If I give in, then how much more demeaning will he be?*

Her recalcitrance at being subjugated caused one of her worst fights with Phillip. He ordered her to get him drinks when he had one of his friends over one evening, and she walked off. By the time he realized she wasn't coming back, his friend had noticed. Later that night, Phillip got sizzling pissed. He told her she was going to do as she was told. She turned her back on him, triggering an extremely violent response. He pushed her down and kicked her, calling her a stupid bitch. She got up and hit him with the stool from her cosmetics dresser, knocking him to the floor. That put him in a rage, and he beat her so badly she couldn't leave the house for a week. So now, she had to deal with another jerk and decided to take Joey's advice seriously.

Joey had been a cop. Through experience he learned abusers and bullies thrived on submissiveness. "So don't let them do it to you," he often counseled. "Once they think that you are an easy target, they'll just keep abusing you. What you have to do is make them know how much pain it is going to cause them to hurt you. All you have to do is be willing to deal with the consequences."

I don't care what happens! I'm not going to put up with overbearing behavior anymore! She took several deep breaths and concentrated on making the night lunch.

The guys were still on deck discussing what needed to be done to finish checking out the boat's operating and safety systems. Rick detailed to Bart the problems he was having cleaning the corrosion in the radio antenna terminals. Eddie explained why he had to go to the ship chandlery down the street for a new water/fuel separator for the diesel generator. He said it took so long because he had to wait for the clerk at the chandlery to find the right housing. Eddie had to replace the entire separator because the inflow fitting had galled. When he went to check it for tightness, it cracked. The sintered bronze filter was okay, but the housing was too corroded to tap a new thread so he had no alternative but to get a new one.

Bart suspected that Eddie had bought something else too. He returned to the boat quite happy. He might have been drinking, using coke, weed, or something. But as long as Eddie didn't use it aboard ship, Bart could care less. He had to. Most of the deckhands were usually into one thing or another. Except Bo who had a lot of other faults but never smoked or used drugs, and he was completely honest.

After about ten minutes of discussing the status of various repairs, Bo realized that he didn't have his coffee yet and yelled down to the main saloon, "Where's my damn coffee?"

But there was no answer. He went down to the galley, confronted Tatianna, and repeated his question, "Where's my damn coffee?"

Having already made up her mind about how to handle the situation, Tatianna turned from the sink and politely told Bo she was busy preparing the night lunch. If he wanted coffee, a freshly brewed pot was in the coffee maker. She turned back to the sink and continued with her food preparation. Bo was pissed. He started to tell her this was bullshit, but Bart was calling him to the deck. He charged up to the deck and looked Bart straight in the eyes.

"What the fuck is wrong with the cook? Who does she think she is?"

Without reacting to Bo's comment, Bart replied, "Bo, we're way behind schedule, and your getting back late didn't help. I want to depart by midnight if at all possible, so forget the damn coffee, put your stuff up, and help Eddie and me check out the mechanical systems. Rick, you're the electronics guy, you check out all of the safety and communication systems."

"This is bullshit," Bo stammered. "What kind of a goddamn cook did you get?" Then he grabbed his seabag and went below. In the galley, he confronted Tatianna again and demanded, "You'd better have a goddamn good lunch tonight!"

Quietly and politely, Tatianna replied, "It will probably be best if you don't use foul language with me."

Glaring at her and turning red, he replied, "What the fuck," and went to the stateroom he shared with Eddie. Neither his size nor temperament was working on this woman.

Bo hadn't finished putting up his things when Rick stepped into his stateroom. "Bart wants to know what's holding you up. He's waiting for you topside."

In the galley, Tatianna could hear Bo yelling, "What the shit is going on here? I leave the boat for a couple of days, and everything is turned upside down. Tell Bart I'll be there in a few minutes."

Rick replied, "Bo, you can put your stuff away later. Bart's waiting for you, and he's already pissed off you were so late getting back. I don't think you should piss him off any more than he already is."

Listening to Bo shouting, Tatianna thought, *Now what have I done? I'm going to be on a boat in the middle of the ocean with this jerk. I'm just going to have to deal with it.*

CHAPTER 9

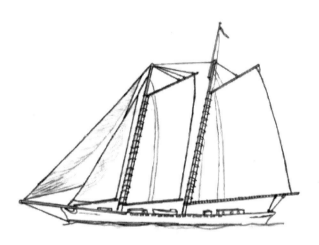

Preparation for departure was behind schedule. Servicing the diesel engine and generator had taken longer than anticipated. Eddie had complications installing the new water pump by himself. Bo should have been there to help, but he had been promised some time off. Rick was checking, as he said, "again and again," all the lines, rodes, anchors, safety rails, fire extinguishers, and personal flotation devices (PFDs). With Eddie, Rick inspected the automatically deployable emergency raft. Then he checked the levels of potable water and fuel. Bart went to the navigation table and laid out several nautical charts, checked the clocks, and printed out a copy of the weather conditions from the weather fax. Using a multimeter, he tested the batteries in all the flashlights, the handheld VHFs, and the automatically deployable EPIRB (Emergency Position Indicating Radio Beacon).

Tatianna had the night lunch ready at 2300. She had a difficult time preparing the food because the electric power kept going off and on. In final preparation, Bart and Eddie were testing all the navigation lights, circuit breakers, and battery connections and running the 27-kilowatt Onan diesel generator. After they cranked over the 400-hp Detroit Diesel engine, she could feel the initial subtle shake in the hull and the very low harmonic vibrations when it was running. She thought the vibrations had a calming effect.

Tatianna felt useless with the sandwiches sitting on the counter untouched, and the crew actively preparing to get under way. She decided to take a sandwich and drink to each of the crew. Bart seemed surprised but pleased. She didn't say anything, and he didn't either. She just stood there without emotion, with the food on a tray. She did the same for Rick, Eddie, and Bo. Bo gave her a menacing look but took the food.

Departure was delayed until 0100 on Tuesday. Tatianna had cleaned the galley, stowed the dishes and cookware, and was about to retreat to her cabin when Bart called for all hands on the aft deck. Before departing, he wanted to go over all the safety procedures starting with the man-overboard drill. He was especially concerned about his new inexperienced cook and explained the procedures more thoroughly than usual. He required that each person show him where the throwable safety floats and PFDs were stored. Everyone was required to take a PFD, put it on, and then place it back in the lazarette. The redundancy of this routine bored the crew, but they knew it was necessary.

Tatianna was relieved to know the captain was so safety conscious. She was dismayed it was Bo, of all the crew, who came to her aid when she needed help in adjusting the straps on her PFD. She was surprised when he spoke softly, clearly, and professionally as he described the purpose of each strap. Her discomfort was heightened when he yanked hard on the straps, throwing her off balance. She felt certain he was doing it on purpose to make her look ungainly.

Bart continued the departure safety drill by reading a list of safety rules, including the requirement that when at sea, and after dark, every person on deck was required to wear a safety harness, no exceptions. After he finished detailing various responsibilities for Rick and Eddie, he gave the command to prepare for departure. The engine cranked over, the navigation lights were turned on, all dock lines were retrieved, and the *DOVE* motored out into the Delaware River.

CHAPTER 10

It was 0645 on Tuesday when the *DOVE* cleared the I-295 bridge over the Delaware River, just south of Wilmington. They had averaged a little under five knots, which wasn't too bad from Bart's point of view. With daylight came increased water traffic and rolling from the wakes of passing boats. Bart was concerned about Tatianna and how well she would be able to handle the movement of the vessel while cooking. Also, Tatianna wasn't experienced on boats and would probably experience some seasickness. As a longtime sailor, he didn't think much about it. *Oh well, everybody has a first time. I just hope she can cut it. This crossing may not go easy.*

Eddie, who had the wheel, didn't have as much experience at the helm as the other members of the crew. Bart was coaching him as they motored down the Delaware. He told him to keep a lookout for the green 5N marker on the east side of Fort Delaware State Park. "The river narrows up quite a bit there, and if there's traffic it'll be close hauled, so try to minimize the roll."

Bart stopped short in coaching Eddie. He was savoring the wisps of fresh coffee and sausage emanating from the galley. He had lost track of time while checking the lateral signage. When he looked at his watch, he was pleased to see it was 0701. Great timing! He was definitely hungry.

Rick came to the helm to relieve Bart long enough for him to have breakfast. Bart was anxious to see how Tatianna was doing with her first breakfast, especially while under way. He had been apprehensive all night, but once he tasted her coffee and bit into one of her flaky biscuits, he was so relieved he took a deep breath and slowly let it out. That didn't escape Tatianna's notice. While working at the sink, she turned her head slightly to look at Bart. His eyes met hers, and he pursed his lips and nodded. She turned back to the sink, nodded also, and continued washing the dishes. No words were spoken, but both of them, for different reasons, relaxed.

At the helm, Eddie asked Rick, "How's breakfast going?"

"She wasn't just a woofing when she said she could cook," Rick replied. "She's made sausage wrapped in crepes with fruit on them, omelets with all kinds of stuff in them, fresh-baked biscuits, coffee, orange juice, butter, jelly, whatever. You would have loved it."

"What do you mean 'I would have loved it'? What's this 'would have' crap? I haven't eaten yet!"

With a grin, while looking through the binoculars for lateral signage, Rick commented, "Well, Eddie my man, she hasn't figured out yet how much food to make, and Bo ate so much there may not be anything left when Bart gets done." Rick, being the most lighthearted among the crew, couldn't miss the opportunity to tweak Eddie.

"That's bullshit, goddamn it! From now on I'm going down first! I don't give a shit who I'm on watch with!"

"Hey! Calm down! I was just screwing with you. There's plenty of food. It's pretty good. Way better than the last cook."

"Don't fuck with me, Rick."

"Eddie! Eddie! Calm down! There's plenty of food, and it's great. I wasn't kidding about the cook not knowing exactly how much to make though. She made way too much. But I gotta tell you, I was really surprised. I didn't expect it. When she came aboard, she looked like she had been in a fight or something, and this morning she didn't smile once. I made a couple of comments about Bart's ability to steer a straight line and keep the boat from rolling while she was trying to cook breakfast, and she never smiled. She nodded but never cracked a smile. She said, 'Yes, that would be helpful.' You get that? 'Yes, that would be helpful.' It's like she's off in never-never land."

"I think she must have bad teeth. When she was talking yesterday, I saw a couple of chipped ones, and she talks funny."

"Yeah, from the looks of her, she probably does have bad teeth. Probably lost them in a fight, so don't aggravate her, or she might beat you up."

"She must have been homeless. Did you see how she clung to that black bag? I've seen that sort of thing on the streets in New York. They don't have much, but whatever they do have it's really important to them."

"I hope Bart knows what he's doing. I think he's still upset over the last cook."

Laughing, Eddie commented, "It didn't help when she pissed Bo off last night either. I can't wait to see when Bo really blows his top."

"Yeah, this could turn out to be an interesting trip! She could lose a few more teeth if she pisses Bo off much more."

When Bart returned to the helm, they were just rounding red marker 28, and Eddie bolted down to the galley to see for himself what Anna had fixed for breakfast.

Rick asked, "How long before we enter Delaware Bay?"

"I figure about three and a half to four hours to the Davis Shoals," Bart responded. "That's pretty much the beginning of the bay. I hope NOAA gives us some straight poop on the weather fax for once. It looks like we're going to have a headwind all the way to the Atlantic, and it's going to be bumpy. If we can maintain about four or five knots, we can reach the Cape Henlopen Light in about ten or twelve hours. After that, it's open ocean to Bermuda. I don't see any serious storms in the forecasts, but there will be high seas."

"So we're gonna motor all the way to Henlopen?"

"Yep! We can make better time getting through the bay, so get some rest. We'll be setting the sails at just about dark."

"Hey, good coffee this morning. I wonder what she did to make it smooth?"

"I liked the biscuits."

"Yeah, maybe she'll work out."

"Yeah, I hope so."

CHAPTER 11

While preparing breakfast, Tatianna had begun to feel nauseous. The passing boats and the pitching and rolling in their wake made her head spin. She realized she was getting seasick. She took more Dramamine, checked the transdermal patches of scopolamine behind her ears, and got through the food preparation without heaving. After cleaning up the galley, Tatianna wobbled to her cabin to rest and change the seasickness patches. Having had little to eat for twenty-four hours, she was feeling weak but had decided the best way to avert serious seasickness was to stay away from solid food. Chicken soup and small amounts of water for the foreseeable future. Maybe some ginger ale. Certainly no coffee.

The small cabin began to close in on her. The air was thick, and it tasted salty. She felt sick and needed some fresh air.

On deck, Tatianna found Bart at the helm with Eddie and Rick sitting and talking. She leaned on the bright brass cover of the binnacle and asked if she could go forward to sit on one of the hatches. Bart asked her not to lean on the binnacle and explained it covered the ship's compass. She stepped back and found a handhold on the railing on the starboard side of the cockpit.

As she started to go forward, Bart asked her to hold back a minute. He said they were finding the name Tatianna too long and complicated. He wanted to know if it was okay if they just called her Anna or Annie or Ann. She turned, reached up high, placed her hand on the main boom to brace herself, and stared at Bart for what seemed a long time. She hadn't focused on her name because she had just taken it.

Part of her hesitation was that most people at home called her Anna. Being called Anna wouldn't give her the new identity she was seeking, but it would be easier to remember.

Slowly, she said in a matter-of-fact way, "Anna sounds okay." Bart stood up straighter. "Okay. Then Anna it will be." All three men nodded their heads in agreement.

Bart was puzzled. Anna was so well spoken and had a delicate air about her. Maybe even sophistication. None of this fit with her looks. But then, this was his first female cook. In fact, she was his first female crew member. Maybe it was a female thing. On the other hand, she was guarded in talking with him. He sensed a catlike wariness that conflicted with the confident defiance he saw last night. It was as if she had two personalities. He decided to leave the situation alone and watch how it was going to play out. He could get rid of her in Bermuda if she became a serious problem.

Without any further conversation, the "new" Anna went forward and sat on a hatch cover.

Rick turned to Bart and Eddie and said, "Did you see that?"

Bart asked, "See what?"

"She doesn't show any expression when she talks. It's like talking to a mannequin or something."

"Rick, I don't give a damn what she looks like when she talks. Just as long as she can talk. Have you shown her all of the boat? We don't want her touching the wrong things, getting hurt, or falling overboard! And uh, Rick! I'm charging you with keeping her and Bo separated. Got that?"

"You've got to be kidding! Why me? What if Bo gets mad at me?"

"Then come to me, and I'll handle it. I have enough other problems and don't need the crew fighting among themselves. On the last trip, you guys were a big pain in the ass, and I don't want any more of it. Right now I'm concentrating on getting to Bermuda on time. So try to keep the level of dissension down."

With the boat pitching and rolling from side to side, Anna felt unsure of her balance and moved to sit closer to the center of the deck. As they passed a large red buoy, numbered 34, the boat began to pitch higher, occasionally sending stinging sea spray across the deck. She grabbed onto a cleat on the side of the foremast for balance.

Anna was cautiously wiping her eyes from the sea spray while trying not to smudge her heavy makeup when Rick came forward. He walked easily on the shifting deck.

"Anna, are you ready to learn about the boat?"

She tried to stand, but with the wind and the movement of the boat, she was becoming dizzy with seasickness. She had to hold the halyards on the side of the mast for balance. She marveled that Rick was simply standing there, not holding onto anything and seemed perfectly comfortable while she couldn't move without support.

"Come on, let's go below, and we'll start with an overall description of what the *DOVE* is and how it works."

"How can you stand like that?"

"Sea legs. You'll get them. Just make sure you keep your legs apart and one foot in front of the other. That'll help you keep your balance. Never lock your knees and try to anticipate the roll so you can adjust your position relative to the position of the boat. Try to keep an eye on the horizon as much as possible and not the boat. That should help a lot."

Hanging on to the gunnel, Anna followed Rick below and took a seat at the dining table. She wasn't ready for this. But in spite of being seasick, she had to concentrate.

CHAPTER 12

Rick brought out a picture of the *DOVE* and showed Anna its overall structure. "The boat itself is an equal-masted, 130-foot, gaff-rigged schooner with topsails configured like classic schooners such as the *HERITAGE*. Her beam, that's how wide she is, is twenty-seven feet; and she has a draft, that's how deep she is under water, of ten feet. The bow spar, the pointy thing on the front of the boat, is about ten feet and can carry two jibs, a type of triangular sail that goes on the front of the boat."

Anna was anxious to learn about the boat quickly and asked a lot of questions. Rick answered patiently. He went over the rest of the ship's operational design and then showed her the ship's accommodations. He started with the saloon.

"Rick," Anna asked, "why do you call this room the 'saloon'? I don't see a bar."

"You know, Anna," Rick answered thoughtfully, "that's a question almost all of our charter guests have asked so I did some research. It seems that a few hundred years ago, the term 'saloon' was used to describe a large elegantly furnished room for entertaining guests. Most aristocrats had saloons in their homes. When ships began to carry paying passengers, the great cabin amidships was decorated comfortably so the guests could entertain themselves and have a nice place to get together. Naturally, they referred to it as the saloon. The riverboats on the Mississippi did the same. As people moved out West, they used the term to describe the large gathering rooms where liquor was served as saloons, and eventually most bars became known as saloons."

After reviewing the contents of the saloon, Rick showed Anna the owner's cabin. It was the most elegant cabin on the *DOVE*. Anna was especially taken with it. The highly polished wood and brass trim combined with the sky blue bedspread and red trim were truly impressive.

Noting the embroidered image of a dove on the bedspread and the inlaid image of a dove on the door of the head, Anna commented, "I really like the name *DOVE*. It seems so peaceful. Is there a story behind the name?"

"Mrs. Pisani named the boat. In fact, she was the one who wanted the boat. Mr. Pisani bought it to please her. I once heard her explain to some guests she wanted a name that combined the concept of flight, because Mr. Pisani works on airplanes, and the peaceful nature of sailing. She said with all the sails unfurled, sailing on the blue water, the boat looked like a swift white bird. So she picked *DOVE*."

"So Mr. Pisani builds airplanes?"

"Not exactly," Rick explained. "Mr. Pisani's main business is designing and manufacturing aircraft parts for the military. He never told us what the parts are. We think they have something to do with the stealth electronics of fighter planes. He also has a string of auto parts stores scattered around the country."

Again, Rick noted that Anna seemed distant to him. Of all the crew, Rick was certainly the most sociable. He had made a couple of jokes he thought would get a response from Anna, but she just looked at him as if they were ordinary statements. Without much thinking about it, he was setting a goal to crack her facade.

Rick went on to explain when Mr. Pisani wasn't using the boat for personal cruises, they conducted charters. Usually for groups of up to eight passengers to help defray the cost of operating the boat. They could take more but found it was too crowded to provide a quality level of service. However, they had to coordinate closely with Mr. Pisani so they didn't conflict with his plans.

Jack Pisani didn't use the *DOVE* frequently. When he did, he usually invited business clients for cruises in different places. The crew had to make sure they had the *DOVE* where and when he wanted it. Sometimes he would have only one or two couples as guests. Other times, he would have as many as four couples.

Rick emphasized, "When the Pisanis board the boat, they expect it to be in shipshape condition and have excellent food and service. Our primary job is to care for the boat and move it to where they want it. For this trip, Mr. Pisani wants it in St. George, Bermuda, and he's going to have two or three couples as guests."

Anna interrupted, "What are his guests like? Are they business people or pilots?" *God, I hope none of them are Phillip's clients!*

"Usually they're people who work in the aircraft industry."

Rick went on to explain, "The Bermuda guests will be exceptionally important people, so be prepared to have some good meals. Bart will have a list of the kinds of food Mrs. Pisani specifies for dinner on special nights. She pretty much goes along with whatever we provide for breakfast and lunch. Those are generally light and informal, even swimwear is acceptable. But dinners are usually dress-up affairs, and the crew has to be dressed up too. Bart will wear his captain's hat and a light blue shirt with khaki pants. After dinner, Mr. Pisani entertains his guests in the saloon or topside if it's a nice night."

Rick showed Anna the captain's cabin, navigation table, radios, engine room, generator, and other operating systems. Anna pointed to the ship's clock on the bulkhead next to the chart table and told Rick that she had to prepare lunch. As she turned to go to the galley, Bo was heading to the cabin that he shared with Eddie but stopped long enough to comment, "Aren't you supposed to be making lunch?" He couldn't miss the opportunity to gain some psychological advantage after the way she had disregarded his position in the pecking order on board.

Rick was concerned about the discord between Bo and Anna, but there was nothing he could do. Saying something to Bo was definitely out of the question. He had never actually seen Bo become physical, but he didn't want to take the chance.

CHAPTER 13

While motoring, there wasn't much to do so the crew relaxed as much as possible. In the Delaware Bay, they were dealing with three- to five-foot seas with a short period wavelength. The short period waves didn't cause much bow action on the *DOVE*. It was the longer period swells of eight feet or more that caused the boat to pitch. The ride wasn't uncomfortable for the crew, but Anna continued having problems with seasickness. In her cabin, Anna was frequently using the small sink. When making lunch, she had to control her urge to vomit. The head aft of the galley was easy to get to, and she tried not to be in a rush to get there. Anna didn't want the crew to see her sick. She was determined to do everything she could to keep from throwing up even if it meant not eating. She didn't realize the crew was beginning to get into their at-sea routine and wasn't really paying attention to her except at mealtime.

For her first evening dinner, Anna wanted to do something special. In the spice cabinet she was delighted to see a gourmet array of spices. Finding a large jar of powdered saffron and coriander, she decided to make paella. She dug deep into the freezer and found chorizos, shrimp, and peas. In the larder were artichokes preserved in oil and canned clams and mussels. She sautéed the sausage and added it to the mix. She had the makings of a real paella. If only there was some Pernod. Rick had shown her Mr. Pisani's liquor cabinet, but that was off-limits. She explained her need, and Bart agreed to let her use some of the Pernod from the cabinet.

Dinner went splendidly from Anna's point of view. Everything came out nicely if not perfectly, and again the men wolfed it down.

But then, under the circumstances, she thought trying to make a perfect meal at sea might not be possible. This was definitely a situation where perfect was the enemy of the good.

Bart told Anna her dinner was excellent. One of the best meals he had ever had at sea. Eddie and Rick agreed. Bo walked off without comment. Anna felt relieved and was beginning to think perhaps she could make it as a ship's cook.

It was getting dark. Eddie announced they were abreast of both the Cape May Light in New Jersey, to port, and the Henlopen Light in Delaware, to starboard. Only open ocean lay ahead. Bart set an initial course of 150 degrees true, to compensate for the wind and Gulf Stream, and called for all hands to set the sails.

The swells were larger in the ocean, but they were much farther apart. This gave a smoother ride. Bart was concerned that the wind was out of the southeast. He originally calculated it was going to take about five days to reach Bermuda. That wouldn't leave much time to service the boat and prepare for the arrival of the Pisanis and their guests. Given the weather conditions, he realized it would take longer.

For the next few days, life on the *DOVE* was a routine of watches and duties. Anna kept to herself as much as possible but made absolutely sure to have the meals ready on time. She stayed on a mostly liquid diet with crackers and over the next few days spent less and less time using the small sink in her cabin.

Anna made it a point not to eat with the crew, and when she needed fresh air, she tried to stay away from the guys, especially Bo. This was hardest with Rick because he wanted to talk with her more than the other crew members. On several occasions, he had asked her about her personal life, where she was from, what kind of name Tatianna was, did she have a boyfriend, had she ever been married, etc. She never answered his questions, repeatedly changing the subject. Rick suspected Anna was in some sort of trouble so he stopped asking her about her background and began explaining various part of the boat and different aspects of sailing.

CHAPTER 14

It was the morning after the *DOVE* had departed Philadelphia when Maroon Espidito saw the TV news. Two police detectives and a woman had been killed in a gunfight with unknown criminals in the older harbor section of Philadelphia. After showing photos of the detectives, the news anchor speculated they unexpectedly interrupted a drug deal and were killed trying to apprehend the drug dealers. The role of the woman was unknown. Her photo was being withheld pending notification of relatives. The anchor mentioned that two other men had been killed in the same area of town. Although the victims had drugs in their car, the police were unable to connect their deaths to the shooting of the detectives.

Maroon leaped up from his stuffed leather office chair and excitedly reached into the breast pocket of his suit for his prepaid cell phone. He had several and used them because they couldn't be traced. He placed a call to the private cell phone of Assistant District Attorney David Kramer.

"Dave here," David Kramer answered quietly.

"Dave, this is Maroon. Was that Tatianna? Did you get her?"

There was a long silence. Then Dave responded in a low voice, "Jesus, Maroon, you shouldn't be calling me here in the office. You know better than that."

Irritated at being reprimanded, Maroon angrily responded, "Just give me a goddamn answer, Dave. Yes or no. This is too important to fuck around with. You said your guys could find her. She took the fucking books."

"What! She took the books? When you asked me to help find her, you didn't say she took the books. I thought she must have skimmed some of the money. Shit! How did you let that happen?"

"Shit. Is that all you can say?" Maroon demanded. "Who the fuck was the woman? Was it Tatianna or not? Your people were on the scene. Who was she?"

"The cops think the woman was a bystander who got caught in the crossfire. That's all they know so far," Dave whispered. "The guys called me when they thought they had found Tatianna and they were getting ready to grab her. Then they hung up. The next thing I heard was two of our detectives had been shot. I don't know who the goddamn woman was or why she was there. Tatianna must have got the drop on our guys and got away."

Slamming his fist on his desk, Maroon yelled into his cell phone, "That bitch stole our goddamn books and killed four of our guys. You better get your fucking people together and find her. And find her quick, or you're going to be joining your fucking dead detectives. Got that?"

The door to Dave's office opened, and his secretary stepped in. She signaled and mouthed the words to Dave that the mayor was coming up to see him about the deaths of the detectives. In front of the secretary, Dave spoke into the phone, "Yes. Great. We'll take care of it," and hung up.

Standing in a mahogany-paneled office, deep inside an older warehouse, Maroon yelled at the wall, "The shithead just hung up on me. Who the fuck does he think he's talking to?" Maroon leaned back in his chair and began to make calls using his office phone. He was giving orders to his best men to scour the area where the detectives had been shot and to find Tatianna.

Maroon's underlings didn't know what Tatianna looked like. She worked only with Maroon. Dave had seen her once in a brief chance encounter at Maroon's office. She wasn't supposed to be there. It was late at night and one of the rare times Dave went to Maroon's warehouse. When Dave unexpectedly appeared, Tatianna scurried out with her face away from him. She stayed anonymous to protect the cartel's information on distribution and payoffs. Maroon set it up that way so no one could take over the organization. He was paranoid about being taken over.

Maroon gave his employees, if one could call them that, a brief description of Tatianna. Short dirty blond hair, overweight, etc. Also, she used a large black bag instead of a briefcase. He told them to go into every store in the area and find anyone who had seen her. They were to bring her back alive. He wanted those books back.

Two days later, Maroon got a call from one of his men. A woman who sort of matched Tatianna's description had bought some boating supplies at a commercial marine store in the harbor area. The sales clerk said someone had beaten her up badly. That was all he knew. The man assured Maroon they made certain the clerk didn't withhold anything.

After several attempts, Maroon was able to get through to Dave Kramer's private cell phone. He told Dave, Tatianna had taken a boat somewhere on Monday night or Tuesday morning.

"Dave, we need to know where the goddamn boat was going. My guys told me it had to be one of the boats tied up at the old commercial docks."

"I'll get back to you right away," Dave answered and hung up.

The next morning, Dave Kramer called Maroon and told him that a seaman on a cargo ship said a sailboat left for Bermuda the other morning. It had been docked between some old freighters in the heavy industrial area several miles from where the detectives were shot. He hadn't actually seen the boat but had a brief exchange with one of the crew at a bar down the street.

"You better be right, Dave! I can send a couple of guys to look for her. We've got to get the books back."

CHAPTER 15

The last few months had been hectic for the coroner's office in Philadelphia, and the staff was pleased Phillip Mueller had waived the need for an autopsy. After all, it was pretty obvious how his wife Annaliese had died. There were numerous witnesses to the accident.

It was Friday afternoon, four days since the horrible accident, and Phillip had just returned from the cemetery near Doylestown. Everything related to her burial went quickly and quietly. Phillip had a small service at the mortuary and invited only a few people to the cemetery.

The police were concerned this seemingly ordinary housewife from an upscale Doylestown neighborhood was carrying a .38-caliber revolver and a box of cartridges, and her husband didn't know anything about it. Phillip seemed to be as perplexed about the gun as the police. In fact, he showed greater emotion when he saw the gun than when he viewed the body. He was definitely stunned. What surprised the police most was his apparent lack of sadness or mourning.

Detectives Finney and Sloan had been assigned to the case and were conducting a routine investigation. It was standard procedure to investigate a death when they found a gun on the victim, whether it was involved in the death or not. They traced the gun to Schwartz's Gun Shop about twenty miles outside the city.

As they entered the shop, Joey Degrassi looked up from his desk behind the display cases and counter. He vaguely recognized the detectives from when he was a uniformed cop in the department.

They recognized him too, and Finney, who was the older of the two, greeted him saying, "So this is where you disappeared to! After you left the department, no one seemed to know what happened to you. Are you okay, Joey? We missed you."

Joey came out from the back of the counter to be more cordial. He told them he had visited the department several times awhile back. It was late in the afternoon, and he only made contact with his old partner, Bob Marino. He went on to offer detectives Finney and Sloan some coffee or soda, but they declined.

"No, we have to get back. We're okay."

Sloan asked why he had quit the force. That seemed to be an important question among all the policemen when one of their fellow officers quit.

"Well," Joey explained, "after my wife Sandy was murdered, I kind of lost interest in being a cop."

"Yeah," Sloan commented. "I remember. She was a loan officer in the bank, wasn't she? That was a goddamn shame."

Joey looked away for a moment, then turned back, and commented in a low voice, "Yeah, there was no reason for the bastards to shoot her. Sandy's desk was off to the side of the lobby, and she was no threat to them. The clerk died too."

Finney asked, "Why didn't you stay on and help catch the bastards?"

"They got killed a week later during another bank heist. After Sandy died, I wanted to kill every son of a bitch who was apprehended, and that wasn't a good situation. So I quit."

"How do you like having a business? Are you enjoying it?" Finney asked.

"Yeah, it's okay. I actually spend most of my time reading books and occasionally selling a gun or two. Mostly shotguns and shells to the farmers."

After reminiscing for a few minutes, Joey asked what brought them out so far from the city. They showed him a photo of Annaliese Mueller's snub-nosed revolver.

"You wouldn't have happened to have seen this gun before, would you?" Finney asked.

"I dunno. It looks like a S&W .38-caliber revolver. What's so special about it?"

"It belonged to a young woman named Annaliese Mueller, who was killed down in the waterfront area of the city. She had a license to carry it, and we traced it to your shop."

Joey's mouth dropped open, and he turned ashen in color. He stepped back to lean against the gun display case. There was a moment of silence as he stared at the detectives. It was obvious that Joey knew Annaliese quite well.

Detective Sloan looked at Joey and said, "So you knew her!"

Joey didn't respond. He was stunned. He continued to stare at the detectives, began shaking his head and muttering, "No! No! This is terrible. This is just terrible!"

"You seem to have known her quite well, Joey. Is that right?" Sloan asked.

"Yes, I knew her. She was a terrific woman. I just can't believe she is dead."

"Why is that?" Finney asked. "Was there something going on between you?"

"She was afraid her husband was going to kill her. When she first came in, she looked pretty bad. One look and you could tell someone had beaten the hell out of her."

Joey looked down and stopped talking for a moment. His voice started to break as he thought about how badly her husband had beaten her up before her first visit to his shop. Finney and Sloan stood quietly waiting for him to continue.

Joey looked up and asked, "Did her husband kill her?"

"No," Finney softly answered. "She died in an accident down near the waterfront. It was pretty gruesome. We were assigned the case after the traffic cops found the gun. It's standard procedure, you know. But what caught our attention was the husband's response. He was arrogant and seemed a lot less distraught about his wife's death than we expected. When we asked about the revolver, he was really taken aback. He was shocked to learn she had a gun. We interviewed the neighbors and a few casual friends. Several of them told us she seemed to always have bruises but covered them up as much as possible and made excuses. And they hadn't really seen her much for several years."

"How did the accident happen?" Joey asked. "She seemed to be a good driver."

"She wasn't in her car. She was a pedestrian and got hit by a truck while crossing the street. The truck came over a small hill going pretty fast, and she stepped out in front of it."

"Did somebody push her? Did you check that out?"

"Oh yeah! A lot of witnesses saw the whole thing. The cops handling the accident were on the ball and kept the witnesses at the scene. They took statements from all of them. It was an accident as far as we can tell. No one was anywhere near her when she stepped out in front of the truck. The truck driver was distraught and more upset than the husband."

Finally, getting to the point, Finney asked, "So how did she come to have a license to carry, Joey?"

"I helped her get it. She was afraid her husband was going to kill her or have her killed so he could get rid of her and not pay alimony. He's some sort of big shot in the finance business and very tight with his money. I taught her how to use a gun and emphasized she should only use it in self-defense."

Sloan asked if Joey had any idea why she was carrying a box of cartridges. "That's a lot of ammunition for self-defense."

"I can't be sure, but it was probably because I ran short on range ammo, and she volunteered to pick some up from Wal-Mart. They have the best prices. Were the bullets fully jacketed?"

"Yes, as a matter of fact they were."

"That's what we used for practice. For personal use, I urged her to use partially jacketed hollow points. That's what you should have found in the revolver."

"You're right, Joey. We were going to ask about that next. When were you going to see her again?"

"I was expecting her last Tuesday, for practice, but she didn't show up. There had been a couple of other instances when she missed her practice session because she thought she was being followed. I was worried but thought she would get in touch with me soon."

"Well," Finney said with an expression of finality, "we have to get back, and it's a long drive in late-afternoon traffic. Everything seems to be in order, but that wasn't the problem anyhow. We're just checking out all the details and didn't know it was you who owned this shop. But I'm glad we met up with you. Be sure to drop by the department. From everything I heard, you were a good cop, and we need good cops. Maybe you ought to think about coming back. With your experience, you could make detective pretty quick."

After the detectives left, Joey stood at the counter for a few moments, staring out the dirty window in a daze. He put the "Store Closed" sign in the door window, even though it was only mid-afternoon, and locked the door.

CHAPTER 16

Joey turned to a cabinet on the sidewall, unlocked it, took out a bottle of Jack Daniel's black label, and got some ice from his under-the-counter refrigerator. He sat back at the desk, poured some of the Tennessee sipping whisky in a glass with ice, took a sip, and began to think about Anna.

When he first met Anna, his wife had been gone almost two years. About a year after her death, he was tired of moping around the house and purchased the gun shop from old man Schwartz. Business was slow. That's why Schwartz wanted to sell it.

To occupy his time, Joey made some renovations to an old coal-mining tunnel behind the shop. The tunnel had been abandoned several decades earlier. Mr. Schwartz had built his shop up against the mouth of the tunnel. Joey thought it would make a good firing range. It went straight back about three hundred feet and was about ten to twelve feet wide and eight feet high. Working by himself, he built a doorway at the back of the shop and wired the tunnel for lighting and air ventilation. There was no vertical air shaft so he had an air-handling system installed that brought fresh air in from the front of the tunnel range and sucked it out from the rear. He vented the exhaust air outside. Since the tunnel was always cool in the summer and somewhat warm in the winter, it didn't need air-conditioning or heating, just good air flow to remove the lead and smoke from the guns.

Joey built firing stations with benches and gun rests and two electric target pulley systems to move the targets from the rear of the tunnel back up to the shooter's bench. His new firing range was not sophisticated but very functional. The tunnel totally deadened the sound from the gunshots.

Joey had almost finished remodeling the gun shop by the time he met Anna. He stayed open on the weekends because that's when the few customers he serviced usually came in. So he closed on Tuesdays and Wednesdays, and for that matter any other days he wanted. He wasn't depending on income from the gun shop because he was living off his limited pension and wife's life insurance. Anything Joey made from gun sales was gravy.

He recalled the Tuesday morning when a silver blue Mercedes pulled up and parked in front of the shop. His regular customers mostly drove pickup trucks. Over his counter, and through the dirty front window, he could see a woman staring straight ahead at the shop. He was confident she couldn't see him due to the signs in the window, the dirt, and the glare. Almost ten minutes passed before the woman got out of the car and tried to enter the shop. She knocked on the door incessantly before finally looking down to see the small "Store Closed" sign. Joey was about to get up and go to the door, but she stopped knocking and went back to the car. But she didn't leave. She just sat there, her arms folded around the steering wheel, her face against her arms, sobbing.

After some time, Joey got up from the desk where he had been hidden from view working on bills and receipts. He went out to the car and knocked on the window. She didn't respond immediately. Then she slowly leaned back against the blue leather seat and opened the window.

When Joey saw her, he immediately realized she had been beaten up. "Miss, are you all right. Can I help you?"

"Yes! You can sell me a gun," she said with tears flowing down her cheeks, making a mess of her heavy makeup.

Thinking fast, he responded, "We don't generally sell guns out here in the parking lot. You should come on in. We can talk inside the shop."

He was hoping to calm her down by inviting her in. Once inside, he had her sit on a chair behind the counter and quietly asked, "Why do you want a gun?

"I want to shoot my husband," she stated flatly.

Joey responded, "Yeah, I think I can see why!"

That was probably not the right thing for Joey to have said. She started to cry again, and Joey tried to console her by offering her some water, which she took and sipped slowly.

With the water and Joey's attention, the woman started to calm down.

Wow! How do I handle this? Joey kept thinking. *I can't let this woman have a gun, but if I turn her away she'll go somewhere else and get one. I'd better get her calmed down.*

"So what kind of gun do you want? I have several kinds from shotguns to pistols." With levity, he continued, "No assault rifles though, I'm sorry to say."

"You're not going to try to talk me out of buying a gun?"

"Well no! That's what I'm in business for, to sell guns."

"You'll sell me a gun?"

"Yeah, but I need to know how you want to use it. I don't want to sell you the wrong kind of gun. One of the major problems people have with guns is that they buy the wrong kind of gun. Then when they need it, they end up getting killed with their own gun. That's not good for business." He said this with a slight amount of humor, trying to cheer the woman up.

He tried to calm the woman down by not disagreeing with her. He had learned that trick as a cop dealing with domestic quarrels. You had to get them calmed down in order to reason with them. It was apparent her husband had beaten her up, but he couldn't determine quite yet whether to call the police. He wasn't a cop anymore. If he made an accusation and she denied it, he could be sued. So he stopped talking and sat quietly waiting for her to respond.

She just sat and looked straight ahead at the wall on the other side of the display cases. He was hoping she was simply distraught and would leave once she calmed down. But then, she looked directly at him and calmly asked, "What kind of gun is best for shooting my husband?"

Joey was thinking that his approach wasn't working. She was persistent.

"That depends. Most any gun will work. Do you want to just hurt him, or do you want to really kill him?"

"I want to kill him."

The decisiveness in her voice startled him, but by then he had become more aware of what he was looking at. This woman had been beaten up pretty badly. She had used pancake makeup to cover up her cuts and bruises. Her eyes were bright blue, but it wasn't easily noticeable because they were bloodshot. She was big, especially compared to him. He was five foot seven inches and a bit thin. He estimated her to be almost six feet tall, and she wasn't wearing heels. Her husband must be pretty big he thought. But he had difficulty determining how old she was. She looked older but seemed young and naive, even vulnerable. He was thirty-six, and he estimated her to be about thirty. Maybe thirty-five.

"How do you want to kill your husband?" Joey was trying to be compassionate in the way he asked her why she needed a gun. "I mean do you want to nail him flat out and go to jail for murder after you kill him, or do you want to be more surreptitious and remain free?"

She looked at him quizzically. "I don't want to go to jail!"

Joey was kind of proud of his question. He thought he had her attention, and it would put an end to her wanting a gun. But it didn't. So he asked her if she would be willing to tell him what, exactly, her situation was.

"I just don't want him to hurt me anymore. I want him to stop. When he's home, I'm always afraid, and I want him to stop hurting me."

"Ma'am, I used to be a policeman, and I've seen a lot of domestic violence. I might be able to offer some advice if you would tell me more about your husband. Perhaps we can find another way to make him stop hurting you, like a separation or divorce."

They talked for several hours, and for the first time in years, Joey felt he was helping someone. He told her he would be willing to sell her a gun, but only after she had proper training and had a license to have one. He understood her circumstances, but a gun might not be the best way to deal with her husband. He expected with time she could be talked out of shooting her husband.

Anna was relieved to have someone to talk to. Her aunt, who had been her primary confidante, passed away several years ago and left her without any family. At about the same time, Phillip started to mistreat her. He chased her friends away, verbally abused her for having them, and more and more frequently threatened to get rid of her. She tried to defend herself, but that usually ended up causing Phillip to become more violent.

—

Joey told Anna if she could come to his shop on Tuesday or Wednesday mornings, he could spend time training her. He gave her a tour of his shooting range, which she thought was really cool. She told him she felt safe in the tunnel. He showed her several types of handguns and offered to let her use his personal guns while she was learning how to handle them. As an ex-policeman, he had accumulated quite a collection that was not for sale. By offering to let her use his guns, she might be less inclined to buy one. If he didn't help her, she would probably go somewhere else, buy a gun there, and end up in jail or dead.

Joey was surprised the next Tuesday morning when the silver blue Mercedes pulled up in front of his shop. He didn't think she would come back but had been hoping she would. It was boring in the middle of the week, and he was lonely in the shop.

He started her lessons by going over the basics of how a gun functions and the different types of cartridges. He took his time. He had her disassemble several semiautomatics and reassemble them. The same with several revolvers. He gave her a textbook on guns, but she hesitated in accepting it. She was afraid to take it home. She suggested she could come early the following week and read the book at the shop.

Over the next year, Joey and Anna spent most Tuesdays, and sometimes Wednesdays, in the tunnel shooting range. She had become, in Joey's opinion, an expert marksman. Her eye-hand coordination was extraordinary. He told her some people just had a natural capability to shoot straight, and she might consider entering some competitive shooting events. Then they started playing gun games. He set up scenarios with different types of targets Anna had to shoot at while lying down, kneeling, or hiding behind barrels or other props. Her favorite game was when both of them worked together to shoot at moving targets Joey had rigged down range. He began to spend his spare time, which he seemed to have a lot of, devising different shooting games and making new targets of villains popping out from behind fake walls or cars. They had to roll on the ground together sometimes to reduce their available target size while pretending to have a shoot-out with villains.

Some of Joey's best times with Anna were when he took her to the paintball range in the woods south of Downingtown. Occasionally they acted as a team to compete against other teams of paintballers in war games. On other occasions, Joey would stalk her, and Anna had to defend herself. She told him it was in the forest when she really began to understand how to use her gun in self-defense. It was after he shot her several times because she had not hidden or shielded herself properly and became an accessible target. She learned when someone was trying to shoot her, she really had to present herself as a minimum target area and calmly return fire. Above all, she had to aim before firing.

To emphasize the shock of someone actually shooting a real gun at her, Joey devised a game where Anna had to defend herself under live fire, using blanks. It was designed to help her overcome the "startle factor" and concentrate on aiming and squeezing the trigger when being shot at. He built special props and installed them in the tunnel. He would position himself at the other end of the tunnel and fire back at her.

Sometimes Anna would come early, and they would go down the road to a country diner to have breakfast and talk about guns and self-defense. He had become her sage. She began to depend on him for moral support and direction. And Anna had become his best friend as well as being his only student.

During one breakfast, after they had been training about four months, Anna asked Joey when he was going to sell her a gun and give her a bill for all the training. She said she had been doing everything possible to keep her husband from getting upset. She felt the training gave her a newfound sense of discipline that allowed her to better control her behavior and avoid provoking Phillip, but he hit her occasionally anyhow.

Joey remembered being caught off guard when she asked for a bill. Anna had filled a huge void in his life, and he looked forward to Tuesdays and Wednesdays like other people looked forward to weekends. He told her all the training came free with the purchase of the gun. Anna smiled brightly then laughed. She squinted her eyes and asked, "And what if I don't buy a gun from you?" For a moment, he felt devastated before realizing she was teasing him. She had never done that before. They both laughed as it became clear between them that they were indeed friends and were enjoying each other's company.

In the month that followed, Joey gave Anna an S&W snub-nosed .38-caliber revolver with a lightweight scandium frame, and they began to use it in training. Of all the guns they used, Anna liked the .40-caliber Glock with the vented short slide the best. She liked it even better than the .38-caliber Beretta Cheetah, which had a fine balance but was a little heavy. The reduced recoil of the vented Glock made it possible for her to improve her groupings on the targets at greater distances. But by the time she took possession of her own gun, she realized that Joey was right. The snub-nosed revolver would be the most reliable and accessible in an emergency situation. Even though it didn't have the firepower of the Glock or the Beretta, its small size would still make it very lethal in up-close defense.

During those last few months, they began exploring trick shooting. Joey felt it would help Anna develop a much higher level of confidence in her shooting skills. He was remembering some of the last training exercises they had when his chair slipped, and he almost dropped his glass of sipping whisky. He looked up, and it was dark out. He felt very lonely.

CHAPTER 17

After four days at sea, Anna was spending much less time at her private sink. It had taken a tremendous effort for her to cook three meals and prepare the night lunch while feeling dizzy and nauseous. The medications and limited amount of food were helping her get past the seasickness. Each day she felt a little better and was discovering what she imagined was the rhythm of the sea, the constant movement of the boat to the swells of the open ocean, and the sound of the water rushing past the hull. She enjoyed hearing the occasional flap of the jib when the helmsman made a course correction. She was even beginning to enjoy the salt spray when she was topside, watching the *DOVE* part the waves in an undulating dance with nature.

One morning, after preparing breakfast and cleaning up the galley, Anna went topside to get fresh air. To her delight, she discovered she could stand up straight without desperately holding onto something stationary. Bo and Eddie were on watch. The mainsails were puffed out to the starboard, and the jib was sweeping well outboard of the gunnel. The sting of salt spray was in the air, and she had to lean into the wind to stand. Anna had the impression of great speed and asked Eddie how fast they were going. He said they were making between seven and eight knots. She asked how fast a knot was. Bo quickly commented it was unbelievable she was on a boat and didn't know what a knot was.

Over the next few days, Anna found herself trying to steer clear of Bo. He was aggressive, and he didn't like her, or maybe just women. But no, it couldn't be women. She had overheard him bragging to

Rick and Eddie about the women he had been with while ashore in Philadelphia. Anna wondered if it was her fault that he was so negative toward her. She hadn't responded well to his impolite demands for special service. She had had that problem with Phillip. *Or maybe it's because he wants to be the dominant male of the crew and I'm not acting submissive. No, I'm not going to do it.* Anna decided it would have to be Bo who learned to get along. She would never be rude or discourteous, but she wouldn't give in to his overbearing demands.

Anna considered Joey her best friend as well as a big brother and perhaps even a father. She missed out on that kind of relationship with her father because her parents died when she was a baby. They were killed in a traffic accident on a narrow country road outside of Lancaster. Her aunt said she survived because her mother protected her during the crash. Her uncle and aunt took her in and adopted her. They were in their late forties and had no children of their own.

Both Anna's uncle and aunt were in poor health as long as she could remember. Their doctors said it was because of all the metal dust they breathed while working in his factory. When Anna was twelve years old, her uncle sold his wire and nail manufacturing business and moved them from Birdsboro to a small house on the west side Philadelphia to be closer to the University of Pennsylvania Medical Complex. He died when she was sixteen.

Although her uncle came from Mennonite stock, he didn't practice the religion except he had always been frugal and saved the little money he made when he sold the business. Phillip was her uncle's financial advisor and had skillfully managed his estate even after his death. Anna felt that she owed everything to Phillip for helping her family survive. If it hadn't been for Phillip, she and her aunt would have been destitute. He had taken a growing interest in her welfare during her mid-teens. Over time, their relationship deepened, and they married when she was eighteen. When her aunt's health began to decline precipitously, Phillip made sure she had good medical care. He told Anna that he was using his own money to pay most of the medical bills.

Anna had difficulty reconciling Phillip's benevolent and caring side with his increasing abusiveness. After her aunt died, Phillip began to excel in business and became more affluent. He provided

Anna with a fine house in an upscale area in Bucks County southeast of Doylestown. He also became more demanding, short-tempered, and violent.

During some of her downtime on the *DOVE*, Anna studied the two ledgers, which were apparently recorded in code. The records in each of the ledgers appeared to document the same transactions but were presented differently and added up differently. They involved huge amounts of money routinely being moved from certain people to others in a complex code of both names and places. It was obvious to Anna the ledgers were records of some kind of illegal activities. She suspected Tatianna was a bookkeeper for a criminal gang. As she studied the second book, she realized money was being paid to an entity not present anywhere in the first book. Then it hit her. *Tatianna must have been siphoning off money and depositing it in her account in that Cayman Islands bank. No wonder they were after her. And now they're after me—and these books! I've got to figure out what to do with all this money and these ledgers.*

CHAPTER 18

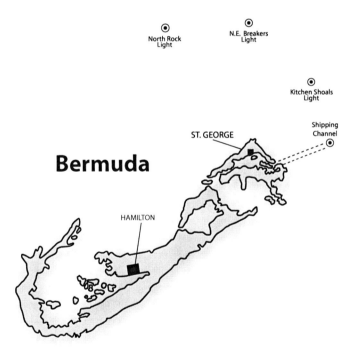

Their transit to Bermuda had taken longer than Bart planned. They had run into headwinds and high seas. It was 0400 on Monday morning when Rick finally spotted the light at North Rock on the northwest coast of Bermuda. A few minutes later, Rick saw the North

East Breakers light due north of the island. In a few hours, the *DOVE* rounded Kitchen Shoals. Bart set a course due south heading for the shipping channel leading into St. George's Harbor through Town Cut. Rick called down to Anna to see if she wanted to come topside for an early morning view of the island of Bermuda. She was about to start breakfast but went up to watch the entry into the harbor. The sun was rising behind the *DOVE*, and the island gleamed brightly. It was a beautiful sight after so many days at sea. She couldn't wait to put her feet on solid ground.

St. George Bermuda

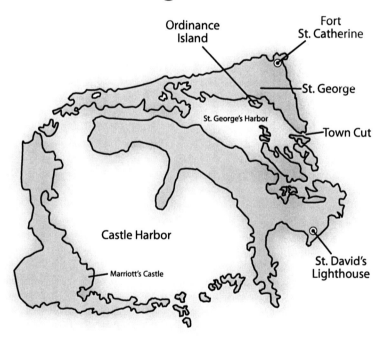

When the *DOVE* reached the outer buoy marking the entry to the channel, Bart called for all hands on deck to lower the sails. Anna went below to prepare breakfast. When she returned, she could see the St. David Lighthouse to the south and marveled at the steepness of the cliffs as they motored through Town Cut. They passed Smith

Island on the port side and tied up at a commercial dock east of Ordinance Island.

After the boat was tied up with the fenders out, and the gangplank in position, the dock master and the customs agent called out for the captain. The dock master had a message from Mr. Pisani who had expected the *DOVE* to arrive in Bermuda the previous Friday. Because of its delay, he had rescheduled his party for the following Friday. He was having three couples as guests and wanted dinner served Friday night aboard the *DOVE*.

Mr. Pisani also wanted Bart to plan for some diving trips on one of the well-known wrecks and some of the patch reefs on the west coast. All the members of his party were experienced divers and would bring their personal gear.

Bart informed the crew they had four and a half days to prepare for Mr. Pisani and his party's arrival. He relayed the food requirements to Anna and told her to make sure everything she needed was on hand. Bo was to start planning the dive schedule and to make sure all the *DOVE*'s air bottles were ready to go. "And," Bart told the entire crew, "the *DOVE* has to be shipshape by Friday morning."

Anna planned to go into town, ostensibly to scout out where to buy food and see what was available. When she crossed the gangplank and stepped on the hard, unmoving dry land, she felt a sudden uneasiness. She was startled by this phenomenon, and it took her several minutes to get used to not having the ground under her move.

Once ashore, she walked out to York Street and looked for the pink-topped pole that designated the stop for buses heading toward Hamilton. Her first order of business was to find a post office and bank. She needed to open an account so she could deposit the cash hidden in her cabin. But to open an account, she needed an address to receive bank statements. On Church Street, she found the main post office and rented a box under the name Anna Meerschmidt. After explaining to the clerk she worked on boats at sea and was often gone for long periods of time, she rented the box for two years.

She then found the Bank of Bermuda just down the block and applied for a checking account using the same name, Anna Meerschmidt. The clerk, a young woman, questioned her because her passport showed her to be Tatianna M. Wolinski. Anna began to tear up and told the clerk Anna was short for Tatianna and Meerschmidt was her maiden name. She was just divorced and trying to reestablish herself under her maiden name. She explained that if her ex-husband found her he would hurt her. The clerk looked at Anna for a moment, studied the bruises on her face, and accepted her story. Anna deposited one thousand dollars. She then rented a safe-deposit box for two years.

After leaving the Bank of Bermuda, she searched for a dentist who could fix her chipped teeth and do it in four days. She wanted to change her appearance in any way she could, and she wanted to do it right away. She had to wait a while to see the dentist, but since she was paying with cash, he was agreeable to the short time frame for the repair work. It was not an unusual request in Bermuda because many of the sailors coming and going didn't have much shore time. The dentist said he would have to charge her extra for the accelerated service, however. She agreed, and he began to prepare her chipped teeth for caps.

The dentist couldn't help but notice the swelling and bruised marks on her face. The bruises were fading in color but were still noticeable under her makeup. He had to be careful when asking her to open her mouth wide because the split on the left side had not fully healed. It looked like the split was going to cause her mouth to be a little wider on the left than on the right. He stopped his preparation for a moment and gently probed the puffy swollen areas above her left eye and on both cheeks.

"You know, Ms. Meerschmidt, Bermuda is a small island, and the medical professionals all know one another."

Of course, Anna couldn't answer. Dentists always seem to talk while the patient can't answer. Can't nod either. Only gurgle.

Anna looked at him quizzically, and he went on, "I have a friend who specializes in cosmetic surgery. He might be able to help you with the swollen areas on your face."

When he completed the preparation, the dentist set an appointment to apply the caps for Wednesday morning. He then gave Anna the name and address of the specialist.

"If you can wait a moment, I'll call my friend to see if he has an opening."

—

The doctor agreed to see Anna Wednesday after her appointment with the dentist.

"Bermuda must be a wonderful place if you can get an appointment with a doctor on such short notice."

"It's like I said, we're friends. Actually, we're fishing and diving buddies so he's doing it as a favor. Also, I explained that I think you need to have him look at the bruises right away. They may be more serious than you think. But be prepared. He charges a lot more than I do."

After the visit to the dentist, Anna looked for a blue-topped bus stop pole for her return trip to the *DOVE*. Poles with blue tops denoted stops for buses leading away from Hamilton. It was a wild ride, with branches hitting the sides of the bus on the narrow roads. She got off at the corner of York Street and Old Maid's Lane, on the north side of St. George's Harbor, and took a shortcut back to the *DOVE*.

CHAPTER 19

The next morning, Anna prepared an especially nice breakfast even though Bart had told her it wasn't necessary. After breakfast, she retrieved the ledgers and ninety thousand dollars from her hiding place. She caught the bus to Hamilton and went to the bank. She deposited the money in her new account and stored the ledgers in her safe-deposit box. She couldn't deposit the ninety thousand the day before because she was opening a new account, and it might have aroused too much attention. Anna left the bank and took the bus back to the north end. Before returning to the *DOVE*, she walked past Water Street and discovered a run-down-looking tavern on the harbor waterfront.

The Windward Tavern was not the kind of place where Anna might run into any of Phillip's clients. It looked like a bar only seamen and sailors might frequent. She needed some place to go, to get away from the crew for a while, relax, and feel free from being discovered. The Windward Tavern appeared to fit the bill.

Maintenance on the exterior of the tavern had apparently been neglected for quite a while, but it had an open-air bar and dining area in the back. Rickety tables lined the heavily cracked concrete slab the management called a patio. The overhead canvas canopy was stained with mold and drooping in some places but seemed to be holding together. At least it shaded the patio from the afternoon sun.

Inside was a long polished mahogany bar with a lot of wooden stools. Five small tables with mismatched chairs provided additional seating. Anna took what appeared to be the cleanest table, moved the dirty ashtray and a couple of empty beer bottles aside, and sat on a chair that felt like it had one leg about an inch shorter than the others. She felt comfortable there in her baggy jeans, blue denim shirt, and canvas boat shoes.

She asked the bartender/waiter for a menu, and he told her they didn't have any. An older man sitting at the bar turned and commented, "You might try the fried fish sandwich. The fish is fresh, but the beef isn't."

Having not eaten hardly any solids for a week, Anna asked if they had soup.

"We got only fish chowder, missus."

"Good, I'll have a cup of fish chowder. Thank you."

"We don't got no cups, just bowls."

"Okay, I'll have a bowl of fish chowder."

Looking at the beer signs hung all about, and the bottles of liquor on the shelves behind the bar, Anna thought, *I might as well celebrate getting out of Philadelphia alive and making it to Bermuda.* She ordered a Heineken beer.

In a straightforward manner, she thanked the man at the bar for his suggestion. He was stocky, probably sixty years old, with longish unkempt silver white hair, and a heavy tan. He needed a shave and spoke with a British accent. After a few minutes, he came over to Anna's table, pulled out one of the chairs, and sat down. He could see this visibly disturbed Anna as she drew back and stared at him.

"Hey, hope you don't mind if I join you. They don't have much business here this time of day, and there's nobody to talk to but the bartender. He's boring, but it gets crazy at night. Mostly seamen and sailors from the boats in the harbor. They don't go to the fancy places up the road. You look more like a sailor than a seaman. What ship are you on?"

"The *DOVE*."

"The *DOVE*? Oh yeah, I saw her come in. She's a schooner, isn't she? Expensive looking too! Where's she docked?"

"On the other side of that island."

"Oh yeah, that's Ordinance Island. You must be at the commercial dock."

"I guess it is. It's pretty big and made of concrete."

"My name is George, what's yours?"

Anna stared at George with squinted eyes and slowly answered, "Anna." This was getting too personal. She was wary and wanted to maintain her anonymity.

"Well, Anna, it's a pleasure to meet you."

At this point, Anna decided George might be lonely and just looking for conversation. He had obviously had a few beers too. She had made a commitment to herself not to talk to strangers, and men in general, unless absolutely necessary. But George was old enough to be her grandfather and seemed like an amiable sort who just wanted company, so she decided not to move to another table or ask him to leave. Besides, the other tables had more cigarette butts and beer bottles on them.

"Do you live here on the island?"

"No, I have a boat over there somewhere," he answered while pointing out toward the harbor.

"What kind of boat is it?"

"It's an old sloop. Her name is *FREEDOM*. I named her that when I retired and decided to roam the seven seas. I've been here about a month. I've been thinking about going to the West Indies in a week or so. Probably St. Thomas first though. It's a long voyage by yourself."

"It must be nice to have no fixed schedule and be able to go where you want, whenever you want."

"Yeah, I guess so."

Anna's chowder and beer came, and the waiter asked if she was okay or would she like another table.

"No, but you could take the ashtray and empty bottles away."

"No problem, missus. Anything else?"

"I think we'll be fine."

Anna was surprised at how good the chowder was and tried to identify the ingredients. She remarked to George that it was excellent. He attributed it to the fresh fish.

"The place doesn't have much going for it except the food. At first I only came here to have a beer, but now I eat here too."

George went on to tell her about the island, the reefs, and the ebb and flow of the nightlife. Then he told her he had come from the Bahamas. "Things were rough there. Lot of problems for sailors.

I left in a hurry and then ran into a storm that tore my mainsail, but I made it into St. George."

"Do you always sail alone?" Anna asked incredulously, thinking that must be why he seemed lonely.

"Yep!" he laughed. "That way I don't have anyone telling me what to do."

George told a few jokes which Anna either did not understand or was displeased to hear.

"You didn't like my jokes?"

"They're okay, George, but I think I've heard them before."

"Oh? I guess I've been at sea too long. I don't know any new ones."

As Anna was finishing her chowder, George got up and told her he had to pick up his sail that was being repaired. He said he had been working on his boat for several days and took the morning off because he had to get the sail.

"George, if you've been here a month, why did you wait so long to get your sail repaired?"

"I didn't. They work on island time here, and it's just now ready."

"Sorry. I didn't mean to pry."

"I'm going to go now, Ms. Anna. If you can stop back by later, we can talk some more. They don't have many women come in here. If you want to visit the *FREEDOM*, she's docked over there."

Anna watched him leave and was thinking that she was not as polite as she could have been. He seemed to be a good person.

After lunch, Anna walked along the north side of the island to see the beach. On the way back, she stopped at a small grocery store to buy some fresh fish.

CHAPTER 20

It was late afternoon when Anna boarded the *DOVE*. She heard women laughing and found Bo, Eddie, and Bart entertaining three young women in shorts and halter tops. Everyone had beers. The tables were littered with ashtrays full of butts, bowls of various junk food, and empty beer bottles. The saloon was heavy with the smell of tobacco and beer. One girl, wearing short-shorts and a low-slung halter top that was barely useful, was sitting in Bo's lap. Eddie was lying sideways against another girl whose top was even scantier. They had obviously been partying all afternoon and didn't seem to acknowledge her presence. The women were giggling and the men laughing.

Anna nodded acknowledgment and walked toward the galley to refrigerate the fish. She was thinking their partying was a lucky break because they hadn't missed her. But then, they probably wouldn't miss her anyway until dinnertime.

Bart looked up as she passed. "Come on over, Anna, sit down and join us. We've had a week at sea, and we're relaxing for a while."

"Yeah!" Eddie added while laughing loudly.

Bo just looked at her. No expression.

From his demeanor, Anna thought Eddie might have been smoking dope. He was, at the least, very drunk.

"Let her go," Bo said flatly. "She's no fun. She'll just be a drag and ruin the party."

"Who is that?" Bo's girlfriend asked.

"Just the ship's cook," Bo answered with contempt.

"Oh!" the girl commented while picking up her bottle of beer. "Has she been in an accident?"

"Probably a bar fight. Don't mess with her."

Anna hadn't expected three extra people to feed, but she probably bought enough fish, if they weren't too hungry. She sautéed the fish in olive oil with fresh-chopped garlic and finished it with a light spritz of lemon juice and a coating of butter that had been simmered with fresh cilantro. To make up for the limited amount of fish, she prepared an extra large bowl of mashed potatoes. Her personal recipe included cream, butter, cream cheese, lime, chopped scallions, chopped garlic, and of course, salt and pepper. She also prepared asparagus, al dente, and biscuits from the freezer.

Anna thought she had prepared a successful meal. They devoured all of the mashed potatoes and asked for more. She didn't expect the women to eat more than the men. And they were rude and arrogant when they spoke to her. They assumed she was there to serve them and made impolite demands for drinks, butter, etc. When Eddie's friend complained Anna took too long to bring her a glass of water, Eddie sat up straight, his eyes enlarged, and he looked at Anna pleadingly not to respond. Bo snickered. Bart had his head down and was eating but stopped and looked out from under his eyebrows to see what was going to happen. Anna turned to Bart with an official-sounding voice, "Will that be all, Captain?"

"Yes, I think we can handle everything from here on out."

Anna went topside, and everyone stopped talking and stared at Bart.

As Anna came up on deck, Rick was returning to the *DOVE* with a bag of purchases. He had been in Hamilton shopping.

"Hi, Anna. Am I late for dinner?"

"Yes, and you had better hurry. The guys have some guests, and there may not be any food left."

As he approached the dining table, Rick saw everyone bent over their plates whispering to one another. He put his bag down and called out, "Hey, guys, I hope you saved some for me." His sudden interruption startled them, and they all turned to look at him. He looked back taking note of the three young women. They were all attractive, and from his vantage point their halter tops were useless.

Bo's date looked down at her breasts and pulled her halter top up, but Eddie's date didn't bother.

"What did I do?"

Bart looked up. "Nothing, Rick. Where have you been?" He really didn't care where Rick had been, but he saw the bag and the question seemed to be the right thing to ask.

"Oh, just in town doing a little shopping. I didn't find much though. I don't expect we'll have a lot of time next week after Mr. and Mrs. Pisani arrive."

"Rick, grab a chair and join us," Bart offered while pointing to an empty chair.

"And who are these young ladies?" Rick asked as he sat down.

Anna was topside and could hear the banter and laughing below. She could hear Eddie's friend commenting that the cook didn't know how to serve guests properly. Then she heard Bo explaining the cook was a barfly.

Those women were rude and unsophisticated. They didn't deserve good table service, but I shouldn't be so sensitive. I've got to be less combative.

Since it was obvious the party was going to go on for a while, Anna didn't want to hang around the boat. She decided to walk over to the Windward Tavern and have a beer.

CHAPTER 21

Old George was right. When Anna entered the tavern, it was busy. Not hopping busy. Just full of people drinking and talking. The music was Calypso and blaring. Even with the soft breeze from the harbor, the smell of beer and cigarette smoke was overpowering. Anna thought it was a good thing the tavern was basically a patio with a cloth roof, or the smell would have driven people out. She noticed there were only three or four women, and they were at the bar talking to several men. She couldn't be sure if the fourth woman was actually a woman. She was heavyset and had long hair. *Could be a woman. Could be a man.*

Beer bottles cluttered the bar and tables, and a few were on the floor. At the far end of the patio, at one of the rickety tables, she saw George and three other sailor types. They mostly had their backs to her and were dressed casually, almost like crew. They seemed to be listening intently to George.

George looked up, saw Anna, and motioned her to join them. It was a nice gesture she thought, since there were no empty tables. The men turned in their chairs. The oldest fellow, the one with a lot of gray hair and a white mustache, got up and retrieved a chair for Anna from the other side of the bar. She walked over and sat down.

"Gentlemen, this is Anna. She's one of the crew on the *DOVE*. These gentlemen are Mike, Frederick, and Doran."

Doran, the thinnest and youngest-looking man, commented, "I saw the *DOVE* when it was entering the channel. Fine vessel. Well kept."

George waved to the bartender to bring over a beer for Anna. It was the same fellow from lunch. He quickly came over to the table with a Heineken.

"Thanks for remembering what kind of beer I like."

"You're welcome, missus! But you be in bad company now. You sure you wanna sit here?" He spoke with a smile that exposed several missing teeth.

At that, the men laughed, and the bartender went back to the bar. It was a busy night, and he couldn't take time for small talk.

Mike, the older fellow with the mustache, asked, "How long will the *DOVE* be in port?"

"I don't know," Anna replied after taking a sip of her Heineken. "The owners are arriving on Friday for a short cruise, and after that I don't know what our schedule will be."

Frederick, who was slightly younger than Mike but balding with gray hair, asked with surprise, "Jack Pisani is going to be here this weekend? I'll have to get over to see him. Where are you docked?"

"On the other side of that small island in the harbor. At the second set of docks. A couple of big deep-sea fishing boats are tied up on the other side of the dock from the *DOVE*."

"That's okay. I know the *DOVE* quite well. Went out on her once. Fine boat, and Jack likes to sail. But he hasn't been here in Bermuda for quite a while. What's he been doing?"

Pushing back a little in her chair, Anna responded, "I don't know. He hasn't actually confided in me."

Everyone laughed. Except Anna. She looked down and pulled her lips tight to make a closed-mouth type of smile. Her tight-lipped smile seemed a bit forced and sometimes vaguely sad or serious but not artificial.

Frederick went on, "Well, when Jack isn't using her, the *DOVE* takes charters out. I saw her over in the Canary Islands several years ago. I guess he's been busy with his businesses. But how is his health? Is he doing okay? Those are high-pressure businesses he runs."

"I'm sorry. But again, I really don't know. In fact, I've never met him. I'm quite new to the *DOVE*. What's he like?"

Frederick leaned forward, crossed his arms, and put his elbows on the table. "Great guy. He can be funny, but he's also a hard boss.

He's Sicilian you know and has a temper. He doesn't tolerate any foolishness from his people. But from what I hear, he's generous and supportive if his employees work hard. His wife is hot. Quite attractive. Much younger and Sicilian too. She's a real pistol, and you really, really don't want to get crosswise with her. Even Jack backs off when she's upset. I'd stay clear of her if I was a crew member on any boat she was on."

Looking concerned, Anna asked, "I hope she doesn't like to cook or monitor the food."

"Oh shit. You don't have something to do with the food, do you?"

"Uhhh. That would be yes," Anna replied while tilting her head and leaning a little bit forward.

"You're not the cook are you?" Mike asked, while wiping beer suds off his white mustache with the back of his thumb.

"Uhhh. That would be yes too."

Frederick looked down at the table, smiled, and shook his head. His head was almost down to his arms on the table hiding a big smile. George, Mike, and Doran were laughing. Then Frederick looked up and told Anna that Jack's wife, Cecilia, prides herself as an excellent Italian cook. "Whatever you do," he said, "don't make any Italian dishes. Cooking is her domain in the family structure, and nobody interferes with it."

Anna bit her lip, shook her head, and looked at Frederick. "Thanks for the heads-up, Frederick. It's a difficult job making everyone happy, and I appreciate any information I can get."

While Frederick was describing Cecilia and her personality, Anna was thinking how similar Cecilia's role in her marriage seemed to her own role with Phillip. Cecilia was probably struggling to maintain some relevant level of status in her marriage. Anna was thinking she understood where Cecilia would be coming from and felt comfortable anticipating her arrival on Friday. But Jack? That would be the big question.

"I was told Mr. Pisani makes parts for the Air Force and has some auto parts stores. So he must be a technical person," Anna remarked while taking another sip of her Heineken.

"He's an engineer and manufactures aircraft parts for the Pentagon. Something to do with electronics for fighter planes. Oh

---

yeah, and he recently bought a string of auto parts stores. Like NAPA but not quite as big."

"So he's a technical person! More inclined to concern himself with the operation of the boat?"

"Exactly. Although he has long discussions with the captain and crew on how the boat is operating, he generally leaves the actual sailing to the captain. Good managers and CEOs make assignments and leave the execution to the staff. That's pretty much how Jack runs his boat when he's on board. I was really impressed with his rapport with the captain and crew when I sailed with him."

Doran, the youngest man, interrupted the discussion about the *DOVE* and asked if George could continue telling them about the recent escalation of piracy in the Bahamas.

George willingly obliged. He liked to tell stories.

"Piracy used to be a major problem for sailors about twenty years ago during the heavy drug trade going through the Bahamas. It let up for a while, but recently it's gotten worse. Especially in the lower islands around Long, Acklins, and the upper Caicos. It's especially bad on the back side of Andros and even in the lower Caicos."

Doran was showing increased interest in the Bahamas and asked George if he had been there recently.

"Yeah, I have. About six weeks ago, I sailed out of Cockburn Town, in San Salvador, and was thinking about going down to the Caicos the next day and then on to St. Thomas. I have some friends there. I was sailing off the south side of Rum Cay, and there wasn't much wind; but there was a small squall moving in from the east, and I was concerned about it. I hadn't intended to anchor in that area, but with the squall coming I thought I would move in close to shore for refuge, maybe even overnight there."

George stopped talking, took a swig of beer, and looked at everyone as they leaned forward encouraging him to go on. "So then, as I cruised closer to the island, I saw a small boat approaching me, astern, with three Bahamians in it. It had a small motor, and they weren't gaining on me very fast, but they were definitely coming toward me. There was nothing else anywhere around. Earlier, I had dropped the jib while looking for an anchoring spot so I unfurled the jib and tried to out run them. But they continued to gain on me.

"When they were about two hundred yards away, I prepared to stop them from boarding me. Fortunately, the leading edge of the storm filled the sails, and I took off. As I was making way and increasing the distance between us, I could see one of them standing in the boat glaring at me."

"That's scary. Is that kind of thing common down there?" Doran asked in amazement.

"When I was anchored in Cockburn, some of the skippers warned me of the increase in piracy, but I guess I didn't pay them enough attention. They said at least a dozen boats had disappeared in the last year, and two of them showed up six months later with new names and Bahamian owners."

Seemingly perplexed, Doran asked, "What about the crew? What do they do with the crew?"

"Kill 'em and throw the bodies overboard. Sharks take care of the rest."

"Goddamn, George, they kill everyone?" Doran exclaimed.

"Yeah, they just want the boats," George answered.

"What are they taking the boats for? Cargo? What's on board? To sell them or what?"

Mike entered the conversation, saying, "I've been hearing about the pirating problem too. Since the crackdown on drug smuggling along the Mexican border, drug dealers are exploring other routes for getting their drugs into the States. American-registered boats are easier to get into the country and offload the cocaine, or whatever, before the Coast Guard approaches them. And if they lose the boat, it's no big deal."

"Yeah, I heard about it too," Frederick added. "Don't you remember the story a year ago, about the big yacht down in Fort Pierce, Florida, with fifty or so Mexican illegals on board? Turned out the boat had been pirated in the Caicos, and the owner and crew had disappeared. The Coasties caught them as they were entering the cut. The crew were Bahamians and Mexicans."

Doran was bent over the table listening intently. Then he asked, "So what do you do to protect yourself? I'm leaving for the Bahamas in a few days and then on to Jamaica. How do you keep from getting hijacked?"

George responded, "Never let anyone get near your boat. And if they try to come aboard without permission, shoot them."

Mike agreed, "Yeah, there's no reason to let them come aboard."

"How do you keep them away? What if they claim they need help or food or something. What do you do then? What about at night?" Doran asked while sitting up straighter. He was becoming agitated, and it was obvious he wanted to know every detail of George's stories.

Without hesitation, Mike answered, "Wave them off and tell them to stay away. Tell them you will radio for someone to come and provide help. If they keep coming, you know you have trouble, and you're going to have to physically stop them."

George interrupted, "I don't know about you fellows, but I keep a nickel-plated, twelve-gauge shotgun and a pistol behind a panel next to my bunk for just such occasions. During the episode over in Rum Cay, I brought my protection up into the cockpit just in case. And don't forget to keep a vigilant night watch. From what I hear, almost all the boarding occurred at twilight or at night. Mostly, just after dark when the crew were preparing dinner and cleaning their boats."

"I keep several pieces of protection on board my boat, the *SEA NYMPH*," Mike added. "In addition to a shotgun and pistol, I have a .30-06 rifle I use when I catch a shark instead of fish. Besides, it has a better range than a shotgun."

Anna asked Mike if the *SEA NYMPH* was a motorboat. "No," he said and smiled. "You're asking because I fish off my boat?"

"Well yes. Can you fish off a sailboat?"

All the men smiled and told her that you could indeed fish while sailing. They felt that fishing from a sailboat might even be better because there was no engine noise or propeller disturbance in the water.

"George, would you have used it?" Anna asked.

"You mean the shotgun? Damn sure would. You don't think the pirates come unarmed, do you? They probably have guns, knives, and machetes. The worst are the machetes. Twenty years ago, there were a bunch of cases where it was pretty well determined the pirates hacked the crew up with machetes. Parts of the bodies were found before the sharks and fish had gotten to them, and there were hack marks and split skulls."

Doran pushed back in his chair, bit his lip, and began to shake his head in frustration. George and Mike sat without speaking but watched Doran. Frederick was taking it all in as was Anna.

Mike then told Doran that if he were approached by pirates, he had two choices. The first was to fight them, and the second was to die.

With that comment, the table went quiet. And then Anna could once again hear the noise, the music, the shuffling of chairs, and the bar customers talking and laughing all around her. She didn't hear any of that while listening to George, Mike, Frederick, or Doran telling the pirate stories.

Mike turned to Anna and asked, "So! It's Anna! Right?"

"Yep, I'm Anna," she said while looking down at the table and her empty Heineken beer bottle.

"How long have you been on the *DOVE*?"

"Only about a week. But what about you? What kind of boat do you have?" Anna asked, trying to change the subject of the conversation from her to him. She was successful.

Mike, like most sailors, took great pride in talking about his boat. Sensing that Anna didn't know much about boats, Mike explained he had a thirty-eight-foot ketch. "It has two masts like the *DOVE*, but the aft mast is shorter and further back on the boat. The *SEA NYMPH* is about ten years old and broad beamed for cruising."

After another beer and listening to storm stories and other boating adventures, Anna said she had to get back to the *DOVE*. The men complained she was leaving much too early and told her she had to come back and drink with them again. She was a good listener.

CHAPTER 22

Under the full moon, Anna had little difficulty finding her way back to the *DOVE*. She stopped for a few minutes to enjoy the brilliant sky. *This is incredible. How come we don't have such a sky back in Philadelphia?* Her thoughts began to meander back home. She stopped looking up and decided to get back to the ship. *I can't think of home right now. I've got to concentrate on disappearing if I'm going to survive.*

Stopping at the gangplank, she looked to see who had the night watch. From the shadows, Rick called out, "Ahoy there, me mate." He chuckled, "State your purpose."

"Asking permission to come aboard, sir," Anna replied lightheartedly.

"Come aboard then and state your purpose," Rick chuckled.

"The boat seems quiet. Is everyone gone?" Anna asked.

"No! They started partying early, and they're hanging out in the saloon or elsewhere. Just as well. We're going to have a lot of work for the next couple of days getting ready for the owners and their party."

"What time are they coming in on Friday?"

"Bart expects them before noon. You'll need to have lunch ready when they arrive."

"How do you think they will feel about having sandwiches? Maybe with some fresh fruit?"

"Sounds good to me."

"Thanks, Rick. See you in the morning," she said as she went below.

Anna was startled to see her cabin door ajar. She was certain she had locked it before she left. She always locked it. When she entered the cabin her concern turned to fear and anger. On the bed were some of her cosmetics and an open box of tampons. Some of the tampons were scattered about on the bedspread and the floor. She saw the door to the small compartment above the bunk was open. It was where she had hidden the guns and ammunition. She almost panicked!

Anna immediately thought she had been found out, and her cabin had been ransacked to find the evidence. She quickly inspected the gun cabinet and was relieved to see the cosmetics still there, along with the cotton balls she had placed in front of the guns. Whoever rifled her cabin didn't see the guns.

Why would they do this? And how did they get in? I locked the cabin door.

Anna went to the captain's cabin and knocked hard on the door—several times. Bart opened the door with a towel wrapped around his waist, looked at Anna, and angrily whispered, "This better be damn important!"

The captain's cabin was small, and even in the darkness, Anna could see the girl in bed sound asleep. "Bart, someone broke into my cabin and rifled through my things. I locked my door when I left, and it was open when I got back. I want something done about it."

"Shit, Anna!" Bart was angry at being disturbed in his cabin. "Does this have to be settled right now? Can't it wait until morning?"

In the dim light, Anna glared at Bart and barked back, "Don't you think it's important someone on this boat broke into my cabin? I don't have much, but my privacy's been invaded."

Bart was startled at Anna's defiant anger. She had been highly respectful of him as the captain of the ship up until this moment, and now she was aggressive and demanding he take action. She was clearly distraught. *Shit, she sounds just like Mrs. Pisani when she's pissed over something.* He backed off his authoritative stance and with a semblance of compassion asked her to wait a moment while he put on a pair of shorts.

They knocked on the door of the cabin Bo was using with his new girlfriend. When Bo answered, Bart asked him to come out and meet with him in the saloon.

Bo looked at Anna, then Bart, and whispered, "What's going on?"

Bart didn't mince words. "Bo, did you go into Anna's cabin tonight?"

"No! What's the problem?"

"Someone broke into her cabin and rifled her things. You didn't go in there?"

"Hell no! I don't bother other people's things. Why are you accusing me?"

Bart agreed with what Bo was saying. *Bo prides himself on his honesty. He has never tried to cover up any mistakes and always told me about problems, even if it was to his disadvantage. But he certainly doesn't get along with Anna. Shit, this is going to get nasty.*

"Well, somebody went into her cabin," Bart stated, "and I'm not going to tolerate it."

"Captain, I don't know anything about it."

Bo rarely addressed Bart as "captain," but when he did, he was dead serious and did it for effect. Bart knew this and could see Bo's rising anger.

Bo turned to Anna and angrily grunted, "Are you accusing me of rifling through your cabin? You don't—"

Bart interrupted Bo by grabbing him on his shoulder and said, "Okay, Bo! That's enough! She didn't accuse you! She didn't accuse anyone. But you two don't seem to get along very well so I checked with you first. That's all there is to it."

Bo calmed down and asked Bart if they took anything from Anna's cabin.

"I don't know. Anna, did they take anything?"

"I can't be sure, but it doesn't matter. What was taken is not the main problem, Captain. Don't you understand? This is harassment. Somebody broke into my cabin, invaded my privacy, and went through my things."

Bo firmly asked, "Yeah, but did they take anything?"

Anna looked at Bo, then Bart, but didn't answer.

Bart looked directly at Anna and asked, "Was anything taken? Was it money or what?"

"Well, I think they took some tampons!" Anna responded, looking somewhat embarrassed.

—

"Tampons!" Bart exclaimed. "You've got to be fucking kidding me! Tampons! And you came disrupting me for tampons! We'll look into this in the morning."

And with that exclamation, he returned to his cabin and shut the door.

Anna was dismayed Bart didn't deem the problem worth dealing with until morning. Bo looked at her contemptuously, shook his head, and returned to his cabin mumbling something about an airhead.

She went back to her cabin, pulled the drawers out completely, checked on the money hidden beside the drawers, straightened everything out, and went to bed.

At breakfast, all three girls were present. Anna had anticipated they would still be there and made extra pancakes and eggs. Everyone seemed to be groggy with hangovers except Bo and his date. He had the night watch from 0200 until 0600 and was wide-awake. He had been topside talking with his girlfriend while on watch duty.

Before anyone left the table, Anna asked Bart if he would please investigate the break-in of her cabin. When everyone looked up at Anna to see what she was talking about, the girl with Bart explained someone had broken into Anna's cabin and taken some tampons. Everyone began to laugh and look at Bo.

Bo slammed his fist down on the table and said, "I don't bother other people's things."

Bart stood up and said this incident was serious, and he wanted to know who went into Anna's cabin.

Eddie's girlfriend sheepishly raised her hand and said she had unexpectedly started her period and needed a tampon right away. She didn't think Anna would mind if she borrowed one.

Eddie explained, "There isn't any place on the north end of the island to buy tampons at night so I thought Anna might have some. She's the only female member of the crew. I didn't think she would get so uptight about it."

Bart angrily demanded, "So how did you get into her cabin? How did you unlock her door?"

"I used the spare master key in the drawer of the navigation table. The one that's for emergencies."

Bart went over to the navigation table, took out the master key, and told everyone from then on only he would have the master key.

—

He turned to Eddie and said, "Come topside with me." Everyone below could hear Bart yelling expletives at Eddie. After a few moments, they came down, and Eddie apologized to Anna. Profusely. So did his girlfriend. Bart, while looking at Bo, demanded that no one will violate anyone else's privacy and to stay away from Anna's cabin.

Bo was angry and glared at Anna. He looked at Bart and demanded an apology for immediately suspecting him. "Just because that stupid—" He stopped short, realizing he was about to say something that could cause a lot of dissension among the crew and really piss Bart off. He also realized that he was talking to the captain, and he was out of order. He looked at Anna and hesitantly choked out a single word. "Sorry!"

Bart studied Bo for a moment. "Sorry about that, Bo. I hope we can get past this episode. Each of us has to honor one another's privacy. We are going to have to come together as a working team. We have only five people manning the boat but should have at least six or seven. And it's time for our guests to depart. We've got two days to get ready for the Pisani's arrival. Let's get to it."

CHAPTER 23

It was Wednesday morning, and Anna had early appointments with the dentist and the doctor. She didn't have time to hang around. The atmosphere on the boat was acrid, and it was just as well she had to leave. She was anxious to have her teeth fixed and didn't want to be late.

The fitting of the caps for her teeth went quickly. The fit was good, and the color matched well. The dentist only had to grind down a couple of small areas on the caps to correct for the bite and make a perfect fit. She was happy with her new teeth, and the dentist encouraged her to smile once in a while.

Anna left the dentist and went to the doctor's office. His news wasn't as good. He x-rayed her face and found there were several fractures in her left cheekbone, the zygomatic arch. He was amazed she didn't complain more about pain there. As soon as he said that, she began to feel more pain. *That's weird*, she thought. *He says it should hurt, and suddenly it starts hurting. A lot!* Perhaps because she was so concerned about her survival she hadn't acknowledged the pain.

The doctor told her the fractures were the primary cause of swelling on her left side, and when the bone healed, the swelling would eventually go down. The other areas of swelling, on her right jaw and cheek, and around her left neck and ear were due to deeply ruptured capillaries and small vessels.

"How did this happen?" He didn't expect an honest answer, and he didn't get one.

"I fell on the boat during some rough seas. I was clumsy."

"Ms. Meerschmidt, come over here to the light box and look at this radiograph. See these lines here and here. And look at the crooked lines in the upper structure of your left eye orbital bones. These are older, healed injuries. You didn't get those by falling down on the boat! These are definitely older injuries."

Anna pursed her lips and stared at the doctor for a moment. Without answering his question, she asked, "Is there anything you can do to fix the swollen areas and help me look better?"

"I can give you some pain medication if you need it. Otherwise, you can put hot compresses on those areas to help blood circulation. In time, they will all heal."

"Thanks, Doctor, but I have been handling the pain. I'd rather not take any medicine if I don't have to. I was hoping there was something you could do to make the swelling go down quickly."

"Ms. Meerschmidt, I don't think you realize how lucky you are that the more recent injuries didn't break your facial bones where you had old injuries. The bone is weak there. So please be careful. I suspect you may have had a minor concussion, and you may still have some minor brain swelling. Have you had buzzing or throbbing in your head?"

"Yes. Sometimes it feels like a hammer banging away, and I have trouble thinking."

"I'm not surprised! Like I just said, you may have some brain swelling. That'll subside over time. Just be careful and stay away from whoever did this to you. If you get hit there again, you could have some really serious damage."

"I'm learning how to walk on the boat when it's bouncing around. I don't think I'm going to have any more accidents."

"Look, Ms. Meerschmidt, I've been practicing this kind of medicine for a long time, and I know what I'm looking at. I'm a specialist in facial reconstructive surgery. That's why your dentist recommended me. If you won't tell me what's been going on, then there's nothing I can do. If something more happens, call my office and tell the nurse you have an emergency. I'll call you right back."

The doctor's words caused the throbbing in her head to become more acute. Anna had a subliminal anger over what Phillip had done to her, mixed with guilt and fear. And when she thought about what she had done to Tatianna, her head hurt more.

On returning to the *DOVE*, Anna wanted to go to her cabin to think about what to do. But Bo stopped her as she crossed the gangplank. "Where the hell have you been? It's lunchtime, and you disappeared. Get the hell down there and get lunch ready. Vacation time is over. We've been working, and we want something to drink and eat."

Bo was right. Anna had lost track of time but still had time to get lunch ready if she hurried. Bo was just taking the opportunity to express his anger at her. She had caused him to lose face among the crew, and he wanted to reestablish his dominant position in the pecking order.

But Anna's anger began to flare, and it showed in her slowly stated response. "Bo! I'll have lunch ready shortly. Just go about your work and leave me alone in the galley."

As Bo turned and walked off, Anna pulled up the sleeve of her denim shirt and glanced at her watch. She was still wearing her gold Rolex watch. Ship's cooks don't wear Rolex watches, especially one with four diamonds in the face. It was only luck she had been wearing long-sleeve, oversized shirts. She immediately hid her left arm and went to her cabin to remove the watch and hide it behind the guns.

Forgetting her watch really spooked her. She thought again about what else she might have overlooked. Joey had told her how the simplest thing could trip up someone on the run. Things that people in hiding might take for granted could cause others to ask questions and blow their cover. She decided to get another watch, something inexpensive that looked like her Rolex.

CHAPTER 24

That afternoon, Anna took inventory of the food supply and developed a schedule and menus for the Pisanis' party. She would have to buy the fresh vegetables and seafood the day before to give her time to prepare both lunch and the first dinner. The fish market promised to deliver the oysters on the half shell before dinner on Friday. She hoped they would be reliable.

Since Mr. and Mrs. Pisani, and their guests, would be arriving late in the morning, Anna decided to have something simple for lunch. Tuna salad sandwiches on croissants with fresh fruit and iced tea would do quite nicely she thought. If they want beer, they can get it themselves from the refrigerator. That would leave her time to prepare a more exotic dinner for their first evening aboard the *DOVE*. Of course, the tuna salad would have to be special if Mrs. Pisani was the connoisseur Anna had been led to believe. She decided to prepare the tuna salad with solid white albacore tuna, hard-boiled eggs, celery, onions, walnuts, a few dried cranberries, a touch of honey, salt, pepper, mayonnaise, and provide lettuce and sliced tomatoes on the side. The dried cranberries would really give it a surprising zip she hoped would be appreciated. She prepared the tuna salad the night before to let the flavors mingle. *That should work out well,* she thought.

Bart was adamant that all the tasks he had assigned be completed before Mr. Pisani arrived. The crew rushed about, sometimes bumping into one another. Anna was ensconced in the galley preparing lunch and the near-formal evening dinner. Just before noon, the crew had completed their tasks and assembled on the deck in clean shorts and shirts to greet the Pisanis and their guests.

Anna was startled to see how young and beautiful Mrs. Pisani was. Frederick said she was hot, but Anna didn't really believe him. After all, she had thought, he was an older man. Mrs. Pisani was wearing white shorts and an azure-colored golfing shirt with an embossed white dove above the left breast. With her long black hair blowing in the breeze, she looked elegant, and she spoke kindly to everyone. After lunch, Anna was apprehensive when Mrs. Pisani approached her as she was clearing the dishes from the dining table.

"You are Anna, right?" Mrs. Pisani asked while studying her in the dim light of the saloon.

Anna was nervous and answered, "Yes, Mrs. Pisani. Was lunch satisfactory?"

"Oh yes. I was intrigued by your use of dried cranberries in the tuna salad. That made a really wonderful difference. I can't wait to see what you have planned for dinner."

Just then, the guests called out for her, and she had to leave. They wanted her to take them to the beach next to Fort St. Catherine for a swim in the surf. Jack Pisani elected to tour the *DOVE*, inspecting most of the mechanical systems.

With guests aboard, the crew had dinner early, and Anna ate before they did. Bart, as captain of the *DOVE*, sat at the table with Mr. and Mrs. Pisani and their guests. Bart wore a light blue dress shirt, open at the neck, without a tie, and a blue blazer. Both the shirt and the blazer had a small red emblem of a dove embroidered on the pocket. Bart wore his jacket slightly rumpled, but that was to be expected on board the boat. Anna thought he really looked the part of a dashing ship's captain.

It seemed odd to Anna that the three guest couples were named Smith, Jones, and Roberts. Perhaps they didn't want anyone to know who they really were, a situation she understood well. But still, she wondered why.

For dinner, Anna had prepared an appetizer of oysters on the half shell showered with lime and a touch of dark balsamic vinegar. The oysters were served with slices of warm Brie and Camembert cheese layered with slices of baked almonds brushed with melted butter. The entree was a medley of scallops and shrimp sautéed in olive oil with fresh garlic and mixed with oranges, olives, and garlic butter, all encased in puff pastry, as is done in Provence. The accompanying vegetables were roasted potatoes basted with garlic-olive oil and topped with cilantro and finely cut chives. Asparagus, under a light blanket of hollandaise sauce, completed the presentation. As for wine, Anna selected a six-year-old Pouilly-Fuisse. To finish the dinner, she served crème brulee with a thin layer of Kahlua on it.

As Anna had hoped, her dinner the first day was well received; and afterward, Cecilia Pisani again complimented Anna on her cooking, specifically the puff pastry. They conversed briefly about the dinner, and Cecilia commented she was amazed Anna was able to prepare a gourmet dinner with the limited facilities available aboard ship. She asked her how she was able to make such a nice crust on the crème brulee. When Anna told her she had borrowed the ship's soldering torch, Cecilia laughed and told her she was ingenious. "I would never have thought of that."

Cecilia was not yet forty but looked much younger. Jack, who was forty-seven, appeared his age. Before she married Jack, Cecilia had been a nurse in the Beavercreek and Kettering Hospitals, just south of Wright-Patterson Air Force Base in Dayton, Ohio, where Jack spent so much time. His manufacturing and machining facilities were closer to Kettering. They had met at a party at the Holiday Inn next to Wright-Patterson. Cecilia was dating a Department of Energy scientist, from the Mounds facility down in Miamisburg, who had been invited to the party Jack was hosting to entertain prospective clients. Jack admired her right away. Not only was she exceptionally attractive, but her straightforward, no-nonsense personality also appealed to him. He hadn't counted on her temperamental and sometimes determined side, but as he later learned, she was Sicilian too.

It wasn't until after dinner, when Cecilia saw Anna in the bright light of the galley, that she could get a good look at her. As they talked, Cecilia was unobtrusively studying Anna's appearance and face. She realized in spite of the rough way Anna looked and dressed, she was actually much younger than she appeared and somewhat sophisticated. Cecilia studied the healing bruises and the puffiness of Anna's face and realized she had artfully covered them with heavy makeup. The injuries were much worse than she first thought. Underneath it all, Anna might be quite pretty. She also noticed the way Anna favored her left side when she lifted various cookware to go into the upper cabinets. Cecilia suspected she had injured ribs. Then Cecilia went topside to talk with Captain Bart.

Jack was complimenting Bart on the dinner and told him not to let the cook get away. His guests were important prospective clients, and anything that made them happy pleased him. He asked Bart to do everything he could to make the cruise go smoothly, not like the last cruise where Mrs. Pisani got so upset.

Cecilia tugged Jack's sleeve and mentioned his guests were waiting for him in the saloon. As Jack left, she asked Bart to stay a few minutes and talk with her. She wanted to ask how he was able to secure a ship's cook of gourmet quality. Anna was better than any of the ship's previous cooks, and she wanted to know a little bit more about her.

Bart told her it was just luck. "I had a 'cook wanted' sign out, and right before we were scheduled to leave Philadelphia, she showed up and applied for the job. She said she could cook, and I figured if she didn't work out, I could replace her here in Bermuda. If worse came to worst, I guess I would have had to have dinners catered."

"What amazing luck," Cecilia replied. "Jack is really pleased. I think she just served the best dinner we've ever had on the *DOVE*."

"Yeah, I've been pleasantly surprised, Mrs. Pisani. Replacing a cook in Bermuda would've been hard to do."

"What other yachts has she cooked for?" Cecilia asked.

"Well, she said she had never been on a boat before."

"Really! She said that? And you hired her?"

"Well, yeah! I was surprised. She didn't try to hide it. So far she's been a 'what you see is what you get' kind of person. She's quiet, hangs back a lot, and tries to be unobtrusive. But she doesn't put up with much nonsense."

Cecilia studied Bart for a moment and then asked, "So how did she get the bruises on her face?"

Bart shrugged, "I don't know, Mrs. Pisani, I've never asked. The crew suspects a bar fight."

"Has she been drinking on the boat? Has she been tipsy or anything like that?"

"No, I guess not," Bart answered while becoming defensive over Mrs. Pisani's persistent questioning. She could see he was uncomfortable with her questions, but she continued anyhow.

"That's odd. Don't you think so?"

"I don't know, Mrs. Pisani. What are you driving at? Why are you so curious about the ship's cook? She's just a barfly who can cook. I've seen a lot of strange combinations working on boats."

"I'm just curious, Bart. Just curious. Please indulge me. Tell me more about her," Cecilia asked while shrugging her shoulders.

Bart replied, "She keeps to herself most of the time, and she doesn't talk to the crew very much. She spends most of her free time in her cabin. Good thing though. She's got Bo pissed off, and she never smiles. The crew thinks she has bad teeth, and that's why she never smiles. Not even at my jokes. And the crew knows they have to laugh at the captain's jokes, right? Half the time I think her head is somewhere else."

"Really. Don't you find that interesting, Bart?" Cecilia asked while leaning back against the gunnel. "She's a drunk who gets into bar fights and gets beat up, but doesn't drink much, is quiet, keeps to herself, and is a gourmet cook. I find that really fascinating. Don't you?"

"I guess so. I hadn't really focused on it. I have a boat to run, Mrs. Pisani. As long as she doesn't make any trouble and cooks good food, I don't really care. Problem is she does cause trouble. She hasn't initiated the problems directly, but she has gotten into a couple of standoffs with Bo. I think the fact she's a woman on a boat is what has caused the problems."

"Really," Cecilia retorted. "You don't think women should be on boats?"

"I'm sorry, Mrs. Pisani. I didn't mean it that way. What I'm trying to say is that the crew isn't used to having a female shipmate, and it's taking a little time to learn to work together."

Bart stopped talking for minute and looked out across the harbor, thinking. Then he continued, "Is there a problem I need to know about, Mrs. Pisani? Is there something she did that I should take care of?" Bart had enough of the questioning and wanted to know what Cecilia was concerned about.

"No," Cecilia said with a bright smile. "I was just so pleased with the dinner that I wanted to know more about her. It's unusual to find a gourmet cook on board a boat. That's all. Oh by the way, did she happen to have a resume or something that I could read?"

"Are you kidding, Mrs. Pisani? A ship's cook or seaman with a resume? No, I just hired her on the spot. As I said before, we needed a cook real bad." Bart was amazed at Cecilia's request.

Boy, women are really strange. They have a good meal, and they have to know everything about the cook. Truly weird.

Cecilia returned to the galley where Anna had just finished cleaning the cookware and dishes. She asked Anna to join her topside where they could talk. They went forward, away from everyone else. It was relatively dark on the bow with only the glow from the aft lighting. They leaned up against the gunnel.

"Anna, I used to be a nurse. I worked in several hospitals in Ohio, just outside Dayton, where I treated all kinds of patients."

"That must have been wonderful. I once thought about being a nurse, but it didn't work out. Do you miss it?"

"To some degree, I do. But that's not why I asked you up here."

Anna was thinking about what Frederick had said when describing Cecilia the other night at the tavern. *Cecilia is an outstanding cook and has a penchant for culinary perfection. Something must have been wrong with the dinner, but she complimented me on the puff pastry and crème brulee.*

"I'm terribly sorry, Mrs. Pisani, for any inadequacies with the dinner. If you will explain how you would like the food prepared, I'll be pleased to make whatever changes you want. I had no guidance for this meal, and I thought a light seafood dinner would be a good introduction to Bermuda. If you—"

Cecilia emphatically interrupted Anna in mid-sentence, "No, Anna. It's not the food I want to talk to you about. You prepared a wonderful dinner. It's you I want to talk about."

Anna backed away slightly, and even in the dim light, Cecilia could see her escalating anxiety. Anna was becoming suspicious Cecilia might know who she really was. Jack Pisani might be one of Phillip's clients. Then she thought she had slipped up somehow and given away her identity. Her mind was racing. *It has to be that they know Phillip, and I've been discovered.* She was terrified and grabbed the gunnel with one hand to steady herself as she backed farther away from Cecilia.

"Anna, from my experience in the medical profession, I found that sometimes it's best to be direct and get to the point. So let me do it here."

Cecilia could see Anna tensing up, narrowing her eyes, and looking fearful. "Anna, the hospitals where I worked were in blue-collar neighborhoods, and I saw a lot of women who presented injury indicators that I see in you. The women often made excuses for their injuries and denied having problems at home, but in the end they usually suffered more violence or were killed. I really hated that and vowed to help abused women whenever I could. And I'd like to help you. I know of some really good programs that could help you."

Anna was stunned, thinking that this woman had x-ray vision.

"Why do you say such a thing? I just had a few accidents. Nothing serious. I've always been clumsy. I'm okay."

Speaking softly, and with concern, Cecilia moved closer. "Look, Anna, we've just met, and I know you're probably not going to trust me or admit to anything. Abused women never do. At least not at first. But I know something's definitely wrong, and you're hiding it. I've seen this sort of thing many times before. Somebody's been hitting you. I know the signs. It's not uncommon in certain neighborhoods, and it's sad. But you are no ordinary ship's cook. You don't talk like one, you don't act like one, and you don't cook like one. So what is going on?"

"Nothing! Nothing's going on, Mrs. Pisani. I'm fine."

Cecilia moved in closer, took Anna's hands, and whispered, "Anna, I want to help you. I really do. I have no tolerance for this sort of thing, and it makes me irate. So if there is anything I can do, please let me know. I won't betray your trust or expose you. I promise. I won't do that."

Quietly, pleasantly, while carefully selecting her words, Anna responded, "Thank you for your concern, Mrs. Pisani. I do appreciate your offer, but I—" She paused in mid-sentence, trying to change the subject. "But about the dinner, did you—"

"You have the dinner covered very nicely, Anna. Whatever you come up with will be fine, I'm sure. I enjoy cooking, especially Italian dishes, and would like to help you occasionally if it won't interfere with your routine. I can even share a few of my favorite recipes.

But let's not change the subject here. I know something bad has happened to you, and I'm offering to help. So please think about what I've said."

Cecilia abruptly returned to the saloon, irritated with herself at not being able to get through to Anna.

Anna stayed behind for a while, shaken by her conversation with Cecilia. She couldn't believe this woman saw right through her. And this was the second person to do so. First the doctor and now Cecilia. She needed to find a better way to cover her tracks and protect herself in case she was discovered to be lying about her true identity.

Anna returned to her cabin and spent hours worrying about her situation and whether she should ask Cecilia to help her. *She seems so sincere! But can I trust her? She knows I'm hiding and hasn't betrayed me. Should I take the chance? I've got to find a way to get the mobsters to stop looking for Tatianna and her ledgers! But Joey said never. What do I do?*

Anna's thinking was interrupted by Bart knocking on her cabin door. He wanted to let her know they were taking the *DOVE* out very early in the morning to do some SCUBA diving, so she should be prepared to fix the next day's meals while under way.

CHAPTER 25

Anna awoke to the shudder of the *DOVE*'s diesel cranking over. It was 0500. Too early to begin breakfast but too late to go back to sleep. She went topside to watch the crew take in the dock lines and prepare for departure. Leaving St. George's Harbor at dawn was beautiful. By the time they got to the outer channel marker, the sun was reflecting off the water and shining on the walls of Fort St. Catherine behind them. As Bart brought the *DOVE* around to a course of 180 degrees true, Anna asked if he was going to hoist the sails. Bart explained that Eddie and Bo were below preparing the diving equipment. He needed to keep the boat as level as possible while they were carrying SCUBA bottles around on deck. They were going to dive on the *HERMES*, on the south side of the island, and then do some shallow-water dives on the patch reefs on the west side.

Bart was feeling friendlier toward Anna after Mrs. Pisani complimented him on his choice of a ship's cook. He told her the *HERMES* was an old U.S. Coast Guard ship deliberately sunk about a mile or so offshore in the mid-1980s and rested upright in about eighty feet of water.

"It's not a big wreck, but it's a popular dive site because it hasn't deteriorated too much. It still looks like a complete ship rather than a pile of rubble. The visibility is usually pretty good. Divers can swim in and out of her pilothouse and take pictures. In the past, our guests liked the *HERMES* dives the best. We'll be there in a couple of hours, and after breakfast we'll get the guests ready for the dive. So make it a light breakfast and prepare some snacks for them after their dives. They'll be hungry."

Bo, as the dive master for the *DOVE*, maintained a large array of SCUBA equipment, including extra octopus rigs with consoles, pressure gauges, depth meters, compasses, and decompression computers. He had extra fins, masks, and wet suits in several sizes. In short, he had everything a diver would need, just in case a guest forgot something or it malfunctioned. The *DOVE*'s dive locker could easily outfit eight divers. The *DOVE* also carried a high-pressure air compressor and a bank of high-pressure storage cylinders for topping off divers' tanks.

Bart took a position seaward of the *HERMES* and dropped the pick. After laying out about five hundred feet of rode, the *DOVE* would be in a position about fifty feet seaward of the wreck. Bo and Eddie hung the dive ladder and positioned a descending/safety line, with a fifty-pound lead ball on a three-quarter-inch twisted nylon line, about ten feet off the bottom. Then they trailed a float, attached to one hundred feet of yellow, floating safety line. With the last of their safety precautions completed, they were ready to begin the dives.

Two of the male guests asked if they had Nitrox on board. Bo pointed out mixing Nitrox on board was complex, and they had opted to support air-only diving. They had a reliable compressor and could stay at a given site for long periods of time. So the divers didn't have to cram in as much bottom time on each dive as they would if on a commercial tourist dive boat.

Bo suited up and prepared to lead the dive. Eddie suited up also, except for the tank and regulator, to act as the emergency support backup diver. He had to monitor the time and be ready to dive in the event of an emergency. Bart and Rick manned the ship topside. Rick's primary responsibility was to monitor the GPS anchor watch indicator circle in case the ground tackle should drag. Cecilia and two of the women declined the invitation to dive, saying they would go for a swim when they were in shallower water. Jack, the three male guests, one female guest, and Bo descended to the wreck.

The three women watched the activity from the deck while Bart walked around the boat to make sure everything was shipshape and to watch for other boats. Anna arrived on deck with lemonade for everyone. She asked Cecilia if she could talk to her in the galley about dinner. In the galley, Anna got right to the point.

"Mrs. Pisani, last night you offered to help me. I've given my situation considerable thought since then. All night actually. If your offer still stands, I'd like to ask a favor."

"Of course! That's great, Anna. I meant what I said, if I can help, I will."

"You said you like to be straightforward so I will too, but I have to be certain you will keep our discussion confidential. It's really important to me that you keep it a secret. I can't emphasize that enough. You have to promise."

"Anna, if I'm to help you, you have to trust me. I've seen this type of situation a number of times before, and I promise to use all possible discretion."

"Okay then. I have an envelope I need to have mailed from someplace other than where I am. Could you mail it for me when you return to the States?"

"I'll be glad to mail it for you. We're flying into New York when we leave Bermuda. Will it be okay to mail it there?"

"Oh yes! That would be perfect. I can have it ready Monday after lunch, just before you leave. I can give you the money for the postage. I don't know how much it will be but—"

Cecilia interrupted, "Anna, I think I can handle the postage. Is there anything else I can do to help? Are you sure the only thing you want me to do is mail an envelope?"

"Yes. If you will do that for me, I will be most grateful."

"Anna, I'm going to give you my personal telephone number in Kettering. Because of Jack's government business, we have unlisted numbers and special security devices to protect him from wire tapping and call tracing. So if you call me at this number, you can be absolutely certain no one else will be listening. Just make sure you use a line that's secure on your end, and that no one can overhear your conversation."

When Anna went topside with Cecilia, one of the women guests took a small digital camera out of the pocket in her shorts and prepared to take a picture of everyone. But Cecilia stepped forward and stopped her.

"Ladies, remember our discussion in the hangar. You agreed there would be no photos taken on the cruise. It's important it not be known your husbands were together with Jack at the same time. It could give away what they are working on."

"Oh yes! We forgot." Anna, half panicked, turned around and scampered down the stairs to her cabin thinking about cameras. She had not taken into consideration people might be taking pictures. *What about other guests who charter the boat? What if they want to take pictures? Boy oh boy, it really is the little things that can trip you up.*

After several dives on the *HERMES*, Bart motored to the patch reefs around Green Flats, about two miles west of Commissioner's Point. The patch reefs were in about thirty feet of water, and they made several dives. One of the guests, Mr. Smith, exclaimed the profusion of beautifully colored fish around the patch reefs was astounding. They were more colorful than at the *HERMES* wreck site. Bo explained the *HERMES* was almost three times as deep as the patch reefs, and the red and yellow colors had been completely absorbed by the deeper water. The tops of some of the patch reefs, on the other hand, were as shallow as ten or fifteen feet, and more of the red and yellow in the sunlight penetrated to those depths.

Collectively, the three male guests agreed; and while laughing, they said they should have already known that since they were engineers. They were just excited with the diving and forgot to think about the physics of light absorption in water.

For the evening meal, Anna suspected the divers would be very hungry. She prepared broiled steaks, mashed potatoes using her own recipe, and steamed broccoli. On Sunday, Jack took the helm most of the time. The male guests had overexerted themselves the day before and were prone to lounge about and enjoy being on such a fine schooner.

After breakfast on Monday, Anna took off for Hamilton to find a stationery store and purchase large manila envelopes. She bought two sizes. Then she went to the Bank of Bermuda on Church Street and retrieved the ledgers from her safe-deposit box. She placed the books in the smaller envelope, sealed it, and addressed it to:

THE DISTRICT ATTORNEY
OFFICE OF THE DISTRICT ATTORNEY
PHILADELPHIA, PA

—

She inserted that envelope into the larger envelope, sealed it, and wrote,

CECILIA PISANI
"PERSONAL"

When she returned to the *DOVE*, Anna barely had enough time to prepare lunch. Cecilia came into the galley and told her she didn't have to hurry. Jack and his guests had gone for a walk to Fort St. Catherine, and the crew had gone for a swim at Tobacco Bay on the north side of the island. Cecilia offered to help prepare the lunch and asked Anna to get the envelope. Anna gave her the manila envelope and explained that when she got to New York, she should open the outer envelope and mail the inner one.

Cecilia was surprised to see the envelope was much larger and heavier than she had anticipated. She originally thought Anna was sending her husband or boyfriend a letter, but this envelope seemed to have books in it. She took the package and placed it in the bottom of her travel bag.

CHAPTER 26

After Jack, Cecilia, and their guests had departed, Bart called an all-hands meeting. He scheduled watch times for ship security and the crew's duties to take on diesel fuel, potable water, and food supplies. He expected to depart for the Bahamas in five days. Three couples from Chicago had chartered the *DOVE* for a week of sailing and diving in the Bahamas and were to be picked up in Freeport, Grand Bahama Island. Before leaving, the crew was free to take unscheduled leave as long as their responsibilities were not neglected, and they didn't stay out overnight without telling him. They would be on their own for eating during the day, giving Anna some time off.

To escape the constant activity of the crew servicing the boat and partying with their new female friends, Anna took several long walks on the north end of St. George Island. She liked to walk to Tobacco Bay and Fort St. Catherine best of all. On one walk, she discovered she had to tighten up the double D-ring belt she had purchased at the chandlery in Philadelphia. Ever since leaving Philadelphia, she had not been eating very much to avert seasickness. That and the constant exercise involved in maintaining her balance on the *DOVE* had led to her losing weight. She was so busy preparing extensive meals and worrying about the money and accounting books she didn't have much of an appetite.

While on her walks, she had time to notice little things. Her face and ribs were healing, slowly but steadily, and she began to feel better about herself. The swollen places on her face were becoming less of a problem too. She also noticed the constant pressure in her head was subsiding, but not the anger over her plight nor the fear she had of being discovered and killed. She continued to worry about the two thugs who had tried to kill her and the other two men who might have been cops. She felt certain someone was still looking for her. She was scared, and the walks on the peaceful beaches of Bermuda helped her think more clearly.

The crew's female friends were staying at the Marriott on the south shore of Castle Harbor. All three of the girls were sharing a single room to save money. There was not much privacy, so two of them stayed on the *DOVE* as much as possible. Eddie and Bo used the ship's primary launch, *L'TL DOVE*, a couple of times to take their dates snorkeling off St. Catherine's. The girls preferred the sturdiness of the solid hull of *L'TL DOVE* to the bounciness of the more practical, inflatable Zodiacs.

On Wednesday night, Anna decided to go to the Windward Tavern and have a beer. She needed to get away from the partying on the *DOVE*. Perhaps old George would be there. As she expected, the place was pretty much full of customers. The music was loud and the air dense with tobacco smoke. When she entered, she stopped and scanned the tables through the cigarette smoke and dim lighting to see if George or one of his friends was there. The bar stools were all taken by people who looked like dockworkers, seamen, and boaters. Except for the two male tourist types, wearing tropical shirts, sitting at the end of the bar looking at her. Perhaps because of her weight loss, they might be checking her out. But they weren't just casually glancing at a new woman entering the tavern. They were obviously scrutinizing her. She spotted George and Mike at a table at the far end of the patio. She walked up and said hello.

"Would you gentlemen object if I joined you?" she said with a tight-lipped smile.

"Hey, Anna! Have a seat," George said as he stood up to pull a chair out for her.

After she sat down, George and Mike both motioned for Anna to lean in closer.

"Anna, we don't mean to pry, but is someone looking for you?" Mike whispered.

Anna pushed back a little from the table, narrowed her eyes, and looked at Mike and George. "Why would you ask me that?" Anna was concerned several people had already figured out something was wrong. *But why is this of any concern to George and Mike?*

"Anna, don't turn around, but—" George warned.

Mike interrupted, "A couple of guys have been coming in here the last few nights asking about a woman who kind of looks like you. The bartender told them someone who might fit the description comes in occasionally."

"And they're sitting at the bar now," interjected George with a serious look.

"Oh no!" Anna exclaimed in a whisper. Her expression was a dead giveaway to George and Mike that she was hiding from someone. She looked terrified even as she tried to regain her composure. She started to look for the men, but Mike held her arm. "Don't turn around, Anna. They're looking this way now, and they're not being cautious about studying you. They're talking back and forth without taking their eyes off you. And they don't look like ordinary tourists either."

"Do you need some help?" George whispered in a concerned tone.

Anna sat still, looking back and forth at George and Mike. They could see she was scared. Very scared. Her eyes were darting back and forth. She was calculating her options.

"Should we call the police?"

"No! Don't do that. Please."

George and Mike both leaned in closer. They knew for sure something was seriously wrong.

"Are these guys police?" Mike asked.

"No! They're definitely not police," Anna whispered back.

"What do you want to do, Anna?" George asked. "Can we help?"

"I think I better get out of here and lose them. If they ask you any questions after I leave, please don't tell them I'm on the *DOVE*. I'll explain it to you later, if I'm still around."

Anna lamented she was not carrying one of her guns. *I have no protection. I should have been carrying my gun. I should have realized they might still be looking for Tatianna.*

Anna got up, slowly pushed her chair back under the table, casually nodded to Mike and George, turned, and walked straight to the exit of the tavern without looking around. Mike and George watched closely as the two men jumped up from their bar stools and quickly followed her.

The parking area in front of the tavern was made up of a loose mixture of gravel, broken shells, trampled down weeds, and dirt. There was a single overhead light at the far corner of the lot with a rusty green overhead shade that provided only a dim, shadowy light for the cars in the parking area.

Once out the door of the tavern, Anna started to run, but her eyes had not accommodated to the near darkness. It was hard to see in the dim light, and the gravelly, loose parking lot surface caused her feet to slip, slowing her down. The two men caught up to her quickly and grabbed her by the arm and by the hair. She yelled for them to let her go and tried to push them away. The shorter of the two men had her by the arm. He pulled out a revolver from his waistband and pointed it at her face while loudly whispering for her to shut up and come with them. It was dark and shadowy, but Anna could see the revolver was a very large caliber gun, probably a .357 Magnum.

She thought about what Joey had taught her. The best time to escape was right away, while they were still vulnerable to discovery and less likely to shoot her. Not later, but immediately.

She punched the taller man in the face and tried to kick the man with the gun who still had her by the arm. He pulled her closer and using the gun slammed her hard across the right side of her face, opening a deep gash. She screamed out in pain and fell to the ground, her mind swirling. He hit her again opening a split in her scalp. There was a loud buzzing in her head and the men looked fuzzy. The man she punched pulled out a knife and yelled, "I'm going to cut you up good for that, you fucking bitch." She could feel blood streaming down the side of her face and neck as she tried to get up. She kept kicking but the man with the gun was holding her down.

Anna was yelling for them to let her go while rolling back and forth trying to get up. She threw gravel at the man with the knife. He kicked her in the face cursing and calling her a bitch. His kick splattered her face and hair with dirt. As she tried to push the man with the gun away, she looked up and saw a fast-moving shadow behind him. Then she heard a heavy muffled thud. The man made a deep guttural sound, fell forward on top of her, and dropped his revolver next to her.

The man with the knife turned toward the moving shadow yelling, "What the fuck," just as Anna pushed the man on top of her aside, grabbed the gun, rolled back, and shot the man with the knife twice. He staggered backward and fell, hitting his head on the fender of the adjacent parked car. He flopped forward and rolled on the gravel toward Anna.

She turned back toward the shadow and saw Mike holding his arm high with a long-necked beer bottle in his hand. George was close behind him with a bottle in his hand. The other man began struggling with Anna to get his gun back from her. He rolled back on top of her and grabbed the barrel of the gun while yelling, "Gimme the fucking gun, bitch!" Mike moved quickly, with the beer bottle raised high, preparing to hit him again but stopped as he heard two muffled gunshots. In their struggle, Anna shot the man in the chest while he had his hand on the barrel of the revolver trying to pull it away. He collapsed on top her, bleeding profusely on her shirt and jeans. She struggled to get out from under him. Gravel and dust kicked up over her as she pushed him off with her feet. Her face, shirt, and jeans were covered with blood, dirt, pieces of dead weeds, specks of gravel, and dust.

"Oh my god, Anna, you killed them both," George whispered while bending over the one with the knife.

"Anna, give me the gun and get out of here," Mike demanded. "Quick! We'll take care of this. You get going! And stay away for your own protection. Stay aboard the *DOVE* and don't leave it."

Anna stood up and looked past George and Mike toward the tavern. The music was still playing loudly, and no one appeared at the door. She scanned the parking lot. It was empty. She looked at the two men lying on the gravel between the parked cars. They didn't move. She looked back at George and Mike.

"Go on, Anna. Give Mike the gun and get the hell out of here. We'll take care of this," George urged while tugging at one of the bodies.

She looked at the bodies once more and without another word handed Mike the revolver and left. Mike wiped the gun down with his shirttail and placed it in the hand of the dead man who had been on top of Anna. Together, he and George arranged the bodies to look like they had a fight and killed each other. George got down on his hands and knees searching the area for any loose items and shuffled the gravel to hide the bloodstains. Mike helped him kick some of the bloody gravel under a nearby-parked car. They both looked around and were relieved to see that no one had left the tavern. Mike looked down at his shirttail. It had blood on it. He tucked his shirt back into his pants, and they walked casually back into the tavern.

George sat down at their table to resume drinking while Mike went to the head to check his shirt and wash his hands. He returned to the table, and they finished their beers. They didn't speak for a while.

George turned slowly toward Mike and with a puzzled look said, "Damn! I can't believe that just happened, and no one seems to have noticed."

Mike carefully looked around the bar and responded, "They're all drunk, George. And the music is really loud."

Anna struggled as she returned to the *DOVE*. The night was dark, and she felt dizzy and disoriented. Her face was throbbing with pain, and everything looked fuzzy. Several times she had to sit down on the road to regain her orientation but was finally able to find her way back. With her head spinning, she had trouble descending the stairs to the saloon.

Bo came out of the galley with a couple of sandwiches and beers. He was heading back to the guest cabin he had taken for himself and his friend. Anna was holding her head with blood dripping down her hand and streaming off her elbow. The upper portion of her denim shirt was soaked red with blood, dust, and pieces of gravel from the parking lot. As she moved some of the gravel fell to the saloon floor. She was unsteady.

"Holy shit, Anna, you're all bloody," Bo exclaimed. He put his food down on the galley counter and helped Anna to a chair. Then he got Bart. Bart and Bo together helped Anna into the galley to use the large sink to wash her face and hands. Leaning over the sink and looking at the red swirling water, she thought she must be badly hurt.

"Damn, Anna, what the hell happened to you?" Bart asked as he tried to wash her face. She pulled her head back and resisted his help for a moment telling him he was hurting her. He told her to stay still so he could wash the blood off her face and out of her hair to find where she was hurt.

"Damn, Anna, what does the other woman look like?" Bo exclaimed in amazement. He was still pissed at the earlier episode where Bart had accused him of breaking into her cabin. But he was genuinely concerned she might be badly hurt, so he backed off.

Bart parted her hair and saw her scalp was split. She had several small but deep cuts next to her eye. He determined the cut in her scalp was only a surface wound, but the wounds next to her eye were more serious. He asked if she was dizzy, and she told him she wasn't. She lied, but she expressed concern for all the bleeding. He told her that cuts to the scalp and face bleed more profusely than cuts elsewhere, but a compression bandage with some antibiotic ointment would stop the bleeding. He poured peroxide on the wound, and the sink filled with a bubbly froth of peroxide and blood.

"You look like you've been in a war," Bo declared while shaking his head. He was trying to be compassionate, but it sounded harsh.

"Thanks, Bo. I hope you're enjoying this," Anna responded weakly with her head almost in the sink.

"I think you may need stitches, Anna," Bart explained. "Maybe we should take you to the hospital in Hamilton to see a doctor."

"No! I don't need to go to the hospital. Can you just use tape and pull the cuts together?"

"I can't use adhesive tape, Anna. It would be in your hair and wouldn't stick," Bart explained. "I can wrap a compression bandage around your head to stop the bleeding. It'll be bulky though."

After placing an antibiotic bandage pad on the cut next to her eye, he wrapped gauze around her head to hold the compression bandage down on the scalp. It was a huge bandage.

"I don't think you will have to wear this very long. The bleeding seems to be stopping just with the antibiotic gauze."

Anna went to her cabin, changed out of the bloody clothes, and then proceeded to the head for a quick shower. She took the clothes to the ship's washing machine to wash out the blood. As she went back to her cabin, Rick returned to the boat and entered the saloon. When he saw Anna's massive head bandage, he stopped short. Bart and Bo were on their knees wiping blood off the floor. Rick stared at Bo. Then he looked back at Anna.

"What happened? Anna? Are your okay?"

Bo answered, "She got into another fucking bar fight somewhere. Isn't that obvious?"

"I don't know about that, Bo," Bart cautioned. "She doesn't have alcohol on her breath. I checked for that. I think she may have been attacked. I wish she would just tell us what happened."

"I don't think she was in a bar fight either," Rick exclaimed. "I don't know what's going on. Something's wrong here."

Bart began to recall Mrs. Pisani's observations. *Anna was a gourmet cook, didn't drink much, and was well spoken and polite. She was a quiet person. Even reclusive. What the fuck happened to her? Could she have been attacked or tripped and fallen down? Judging from the way she maneuvers herself on the deck, she can't be that clumsy. At some point, I've got to get her to talk to me.*

Bo picked up the sandwiches and drinks he had placed on the galley counter. He wouldn't admit it, but he did have great concern about what had just happened to Anna, whatever it was. He wouldn't want any of his fellow crew members to get hurt, but he was wondering why it seemed only Anna had a problem.

Back in her cabin, Anna was pondering what had happened. She was thinking how lucky she had been George and Mike had helped her and worried they were going to get into trouble. She need not have worried. It was over an hour before the bodies were found in the poorly lit tavern parking lot and only after several cars had left.

When the police arrived, they questioned everyone in the tavern. They asked if anyone knew the dead men or had seen them in the tavern. The bodies had no identification on them but lots of money. In front of the police, Mike asked George if the dead men might be the same two guys who were arguing over in the corner earlier that evening. The police overhead him and then asked a couple of drunk seamen in that part of the tavern if they had seen two men arguing. They said they had. The police decided that the two men had killed each other in a fight but were perplexed they found only one gun. The other gun must have been picked up by one of the customers who left the tavern. The important part of their assumption was the two men killed each other, and their deaths didn't involve George or Mike

—

130

CHAPTER 27

In New York City, it was Thursday morning before Cecilia had some spare time. She left her hotel and hailed a taxi to go to a nearby post office. She approached a high table, up against a marble-clad wall, and opened the large manila envelope. The address was not at all what she expected to see. *The District Attorney in Philadelphia? Why is Anna sending a package to the District Attorney?* This was much more serious than she had expected. Anna was adamant that she would not tell anyone. Her plea seemed much more ominous now. Cecilia began to consider it might not be Anna's husband or boyfriend who had beaten her up.

Cecilia debated with herself on whether to open the envelope and see what was inside. After a few minutes of consternation, she placed the outer envelope in her briefcase and went to the counter to ask the clerk to provide the zip code and mail the envelope first class.

Back in her hotel room, Cecilia wondered what Anna could be sending the district attorney, and what might happen after the DA got the package. She suspected it was going to stir up a lot of trouble. She called the Philadelphia Chamber of Commerce to ask them for the name and phone number of the main newspaper in Philadelphia. She ordered a subscription to the *Philadelphia Inquirer* to be mailed to her home address in Kettering.

On Saturday morning, the *DOVE* motored out of St. George's Harbor, through Town Cut, out the shipping channel, past the outer channel marker, and set a course of 180 degrees true—due south. The early morning sun glowed brightly and reflected off the buildings and hills of Bermuda.

Bart called for all hands to prepare for hoisting the sails. Anna didn't go topside and help uncover the sails. It was something she started to enjoy doing, but not that morning. Bart turned the *DOVE* into the wind and powered down. Then he called out to hoist the mainsail. The crew acted quickly. With practiced precision, they hoisted the main gaff boom and mainsail and then secured the halyard and the mainsheets amidships. When the foresail was hoisted, and its halyard and sheets secured, Bart called for all hands to prepare to fall off and run with the wind. The crew let off the main and foresail 45 degrees to starboard to catch the wind. They sailed on a broad reach of 230 degrees until they were due south of the Gibbs Hill light and then set a course of west by southwest, 245 degrees, for the Northeast Providence Channel between Great Abaco and Eleuthera, Bahamas.

Bart was pleased to have a following wind almost exactly on course for the Bahamas. It would provide a great ride without all the tacking he had to do on the trip over to Bermuda. And there wouldn't be any wind-driven salt spray from the waves breaking against the bow.

It was amazing the wind was predicted to blow in that direction for almost a week. Bart hoped the prediction would hold. He had the crew set the mainsail fully to starboard and secured the boom with a portable boom vang anchored to a deck tie-down near the gunnel. Then the foresail was set fully to port and the boom secured with an outboard boom vang. Sailing wing on wing with the gaff sails up, he ordered the giant spinnaker be hoisted and the *DOVE* sailed with the wind toward the Bahamas.

Bart was seriously concerned about Anna's plight. The swelling on the right side of her face was improving, but he could see her wounds were still painful. The bandages were off, and the cuts were healing, but Bart suspected she might have a broken or fractured bone in her cheek.

Anna didn't complain about her pain so Bart was at a loss for what to do. She did her job and went immediately back to her cabin. No talking while making the meals. She didn't come topside or spend any of her free time in the saloon. Bart thought about Rick's admonition not to jump to the conclusion that Anna had been in a bar fight and decided to try to find out what had actually happened. *Nothing I've done has been successful in getting her to talk. I must not be approaching her the right way. Perhaps I've been intimidating her and causing her to withdraw from the conversation. If I have her share my watch at the helm and teach her about steering the boat, maybe she will loosen up and explain what happened back in Bermuda. Or maybe even before she joined the crew.*

Bart was pleased that Anna liked taking the helm. He discovered she was a quick study and was enjoying learning the various aspects of sailing. As the days went by, Anna was also spending more time topside under Rick's careful tutelage. The salt air helped her wounds heal quickly. While Anna appreciated Bart's willingness to take the time to teach her the basics of sailing, she continued to deflect his effort to get her to talk. Bart was becoming increasingly frustrated by his inability to crack her façade.

With the following winds, the *DOVE* was making good time, and Bart was ahead of schedule to pick up the new charter in the Bahamas. At night he lowered all the sails except the main so there would be less work for the crew. He was not in a hurry.

CHAPTER 28

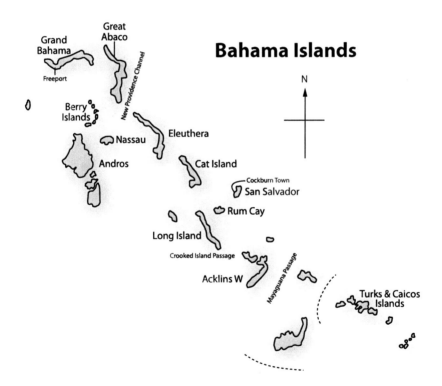

Bahama Islands

Grand Bahama
Great Abaco
Freeport
New Providence Channel
Berry Islands
Nassau
Eleuthera
Andros
Cat Island
Cockburn Town
San Salvador
Rum Cay
Long Island
Crooked Island Passage
Acklins W
Mayaguana Passage
Turks & Caicos Islands
N

Anna was fascinated with how the ship's activities at sea quickly became so routine. Each crew member took his turn at watch and performed his assigned duties. They became a part of the machinery of the boat. On the trip to the Bahamas, the sea was relatively calm compared to the pitching and rolling on the passage to Bermuda.

Cooking was much easier standing on a level and unmoving surface. Even the pots and pans behaved themselves, but it didn't last long. The sky soon clouded over, the wind shifted, and the seas kicked up. The spinnaker was lowered, and the inner jib was hoisted. The *DOVE* heeled hard over to port, and they sailed on a starboard beam reach.

Goddamn weather forecasters, Bart thought. *I wish they could get it right for more than a few days.*

As they neared the Bahamas, the wind lightened again, and sailing was smoother. When they entered the channel between Abaco and Eleuthera, Anna went topside. She was excited to see land again. The approach to the Bahamas was especially imposing.

Bart came up on deck in a foul mood cursing to himself about something Anna couldn't decipher. He normally didn't curse much. As the captain of a vessel, he had to show some decorum. Anna had admired that. But he was upset and told Bo, who had the helm, he had just made contact with their marine agent in Lucaya, Grand Bahama. The Koroguru Group, which had reserved the charter, had to reschedule for a later date, maybe in a month or so. They realized they would forfeit their deposit, a substantial sum, but had no choice, for business reasons. They asked if they could also change their pickup port.

Forfeiture of their deposit helped take some of the sting out of losing the booking for Bart. The number of charter cruises had been down for about a year. Mr. Pisani had offered Bart a bonus if he could get more charters to offset the cost of operating the *DOVE*. Mr. Pisani liked to sail, and he always wanted to have the boat at his disposal, but he was a businessman and sought to reduce his company's cost for maintaining the *DOVE* as much as possible.

The Koroguru Group had arranged to be picked up in Freeport, but there was no longer any reason to go there. A thunderstorm was brewing around the Berry Islands and the upper Tongue, so Bart opted to spend a day or two in Nassau to rest and restock the galley after the passage from Bermuda. They docked next to several large luxury motor yachts in the harbor adjacent to the Atlantis Resort on Paradise Island. It was late in the afternoon, and the crew wanted to go into town and visit the bars before the storm moved farther south and hit Nassau. Nassau was more of a party town than Bermuda and had a lot of young tourists. Anna volunteered to take the first evening security watch. They had enough food and supplies so there was no immediate need for her to go ashore.

Early the next afternoon, Bart contacted the agent in Lucaya. The agent had been working with the Koroguru Group to reschedule their charter. He said they decided on a two-week cruise out of Charlotte Amalie, leaving in three weeks with stops in Virgin Gorda, St. Maarten, Montserrat, and Barbados. They wanted to know if there could be some flexibility in the actual departure time to accommodate their business requirements. Since he had no other bookings, Bart agreed.

The crew used every opportunity to go into town. Rick went to the beach one afternoon and invited Anna, but she declined. Although she had lost more weight, she wasn't comfortable with the idea of wearing a bathing suit. Or even shorts for that matter. Besides, she didn't want to encounter anyone in Nassau who might recognize her. Instead, in the evenings she walked down to the waterfront and found taverns that didn't cater to the tourist trade. When anyone spoke to her, she was unresponsive or changed the conversation. She didn't want to talk to men and preferred to simply sit, drink a beer, and listen to the sailors' yarns.

Stories of the drug trade and yacht hijackings were rampant. After the United States clamped down on it along the Gulf Coast and Mexico, the drug and human smuggling traffic had increased dramatically in the Bahamas. Human trafficking was especially profitable. There were no retaliatory consequences for the loss of human cargo because the payment was up front, unlike the loss of cocaine for which the payment came after it was sold. But the traffickers still needed boats, the bigger the better, to get the cargo to the States. Some of the yacht captains were making arrangements for tighter communications with one another and for rafting up during overnight anchorages. Boaters and sailors were concerned the Bahamian government was trying to keep the problem out of the media and wasn't doing enough to stop the piracy.

Bart had three weeks to get to Charlotte Amalie to pick up the Koroguru Group so he decided to slowly cruise through the relatively weather-protected waters of the Bahamas and the Turks and Caicos. They could readily find shelter from sudden storms if they sailed among the islands, rather than the open Atlantic. The *DOVE* could easily take the rough weather, but there was no need to beat the crew up in a storm. By sailing only in daylight, he also could reduce the stress of round-the-clock watches. After they picked up the Koroguru Group, the crew would have their hands full for two weeks, and it would be good to give them a rest. Two days later, the *DOVE* departed Nassau.

CHAPTER 29

Bart sailed southward through Exuma Sound. The sky was overcast, and the wind was generally light except for several short squalls off Cat Island. Under the drive of light wind, the *DOVE* wasn't making much way. As they sailed into Crooked Island Passage, the wind kicked up, and it rained heavily as it often does in the islands. As quickly as it started, the sea state calmed, and small patches of blue sky appeared. But another storm was on the horizon to the north. With no need to hurry, Bart decided to anchor early off the east side of Acklins Island.

It was almost dark when Anna had finished cleaning the galley and retreated to her cabin. Under the lightly overcast sky, the faint red and bronze color of the sky to the west had disappeared and was quickly overtaken by dark purple and finally blackness. Bart had shut down the generator for the night and switched over to the 12-volt battery-operated system. It was dim, but everyone liked the quietness and warm atmosphere of the less-intense lighting. Shutting down the generator also conserved expensive diesel fuel and reduced the cost of operating the *DOVE.*

With no generator, there was no air-conditioning. The ventilation tubes on the deck had to be positioned to catch the breeze, and the cabin portholes had to be open. Anna could smell the soft ocean breezes and hear the quiet, rhythmic lapping of small wavelets against the hull. It was mesmerizing. In the lower islands of the Bahamas, the nights could be deeply dark. And this night, with only a half moon, was no exception.

Bart went to his cabin to study the charts of the West Indies for the next charter. Rick was organizing the ground tackle in the anchor locker under the bow. Eddie and Bo were cleaning the aft deck. Eddie was mopping on the port side, listening to his iPod, and humming to himself. Bo had a long-handled scrub brush and was working on the starboard side. He too was listening to an iPod. They were both happily preoccupied with their music and activities and oblivious to anything around them.

Anna sat on her bunk, resting against the outer bulkhead as she usually did when she read. As she leaned over to turn on the small brass reading lamp, she felt a subtle thunk against the hull. She stopped to listen then heard what she thought was scraping on the side of the *DOVE* and splashing sounds out of sync with the previous rhythmic lapping of wavelets. It was quiet, but she felt sure something had bumped up against the *DOVE*. She turned and looked out the porthole. She had a fleeting glimpse of the stern of a small skiff drifting close to the hull. It had a small outboard motor, but it wasn't running. Then it was gone. The skiff had been almost impossible to see in the darkness. She looked again, but there was nothing. She thought for a moment she was imagining things, but then there was the soft scraping sound again. Something was definitely sliding up against the hull.

Everything Anna had heard at the tavern in Bermuda and the bars in Nassau suddenly came rushing into mental focus. It took only a moment for her to suspect they were being boarded by pirates. She opened the small cabinet over her bunk, swiped out the cosmetics and tampons, and retrieved the Glock. Moving quickly, she turned out the only light in the saloon and cautiously climbed the steps to the deck.

Standing in the doorway to the deck, she could see Bo jabbing his long handled scrub brush to fend off a short dark man with a machete. The man was wearing only shorts and was swinging the machete at the brush handle. Bo had dropped his iPod on the deck and was screaming at the Bahamian to back off. At the same time Anna glanced to her right to see Eddie protecting himself with a deck mop while backing up from another man with a long knife. The deck was soapy where Eddie had been mopping and the Bahamian had difficult footing. Eddie was yelling for help while holding on to the port gunnel with his left hand to keep from slipping.

Anna yelled, "Bo, drop! Bo, drop now!"

Instinctively, Bo dropped to the deck, and his ears shattered with the report of two .40-caliber gunshots. The sound was explosive and immediately over his head. His ears were ringing, and his pulse was pounding as he scrambled backward on his butt, feet, and hands until he bumped into Anna's legs. Bo's eyes never left the man as he dropped the machete, grabbed his chest, and began to collapse onto the deck spitting out blood.

The man on the port side instantly stopped trying to stab Eddie, spun toward Anna, grabbed a revolver from the back of his waist band, and tried to take aim at Anna. Bo slid around behind Anna as she dropped to one knee, brought up her left hand to brace her grip on the pistol, and took aim. The Bahamian fired two wild shots at her while trying to fend off Eddie who was hitting him with the soapy mop. One bullet hit the outer wall of the main cabin next to Anna, and the other hit the main boom above her.

Anna didn't flinch. The man scrambled to the deck and tried to shield himself behind an open hatch cover. Anna fired twice. Her shots penetrated the hatch cover, and the man rolled out on to the deck screaming in pain. Everything went dead quiet for about four seconds. To Eddie, it was like an hour. Bo, still on his butt, was wide-eyed. The man in front of Eddie was holding his left shoulder with his right hand, but he still had his revolver in his hand. Suddenly there was the deafening blast of three more gunshots right above Bo's head. Anna shot the man three times in the chest. He laid still with blood flowing onto the soapy deck beneath him.

There was a loud thud and a scrapping noise at the rear starboard gunnel. Bo jumped up and started toward the sound.

"Bo, back away. Stay back," Anna shouted.

A grappling hook was digging into the gunnel with a line attached to a small wobbling boat. A man in the boat was trying desperately to detach the grappling hook from the *DOVE*.

Bo watched in awe as Anna ran quickly and deftly toward the grappling hook. No hesitation. Eyes and gun focused on the skiff. Bo moved closer and started to look down at the skiff but felt Anna strongly pushing him aside and telling him to move. She sounded surreal. No emotion. No panic. Bo moved quickly back behind Anna while trying to decide what to do. Eddie was staring at the dead Bahamian in front of him and the blood flowing into the soapy water forming bright red bubbles on the deck. As she reached the gunnel, Anna saw a white man with an unkempt scruffy beard, standing on the front seat of the small boat, trying to balance himself while attempting to undo the stuck grappling hook from the gunnel.

Anna cautiously peered over the side of the *DOVE*. Bo moved in next to her, but she pushed him back again. "Bo, get back."

Looking up, the man saw Anna with her arms bent upward, holding her Glock with both hands alongside of her head. He grabbed his short-barreled, nickel-plated shotgun and pointed it at Anna. Anna leaned over the gunnel and shot twice, hitting the man in the left side of his neck and chest. As he fell into the skiff, he fired the shotgun into the empty air. Landing with his head and arm hanging over the side of the skiff, he dripped blood down the inside of the freeboard and into the bilge water of the skiff. He didn't move. The bilge water began to reflect the red sheen of blood spreading outward and around his body.

Everything went quiet. A deafening quiet. Bo was shaking and looking wide-eyed at the bodies and then at Anna. Eddie was standing frozen with the mop handle still in his hand staring at Anna. The whole event had taken less than forty seconds. Eleven shots had been fired. Three men were dead. And now only quiet.

The silence was broken by the pounding of Bart's feet hitting the deck. "Holy shit! What the fuck is happening up here? What's all the shooting?"

He saw the Bahamian and the blood spreading out on the starboard deck. Bo's deck shoes were covered in it. He looked over at Eddie who was standing frozen, staring at Anna. He saw the other Bahamian slumped over on the deck in the red bubbling soapy water. For a moment, he couldn't speak. He just looked. All he could say was, "Holy shit!" Bo and Eddie began yelling, almost jabbering, about what had just happened.

Rick came running from the anchor locker and was trying to decipher what Bo and Eddie were yelling about. It took a few seconds for his eyes to accommodate to the low light. He saw Anna standing with her back to him. Her right arm was hanging down, and in her hand, he saw a pistol with light whiffs of smoke wafting upward from the downturned barrel. His first thought was Anna had shot Bo. He started to say something, but as he got closer he saw the blood on the deck and the dead Bahamian behind Bo.

Tucking the Glock into the back of her waistband, Anna broke the silence, "Bart, we have to turn off all the lights and get out of here as fast as possible. Bart! Bart! We have to get out into international waters." She turned to Bo. "Bo, make sure the skiff is tied securely to our boat. Eddie, you and Rick get these bodies into the skiff. Tie all of them together and then to the boat."

"Holy shit. This is unbelievable. Unfuckingbelievable." Bart was having trouble comprehending what had just happened. A minute ago he was in his cabin, half asleep, studying charts. Now dead men and blood were on the deck, and the ship's cook was telling him what to do.

Quickly, Bart became engaged and exclaimed, loudly, "The fucking Bahamian police won't care whose fault this was. We have to get out of here. Now!"

Bart glanced at Anna for only a second and then went below to turn out all the lights except a single small light over the helm. He figured they needed it to move the bodies.

In the eerie silence and dim light, Rick and Eddie moved the Bahamian from the port side and were about to dump the body over into the skiff when Anna stopped them. To her own astonishment, she was unflustered and in full control of the situation. She was just doing what she had done so many times during the shooting games she played with Joey. He trained her to be calm and take control of the situation, and she was doing it. She told Rick and Eddie to make sure there would be no chance of the bodies slipping into the water and drifting away. "They need to be tied to the skiff, and you have to make sure there is nothing in the skiff that can be traced back to the *DOVE*. And nothing left on the *DOVE* that could be traced back to these dead Bahamians."

Eddie went to find some spare rope, with the earphones to his iPod hanging down and banging against his knees. Anna told Bo to help Bart get the boat under way. Bart cranked over the diesel engine. Bo went to the bow to operate the winches and haul up the anchors while Eddie returned with fifty feet of nylon rope. Rick went over the side and boarded the skiff, while Eddie and Anna slid the bodies over and lowered them down to Rick. Rick tied the bodies together to the skiff and to the small outboard motor on the stern. Rick was about to climb back onto the *DOVE* when Anna asked him to make sure the skiff was secured firmly to the *DOVE*.

"Rick, we don't want the boat to get loose while we are towing it out to sea."

Bo returned to the helm and told Bart the anchors were secured. Bart switched off the one remaining light, engaged the prop, and headed east and out to sea through the Mayaguana Passage. He told Bo he needed a sharp lookout in the darkness, and Bo went forward and stood watch. As they got under way, Anna retrieved the Bahamians' knife, machete, and gun and carefully dropped them into the skiff.

As soon as they were under way, Anna told Rick and Eddie, "We have to clean up the blood right away. Can we do it in the dark?"

Rick connected a hose to the seawater bib and started hosing down the deck. In the darkness, Anna and Eddie scrubbed the deck with soap, a brush, and a mop. Rick kept a strong flow of water washing the blood into the sea.

At about 0300, the *DOVE* was in several thousand feet of water in the Atlantic Ocean and came to a stop. Bo boarded the skiff, and Eddie handed him an old spare anchor. Bo secured the anchor to the line that tied the bodies, boat, and motor together and chopped several holes in the bottom of the skiff. As it took on water and began to sink, he climbed aboard the *DOVE* and cut the line that held it to the *DOVE*. Everyone stood quietly at the gunnel and watched as the small boat with its grizzly cargo slowly sank in two thousand feet of water.

No one tried to sleep, and no one talked about what had just happened. They just kept motoring southeasterly toward the Virgin Islands.

With Bart at the helm all night, and Bo, Rick, and Eddie keeping watch for other vessels, they were tired and hungry. At dawn, they smelled the aroma of fresh coffee wafting up from the galley. Anna was also preparing eggs, grits, and biscuits.

Bart told the guys to have breakfast first. He would stay at the helm and eat after they came back. He thought steering the boat would keep his mind off the madness of the night before. But it didn't. His mind kept going over the events. *She was so methodical and precise in handling the situation. She acted like a pro and knew exactly what to do. And she showed no emotion after shooting the pirates. It's as if she has two personalities.* He knew Anna had done the right thing, but he was having trouble accepting the reality of it all. *Three pirates were dead. Maybe she's a secret agent. Or a spy. What else could it be? But she saved our lives. And the boat.* His mind was racing to find an explanation for her deadly professional performance. *And what about Bermuda? What was that all about? She couldn't have just fallen down. The cuts and gashes on her face couldn't have dripped enough blood to have soaked her jeans like they were. Is somebody after her? And how the hell could she be making breakfast as if nothing had happened last night?*

While Bart was having breakfast, and before cleaning up the galley, Anna went topside. She asked Rick and Eddie to scrub down the deck again and use plenty of bleach to get rid of any bloodstains in the cracks in the wood. She told them they had to inspect every inch of the boat for any trace of what had happened, including the sides of the boat. She asked Bo if he could cut out and repair the sections of the hatch cover, the boom, and the main cabin entry that had bullet holes in them.

Bo looked at the holes and said he could drill the bullets out, fill the holes with wood putty, and varnish over them so no one could detect any damage. He said he could do the same for the gunnel where the grappling hook had gouged the wood. They spent most of the morning switching helm duty, cleaning the deck and gunnel, and repairing the wood.

After lunch, Bart brought the *DOVE* to a full stop. The sea state was only a half foot, and the wind was from the east and light. He let the *DOVE* drift and called for an all-hands meeting in the saloon to discuss what had happened. The crew was not making their usual jovial comments. They just sat quietly and listened. Bart was serious and uncharacteristically authoritative. He told them absolutely nothing happened last night. The *DOVE* was never near Acklins Island. When they left Nassau, they sailed around the southern tip of Eleuthera and took the ocean route to the Virgin Islands. If there was ever a question about the repairs, it happened during bad weather on the transit from Bermuda to Nassau. "Got that? Is that clear?"

Everyone agreed.

"There can never be any mention of the things that didn't happen last night," Bart demanded again. "Is that totally clear?"

Everyone agreed again.

"Okay! We're going to sail to St. Thomas and wait there for the Koroguru Group charter. If all goes well, we should have about a week and a half to two weeks before they board. I'm planning on anchoring out on the east side of the island, in Red Hook Bay, and using the dinghy to get to shore. That should give us some additional time for Bo to make sure the repairs are flawless. I know you are going to go ashore or into Charlotte Amalie for beer, but I don't want you to get drunk. That applies especially to you, Eddie."

Bart brought the *DOVE* into the wind and commanded the sails be hoisted. The wind was light, and the *DOVE* began sailing slowly to the Virgin Islands. They had plenty of time. There was no hurry.

The next morning, as Anna was preparing to serve breakfast, Bo came into the galley and began helping her take the food to the table. She stepped back and watched in surprise. Bo came back to carry more food to the table and saw her watching him. He grinned and asked if there was anything else he could do to help. She gave him what the crew had come to know as her best smile, tight lipped with a nod. Pleasantly, she told him she was the cook. He should sit down and have breakfast, which he did. Breakfast was quiet. No chatter.

She was pleased Bo was being friendly, but it had not fully dawned on her why. She viewed the episode in the Bahamas as an act of self-preservation. That Bo felt she saved his life hadn't entered her mind. In fact, she thought Bart and the crew might be mad at her for causing so much trouble. She had so many concerns for her safety she couldn't think logically.

After breakfast, everyone took their dishes into the galley. They normally left them on the table, and Anna cleaned up after them. Anna objected, telling them the galley was her territory, and they should stay out of it. After the galley was cleaned and the cookware put away, Anna went up on deck for fresh air. The *DOVE* was barely heeled over, and the pitch of the bow was slight. She began to wonder if she still needed her scopolamine patches and decided not to wear them anymore.

While standing at the gunnel and looking out over the water, Bo told her it was probably about time she got more formal training on how to sail. And so, for the next few days, Bo spent his spare time teaching Anna about ropes, lines, knots, sails, sailing, and boating. He was very polite to Anna. Everyone was. The Bahamas had been a turning point.

CHAPTER 30

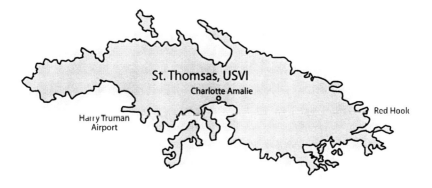

Rick had the best eyes for finding land, and he was the first to call out St. Thomas was in sight. It was late afternoon when they sailed around Little Hans Lollik Island and Thatch Cay. Bart anchored in the outer fringe of Red Hook Bay, past the smaller moored sailboats. Only one other large sailboat was in the bay, and it was near the mouth of Vessup Bay, a small harbor to the west. Anna admired the ketch as would anyone. It was a sixty-two-foot center cockpit ketch, flying the U.S. and British flags. Red Hook Bay looked like a boater's paradise. Clear water, well protected from storms, and surrounded by a mountainous island. Anna was impressed. She thought Bermuda was beautiful, but this could be even nicer.

After setting the anchors, Bart asked if anyone wanted to take the launch ashore. Eddie and Rick jumped at the chance and took *L'TL DOVE* to the dinghy dock. They wanted to find a bar, have a few beers, and spend a little time on land. Bo, who usually was among the first to go ashore to find a bar, hopefully with women, elected to wait until the next day. He said he had to inspect the damage to the boat and make a list of supplies needed to complete the repairs.

Anna declined because she was afraid of bumping into someone who might recognize her. Since she sent the ledgers to the district attorney in Philadelphia, she hoped the criminal thugs would learn Tatianna no longer had the books and stop searching for her. But she still might be seen by someone vacationing in St. Thomas who knew Phillip.

Anna needed to go ashore though because her jeans and shirts were getting too baggy. Her restrictive diet and the constant activity of working on a sailboat were having a significant effect on her weight. All to the good she thought. She had gained a lot of weight after her aunt died, and Phillip started abusing her. She lamented having been so slack about her appearance and vowed to never let it happen again.

The next morning, Anna asked Bart if she could go ashore on the launch with Bo. Bo had become so attentive and polite she actually found herself beginning to enjoy his company. Then she turned to Bo and asked him if he would mind if she went along. He pleasantly agreed but explained he wouldn't be ready to go for a few hours. She asked if he would mind teaching her how to operate the launch, *L'TL DOVE*, or one of the rubber dinghies (Zodiacs) when they went ashore. He again agreed with a smile. Bart informed Bo he was going ashore to make a slip reservation with the Harbor Master in Charlotte Amalie and go to the bank. He expected to be back by noon. Bart took one of the Zodiacs they had inflated earlier and went ashore. He thought Anna would feel safer in the ship's launch, *L'TL DOVE*.

While waiting for Bo, Anna joined Eddie on the foredeck where he was sorting the ship's supply of spare lines. He had made a mess in the anchor locker in his frantic search for rope in the Bahamas. He had promised to teach Anna how to braid and whip stranded nylon line, and this seemed like the perfect time.

Eddie laid out several one-hundred-foot coils of new three-quarter-inch stranded nylon rope that needed to be whipped.

—

The coils were heavy and had been wrapped tight around the middle to hold the loops together. He explained to Anna that whipping was the term for wrapping the ends of a rope with small stuff (waxed whipping twine) so the ends wouldn't unravel. He brought out several colors of whipping twine and began to show her the procedure.

Unnoticed by the crew was a gray inflatable Zodiac, with three men in it, leaving the big ketch with the U.S. and British flags. It motored slowly to the *DOVE* and bumped quietly against the starboard side. One man climbed quietly aboard with a line. He tied it to the gunnel, and the other two men came aboard. They walked toward Eddie and Anna, sitting on a hatch near the bow. Bo was on the other side of the *DOVE* working on the damaged hatch cover when he looked up and saw the men. He recognized the smaller man leading the other two. Bo quietly put down his tools and walked forward on the opposite side of the boat from the three men.

As the men got close to Eddie and Anna, the smaller one, at about five feet eight inches tall, with light-colored sandy hair, well tanned, and wearing a faded blue T-shirt, yelled at Eddie, "Eddie, I thought it was you. I've been looking all over the goddamn islands for you. Where's my fucking money?"

Backing up from the man, Eddie yelled, "Jimbo, how the hell are you doing?"

"Don't give me any of that how-do-you-do shit. Where's my fucking money?"

As Eddie backed up toward the bow, Jimbo continued to move forward and abreast of Anna who had been sitting on the hatch cover working with the coils of rope. The other two men stayed back about ten feet as if to guard a retreat and to watch Bo who was now standing on the other side of the bow hatch watching the confrontation of Jimbo and Eddie. One of them crossed his arms in a defiant gesture to Bo.

"Look, Jimbo, I told you I'd get the money, but I haven't been back here in a while. I can get it, but I don't have it right now."

"The Colombians don't put up with this kind of bullshit, Eddie. They kill assholes who try to cheat them, and when you disappeared I was left holding the fucking bag. I had to cover for you, and you fucked me over. You owe me thirty-seven hundred dollars, and you're going to give it to me right now, or I'm going to cut your fucking balls off."

Jimbo pulled a large diving knife out of its sheath and started to approach Eddie with the knife pointed at him. He was yelling at Eddie, "Give me the fucking money now."

When Anna saw Jimbo draw the knife, she instinctively grabbed one of the one-hundred-foot tightly wrapped coils of rope. Using a roundhouse swing with her whole body, she slammed Jimbo on the side of his head with the coil. He had barely finished his last words "the fucking money now!" when the heavy coil of rope hit him. It knocked him sideways, and he lost his balance. He stumbled and fell, hitting his head against the hatch cover, dropping the knife, and rolling onto the deck.

Anna jumped on top of Jimbo, putting her legs and knees on either side, and rolled him over face-up. She put her weight on his chest, grabbed the knife, and put the blade to his throat.

Bo jumped on top of the hatch cover screaming, "No! Anna, no! Don't kill him. Please don't hurt him!"

Eddie was shocked to see the situation shift so suddenly and joined Bo in yelling at Anna not to kill Jimbo. "Anna, please don't hurt him. I know him."

The two men standing back were caught totally off guard. They were surprised to see Jimbo draw the knife but didn't think he would hurt Eddie. Before they could react, Anna already had Jimbo on the deck with his knife to his throat. They stood frozen not knowing what to do.

Jimbo laid still, eyes wide open, feeling the blade pressing down on his throat. Anna's face was only inches from his. She was saying something, but his attention was focused on the pressure of the blade on his throat. He tried to resist, but as he did he felt the pressure of the blade increase. It felt like it was cutting into his throat, so he stopped struggling. Slowly, he began to hear Anna saying something as Bo and Eddie stopped yelling. In a cool, demanding voice she was asking, "Who gave you permission to board this boat? You don't come on our boat and threaten our crew. You understand that? Tell me you understand."

Jimbo didn't answer. He continued to feel increasing pressure of the blade on his throat. He could hear Anna talking to him, but he couldn't respond.

———

Bo had moved next to Anna. Bending down he was asking her in a low but intense voice to please not hurt him. He could see the blade was pressing against Jimbo's throat but not cutting him.

It finally hit Jimbo he could die, and he stuttered, "I'm sorry. I should have asked permission to come aboard. I'm sorry."

Anna slowly let up on the pressure of the knife on his throat.

She stood up and backed away. She stepped up onto the hatch cover alongside Bo, still holding the knife, and told Jimbo, "Get off the boat. And take these two with you."

Jimbo slowly got up holding his head where he had hit it on the hatch cover. He looked at his hand and saw a small amount of blood. He checked his throat, and there was no blood. Then the three of them went back to where they had tied off their dinghy, and, as the other two men got into it, Jimbo yelled back, "This is not over, Eddie. You're going to pay up what you owe me."

As Jimbo got into the Zodiac, he stopped again and yelled, "And you tell the big bitch I'm going to get her too. We'll be looking for her. This is total bullshit. You're not fucking me over again. You owe thirty-seven hundred dollars, and you're going to pay it back."

They pushed off, and as they started to motor away, Jimbo looked back and saw Anna throwing his knife in the water.

Unnoticed by everyone, Rick, who had been cleaning the electrical connectors under the binnacle in the helm, had picked up Bo's hammer and a large screwdriver and had carefully walked along the opposite side of the boat. He watched what was happening but couldn't see that Anna had a knife at Jimbo's throat. He could tell that whatever was happening was dangerous and was prepared to come to Anna's aid if needed.

Bo turned to Eddie and demanded to know what was going on. Rick joined in and wanted to know if Eddie was using drugs. They were both yelling at Eddie. Bo grabbed Eddie's T-shirt and started cursing at him while Eddie was apologizing over and over.

Bo pushed Eddie away and turned to Anna. "I thought you were going to cut his throat. You scared the shit out of me."

With her now-trademark tight-lipped smile, she said, "I couldn't do it. The knife was too dull."

Bo, Rick, and Eddie stared at her for a moment in disbelief, and then Rick broke out laughing. "I guess he won't mess around with Anna again."

Bo smiled, laughed a little, and then stopped. "This is a really serious problem. It's nothing to be laughing about."

"You owe him thirty-seven hundred dollars?" Anna asked Eddie.

"Yeah, but I'm going to pay him back."

Rick asked, "And the Colombians are involved?"

"I didn't know Colombians were involved."

"When the fuck were you going to pay him back?" Bo angrily demanded. "The Colombians don't take prisoners, dumbhead. They kill people. Are you out of your goddamn mind? You've got to fix this problem right away. I don't care how you do it, but you've got to fix it right away before you get us all killed. This is damn serious shit, and I can't believe you've done this to us."

"I know I have to fix it, but I don't have the money right now. I don't know what to do."

Bo got closer to Eddie. "Did you ever have it, Eddie? Did you ever have the goddamn money?"

Rick joined in, "Eddie, getting involved with drug dealers puts us all in danger. These guys will kill over a few dollars, much less thirty-seven hundred. It isn't just the money. They kill to protect their image. And they could be looking for the *DOVE.* This is bad. This is really, really bad."

"I'm sorry, guys. My girlfriend in Puerto Rico asked me if I knew how to get some coke and said she would pay for it. I asked Jimbo to help, and he got it for me. I thought it was his. I didn't know the Colombians were involved. I was going to pay him the next morning when I got the money from my girlfriend. But when I gave her the coke, she ran off with it. The *DOVE* was leaving San Juan that night, and there was nothing I could do. I had to leave."

"Eddie, that girlfriend ran off almost a year ago," Bo admonished. "How long have you owed Jimbo the money?"

"Since Puerto Rico."

"You've owed him the money for almost a year? They've been looking for you for a year?"

Bo cautioned, "Look, guys, we're in deep shit. Even if Eddie pays up now, Jimbo is going to want to get even for what just happened." Then he turned and stared at Anna. So did Rick.

"Anna, they're going to be looking for you too. This isn't good." Bo's voice was accusatory.

"You're right, Bo. I just should have let him cut Eddie's balls off. Right? Maybe the next time I will!"

Once again, Bo was surprised by Anna's defiance. She stood her ground. He knew she was right and did the right thing, but it happened so fast. Jimbo might have stabbed Eddie in a fit of rage, but she prevented it from happening. The thing that bothered him most though, and Rick too, was she acted to save Eddie, without hesitation, and they didn't.

Bo was thinking, *How come I didn't do something? What's wrong with me? You really have to admire her. She's one hell of a woman. But where did all this come from? She doesn't look that capable.*

They stood quietly staring at Eddie. Eddie realized he hadn't thanked Anna for protecting him, even if doing so might have caused a lot of problems. So he thanked her and apologized again for putting everyone in danger.

But Anna couldn't hear Eddie over the raging thoughts reverberating in her mind. *Oh no! Now I may have another group of people trying to kill me. This is too much. I've got to do something. How do I get Jimbo to back off?*

Anna offered, "Eddie, maybe I can help. I have some money saved and may have enough for you to pay Jimbo back. But you'll have to repay me. Can you do that?"

Bo looked at Anna incredulously. He was mystified that she had that kind of money. When she first came on board, he thought she was penniless. No one else on board had that kind of ready cash. The more he learned about Anna, the more of an enigma she became. But in his changing view, it was all positive.

Anna looked back at Bo, tightened her lips, and shrugged her shoulders.

Rick said, "That would be a great solution, Anna. But what if Jimbo is so pissed off just getting his thirty-seven hundred dollars isn't enough. He might want revenge."

"Well, let's go see if it will work," Anna answered. "Bo, can you get the launch ready? Eddie, you need to take me over to Jimbo's boat. I think this could be the solution to the problem."

"Uh, Anna," Eddie responded, "maybe somebody else should take you over. They might do something if I'm there."

"No, Eddie. It's your debt, and you should be there."

Anna went to the galley and got two small paper bags. Then she went to her cabin, locked the door, and put thirty-seven one-hundred-dollar bills in one bag and twenty more in another. She stuffed the paper bags in her jeans, under her shirt, and made sure it was well tucked in.

Eddie and Anna approached Jimbo's ketch and called out. There was a scrambling of men about the deck, and then Jimbo came to the gunnel. He was surprised to see Anna and Eddie in the *L'TL DOVE*.

"Well! It's the Big Bitch and the Dead Man. You better have my fucking money."

Anna called out, "Permission to come aboard, Captain?"

"Yeah, Ms. Big Bitch, come on up."

"Will you guarantee my safety if I come up?"

She said it loud enough that the entire crew could hear her.

"Yeah, come on up."

Anna boarded the ketch, leaving Eddie in the launch. She asked Jimbo if they could talk privately. They went to the bow, away from everyone. Anna, in a low voice, asked Jimbo if he would leave Eddie alone if she paid his debt.

"He owes me a lot more for the trouble he caused me. That son of a bitch took advantage of our friendship and then skipped out leaving me to deal with some very nasty people."

"He explained to us that he got the coke for a girlfriend in Puerto Rico who stiffed him and took off. He didn't have time to find her because the *DOVE* was leaving port. He didn't mean to cheat you, Jimbo. And he's really, really sorry. But the important thing is what will it take to set everything right again?"

"I had to pay off that debt myself. And it wasn't easy. If I hadn't, the Colombians would have killed me and gone looking for him, and we would both be dead by now."

"Yes, but would paying you back the thirty-seven hundred now solve the problem?"

"If I get the money, it will solve that problem, but I'm still going to beat the shit out of him for almost getting me killed."

"Fair enough. He deserves to have the shit beat out of him. I might even help you do it," Anna teased Jimbo.

"Oh, I'd love to see that," Jimbo said with a loud laugh.

"I have the thirty-seven hundred here." Anna unbuttoned the lower button on her shirt and removed the bag with the thirty-seven one-hundred-dollar bills in it.

"Damn! You have the money right here? Awesome!"

He looked in the bag and saw the crisp one-hundred-dollar bills and smiled. Then he had some choice words about what a shithead Eddie was. He couldn't resist calling Eddie names because he had been looking for him for so long.

Anna moved closer to Jimbo, almost touching foreheads. Speaking even more quietly, she whispered, "Jimbo, now that we have that out of the way, what would it take for you to be happy and completely forget the whole thing?"

Jimbo squinted his eyes, leaned forward, and whispered back, "You can bring that son of a bitch up here and let me beat the shit out of him right now. How about that? And you can help if you want."

"Well, I can't do that. We would have to find another deckhand. I hear they are hard to find down here. But would you rather beat the shit out of him or have another two thousand dollars as interest on the loan?"

"Are you kidding me? Two thousand?"

"Yep!"

"I'll take the two thousand."

"And then everything is copacetic?'

"That depends!"

"That depends on what?"

"On what copacetic means."

Anna tensed her lips, shook her head, and said, "It means everyone will be happy. We can drink a beer on it. Is that okay?"

"Okay, I'll go for that. But I've got to have the money first."

"Just one more thing, I don't want you telling anyone, not anyone, that I paid you any extra money. Can you do that? Otherwise, you'll have to settle for just beating up Eddie."

"So the Big Bitch saves the little shithead? Okay, consider it done."

"And one more thing, Jimbo. I'm really terribly sorry about what happened this morning, but I thought you were going to hurt him. I didn't mean to harm you."

"I've been thinking about it. I have to tell you I don't normally go around threatening people with knives. I was so pissed at Eddie I couldn't help it. We were close friends, and he screwed me. I've been thinking about it for a year. I'll tell you what. If I ever have anyone threaten me, I want you on my side."

With the agreement secured, Anna took the other bag out of her shirt and gave it to Jimbo. He smiled more broadly than before. Then he asked her to come below and have a beer with him. Anna agreed and asked if they might invite Eddie to join them, but Jimbo balked and told her that would be going too far.

They sat in the dining area of the *ANDROMEDA* drinking beer for about fifteen minutes.

"*ANDROMEDA* is an unusual name for a boat, isn't it? There must be a story behind it."

Jimbo explained the British owner wanted to get as far as possible from his work and thought only another galaxy would be appropriate. So he looked up the nearest galaxy and named his boat after it.

After finishing their beers, Anna climbed down to the launch. Jimbo started yelling at Eddie, "If it hadn't been for the Big Bitch you would be dead. You can thank her for saving your scrawny ass."

When they returned to the *DOVE*, Bo and Rick wanted to know how it went. Bo was especially concerned and asked, "Did Jimbo agree to drop the vendetta?"

"Yes," Anna announced. "He's actually a pretty nice fellow. He has been stewing for a year that Eddie almost got him killed. He just lost his temper. That's all. He's happy now."

Eddie was feeling exuberant over the outcome of Anna's negotiations with Jimbo. "Thebb negotiated the whole thing, and I promise I'll pay her back."

"Who's Thebb?" Rick asked.

Anna looked at him quizzically.

"The Big Bitch! You know, Thebb."

"Thebb?" They asked again.

156

"Yeah! That's what Jimbo's crew called her while I was waiting in the launch."

Jimbo's crew had disparaged Eddie as a pussy, among other things, for having to have Thebb save him from Jimbo. They didn't call her a girl. Just Thebb. Eddie countered if they didn't lay off him, they would have to deal with Thebb themselves. One of the crew looked over at Thebb, who was almost forehead to forehead with Jimbo and deep in conversation, and commented he would like that. Eddie looked at her and realized Anna had lost some weight and did look attractive, even in her baggy jeans and denim shirt. He hadn't thought about it before.

Bo reprimanded Eddie, "Her name is Anna."

Listening to the guys talk, Anna began to think this could be an escape from her actual name. Most of the people she knew in Philadelphia called her Anna instead of Annaliese. Joey had said anyone trying to become anonymous needed to have a new name right away.

Anna spoke up, "Wait, fellows. I kind of like it. It's unusual, don't you think? It has a nice ring to it—Thebb. From now on I'm Thebb Meerschmidt."

Rick squinted, "Meerschmidt? I thought it was something else. Something like Wolblaski or something?"

"No! It's Meerschmidt. Whatever gave you that idea, Rick? Thebb Meerschmidt. I really like Thebb. From now on, call me Thebb."

"Boy, Bart's gonna be surprised to have to deal with a new name."

Bo stood quietly, in amazement. *Is it because she's a woman she can change her name so easily? I thought, for sure, that her name was Wolinski. There's got to be more to it.*

Rick looked up. "Uh, speaking of Bart, here he comes now. What are we going to do?"

Thebb spoke up, "If you all agree, I suggest we tell him everything. That way we don't have to remember to not mention it. Just be up front with him and tell him what happened. He'll understand."

Bart threw a line to Eddie and came aboard.

"Why are you all standing there looking at me? What's happening?"

"Well, to start with," answered Eddie, "meet Thebb pronounced Thee-bee!"

Bart looked at Thebb and then back at Eddie. He was having flashbacks to Bermuda and all the blood. Then the Bahamas. No one said anything, and Bart kept thinking, *What do I do now? She must be a CIA agent or something. Maybe she's in a witness protection program. It doesn't matter. If she wants to have a new name, she can have it. We can just say it's a nickname.*

Bo began to explain what had happened and how Thebb loaned some money to Eddie so he could pay off his debt to Jimbo.

Bart turned to Eddie and told him he's a lucky son of a bitch. "Jimbo knows a lot people all over the islands and he has a lot of connections. Many of them are not nice people. That's how he has stayed out of trouble so long. You'd better not piss him off."

After a moment of silence, Bart continued, "I was wondering what was going on. As I was pushing off from the dinghy dock, Jimbo was coming ashore, and he said to tell the Big Bitch he wants to have another beer with her. I couldn't figure out what the hell he was talking about, but I guess this explains it."

Thebb was listening intently. Especially to the part where Bart said Jimbo had connections all over the islands. *So Jimbo has connections. I wonder what kind of connections he has?*

CHAPTER 31

Several days after the Jimbo incident, Bart called the crew into the saloon to pay them for the last month's work. Because they were so often at sea, there was no set schedule for paying the crew. Bart usually paid them when they were in a port with good banking facilities. He already knew Bo and Rick preferred to be paid with a check, and Eddie wanted cash. But he didn't yet know Thebb's preference so, with everyone there, he asked her first.

"Cash, check, or automatic deposit from Mr. Pisani's office?"

"Can you write a check made out to Thebb Meerschmidt?"

Bart looked quizzically at her and told her he thought her last name was Wolinski.

"Whatever made you think that, Bart? It's Meerschmidt."

"I don't know, Thebb. When you first came aboard back in Philadelphia, I must have been busy preparing for departure and didn't pay enough attention. Thebb Meerschmidt it is." He was trying to give credence to her claim her name was always Meerschmidt. He knew for sure she originally said Wolinski because he wrote it down in his log.

Bart was now certain Thebb was running or hiding from someone or something. It was becoming more obvious the longer he knew her. He considered the possibility it could be the police, but that scenario didn't add up. *She definitely isn't who she says she is. How could Mrs. Pisani have figured that out so quickly? And how could a ship's cook be so proficient with a gun?*

By now Bart had developed high respect for Anna and knew he owed her a debt for saving the *DOVE* and the lives of the crew back in the Bahamas. Also she was a damn good cook, the best they ever had. If she wants to have a new name and hide out on the *DOVE*, he would do everything he could to help her. He also realized, for the first time, he was going to have to protect her identity. And so would the crew.

Thebb had been practicing how to operate both the *L'TL DOVE* and the Zodiacs. She liked using the rubber dinghies better because she was afraid the fiberglass hull of *L'TL DOVE* would mar the sides of the bigger boats when she came alongside to board them. With her newfound skill in operating the dinghies, Thebb went ashore and took a taxi to the Ron de Lugo Federal Building on Veterans Drive in Charlotte Amalie to get a passport application. After that she went to the post office to rent a box and then to the Bank of Nova Scotia. She opened an account under the name Thebb Meerschmidt, deposited her first-ever paycheck, and transferred ten thousand dollars from her account in Bermuda to her new account.

Thebb then stopped at a couple of clothing stores and bought some new jeans and shirts. Every day, her appearance was improving. Her weight was dropping, and her face was healing and thinning. She began to look attractive again, even if scarred and somewhat overweight. She hoped better fitting jeans and shirts would make her look less dowdy.

When her errands were completed, Anna took the rubber dinghy out to the *ANDROMEDA* to talk with Jimbo. After being invited aboard, she told Jimbo that Bart had relayed his message about having another beer with her. She suggested they go into town, and Jimbo agreed. They took a cab to a waterfront tavern Jimbo frequented.

The tavern was in the industrial waterfront area. Jimbo assured Thebb it wasn't a place tourists frequented. After a few beers and listening to some of Jimbo's stories (all sailors seemed to love to tell sea stories), Thebb concluded he was actually rather easy going and friendly. *That must be why he has so many connections.* She decided his "almost attack" on Eddie was just for show to impress on him how pissed off he was. She was right. Jimbo told her how upset he had been his buddy almost got him killed. And he apologized again for causing such a commotion.

"So, Jimbo, is it true you have a lot of connections?"

"You could say I do. I've been working in the islands for a long time and have gotten to know a lot of people. If you're straight with them, and watch their backs, they—"

"Are any of them important? Like, I mean, officials or that sort of thing?"

"Well yeah. I guess you could say that. I have a few acquaintances in the government."

"Jimbo, could you get me an official birth certificate from the Virgin Islands? I will be willing to pay for the service."

Jimbo just sat for a minute, looking at Thebb. Then he looked out the window at the water. Then back at her.

Thebb could see she had blindsided him with her request.

"It's really important to me," she continued. "You know how scared you were when you thought the Colombians were on your case? How they might kill you? I have a similar problem, and I really need a new birth certificate. Right away."

"It seems to me if someone is chasing you, he may be the one in danger," Jimbo said with a wink and a smile.

"Come on, Jimbo! I'm deadly serious. I really do need a new birth certificate. Can you help me?"

"Well, I might be able to help. It could be expensive though."

"Like how much?"

"Could be several thousand dollars."

"Would it take long?"

"Might not, but I'll probably have to put some money up front to get it done."

"And what about your cut?"

"Thebb, I didn't expect the extra money you gave me the other day. That was great. It blew me away. So I don't need any more. Actually, I didn't even expect to see the thirty-seven hundred dollars again."

"Then you'll do it?"

"Yeah! But you have to agree to have a beer with me again on the *ANDROMEDA*."

Thebb wrote out her new name and birthdate along with fake names for her father and mother. She gave the paper slip to Jimbo along with one thousand dollars for up-front money. Then she asked

—

if he could get two official copies because she would have to submit one for a passport and needed another for a driver's license. She emphasized how critical it was to keep the transaction totally secret. Based on Jimbo's protection of Eddie, even when he thought Eddie had screwed him, Thebb gambled she could trust him. She actually had no other options.

Two days later, Thebb pulled up alongside the *ANDROMEDA* in one of the *DOVE*'s Zodiacs. She threw a line to a member of the crew and asked for permission to board.

Jimbo took her to the bow and told her the birth certificates were ready. He was just getting ready to go over to the *DOVE* to let her know. It was going to be twenty-five hundred dollars. Two thousand for the first one and another five hundred for the second. She went back to the *DOVE* and got the remaining fifteen hundred dollars for the birth certificates, plus another thousand for Jimbo, even though he said he didn't want a cut.

They went into Charlotte Amalie in a cab that smelled of mold, just like the one they had taken a few days earlier. Thebb waited at the tavern while Jimbo got the birth certificates. Upon his return, she left the tavern and made copies of her completed passport application at the local copy shop, bought some stamps, had her passport photo taken, and mailed the application. She hoped she would have a new passport waiting for her when the *DOVE* returned to the Virgin Islands after dropping off the Koroguru Group in Barbados.

She went back to the tavern and found Jimbo. She gave him the extra thousand dollars for helping her and emphasized again the importance of total secrecy. Jimbo hesitantly took the money telling her she didn't have to pay him. He wanted to do it as an apology for pulling the diving knife on Eddie. He told her again he didn't know what had come over him. He said he had never been so scared in his life as when she had his knife to his throat.

Thebb pursed her lips in a tight-lipped smile and said, "Jimbo, you were never in real danger. I couldn't have cut your throat anyway."

"Really? Why not? I was scared as hell."

"Yeah, but the blade was really dull."

Jimbo laughed and exclaimed he only carried the knife for show anyway. He never really used it for anything except to open beer cans.

She was about to leave when Jimbo asked if her name "Thebb" was Egyptian. She explained it was actually an acronym.

"An acronym? What's an acronym?"

"It's a word formed from the initial letters of a string of other words. Thebb stands for 'the Big Bitch.'"

"You're kidding! Really?"

"So, Jimbo, what's your name? Jim, James, what?"

"Kelsey James Bohansen. But I go by Jimbo. Thebb, how do I get in touch with you? I don't want you to sail away and not see you again. You're the most exciting person I've met down here."

"And I want to see you again too, Kelsey James Bohansen. You're actually a nice person, very different from when we first met. You really need to show that side of yourself more."

Two days before the Koroguru Group was to arrive, Bart began preparations to move the *DOVE* to the commercial docks in Charlotte Amalie. Prior to departure, Jimbo motored over in his dinghy to ask Eddie to have a beer with him. When Eddie saw Jimbo, he was apprehensive, thinking Jimbo might still want to hurt him. Jimbo only wanted to patch up the friendship with Eddie that had begun in grade school. However, Jimbo had an ulterior motive in visiting the *DOVE*. He wanted to see Thebb again.

After a quick beer with Eddie, Jimbo disembarked the *DOVE*. As he climbed down to his dinghy, Jimbo asked Thebb to be sure to find him when they returned to St. Thomas. It was his home base, and he looked forward to seeing her again.

CHAPTER 32

Virgin Islands

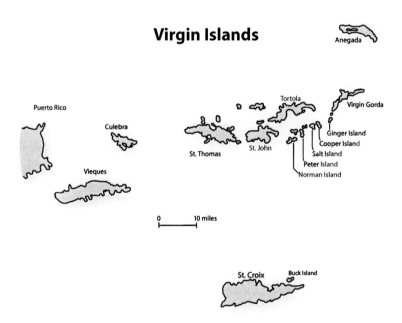

The Koroguru Group boarded the *DOVE* in Charlotte Amalie just before noon. They weren't what the crew expected. They were in their middle thirties, highly energetic, and arrogant. Only one of the three couples, Akiya Megumi and his wife Mitsu, had any Japanese ancestry, and they were both native-born Americans. One of the men, Billy Moffet, was especially arrogant and demanding. As soon as he came aboard, he dropped his baggage on the deck and told

Eddie to put his and his wife's luggage in their stateroom and get him a beer.

Before Eddie could respond, Bart interrupted. He asked the guests and crew to gather immediately in the saloon for a pre-cruise briefing. Normally Bart would have waited until the guests were settled in before holding his briefing. Billy Moffet's actions prompted him to change his routine.

Once all the guests were seated, Bart introduced the crew and guests to one another. He explained there were no maids, stewards, or other personal services available on board. Guests were required to handle their own luggage unless it was especially cumbersome. The crew were sailors and were needed to sail the boat and provide for the guests' safety. He told them where drinks were stored and when meals would be served. He went on to describe the procedures for operating *L'TL DOVE*, the Zodiacs, and the diving equipment. If they wanted to help with the rigging or man the helm for a short interval, they had to get permission from the captain and no one else.

The guests acknowledged what Bart told them. He could see the women expected more services than he was promising. He told them to stow their belonging and come topside for a safety briefing. A safety drill would be conducted each time they left a port.

It was early afternoon when the *DOVE* departed Charlotte Amalie Harbor. Later that day, Bart anchored on the west side of a small sandy-beach island in Leinster Bay, on the north side of St. John Island, in the U.S. Virgin Islands. It's an exceptionally beautiful bay, with clear blue water and clean, isolated sandy beaches. The crew ferried their guests to shore where they walked on the beach and viewed the mountainous horizons of St. John Island on the south and Tortola Island to the northeast. The men swam and snorkeled on the shallow reefs. The women chose to sit on the beach and watch. When the guests returned to the *DOVE*, they were happy. They hadn't expected to be able to go to the beach so quickly.

In the morning, Rick and Eddie took the guests back to the island in the Zodiacs to swim and walk the beach before continuing on. While the guests were ashore, Bo asked Bart if Thebb could help in sailing the ship when she was between meals. Bart was surprised at the request, but when Bo promised to closely supervise her, he hesitantly agreed. While Bart had full confidence in Bo, he was concerned that helping Thebb could interfere with Bo's responsibilities for the safety of the guests. He told Bo he had to be extra vigilant with this group. They seemed overly confident and weren't paying close attention to his directions.

After leaving Leinster Bay, Bart sailed to the Baths, on the southwest tip of Virgin Gorda. No charter cruise could be complete without anchoring off the boulder-strewn beaches of the Baths. After a day ashore, the guests clamored back aboard the *DOVE*, excitedly talking about swimming among the huge boulders. That night, Thebb attempted to make a gourmet stir-fry dinner that didn't turn out as well as it could have. Mitsu Megumi offered to help her prepare dinner the next time she was going to serve an Asian dish. Always eager to learn new cooking techniques, Thebb readily accepted. Bart had concerns about letting guests in the galley, especially while under sail. But Thebb assured him that she would provide close supervision.

On the next few legs of their cruise, Bart planned to anchor at Little Dix Bay and then in North Sound so the guests could go ashore and have dinner at the Bitter End Yacht Club on Virgin Gorda. After leaving North Sound, he planned to turn north, then east around Anegada, and do some ocean sailing. They would sail around Sombrero Island, past the east end of Anguilla, and on to Philipsburg, St. Maarten, where they would anchor in Great Bay on the south side of the island.

Bart sailed the *DOVE* into the North Sound of Virgin Gorda in mid-afternoon. Under full sail, he cruised through the west passage and anchored near the middle of the sound. The sight of the mountainous terrain surrounding the sound made it feel like a lake. There was a pervasive sense of privacy. At twilight, the guests boarded *L'TL DOVE*, and Eddie ferried them over to the Bitter End Yacht Club for dinner ashore. The launch wasn't designed to carry seven adults. Although the sides were relatively high, with the excessive weight there was less than a foot of freeboard. But the water was flat and the wind calm, so Eddie had no difficulty keeping it steady. Besides, they were adults and sat still, unlike kids who likely would be moving about and tipping the boat from side to side.

When they returned to the skiff after dinner, the entire Korogiru Group, wives included, were inebriated and started running up and down the beach. They were laughing, giggling, and singing. Eddie had a hard time getting them corralled. Once they were back in the launch and headed for the *DOVE*, he found their singing contagious and joined in. Suddenly, Craig Williams stood up to wave his arms and sing to the sky. The center of gravity shifted, and the launch lurched heavily to starboard. Craig fell out, splashing everyone in the launch. All singing stopped. Eddie had to give instructions for the guests to lean to port while he helped Craig back into *L'TL DOVE*.

With Craig safely back in the boat, they started laughing and singing again without regard to the fact he was dripping wet. Before Eddie could start the outboard motor again, Janna Williams, Craig's wife, asked Eddie to sit still so they could look at the stars. Only a partial moon was visible, and the stars were exceptionally bright. She unexpectedly stood up and started stripping her clothes off, telling everybody Craig was already wet, and they should all go skinny dipping under the starlight.

Eddie was panicking and tried to talk them out of swimming at night. "It ain't safe! Stay in the boat," Eddie kept repeating to no avail. Before he could throw out a safety line with a float, they were diving into the clear water. Akiya and Mitsu were marveling at the phosphorescence of their movements in the water while laughing and splashing Eddie in the boat. Eddie tied several PFDs to lines and threw them in the water for additional safety. Then he called Bart on the portable VHF to tell him what was happening and ask for help. If anything went wrong, he might not be able to handle everyone by himself in the dark. Bart called Bo and Rick topside and had them lower one of the Zodiacs into the water and prepare to help Eddie.

"Bart, what do I do?" Eddie called over the VHF radio. "They're all buck naked. How do I deal with the women?"

Bart was going to have Bo and Rick take the Zodiac over to assist Eddie. When Eddie said the women were naked, he asked Thebb to help. She agreed and climbed down into the Zodiac. She accompanied Rick who took two of the ship's waterproof diving lights, a portable VHF, and swim fins and paddled out to assist Eddie. They didn't use the diving lights because that would reduce their night vision. They used oars to prevent the possibility of injuring someone with the prop. The starlight was bright, and they could clearly see everyone in the water, swimming and splashing and yelling at one another. The water was aglow with phosphorescence. They were a happy group, singing and laughing in the dark water. Rick drifted close to Eddie and *L'TL DOVE*, using his swim fins to maneuver the rubber boat.

On board the *DOVE*, Bo was using binoculars to watch the group and be ready with additional support. Using the VHF, Bart was telling Eddie to encourage the guests to get back in the boat but to be polite and accommodating. Eddie said he was pleading with them to get in the boat, but they continued to ignore him.

Bart, resigned to the group's unexpected skinny dipping, advised Eddie, "Just get them back on board as soon as you can. It's not safe to be swimming in the dark. Rick and Thebb are there to help. Try to use the Zodiac to get the women out of the water."

The *L'TL DOVE* had high freeboard when empty, and Bart was afraid the inebriated guests would sink it trying to get back in. The men were able to climb back into the launch, but the women found it easier to slide into the rubber Zodiac. Unfortunately, their clothes were in the *L'TL DOVE*, but they were too drunk to care.

Back aboard the *DOVE*, the guests got dressed and went to the saloon for more partying. Bart asked if they were okay, and they all excitedly told him they just had a great time and laughed. Bart shook his head and went topside.

While the guests were drinking more piña coladas and daiquiris down below, Rick was telling Bart and Bo how funny it was trying to get drunk, naked, and slippery women into the dinghy. Thebb told the guys they should have thought to take towels. Bart was exasperated. "I didn't expect them to get drunk, strip naked, and go swimming in the middle of the night. What if something had happened? We weren't prepared to deal with an emergency in the dark, and somebody could have drowned."

Thebb decided to make some hors d'oeuvres for the guests. While she was placing the food on the table, the women were excitedly telling her the captain was absolutely right about a smaller sailboat being a great experience. Janna enthused they could never have gone skinny dipping while on a large commercial cruise ship or see the stars so brightly at night. Mitsu Megumi was absolutely mesmerized by the brightness of the stars, something she had never seen before, even on previous cruises on large ships. Janna went on to say swimming in the warm water with the phosphorescent light from their movements was truly psychedelic.

The women told Thebb they thought Captain Bart would have reprimanded them for their little escapade. They were surprised he only asked that they let him know in advance so he could take precautionary measures for their safety. Thebb politely reiterated they should talk to the captain when they wanted to go swimming, especially after dark. "Sharks like the warm water too. Especially at night."

The women sat quietly, looking at one another. "I guess we didn't think about that, did we?" Janna meekly remarked.

As Thebb was giving her advice, Bart entered the saloon and overheard her. He added, "Thebb's right, folks. We don't want to dampen your fun. We just want to make sure you get back home safely with all your body parts."

The next morning, Bart navigated the *DOVE* out the North Channel, leaving Virgin Gorda behind. It was late in the morning before the guests began to appear in the saloon. Janna wanted a Bloody Mary to deal with her hangover. Then everyone wanted one.

As they sailed around Necker Island, south of Anegada, and headed east, there were mild winds, moderate seas, and clear skies all the way to St. Maarten. Thebb was surprised at how much Billy Moffet's attitude had changed after their visit to Virgin Gorda. The crew now had him helping with the sails and let him take the helm for short periods. Akiya Megumi, who seemed to be in charge of the group, had a similar attitude change. In fact all the guests did.

On the trip over to St. Maarten, Bo began to spend more time with Thebb. He initiated conversations about sailing and his experiences. They were mostly one-way conversations because he couldn't get Thebb to talk about herself. He tried, but she always changed the subject. To Bo, she was a delightful mystery.

During their watch one night, Bo confided to Rick that he had never met a woman before who was so quiet and unassuming and yet so capable and independent. He started to tell Rick that ever since the . . . He stopped in midsentence, remembering the event in the Bahamas had never occurred.

Rick smiled and with a low chuckle commented, "Bo, you really like her, don't you?"

Bo stared at Rick for a moment, looked down at the deck, and nodded affirmatively. "Yeah, I do. She's not the person I thought she was when she first came aboard. She's polite and does her job quietly, but you don't dare cross her. Yeah, I do like her—a lot."

"Yeah, I do too. We're lucky to have her."

Having a personal conversation with Bo about women was a totally new experience for Rick. They had been sailing together for about a year and a half but never had a close relationship. He decided to take the conversation a step further and asked Bo if he thought Thebb could be hiding or running away from something. "There were all those bruises, and her face was beat-up when she first boarded the *DOVE*. And then in Bermuda. All that blood?"

Bo shook his head. "Yeah, she looked really messed up. And if we catch the son of a bitch who beat her up, we ought to—"

Rick interrupted him in mid-sentence, "Wait a minute, Bo. I don't think I want to tangle with the guy who was able to beat Thebb up." They both laughed a little.

"Yeah, Rick, you're right. I think she's hiding out from someone or something. I don't know what it is, but it must be a really dangerous situation. She's like a cat in a house full of screen doors. And the gun. She doesn't have a gun for the fun of it. And she definitely knows how to use it. I was in the military and never saw anyone shoot better. But it doesn't matter! Whatever her problem is I'm going to look out for her. Everyone is. Right?"

CHAPTER 33

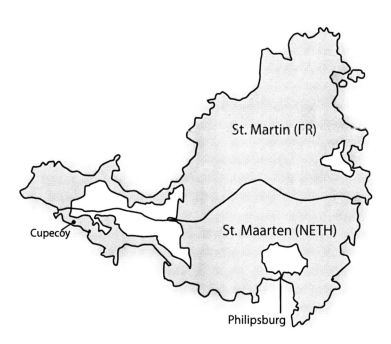

St. Martin (FR)

St. Maarten (NETH)

Cupecoy

Philipsburg

It was late in the afternoon when the *DOVE* tied up to the long commercial pier on the east side of Great Bay at Philipsburg in St. Maarten. After the fenders were deployed and the gangplank lowered, the Koroguru wives invited Bart and the crew to go out to dinner with them later that evening. Susan Moffet said she had read about an excellent restaurant and casino in Cupecoy, which wasn't too far away. Bart said that he would extend the invitation to the crew, but they would have to wait until the crew washed down the deck. The women went back to their cabins to freshen up. Their husbands elected to help the crew. They wanted the full sailing experience.

When Bart told Thebb about the invitation, she immediately volunteered to take the security watch. Bart reminded her it was Eddie's watch, and she should go with the crew. "Besides," he told her, "you've been doing all the cooking. This will be an opportunity to get away from the galley for a while."

"Bart, I don't have anything to wear. I only have jeans and canvas boating shoes. I can't go to a restaurant in jeans," Thebb pleaded.

Just then Janna came topside and overheard Bart trying to convince Thebb that wearing jeans wasn't a problem. She could buy some clothes in Philipsburg or Cupecoy. Janna interjected, "St. Maarten is a very casual place. We are all planning on wearing jeans too."

"Thanks, Mrs. Williams," Bart answered, showing he was pleased for her support.

"It's Janna, Captain."

Bart turned to Thebb. "I'm sure jeans will be okay as long as they aren't full of holes and greasy. No one will mind."

Thebb reluctantly agreed to go to the restaurant, but Bart could see she wasn't pleased.

When the women came topside, Janna was wearing jeans with decorative scrolling. Thebb recoiled, saying her jeans were not the same, and she should stay back. She was trying desperately to avoid going any place where she might be recognized, but the women stepped in. They escorted her down the gangplank onto the long pier where their husbands and the crew were waiting to walk to the taxi stand.

The two taxis were jammed with five people each, but the cabbies seemed okay with it. They headed off to the Le Island restaurant in the Atlantis Casino in Cupecoy. The restaurant was only a few miles to the west. It was popular because it adjoined the casino and also served French-style island food.

As they entered the dining room, Bo watched as Thebb scanned the surroundings, studying all the diners. He was becoming much more aware of her constant alertness, so he too scanned the tables. Then he noticed Thebb was also checking out the exits. When they were being seated, Thebb made a subtle effort to take a seat with her back to a wall so she could see the entire dining room and not be surprised by someone coming up from behind her. Bo saw what she was doing and took a seat next to her. No one else seemed to notice.

The Koroguru folks ordered martinis, daiquiris, yellow birds, and piña coladas. Thebb had a glass of house red wine while the rest of the crew drank beer. Bo and Rick were asking Thebb if she could teach them how to select wine sometime. Akiya joined in and explained he was an electrical engineer and never seemed to have had time to study wine. As if challenged by the claim engineers worked too hard to study wine, Janna pointed out she was a lawyer and didn't know much about wine either. Quickly, the other guests chimed in that they didn't have time to learn about wine. Billy Moffet leaned over the table and told Akiya it was his fault for working them so hard. That was when the crew realized they all worked for the same company, including some of the wives.

Akiya offered to buy a selection of wines for a wine-tasting party one night aboard the *DOVE*. Everyone thought it was a great idea. Thebb agreed and raised her glass as if to toast them.

The waiter brought several baskets of miniature croissants accompanied by butter mixed with minced shallots, lemon, and fine herbs. They all ordered a second round of drinks, except Thebb. The group was happy. It was a relaxing atmosphere to carry on conversations with one another. They had nearly finished their second round of drinks when the waiter finally returned to take orders for appetizers. They ordered foie gras, goat cheese wrapped in puff pastry, and other delicacies.

As they were ordering, and making a show of it, a group of three couples entered the restaurant from the casino on the far side of the restaurant. The maitre d' guided them to a table on the opposite side of the room. Bo noticed Thebb tensing up. She bent over to face her plate and turned to Bo. "Bo, please pay for my wine. I have to go. It's an emergency." She got up and slid her chair back under the table. Without a word to anyone, she headed for the side door on the opposite side of the restaurant from the newly seated trio of couples. Bo quickly excused himself and followed, trying to block Thebb from the view of the newly arrived diners.

Outside the restaurant, Bo could see Thebb was visibly shaken. Her eyes were wide, and she was tense. He asked her what was wrong.

"Nothing serious, Bo. It's a female thing. I have to get back to the *DOVE*. Right away."

"Thebb, was there someone in that group of people you know?"

He had to move fast to keep up with her as she sprinted to one of the cabs waiting near the entrance to the casino.

"I'll be all right, Bo," she yelled back. "Why don't you go back in and enjoy your dinner. I'll be okay."

"No! You wait here while I tell Bart we're returning to the boat. I'll say you suddenly feel sick."

As Bo reentered the restaurant, one of the trio of couples was standing at the group's table talking with Bart. The woman appeared to be in her late thirties. She was well dressed and wearing diamond earrings, an expensive-looking gold and diamond necklace, and a diamond bracelet. She was attractive and obviously well-off. The man was older. Probably in his late forties. He had some gray hair and was wearing a light blue golf shirt, a perfectly fitting blue blazer with white slacks, and white shoes. As Bo approached the table, the woman was asking Bart about the lady who had just left his table. Bart glanced over at Bo and then looked up at the woman. He awkwardly replied she was a friend and asked the woman why she wanted to know.

"She reminded me of a friend of ours who passed away recently. She bears such a striking resemblance I thought she might be her sister or a relative, or—"

Bo interrupted the woman, "Are you from Chicago?" he asked in a pleasant tone.

"No! We're from Philadelphia," the woman responded in excellent English. "Are all of you from Chicago?"

Bo kept everyone at the table from answering by quickly responding, "Oh yes. This is our first time here. It's a wonderful place. How about you?"

Rick was staring at Bo with his mouth open. The Koroguru folks, both the men and women, were looking at Bo with puzzled expressions. Bo looked back at them and smiled.

The woman continued talking, her curiosity unabated. "Actually, we have been here before. We come here for the casinos. In fact, we just left the casino here in Cupecoy. It's very nice, but about the woman who just left . . ."

Bo interrupted the woman again, "She's just checking on our children. One of the kids isn't feeling well. Too much sun I guess." Bo cocked his head, wrinkled his forehead, made a questioning face, and continued, "You asked if she has a sister?"

"Well yes."

Smiling, Bo responded, "She has often said she wished she had a sister. Unfortunately, she only has two younger brothers."

"Oh, we're sorry to have bothered you. We'd better get back to our friends. It was just a shock to see someone who looked like she could be our friend's sister."

Bo couldn't stand it anymore. He had to ask, "I'm sorry for your loss. You must have been good friends. But tell me, how did your friend die? I hope it wasn't a long illness?"

Rick leaned forward to hear better. Bart put his hand on Rick's shoulder and squeezed hard. The Koroguru Group were silent and continued looking at Bo and the woman. Janna had put her head down to stare at her plate, but she was listening very carefully to what was going down.

The woman looked a little surprised at Bo's overly curious question. "No, it was a terrible, terrible accident. She was so young and—"

The woman's husband interrupted and spoke for the first time, "It was a freak traffic accident. She was a pedestrian and got hit by a truck. She was the wife of our executive vice president, and it just destroyed him. Everyone at our firm was devastated. My wife, Denise, here, works closely with him so she knows more about the accident than anybody else."

Bo responded with considerable concern and empathy. "That's a terrible story. We're all sorry to hear of your loss."

Bart, Rick, and the Koroguru Group started nodding their heads in sympathy.

The man tugged on his wife's arm and pulled her away. "Come on, honey, we have to get back to our friends before they think we've abandoned them."

Bo turned to Bart and said, loud enough that the departing couple could hear, "I should go help my wife with the kids. Be back in a little while."

Outside the casino, Thebb was nowhere to be found, and Bo wasn't surprised. She had caught a cab back to Philipsburg. He got another cab and followed.

Back at the table, Janna asked Bart, "What just happened?"

Before Bart could answer, Rick intervened, "When Bo has a few drinks he does odd things. He probably thought those people were being rude and gave a ridiculous answer to be funny. Did you see him smiling when he told those people he had kids? We have to watch out for him when he has had a few drinks. You have to help us."

"They were kind of rude," Bart added, "but that's no excuse for what Bo did. I apologize, and I'll speak to him when we get back to the boat."

Janna wasn't buying Rick's story, and she wasn't to be put off. "That was such a sad story they told. The woman was obviously distraught over the loss of her friend. You should tell Bo not to be so mean next time. So what's the real story, and where is Thebb? She should be here to enjoy dinner without having to cook. Is she okay or what?"

"I don't know," Bart answered. "She hasn't been feeling well the past few days. I think it's a female thing. I asked Bo to go check on her."

Jumping out of the cab at Philipsburg, Bo ran down the long concrete pier and up the gangplank to find Thebb sitting next to Eddie looking out over the city. He was winded and breathing heavily as he stood in front of Thebb, taking a moment to catch his breath.

Without acknowledging Eddie's presence, Bo reached out and took Thebb by the hand. "Thebb, how about going for a walk with me out on the pier?"

Thebb looked cautiously at Bo and hesitantly accepted his invitation. "Bo, are you sure you want to go for a walk? You just ran the entire length of the pier. Do you need more exercise?" She suspected he was going to ask about the people in the restaurant and didn't really want to go. She also didn't want to get into an argument in front of Eddie.

When they got to a place far enough down the pier that they could talk without being overheard, Bo confronted her, "Thebb, you know those people, don't you?"

Instead of the deflective-type answer she usually gave, Thebb moved close to Bo, squinted her eyes, and responded in a low, angry, and aggressive voice, "Bo! Back off. This doesn't concern you. You don't know what you are doing."

"Listen to me, Thebb. I just covered your ass back there. I told those people we were married, and you went to check on the children. I think they bought my story, but I don't think our guests did. So tell me straight. You know those people, don't you?"

"I'm telling you, Bo! You've got to listen to me! You can't get involved with me. You don't know what you're doing."

"I already am, Thebb," Bo said softly. "That woman thought you were the sister of a friend who got killed in Philadelphia in a traffic accident. I told her we were from Chicago. I want to know what's really going on. Someone's after you. Am I right?"

With the overhead pier lights reflecting on the tears running down her cheeks, Thebb moved even closer, almost nose to nose. "Goddamn it, Bo. Stop. Will you listen to me? You can't get involved with me. It's too dangerous, and I won't let you do it."

Bo's obvious concern was comforting, but his attempt to break her anonymity was terrifying. The tension of trying to hide in plain sight was overwhelming, and he was trying to expose her. She pushed him away and began to cry as she ran back to the *DOVE* and the relative safety of her small cabin. She sat on her bunk rocking back and forth, asking herself, *Now what do I do? What would Joey tell me?*

As Bo climbed the gangplank, Eddie asked what was going on. "Thebb just ran up here crying. What did you say to her?"

Bo pushed Eddie out of the way and said, "Go back to your post, Eddie. This doesn't concern you."

The sudden banging on her cabin door jolted Thebb. She opened the door to find Bo with his elbows leaning against both jambs.

"You can't just run away from me like that, Thebb. I know there's something really serious you're hiding, but I'm not going to pursue it. You have a right to your privacy, and I shouldn't have pushed you. I won't do it again. But if you need any help, I'm here to support you. Just promise me you'll ask."

Thebb's consuming fear of being discovered and killed and the shock of seeing one of Phillip's close associates at the restaurant were almost more than she could endure. Bo's offer of help was like a hand offered to a drowning person. She wanted to reach for it but feared she would pull him under with her. She wrapped her arms around Bo's chest, put her head on his shoulder, and cried. "Thanks, Bo. I really appreciate your help. I really do. You're a good person."

She stood for a moment, just holding him. He put his arms around her and held her tight. She continued, whispering, "Please don't ask any more questions about me or my past. When the right time comes, that is, if the right time comes, I'll tell you whatever you want to know. I just hope you will still be interested in knowing by then. But for now, Bo, all you need to know is that I'm Thebb Meerschmidt and a little weird."

"Okay, Thebb," Bo agreed while wiping her tears with one hand. "No more personal questions."

Thebb loosened her arms and started to back up, but Bo continued to hold her tight and gave her a heartfelt hug. She put her hands on his chest and gently pushed him away.

Bo let go, got two beers from the galley, and went topside to join Eddie in his security watch. They sat quietly, drinking their beers, waiting for the charter group, Bart, and Rick to return.

The Koroguru Group took a long time to finish dinner and were in a good mood when they returned to the *DOVE*. They tried to get the taxi drivers to drive out on the pier, but the drivers refused. The group had to walk the length of the pier. Bo and Eddie watched as the singing and slightly staggering group approached the gangplank.

In spite of her tipsy condition, Janna called out to Bo, "How's Thebb? Is she okay?"

"Yeah, I think she's okay. She's resting in her cabin."

CHAPTER 34

West Indies

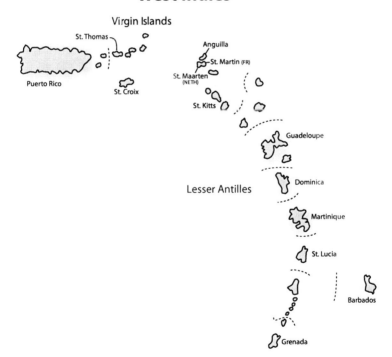

It was early in the morning and still dark when Janna and Craig Williams felt the shudder of the Detroit Diesel engine cranking over. A few moments later they felt the *DOVE*'s slight roll as Bart maneuvered her out of Great Bay and into the Caribbean Sea. They rolled over and went back to sleep. At 0700 Thebb had breakfast ready to serve, but only Billy Moffet and Akiya Megumi came to the table.

After breakfast, Billy and Akiya took turns at the helm under Bo's guidance. They helped in hoisting the sails and manned the sheets as the *DOVE* switched over to wind power. Apparently suffering from hangovers, the other members of the Koroguru Group took all morning to emerge from their cabins. They missed breakfast but were ready and waiting when Thebb brought lunch to the table. Eddie took the helm. Bo and Rick joined Bart and the Koroguru Group at the table. Thebb stayed in the galley fussing over a dessert.

After lunch, Bart laid out a set of nautical charts on the navigation table. He called the Koroguru Group over to the table and presented them with his proposed itinerary for the remainder of the trip. He suggested they sail southwest to Saba, Saint Eustatius, and Nevis on the south side of St. Kitts. Depending on the wind and weather, he proposed that they stay overnight offshore of one of the islands. He favored Nevis and remarked it was an especially interesting island because of the high volcano and the small size of the island. "When we leave Nevis, we have a long way to go so we will sail on the lee of the Lesser Antilles toward Barbados. We can stay overnight on the lee of the nearest island depending on weather, wind, and time. We may have to sail at night to keep to our schedule. If we do, I think it will be an enjoyable experience."

Billy Moffit and Akiya Megumi had become sailing enthusiasts and wholeheartedly agreed.

Billy remarked, "Captain, we can sail all you want. Akiya and I would like to spend as much time as we can helping the crew."

Craig Williams commented, "Geez! I guess you're gonna want to buy a sailboat when we get back."

"That's a great idea," Billy responded enthusiastically. "Lake Michigan is a fantastic place to sail. I don't know why I didn't start sailing before. This cruise has been a real eye-opener, and now it's almost over."

During the remainder of the trip, Bart made sure Billy and Akiya had plenty of time manning the helm.

It was approximately noon when Bart maneuvered the *DOVE* up to the commercial dock in the Port of Bridgetown on the southwest corner of Barbados. The Koroguru Group had flight reservations for 7:00 p.m. at the Grantley Adams Airport. By the time the *DOVE* tied up in Barbados, everyone in the Koroguru Group had learned a lot about sailing, even the women. Susan Moffet told her husband, Billy, she looked forward to getting a sailboat.

Bart apologized that the last portion of the cruise did not include more island hopping, but there wasn't enough time. He pointed out Barbados was a long way from St. Thomas. He encouraged them to schedule a cruise on the *DOVE* the following year, telling them they were now sailors and could take over the crew's duties. Everyone laughed as they walked down the gangplank and waved good-bye.

After the *DOVE* was securely tied up, Bart gave the crew the night off as a reward for making the Koroguru charter so successful. Thebb decided to go ashore and buy some new clothing. Faced with the dilemma of having to use Tatianna's passport, she decided that Bridgetown was large enough, and busy enough, to safely go shopping. She would stay away from the upscale boutiques. Instead, she visited Cave Shepherd, a large department store, and ended up buying more jeans, denim shirts, a pair of shorts, canvas boating shoes, and some blouses.

While looking at herself in the full-length mirror in the women's dressing room, Thebb realized she had slimmed down a lot more than she thought, given she had only been on the *DOVE* a few months. Her face was almost healed, and she was beginning to look like she did before she got married. Very pretty actually. The doctor in Bermuda had said that the bumps and puffy areas on her face would diminish over time, and they had. Especially the wide swelling that had bothered her the most. Oddly enough, the scar at the left edge of her mouth, where Philip had split her lips and cut part of her cheek, seemed to be an improvement to her looks. It gave her a little bit of character. *Anyway, I can't do anything about it so I might as well like it.*

No trip to a department store could be complete without a visit to the cosmetics counter, and Thebb complied with the unwritten requirement. She was developing a healthy-looking tan, and with her face less bruised, she needed a different foundation. She left Cave Shepherd and walked down Broad Street feeling a lot better about her looks. Very upbeat.

As she boarded the *DOVE*, wearing her new jeans and with the new makeup, Rick commented she was looking nice. She was pleased but gave him an indifferent look. He smiled knowingly. He knew she wasn't going to respond to a compliment, but he did it anyway. Bo passed her as she approached the stairs to the main saloon and turned around to look. She glanced back at Bo and nodded with her tight-lipped smile. Rick subtly acknowledged to himself that she responded differently to Bo.

CHAPTER 35

The next day, after breakfast, Bart called for an all-hands meeting to map out their return to St. Thomas. He had contacted the *DOVE*'s marine agent to tell him the Koroguru charter was completed, and he intended to return to St. Thomas to wait for another charter.

Thebb was pleased. She needed to get her passport and driver's license so she could dispense with Tatianna's identity. Eddie was happy because he used to spend a lot of time in St. Thomas and had a few friends there. At least he used to have friends there before the Jimbo incident. Bo was agreeable, and Rick seemed to be pleased to stay anywhere in the islands.

Bart laid out the route he proposed for their sail back to St. Thomas. "When we leave Barbados, we'll take a heading of west by northwest, skirt around the south end of St. Lucia, and then head north staying on the lee of the islands. We won't be in a hurry so we can lay over in the evenings or find shelter if we get bad weather. No sense in killing ourselves. We can enjoy the trip back. We've been pretty lucky, weather-wise, with the Koroguru charter, and I hope it'll hold till we get back to St. Thomas."

This would be the kind of trip the crew liked best. Sailing without demands or guests. Just enjoying the trip. They could probably anchor up in a cove somewhere and do some swimming, diving, and leisurely maintenance.

"Okay then, get on it. Let's restock the food larders, refuel, take on water, and prepare to depart at noon," Bart ordered. "Rick, you go with Thebb and help her restock the galley. I'll wait until Rick and

Thebb return with the food before we move over to the fuel dock. We'll depart from there."

Rick and Thebb, pulling up to the *DOVE* with a taxi full of food, were surprised to see a small crowd had gathered around the *DOVE*'s gangplank. Bart and Bo were on the dock talking to the group, all of whom had their backs to the oncoming taxi. As they got closer, they could see that it was Akiya, Billy, and the rest of the Koroguru Group. Their flight had been delayed overnight due to mechanical problems, so they got hotel rooms and went out for dinner. In the morning, the airline informed them the delay could be another forty-eight hours. Faced with a long wait to leave Barbados, Billy suggested they check to see if the *DOVE* was going back to another island where they could catch a flight to Chicago. His motive was obvious. Akiya liked the idea even if it would require they all take another week of vacation. He had been bitten by the sailing bug.

When Bart told them he was returning to St. Thomas, they began negotiating a return cruise with him. Being ever mindful of the need to supplement the cost of operating the *DOVE*, and his bonus, he was pleased to have another charter.

Billy and Akiya asked if they could participate more in sailing the *DOVE*, even if it cost more. They could learn a lot on this trip. Bart agreed, "You're going to spoil my crew if you spend too much time sailing the boat." They laughed excitedly and departed to retrieve their luggage from the hotel.

There was the familiar light shudder and rumble of the 400 horsepower Detroit Diesel engine as it cranked over. Bart ordered that all lines be taken in, and they motored away from the fuel dock, out of the harbor, and set a course for the south coast of St. Lucia. After clearing the harbor, Bart hoisted the mainsails and foresail and then ordered that the huge spinnaker be raised to take advantage of the following trade winds. That was an experience Billy and Akiya had not had. Once set, everyone came topside to see it. With excellent weather and favorable winds, the *DOVE* made good headway and turned the corner around St. Lucia to head north, staying in the lee of the islands.

While sailing southeast of St. Croix, Janna Williams sought out Thebb in the galley and complimented her on the exquisite cuisine she had prepared during their cruise. Thebb thanked her and suggested she and her husband cruise with them again. Janna then gave Thebb one of her business cards, explaining she was a corporate lawyer with the Koroguru Group but had a lot of legal experience in other areas such as family law. She went on to offer her services should Thebb need a lawyer.

"Thanks, Janna, but I don't need a lawyer."

"Well, you know lawyers, we're always passing out cards and drumming up business. We're not like doctors. We have to let people know how to find us. One never knows when they might need an attorney. Just keep the card."

"Thanks again, Janna, I'll keep your card as a remembrance of your visit with us."

Arriving at St. Thomas, Bart tied up the *DOVE* at the commercial docks in Charlotte Amalie. The Koroguru Group gathered their luggage and placed it near the gangplank. Bo suggested they use duffel bags on their next trip. Billy agreed and then asked if they could get a couple of group photographs with the crew. Thebb had just come topside and offered to be the photographer. When they tried to get her in one of the photos, she repeatedly declined. "You don't want a picture of the ship's cook. Here, I'll take another picture of all of you with the captain of the *DOVE*. That will make a much better picture." Bo helped divert the group's attention by telling them he was ready to help take the luggage down to the dock. Janna gave Thebb a hug and reminded her of what she had said before they docked. "Remember, Thebb. If you need an attorney, I want to help you."

CHAPTER 36

Cecilia Pisani had been receiving the *Philadelphia Inquirer* for about three weeks. Sometimes she would go for three or four days without getting a copy. Then the mailman would deliver all the back issues at the same time. She suspected the mailman only delivered her newspapers when he had an otherwise light day. But she reasoned it didn't really matter. She was only trying to learn if her suspicions were correct and if there were any repercussions from the envelope she mailed in New York.

In the first of a new three-day pile of issues, the headlines blared the mayor and district attorney of Philadelphia jointly announced they had broken a hundred-million-dollar-a-year drug operation. The article described how, through diligent investigative work, the district attorney's office had uncovered a pervasive network of bribery and drug dealing involving city officials. The district attorney had indicted two city commissioners, the police commissioner, half a dozen policemen, and eight members of a Philadelphia drug ring. The second issue in the pile of newspapers didn't have much more information but recounted, through an interview with Principal Assistant District Attorney David Kramer, the importance of the breakthrough in the city's ongoing fight against drug-related crime.

It wasn't until the third issue any mention was made of accounting records. The records revealed the involvement of certain city and police officials in a vast drug-smuggling cartel that had ties directly into New York, Chicago, Miami, and Colombia.

The article revealed the drug cartel had recorded sales, payoffs, and bribes in a sophisticated, multilayered code. The city's crime laboratory was only able to decipher the first two layers of the code, but those layers identified certain city officials and the amounts and dates of the bribes. Two other layers were based on an alphanumeric code that changed from page to page. That part of the code was incredibly complex and seemed to be generated by several algorithms similar to the German enigma code of World War II. The crime lab was continuing to work on the code which, when deciphered, could implicate other high-level city officials.

Cecilia sat transfixed, asking herself, *Did the envelope I mailed for Anna contain the records they are talking about? Could Anna have been the cause of all this?*

With increasing anxiety, Cecilia continued to read. Through intensive interrogation, the DA's office had learned that a certain Maroon Espidito was the head of the Philadelphia section of the drug cartel. The informants were mostly lower echelon thugs and street dealers who had cut a deal for reduced charges. They claimed it was Espidito who had killed two gang members several weeks earlier in a dispute over drug money. It was a gangland, execution-style shooting in an industrial section of the city near the waterfront.

Other informants fingered two detectives, who were gunned down that same morning in the same area. Initially, the police had thought the detectives were investigating the murder of a homeless woman when they inadvertently stumbled into a drug deal and were gunned down. The police later determined the woman was an innocent bystander. She was killed by stray gunfire during a shoot-out between the detectives and Espidito following a heated argument earlier that morning. The combination of the operatives' testimony and decoded information in the cartel's books led to a massive investigation of corruption in the police department.

Cecilia couldn't believe what she was reading. *If the envelope that Anna sent to the DA's office had the drug cartel's books, she must be in a lot of trouble. Maybe that's why she wouldn't say who was beating her up. Oh damn!*

She continued reading. The DA's office had established a special prosecutorial team to oversee the city's effort to find Espidito and whoever created the complex accounting codes. Finding the accountant was a high priority as well as uncovering any other

—

city officials involved with the drug cartel. David Kramer, the senior assistant DA, was appointed to head up the team.

Maroon Espidito was considered to be armed and dangerous. The police initiated a massive manhunt to find him. The DA's informants believed he had escaped the city and gone back to Colombia. The police were also looking for the mystery accountant who was reputed to be a critical link in the murders and other drug cartel activities. The accountant was believed to be hiding out in New York City.

This jolted Cecilia. *New York City! Oh my god! It was Anna's package.* She sat up straight and slammed the paper down, accidently spilling her coffee on the other issues of the newspaper. She was taking deep breaths when Jack walked in and asked what was happening.

"I'm just clumsy. I'll clean it up," she snapped.

"Why are you upset with me, and why are you reading a Philadelphia paper?" Jack asked as he tried to help by picking up some of the soggy newspapers.

"Put that wet paper down, honey, it's dripping all over. I'm upset because I just spilled coffee on my dress. And if you must know, I heard this paper usually has great coverage of cultural events planned in the Northeast. I'm just checking in case you have any meetings coming up soon in Philadelphia or New York. Maybe we could go see a good play, and I could also do some shopping. Now get out of here. I spilled the coffee, and I'll clean it up."

"Oh!" Jack had learned to back off when Cecilia was agitated.

"I have a meeting with the Air Force today in Washington and may be a little late getting back home tonight. I've got to catch a flight out of Wright-Pat this morning so I have to get going. I'll call you if I'm going to be delayed." He gave her a kiss and left the house.

As soon as Jack left, Cecilia grabbed the newspaper and continued to read the article to the very end. She sat back in her chair not seeing anything, just thinking. *Of course, they would be looking in New York. The postmark is from New York.*

She realized the police would use the postmark to find the post office where the package was mailed and interrogate the clerks. *Would they remember me? Did I ask for the zip code for Philadelphia or for the district attorney's office in Philadelphia? Which was it? Maybe it doesn't make any difference. Maybe it does.*

—

Cecilia was distraught and panicking. But then, she reasoned, it would be impossible to track the ledgers to her. After all, she didn't give them her name, and she used cash to pay for the postage. *But the outer envelope? It had my name on it. Did I throw it in the trash at the post office? What the hell did I do with the outer envelope?*

Then she remembered. There was no trash can near the table in the post office. She put it back in her briefcase and disposed of it when she returned to the hotel. Nonetheless, she was shaken by the news articles and wondered, *How in hell's name did the ship's cook, Anna, get involved with a drug cartel? Maybe this whole thing's a cover-up, and she's hiding from the mob! Oh my god, the mob could be looking for the DOVE!*

Cecilia picked up the newspapers, still dripping with coffee, and took them to the kitchen where she carefully blotted out the coffee stains, salvaging what sections she could. She stood at the kitchen counter staring at the upper cabinets only a foot in front of her. *Is Anna the accountant? She doesn't seem to be the accountant type. I just can't see her being involved with criminals. Why would she give her records to the district attorney? None of this makes any sense. But she is in deep trouble, and somebody has been beating the hell out of her. How does this all fit together?*

Regardless of what Anna had done, or not done, Cecilia knew she had to keep Anna's secret. If she didn't, Anna could be killed and so could she.

CHAPTER 37

Thebb was anxious to go into town as soon as the Koroguru Group had disembarked so she could get her passport under her new name. It would relieve some of her worries about being discovered as either Tatianna or Annaliese. But she would have to use Tatianna's passport once more to enter Charlotte Amalie. They probably could have circumvented customs altogether if they had anchored in Red Hook Bay, like the last time they were in St. Thomas. That would have required ferrying the Koroguru luggage to shore in the skiff. Docking at the commercial docks was more convenient for the guests. It was closer to the airport, and cabs were readily available.

Bo, Rick, and Thebb went to the customs counter together. Bo and Rick wanted to get a beer at a local harbor-front bar and relax before Bart decided to move the *DOVE*. They invited Thebb, but she declined explaining she needed to run a few errands. When they reached the customs counter, Thebb hung back, letting Bo and Rick go first. She scanned the surroundings and checked for any familiar faces or suspicious situations. The customs agent was an islander. He was short, bored, and not particularly friendly. He was the typical functionary. Robotic. He was not interested in the reasons why, only that the process be completed as described in the rule book. No exceptions no matter what the reason. No thinking. Just follow the routine.

Bo stood at the weathered wood counter for about five minutes before the agent returned from a small glass-enclosed office behind the main counter. There was no air-conditioning. Only a large oscillating fan in the corner of the room. The agent lethargically

---
190

processed his passport with little interest. He mechanically asked if he was Dieter Boarman and if he had anything to declare. Same for Rick. When Thebb presented Tatianna's passport, however, the agent showed interest. He asked no questions, but he looked at Thebb and took the passport into the small office behind the counter. Thebb's heart started to race. Bo, standing behind the yellow line past the counter, watched with alertness. His view was limited, but he could see the agent through the large tinted glass window on the front of the office. The agent was bending over a desk and checking something. He returned to the counter and asked if she was Tatianna Wolinski. She answered yes. He looked at Tatianna's photograph in the passport. Then at Thebb. He resumed the same sapless, attitudinal demeanor he had exhibited with Bo and Rick and asked if she had anything to declare. After she answered no, he returned her passport. She left the customs office with Bo to join Rick who was waiting outside.

When the clerk asked Thebb if she was Tatianna Wolinski, Bo felt the hair on the back of his neck stand up and his ears burn. He remembered Bart asking her about her name when he was writing her first paycheck. She had come on board using Wolinski but later changed it to Meerschmidt.

Then it hit him. From his limited understanding of German, he realized that Meerschmidt was deliberately constructed. "Meer" in German meant sea or ocean, and "Schmidt" meant a worker or a smith, as in blacksmith. She had cleverly constructed her name after joining the crew of the *DOVE*—sea worker.

Bo thought hard for a moment, *Maybe Wolinski isn't her real name either! She's more mysterious than ever.*

He didn't know why, but somehow this sudden revelation made him feel closer to Thebb. He thought about their argument on the pier at Philipsburg when she told him not to get involved with her because it was too dangerous. He felt he had a better understanding of how hard she was trying to disappear. From what or whom, he didn't know.

Once outside the custom's office, Bo cautioned, "Thebb, I didn't like the way that agent handled your processing. Maybe Rick and I should go with you."

"No! I don't think you need to worry. Please go ahead with what you were going to do. I don't expect to take too long, and I'll be back to the *DOVE* in a few hours."

"Okay! But be careful, Thebb. You know where to find us if you need help."

Bo and Rick knew better than to press Thebb to have a beer with them. She rarely joined them ashore. They had figured out she avoided places where there would be a lot of people. It had become unmistakably obvious in St. Maarten.

Thebb was anxious to get to the post office to see if her passport had arrived and didn't want company. She knew Bo, and all the crew for that matter, had become protective of her and were concerned for her safety. But she needed to be alone for some of her errands.

Thebb was elated. The passport had arrived. She took her new passport and went immediately to the Virgin Island's DMV office to get a driver's license. As usual, they were operating on island time and showed even less interest in processing her than the customs agent. She would have to return in the morning to take the driving test. So she took a copy of the *Driver's Education Booklet* and returned to the *DOVE*.

CHAPTER 38

After Thebb left the custom's office, the agent placed a call to his supervisor. The agent reminded the supervisor he had been asked to be on the lookout for a woman by the name of Tatianna Wolinski. "She was on da list in my office."

"Ah yes. I remember," the supervisor answered.

"Da woman just passed through da gate," the agent casually explained.

"Very good. You did very good," the supervisor replied with indifference and hung up.

The supervisor then dialed the personal cell phone number for the principal assistant DA in Philadelphia, David Kramer.

"Yeah. This is Dave."

"Mr. Kramer, this is the director of the customs office in Charlotte Amalie, St. Thomas."

"Do you have information for me?" Dave answered with enthusiasm.

"Yes, I do. An agent in our harbor office just processed the woman you were looking for."

"Really," Dave exclaimed. "That's great work. We won't forget your attention to our request."

"Thank you, Mr. Kramer. Do you want us to do anything else? You didn't request that we hold her or anything."

"No! Not at this time. We are just trying to track her right now. It's important she doesn't know we are following her. That would ruin our surveillance effort and compromise our overall investigation. But thanks for your offer."

"We are always ready to help when the law enforcement offices need it," enthused the supervisor. "Don't hesitate to call on us if you need additional help."

"Thanks. I'll keep that in mind."

Dave leaned back in his high-backed office chair and gloated. He had personally called the customs office directors in Puerto Rico and the Virgin Islands hoping that Tatianna might show up there. All his information indicated she probably escaped from Philadelphia on a boat. A boat could be going to any one of the islands, he reasoned. After all, she couldn't stay at sea forever. If she used her passport, he might be able to find her. It was a shot in the dark, but he thought it could pay off. *Who would have thought the Virgin Islands office would be so efficient? We're going to get that bitch before she does something with our main set of books and foreign accounts.*

When the DA bypassed him and sent the ledgers directly to the crime lab to be deciphered, Dave thought he might be a suspect. He had almost panicked and made plans to escape the country. He prepared to empty his safe-deposit box of his stash of cash and deposit it in his foreign accounts. Mostly in Switzerland. When the crime lab couldn't decipher all of Tatianna's codes, he put his plans on hold. He felt sure they would never decipher her special codes. She was a genius in the way she encrypted her accounting books. Maroon had told him of her exceptional talent for managing their accounts. In addition to being an expert cryptologist, she spoke several languages, including Spanish, German, and Polish. But she could also be vindictive!

The main question Dave had asked Maroon, and himself was, *Why the hell did Tatianna turn over the books to the DA and then disappear? What the hell had happened? How could this have helped her? She's on the run now. And why only the doctored books for Philadelphia and some of the minor satellite operations in other cities? What about the main set of books involving the cartel's Swiss bank accounts and money-laundering operations in Miami?*

Before Tatianna disappeared, Maroon had told Dave he suspected she was skimming their money, but he couldn't be sure. Not the Colombians' money, but theirs. He estimated that over a million dollars was missing. But her books were so slick it was impossible to tell. It could be more.

After Tatianna disappeared, Dave had reiterated to Maroon, "If she exposes the main set of books, the cartel will kill us both. There won't be any escaping from the Colombians if they find out we haven't been reporting all the drug transactions." Dave and Maroon had been skimming some of the drug money for the past several years. This was something the Colombians took very seriously. They would find them and there wouldn't be any way out.

Dave picked up his cell phone to call Maroon.

With his customary politeness, Maroon answered his cell phone, "Yeah, what do you want?"

"I found her. She's in St. Thomas," Dave said in a low and hushed voice.

There was a short silence.

"That's fucking great work, Dave. How long has she been there?"

"She just checked through customs. It's a great piece of luck. I can hardly believe it. She used her own passport. I thought she would have been smarter than that. This is a great break."

"I knew the bitch would slip up eventually."

"Maroon, I think I figured out why she sent the books to the DA. She was trying to get us killed. No one knew about her except you and me. If we were out of the picture, she wouldn't have to worry about us or the cartel. I told you she was devious, but you didn't listen to me. So make sure you fix our problem this time. For good."

"Yeah, I hear you. That fucking bitch is going to pay."

"I hope to hell you can find her before she disappears with the main set of books and money, Maroon. So don't kill her before you get the books."

"She ain't gonna get away. I've got some contacts down there, and we're gonna get her this time."

Dave leaned back on his chair, swiveled around, and looked out the great Palladian window next to his desk. He was both pleased and worried. He knew that Tatianna was extremely dangerous. She didn't usually make mistakes. They better take full advantage of this one before she caused more problems. She had been responsible for the arrest of nineteen cops, several city officials, and a dozen of Maroon's guys. The number of arrests kept increasing as the laboratory deciphered more of the ledger entries and Maroon's gang members began talking. In addition to Maroon, only Tatianna could connect him with the drug operation. He had made sure of that. But Tatianna could put him away for years or have him killed. She had to be dealt with right away.

Maroon knew Tatianna held the keys to the Philadelphia and Miami operations so he had to be careful in dealing with her. She had a temper too. He had a fight with her the morning she disappeared. He had demanded she give him a full report of what was in the books. But she told him to fuck off and not to accuse her of cooking the books. She slammed the door to his office when she left. That pissed him off, so he had a couple of his guys follow her to let her know he was watching her. He now realized it hadn't been a good idea because they weren't his smartest guys. They probably spooked her. Maybe she thought they were going to kill her and take the books. But whatever the reason, it didn't matter. Now he was going to get her for sure. She killed four of his people in Philadelphia, and the two he had sent to Bermuda disappeared. They're probably dead too. He had underestimated her. She was a hell of a lot more dangerous than he had previously thought.

CHAPTER 39

Thebb was looking forward to getting her driver's license as she prepared breakfast. It was no longer unusual for Bo to ask her if he could help her in the galley after breakfast. His offer almost always met with the same result. She pleasantly declined. That morning, however, she asked Bo for some help. She needed someone to rent a car she could use to take the driving test.

Passing with flying colors, Thebb got her much-valued driver's license. It was a convenient piece of identification she so desperately needed. She dropped Bo off at the commercial dock and drove out to Red Hook to see if the *ANDROMEDA* was anchored in the harbor. She wanted to visit Jimbo, whom she now thought of by his given name, Kelsey. When she got to the harbor, she realized she should have brought a portable VHF radio to call him. Her only alternative was to try and get someone's attention on the *ANDROMEDA*. She stood on the dinghy dock and waved, but no one was on deck to see her.

An older gray-bearded man working in the cockpit of a smaller weatherworn sloop anchored nearby noticed her waving. He looked over at the *ANDROMEDA* and saw the decks were clear, so he motioned to the woman on shore. He got in his rubber dinghy, cranked up the small Yamaha outboard, and motored over to the dock.

"Oh my goodness, George. Is that you? I almost didn't recognize you with a beard. It looks good. More nautical and distinguished."

"Yeah, I got tired of shaving at sea. You've changed too. I thought it was you on the dock so I decided to come over and give you a lift."

"This is wonderful. I've been thinking a lot about you, and I'm really happy to see you. What are you doing in St. Thomas?"

"Join me for a cup of coffee on *FREEDOM*, and I'll tell you all about my recent exploits."

Thebb was delighted to see George. She hugged him to let him know how pleased she was. Once aboard *FREEDOM*, with coffee in hand, she asked how things went in Bermuda after the incident in the parking lot.

"Nothing happened! It was the weirdest thing, Anna. The police decided the two men had been in a fight over drugs and shot each other. They didn't have any identification. One man had drugs on him and the other had a ton of cash. The police theorized they had a fight over a drug sale. No one in the tavern was actually sober enough to tell the police anything. The police wondered why there was only one gun since they were both shot. They assumed that one of the customers must have picked up the other gun on the way out. I don't think they were going to do a ballistics test. They try to keep any news of violence on the island quiet so they don't upset the tourist trade."

"I have been really worried about you and Mike. You might have gotten in trouble for saving me. If you hadn't come out to help me, those men would have killed me."

"I'll tell you, Anna, that was the most incredible thing. We were so damn lucky I couldn't believe it. Mike kept telling me not to worry, and he was right. We were just a couple of drunk old fools drinking beer at the tavern, and the cops didn't pay any attention to us."

"George, I really, really appreciate what you and Mike did, and I'll never forget it. I can never repay you. You and Mike saved my life."

"Anna, we couldn't let—"

Thebb interrupted, "By the way, George, my name now is Thebb Meerschmidt. I don't go by Anna anymore. It's too dangerous."

"That's a great move, Thebb. It's good you have a new name. I'm not going to ask why those men were looking for you, but the farther away you can stay from your old identity the better."

—

"Yeah, I figured that too. It was just luck the name 'Thebb' came up in a conversation with the crew so I took it."

"You know, Thebb, I almost didn't recognize you. You've lost a lot a weight, got a tan, and have longer hair. And if you don't mind an old man saying so, you're looking damn good now. The bruises and bumps are gone too. With your new name, maybe your problems are behind you."

"Thanks, George. Another nice thing is the crew on the *DOVE* haven't really mentioned anything about the changes."

"That's incredible! I didn't know blind people could sail a boat," George said with a lot of laughter.

Thebb nodded yes to George's laughter and said, "You're a good man, George, and I can't tell you how much it means to me to see you again."

After they talked for a while, George asked Thebb if she was trying to get the attention of someone on the *ANDROMEDA*.

"I'm trying to meet up with Kelsey Bohansen, the captain of the *ANDROMEDA*, but I forgot to bring a portable VHF."

"I met the guys on the *ANDROMEDA*, but I don't remember a Kelsey,"

Thebb gave her usual tight-lipped half smile and explained, "He's also known as Jimbo, but I prefer to call him by his real name. Jimbo sounds too rough for such a nice guy."

"Oh," George answered. "I see. You like this fellow, huh?"

With cocked eyebrows, Thebb answered, "Now, George, don't get ideas. We're just good friends. He struts a bit and tries to present a swaggering image, but he's really an okay guy." *And he's reliable.* A thought she didn't relate to George.

"I'm sure he is," George replied with more laughter. "Why don't I give him a call on my radio?"

"This is *FREEDOM* calling *ANDROMEDA*. Come back. This is *FREEDOM* calling *ANDROMEDA*. Come back."

After a few minutes of silence, George's radio crackled. "This is *ANDROMEDA*. What can we do for you, *FREEDOM?*"

"We are looking for Kelsey."

"Sorry, *FREEDOM*, but there's no Kelsey aboard," came the crackling reply.

"How about Jimbo. Is Jimbo there?"

———

"Yeah. Let me see if he's up yet."

After a few minutes, a reply came, "This is Jimbo."

Thebb took the microphone from George. "Kelsey, this is Thebb. Can you join us for a cup of coffee?"

"Great, Thebb, you made it back. I was hoping I would see you again. Where are you?"

"Oh, about a hundred yards away on the *FREEDOM*. If you will come up topside, I'll wave."

Kelsey motored over to *FREEDOM* in his dinghy and called out, "Permission to come aboard, Captain?"

Once aboard, Thebb introduced George and Kelsey.

"The *ANDROMEDA* is a fine-looking vessel," George pointed out. "Very clean, unlike *FREEDOM*. Have you been here in Red Hook long?"

"We've been anchored here for about two months. Our last charter cancelled, and the owner wants us to just wait until he's ready to sail her again," Kelsey answered with a frown.

"I need some mechanical work on my engine," George stated. "Can you recommend a good place to go in Charlotte Amalie?"

"I have some contacts in town who can probably find someone. When I get back on the *ANDROMEDA*, I'll look them up and give them a call. Do you need the work done right away?"

"Sooner will probably be better," answered George. "Nothing critical. Just some minor things, but it's always best to be prepared to go to sea at any time."

"I have to get back to the *DOVE*," Thebb said. "Can I hitch a ride to the dinghy dock?"

Kelsey eagerly volunteered to ferry her back. He told George he would contact him, helped Thebb into the dinghy, and pushed off for the dinghy dock. On the way, he asked her where Bart was going to anchor the *DOVE*. She told him it was her understanding he was going to move back to Red Hook the next afternoon.

"Right now, we're tied up on the other side of one of the commercial docks in the main harbor. It was all Bart could get when he called for a slip. The facilities there are pretty much run-down, but at least they had a few available slips. There are a lot of old dilapidated buildings on either side, and Bart worried about rats crawling up the dock lines. He told Eddie to put some sort of antirat cups on them. I really hope we can move tomorrow."

Kelsey edged up to the dinghy dock, and Thebb got out and waved good-bye. "I hope to see you tomorrow," he called out.

After returning the rental car, Thebb took a taxi to the *DOVE*. It was early afternoon when Thebb entered the saloon. She was surprised to see Cecilia talking with Bart and the crew. Cecilia turned and said hello.

"Hi, Anna. I hear you had a great cruise with the Koroguru Group. They told the marine agent they had the best time of their lives and especially enjoyed your cooking. Good job," Cecilia enthused.

"Thanks, Mrs. Pisani. I'm pleased they had a good time. We all hope they will join us again," Thebb responded with an open confidence Cecilia hadn't seen before.

"Anna, please call me Cecilia. Mrs. Pisani is a bit too formal when we don't have guests on board."

"Thank you, Cecilia, and please call me Thebb. I don't use the name Anna any longer. Everyone calls me Thebb now."

Cecilia cocked her head, squinted her eyes, looked directly at Thebb, and replied, "I see. So Thebb it will be. Is this a nickname, or is it now your formal name?"

"It's formal," Thebb replied. "It was kind of an accident that I became known as Anna. I shouldn't have let that happen."

Bart and the crew were looking back and forth between Cecilia and Thebb. Bo was especially curious about how Mrs. Pisani would take to Thebb's new name. She did it with such aplomb it was hardly noticeable. Almost like she expected it. Actually, she didn't expect it, but it didn't surprise her after reading about the drug busts in Philadelphia.

Cecilia returned to her discussion with the crew. "Well, as a celebration of your successful cruise with the Koroguru Group, I would like to take all of you out for a fine dinner."

Bart said one of the crew would have to stay aboard for security watch. Before anyone else could respond, Thebb, as usual, volunteered. Cecilia pointed out the one crew member who needed to go out to dinner would be the one who has been preparing the meals on board. Bo interjected he would stay behind with Thebb.

Then Rick said he would too. Cecilia looked at the crew and then turned to Bart.

"Bart, you must be a wonderful captain. Your crew doesn't want to leave your ship. Okay! Let's stay aboard the *DOVE*, and I'll make dinner," Cecilia authoritatively stated.

Thebb offered to help, pointing out Cecilia might not know where all the supplies were. Thebb added a sweetener saying she wanted to learn some of Cecilia's gourmet-cooking secrets. What could Cecilia say after that? She agreed. While preparing dinner, Cecilia quietly told Thebb she needed to talk privately with her after dinner. "A lot of things have happened since I mailed your package in New York, and you need to know about them."

That last statement caught Thebb's attention and scared her.

CHAPTER 40

Maroon ended his conversation with David Kramer by closing his cell phone cover with a loud snap. He was pumped up over the news Dave had tracked Tatianna to St. Thomas and realized he had to act fast. Finding her in St. Thomas was too important to delegate to his men. She was obviously too crafty for them to handle. He would have to do it himself.

Maroon opened his safe and removed his personally coded directory of important contacts. Even Tatianna hadn't seen it. Since only he knew the algorithm to decipher it, he felt the information was safe. He paused and studied the directory for a moment remembering the police crime lab had broken some of Tatianna's codes, and she was a genius with codes. He had wanted to have her develop a code for him but decided against it since he needed total secrecy for his private contacts. He thumbed through the directory to find the number for his contact in Puerto Rico.

"Buenas tardes."

"Isabella, this is Maroon."

Isabella was petite, attractive, and sensuous. With her long dark hair and warm complexion, she was a striking Latin beauty. She was a professional facilitator and had lots of connections. Many people owed her big favors. She was highly effective in conducting successful transactions with authorities throughout the Caribbean. Always for a handsome profit. She was able to avoid scrutiny because she usually did not become directly involved in criminal activities, and, of course, she paid the officials well. That was one of the reasons her fees were so high. She was well-known by both the cartel and authorities but was not acknowledged by the police or the many politicians she dealt with. Her reputation for secrecy was unequaled. It was ironclad. Her clientele knew that reneging on a payment could be fatal.

Maroon explained he needed her expertise, contacts, and access to certain "equipment" to fix a problem in St. Thomas. She said she understood and could help, but that type of assistance was very costly. Maroon emphasized it was a very sensitive operation and had to be done as quickly as possible. He needed the highest level of competency. He would be pleased to pay whatever it took, but he wanted her personally to set it up and work with him in getting it done. No one else would do.

Isabella balked at Maroon's request. "Maroon, you know that I don't do that! I can set it up, but I don't usually help do the actual work."

Maroon heard the word "usually" and pressed ahead. "Isabella, this is a unique situation and involves finding a woman. A very crafty and dangerous woman. No one else has your level of expertise. I will pay for your on-site help. This will be a very profitable business deal for you."

After learning more about the elusive Tatianna, Isabella cautiously agreed to help. If Tatianna was as smart as Maroon said, the project would be challenging. The challenge appealed to her ego. She gave Maroon directions for meeting her and told him to be prepared to make a fund transfer when he got there. Clients had to pay up front in her business. Maroon agreed and told her he would book a flight to San Juan right away. He would call her with a list of the equipment he needed and his arrival time.

Maroon was standing at the curb in front of the arrival terminal of the Luis Muñoz Marin Airport in San Juan when a black Aston Martin pulled up in front of him. The window rolled down, and Isabella told him to get in. They didn't talk, and they didn't go far. She pulled up in the parking lot of the Banco Popular de Puerto Rico on Calle Loiza, and they went in to make the fund transfer.

After Maroon transferred the required payment, Isabella drove to the general aviation hangar at the airport where she had hired a private plane that would fly them to Charlotte Amalie. The equipment needed for the business transaction was already aboard the plane. It included several semiautomatic pistols, a .357 Magnum revolver, and a sawed-off pistol-handled shotgun. She carried a Walther PPK, anniversary model. It didn't have the punch of a .357 Magnum, but it was .38 caliber and to her liking. She felt it was the kind of gun a lady should carry.

It was almost noon when Maroon and Isabella arrived at Harry Truman Airport in Charlotte Amalie. They taxied over to a remote hangar and quickly exited the plane. A delivery truck and driver were waiting inside the hangar. When they left the airport, Isabella told the driver where to drop them off. They picked up a plain tan sedan and drove to a house overlooking Crystal Cove on the north side of the island. It would serve as their operations center. On the drive, Maroon explained in more detail why he was there and gave Isabella a general description of Tatianna. Isabella suggested Tatianna probably changed her appearance. She could have dyed her hair and might be a brunette. And she might also be wearing glasses.

"You're right," Maroon agreed. "I hadn't thought about that. It's gonna make finding the bitch harder."

"And from what you have told me, we should check out the sailboats in the harbor."

Once inside the house they lost no time. Isabella began using one of her many prepaid cell phones to make contacts. Maroon was anxious to start searching, but Isabella cautioned him that they first needed to have a plan. "I have contacts on St. Thomas who can help us. We'll start looking for the woman after I make a few more calls."

CHAPTER 41

———————

Cecilia prepared an Italian seafood dinner of fresh red snapper baked in a tomato-based pesto sauce and served over fusilli pasta. Thebb helped by preparing pasta figioli, salad, and garlic bread. There was too much traffic in and out of the galley for beer and chips and for a meaningful conversation, so Cecilia held to her original plan to talk to Thebb after dinner.

While they were preparing dinner, Kelsey came aboard. He said he wanted to talk to Eddie, but he really wanted to see Thebb. Bo wasn't pleased and told him the owner was aboard. Kelsey didn't expect to see one of the owners and tried to leave, but Cecilia caught him and insisted he stay for dinner. There would be plenty of food she insisted. Bo suggested that he and Jimbo (he refused to call him Kelsey) go topside and talk with Eddie. He said Mrs. Pisani and Thebb were busy preparing dinner. It did not escape Cecilia's notice that Bo was trying, ever so discreetly, to separate Kelsey and Thebb. *Hmmm! This should be an interesting dinner*, she thought.

After Bo and Kelsey went topside, Thebb and Cecilia heard a deep husky voice calling for permission to come aboard. Thebb surprised Cecilia by instantly dropping what she was doing to go topside. Cecilia wondered who so instantly got Thebb's attention. *Must be another new boyfriend.*

As she continued preparing dinner, Cecilia realized Thebb had slimmed down a lot, and her face was almost healed. Her hair was much longer too. The sun had bleached it to a light blond color that offset her powder blue eyes. She thought if Thebb would make any attempt to improve her appearance, she would be very pretty. Cecilia

———

decided she had to get Thebb out of the baggy jeans and denim shirts she always wore. It was hard to tell she was a woman.

A few minutes later, Thebb introduced George to Cecilia in the galley. Cecilia wasn't able to hide her surprise at seeing this older, gray-bearded man. George wasn't expecting to see anyone other than Thebb and was not dressed for the occasion. He was wearing shorts and a T-shirt. With grease marks on the shorts and an unkempt beard, he looked like a street person. Cecilia was taken aback as Thebb introduced him as her very good friend.

George was surprised too. He hadn't expected the owner of the *DOVE* to be so young and attractive. He immediately apologized for his appearance and explained he had just brought his boat, *FREEDOM*, over to the harbor for some minor mechanical repairs. She's tied up at the mechanics dock about a hundred yards away. He saw the *DOVE* and decided to drop by to say hi. When he tried to excuse himself and leave, Thebb insisted he stay for dinner.

"George, you have to stay for dinner and meet Captain Bart and the crew. There's plenty of food for another guest, isn't there?" Thebb excitedly asked Cecilia.

"Oh yes, there is. Please stay for dinner, George," Cecilia answered. "I'm sure it's going to be a fun evening." *What's going on here? First, Kelsey and now this old sailor and Bo. I can't wait to see what dinner is going to be like.*

The dinner went well. Lots of sea stories from George and Bart. Each trying to outdo the other. Kelsey had his share too, as did Bo. Cecilia relished the spontaneity and camaraderie among the sailors. Dinners at home with Jack and his friends were more formal and lacked the easy discourse she was enjoying aboard the *DOVE*. She had been on the *DOVE* many times before but had never seen such cohesion among the crew. They really enjoyed one another's company. Thebb rarely spoke, but when she did, everyone listened intently. They seemed to pay her special deference. Cecilia was wondering if Thebb was the spark that united everyone.

It was still light after dinner. Rick wanted to go barhopping in Frenchtown and listen to live island music. He invited everyone to join him, and all the men except George accepted. George said he wasn't dressed appropriately so he would just visit with the ladies. Cecilia wasn't pleased George wanted to stay and talk with Thebb.

She wanted to show Thebb the newspaper articles from Philadelphia and find out if the envelope she mailed in New York was what precipitated all the arrests for drug trafficking in Philadelphia. She felt she had a vested interest in knowing the truth because she could be culpable too. She pulled Thebb aside and politely told her to ask George to leave so they could talk about the envelope.

Cecilia was dumbfounded by Thebb's refusal to ask George to leave. Thebb said he was a very special friend and confidant. She trusted him implicitly and felt Cecilia could speak freely in front of him. Cecilia agreed even though she was reluctant to let anyone but Thebb know what had happened in Philadelphia.

In the owner's cabin, Cecilia said she believed the large envelope she mailed for Thebb in New York, addressed to the DA's office in Philadelphia, contained accounting ledgers.

"You opened my package?" Thebb exclaimed with a fearful look and a very alert posture.

"No! I didn't open your package," Cecilia responded defensively. "I didn't have to. A few weeks after I mailed the envelope, all hell broke loose in Philadelphia. Lots of drug dealers, cops, and city officials were arrested."

"What has that got to do with the envelope?" George asked.

"Just this!" Cecilia said as she handed them copies of the Philadelphia newspaper articles.

Thebb and George read the clipped articles about the drug cartel and the many police officers and city officials who had been arrested. Thebb was quiet, and Cecilia could see she was stunned, speechless, and afraid. Occasionally, Thebb shook her head in disbelief. While she suspected Tatianna had been involved in criminal activity, Thebb had no idea it was so far-reaching. She had tears running down her cheeks. George kept muttering, "Wow, holy shit, goddamn," and other obscenities as he read the articles.

When they had finished reading, George sat staring at Thebb. She seemed unwilling to look directly at him or Cecilia. After a moment of silence, George grabbed Thebb, gave her a bear hug, and told her she was one hell of a woman.

"Wow! Unbelievable! What do you think, Cecilia? She's one incredible woman, isn't she?" he asked.

"Yes she is," Cecilia answered with skepticism. "But I need to know if you were involved with those ledgers, Thebb?"

"No! Not exactly. I just accidentally came across them and thought the authorities ought to have them. I really can't explain any more than that. I've never been involved with drugs or any of the people in those newspaper articles."

"Then who beat you up, Thebb? Was it one of those drug criminals who beat you up?"

"No! It had nothing to do with the drug dealers. I was just clumsy and fell."

"No, no, no, Thebb! That won't wash! Dammit! You can't fall down and get those kinds of injuries. I was a nurse, remember. Did one of those guys beat you up?"

Thebb just sat, staring at the engraved dove on the mahogany door in the master cabin. It was inlaid with a silvery metal and looked peaceful. Her head started to throb again, something she had been free from for a number of weeks. But now it was pulsating, and she could actually hear and feel her heart thumping. She was trapped. She couldn't go home because Philip would try to kill her, and she couldn't get involved with the drug bust in Philadelphia or the drug dealers would kill her.

When will this end? It just keeps getting worse. Now Cecilia knows about the accounting books. I wish I could just jump overboard and swim away.

Cecilia watched as Thebb bit her lip and just stared out into space with tears running down her cheeks.

George hugged Thebb again and wiped some of her tears away. He turned to Cecilia. "Look, Cecilia, if Thebb said she wasn't involved then she wasn't involved. Period. But that doesn't matter right now. What does matter is the drug cartel may think she had something to do with the DA getting their books. And they may be trying to find her. We should have a plan for what we're gonna do."

George was thinking about what had happened in Bermuda and realized the two men who had attacked Thebb in the tavern parking lot were probably sent there by the drug cartel. It all fit. If she was involved with any of those people, she was in really serious trouble. He and Mike had no doubt the two guys at the tavern fully intended to hurt her. Badly! Maybe even kill her. He didn't know how she got herself entangled with the drug dealers, but he felt certain it wasn't intentional.

They all sat quietly, thinking. Then Cecilia, looking puzzled, asked George, "So what makes you think they might be looking for Thebb? The police in Philadelphia already have the books, and lots and lots of people have been arrested. Very important people."

Again there was silence as Cecilia continued to stare at George. Then she looked at Thebb and said, "There shouldn't be anyone looking for you. Unless—"

More silence.

"Unless there are more books! Are there more books, Thebb?"

Thebb sat up straight, and her eyes grew wide. "More books?" Then she stared at the floor and mumbled, "Could there be more books?" She stood up and looked directly at George. "Oh my god! More books? Why would they think that I have them?"

Thebb had never considered the possibility of additional books, but suddenly images of the Cayman Islands bankbook and key flashed across her mind, and her head started to pound again.

Cecilia and George sat transfixed, watching Thebb standing and mumbling about the possibility of more books. She looked like she was in agony. Then there was more silence.

George broke the silence, "From what I just read, some gang members might still be at large, and they may want to get even with whoever gave the books to the DA."

"So what do we do now?" Cecilia asked, resigning herself to the fact she wasn't going to get a definitive answer out of Thebb.

George turned to Cecilia. "For now, let's just stay alert and think about a plan. If anyone is looking for Thebb, we should be ready to protect her. Besides, how would they know where she is? And she has a new name. I don't think there's a problem."

"Thanks for showing me the clippings," Thebb said to Cecilia. "I had no idea what was happening back in Philadelphia."

George added, "Cecilia, you're a strong and caring woman. I'm really impressed you were willing to get involved and help Thebb. Not many people would do that."

CHAPTER 42

The three sat quietly in the master cabin. Cecilia was thinking it had been one hell of a confusing day. Her suspicions about the package had been confirmed. She met Kelsey and George. And Thebb had become more mysterious. Cecilia questioned why Thebb was so desperately hiding her real identity. It was obvious she was hiding from the drug dealers, but there was something else she was even more afraid of. She appeared to be both very strong and very vulnerable at the same time. And George was totally infatuated with Thebb. Why was that? He must be thirty or forty years older than she was. What had she gotten herself into? So many questions were left unanswered she wondered why she had come down to St. Thomas in the first place.

George interrupted the silence, "I'm dirty and should never have come over without changing clothes. I better get back to my boat and clean up."

"Don't worry about your appearance, George, just please stay close by. I really missed seeing you the last few months."

Cecilia sat wondering, *What's this all about? Why has she missed seeing him? Maybe he's a relative?*

Suddenly there was a thumping topside. "Somebody's coming aboard," Cecilia whispered.

It was the crew and Kelsey. They proceeded noisily down to the saloon, and Cecilia went out to meet them.

"You fellows are back early?"

Bo stepped forward and with a concerned look asked, "Where's Thebb? Is she here?"

Thebb left the master cabin with George close behind. As she entered the saloon, she heard Bo asking for her, and his voice seemed anxious. That scared her.

"Thebb, there's a man and a woman going from bar to bar looking for a woman who kind of fits your description," Bo said with strong concern. "Kelsey has some contacts who said they are offering money to bartenders, waiters, and maitre d's to be on the lookout for her. They're promising a thousand dollars to anyone who can help them find her."

Kelsey joined in, "Thebb, from what my contacts are saying, these are definitely bad people. One said they gave him the shivers with the intensity of their search. Could they be looking for you?"

Bo interrupted Kelsey, "Thebb, the woman they're looking for is closer to what you looked like back in Bermuda. They're describing her as having short blond hair, or possibly short dark hair, blue eyes, and overweight. Sorry about that, Thebb, but it was their description. They're describing her as about five feet, six or seven inches. A little bit shorter than you but close enough."

Kelsey spoke up, "The scary part is my contacts said they also thought she might be on a sailboat."

George nudged Thebb to the side, stepped forward, and said, "I think we're dealing with a case of mistaken identity, but it doesn't matter. The thugs are searching for someone who looks similar to Thebb. These are dangerous people who don't care who gets hurt. We better be alert and prepared to respond in case they discover Thebb and decide she's the one they want." George spoke with such authority everyone stood quietly listening to him.

It had jelled in George's mind that Thebb had somehow, inadvertently, crossed paths with drug dealers and ended up with their accounting books. *She says she's not the person they're looking for. I believe her, but it doesn't really matter. She tried to do the right thing by sending the books to the DA, but she has caused an uproar.*

Thebb had receded to the outer edge of the group and hadn't said a word but was listening intently.

Bart had been quiet but was paying close attention. He said the first thing they needed to do was put people on watch, topside, right away. "Rick, you take the first security watch and keep a keen eye out for anyone hanging around the boat. Everyone else should stay alert and be prepared in case we have to move the *DOVE.*"

Kelsey asked Bart, "Where do you plan on anchoring?"

"I don't know yet. I have to study our options. But we have to be ready to leave on a moment's notice."

Bart went to his cabin to study his charts.

Eddie and Kelsey went to the galley for something to drink.

Bo started to go topside, but Thebb grabbed his arm and asked him and George to join her for a moment in her cabin, as small as it was. She was scared and was about to expose one of her closest-held secrets. Once inside the cabin, with the door shut and the two men sitting on the bunk, she opened the small cabinet above the headboard of the bunk. She removed a few feminine supplies and placed them on the bunk. Bo and George watched cautiously. Then she removed the Glock, the Beretta, and several boxes of ammunition.

"Bo, have you ever used one of these?" Thebb asked as she handed him the Beretta.

"Well yeah, but do you think we need this?" he asked incredulously.

George responded, "Absolutely."

"Thebb, if you're not involved with these people, how come you have these guns and all this ammunition?" Bo asked while staring at the Beretta in his hands.

"Bo," Thebb stated, taking on the same unemotional air of authority he had seen back in the Bahamas, "this is necessary. Do you know how to use a semiautomatic pistol?"

"Well yeah, but—"

Thebb interrupted him, and with a determined look, she explained the gun had a round in the chamber and fifteen in the clip. "The safety is off, and you should keep it off. The Beretta has a double-action trigger. It will cock the hammer for the first round. Just don't pull the trigger until you are ready to shoot somebody. Hopefully, you won't have to."

With that, she pulled her shirttails out and tucked the Glock in her waistband. "George, do you still have a shotgun on board the *FREEDOM?*"

"Of course," George answered while watching in amazement as Thebb took charge like a military officer. "I have a revolver too, but it doesn't have the firepower you have here."

"That's good. Can you keep it at the ready?"

As George was leaving her cabin, Thebb asked Bo to stay for a few minutes. She told him about the newspaper articles and why they all might be in danger. She explained it was only happenstance that she ended up with the drug cartel's accounting ledgers. She thought it was the right thing to do to mail the ledgers to the DA, but it put them all in danger. She apologized for the problems she was causing and stressed the situation was very much life threatening.

"Bo, you have to be ready to use your gun without hesitation. You can't wait and give the drug dealers a chance to react. You have to act immediately."

She continued, giving him some of the pointers Joey had so aptly taught her. "Don't hesitate," she emphasized several times. "Hesitation will get us killed. And aim at what you want to shoot."

George left to go back to the *FREEDOM.* He was tied up on the next pier over from the *DOVE.* Rick had the security watch and was sitting on a hatch cover scanning the harbor when George left the *DOVE.* Before he reached his boat, George noticed a motorboat, about twenty-one feet long, quietly tying up to the dock behind the *DOVE* but farther out in the darkness.

This wasn't an uncommon occurrence. Boats sometimes came and went after docking for only a few hours. But not so much after dark. With unsavory people searching for someone who looked like Thebb, George was alert for anything unusual. He stopped in the shadows and watched as three men, islanders, walked leisurely down the dock toward shore. They didn't seem to be a threat, and he relaxed.

The concrete dock was long and dark. It was common in the islands to have minimum lighting on the docks. Lighting was expensive, and the marine facilities usually provided as little as they could get by with. Besides, boaters sometimes complained about too much light when they overnighted at the docks. Harbor masters used that as an excuse to cut back. This dock had only a single light post at each end of the long pier, and the *DOVE* was tied up closer to the shore than to the middle of the dock. Bart usually docked on the port side of the *DOVE*, and for this docking pier he had to position her with her bow pointed out toward the bay.

Rick carefully watched the men walking down the dock but relaxed when it seemed they were walking to shore to visit a bar. However, when they got abreast of the *DOVE*'s gangplank, two of them rushed up onto the deck. The third man stationed himself at the foot of the gangplank. Rick jumped up and tried to intercept them. "You can't come aboard! You can't come aboard," he yelled as he tried to get between the men and the stairs to the saloon. Without slowing down, one of the men slammed Rick hard on the side of his head with a pistol. Rick fell making only a low thunking sound as he hit the deck, semiconscious and bleeding profusely.

The men raced down the stairs and into the saloon where Cecilia, Eddie, and Kelsey were sitting and talking. Bart was in the captain's quarters. The men ran immediately to Cecilia. One man grabbed her with his left arm around her throat and a knife in his right hand. The other man had a large semiautomatic handgun. Eddie and Kelsey knew enough about guns to surmise that it was a .45-caliber pistol. They stood frozen.

"You be Tatianna?" the man with the gun demanded of Cecilia.

"No. Let go of me," she screamed as she struggled to get loose.

Bart heard the commotion and opened his cabin door. When he saw what was happening, he demanded that the men release Mrs. Pisani immediately. The two men were yelling for everyone to get down and not move. They yelled so loud that George heard them across the short body of water that separated the two vessels.

Cecilia was screaming. The man with the knife was yelling in Cecilia's ear, "Shut de fuck up, or I cut yo throat." Cecilia continued to struggle but shut up. The man lifted her up by her neck so that only her toes touched the saloon floor. She was having difficulty breathing.

Bo and Thebb heard the struggling and yelling, and Bo started to open the cabin door. Thebb stopped him and put her ear up against the wall. Bo did the same. The yelling had stopped, and they could hear the men demanding to know if Cecilia was Tatianna. She kept telling them there was no Tatianna on board, but they wouldn't listen.

"We know you be Tatianna, and you be coming with us," the man with the gun said as they began dragging Cecilia up the stairs. Thebb

—

cracked the cabin door open in time to see them going up the stairs with Cecilia who started screaming and kicking again. Thebb and Bo opened the forward hatch and climbed out onto the deck.

Thebb whispered to Bo, "Can you jump to the dock and get in front of them? If you can get on the dock, you can stop them from leaving the boat. I'll back you up from here on the foredeck."

It was a long jump, but Bo made it. He landed awkwardly and twisted his ankle slightly. He took cover next to the large steel trash container positioned against one of the dilapidated buildings on the dock.

As the men got to the main deck and were trying to reach the gangplank, Rick had regained consciousness and jumped the man with the gun. But the man hit him again, pushed him to the deck, pointed the gun at him, and yelled, "You stay down or I shoot you."

The third man, who had been on the dock, came up the gangplank to help carry the struggling Cecilia. As he reached the deck, he heard Bo yelling from the dock for them to drop their guns and release the woman. Two of the men started shooting at Bo in the darkness. They couldn't see him, but they shot in the direction of his voice. Bo took cover behind the trash container and fired back, missing the men who were crouching and trying to get behind the gunnel. One man started to go down the gangplank while shooting toward Bo. The pings and clanks of the bullets hitting the steel container kept Bo from returning fire.

Thebb was at the bow of the boat and unseen in the darkness. She rested her hands on the gunnel and took aim. It would be a long shot for a pistol at a moving target with limited lighting, but Thebb had the gunnel as a bench rest. She aimed carefully and shot twice from the front of the boat. The man's gun dropped to the gangplank and bounced downward onto the concrete dock. The man, looking surprised, rolled over the handrail and fell on the dock partly blocking the gangplank. He laid still. The other two men spun around to face the shooter in the darkness on the bow, and a single shot rang out from the dock box. One of them cried out, "I'm hit. I'm hit. Oh shit, they shot me." He turned and tried to escape down the gangplank. Another shot rang out from farther up the dock. It was from George's .38-caliber revolver.

The men started yelling to stop shooting, or they would kill the woman. Dragging Cecilia down the dock, they made it past Thebb. In the darkness, there was no clear target. If Thebb had shot at them, she might have hit Cecilia. Bo kept yelling at the two men to stop, but with the partial light and the men twisting and running, he couldn't shoot either. After the men passed him, Bo ran after them hoping to get an opening for a shot, but one of them shot back at him. He saw the muzzle flash and heard the report. He also heard the bullet ricochet off the concrete nearby. He was in the open and vulnerable. He dropped to a lying position on the concrete and looked for an open shot, but the men used Cecilia as a shield.

The two island men made it to their boat and motored out of the harbor. They headed for the open Caribbean, leaving their accomplice behind.

Kelsey, Eddie, and Bart came topside and were yelling, "Did they get away with Mrs. Pisani?" Bo ran back to the gangplank and saw the injured kidnapper on the concrete. He yelled to Thebb, "Thebb, are you okay?" She yelled back, "I'm okay. Has anyone been shot?" Each of the men, except Rick, yelled back, "I'm okay!" Rick was sitting on a hatch cover holding his head and bleeding. Kelsey took his shirt off and used it as a bandage to stop Rick's bleeding. "Are you okay? Are you okay?" Kelsey kept asking Rick. Bo stepped over the kidnapper and ran up the gangplank. "They got away with Mrs. Pisani!"

Thebb came running down the port deck asking Bo if he got a shot at them. Bart was asking Rick if he had been shot. Rick said he hadn't been shot, but he felt like it. He thought that he was okay.

George approached the *DOVE* carefully and inspected the man lying at the foot of the gangplank. He yelled up to Bart, "Captain, this one's still alive."

Kelsey and Eddie helped Rick down into the saloon and laid him on the floor. Bart removed Kelsey's makeshift bandage to see how badly Rick was hurt. As Rick tried to sit up, Bart told him to lie back down. "You're bleeding a lot, and we've got to stop it right away." Rick looked at the blood on his shirt and lay back down on the floor with his eyes half open. Blood had spilled on the deck, the stairs, and all over Rick.

Thebb yelled to George and Bo, "We have to got the wounded man on board and get out of here right away." George picked up the man's gun, a 9-millimeter Beretta. Thebb ran down the gangplank and helped George and Bo carry the wounded man down to the saloon. He was big and heavy and difficult to get down the stairs. They laid him on the floor near Rick. Bart grabbed some towels from the galley and began trying to stop the man's bleeding.

"Bart! We have to leave right now," Thebb urgently advised Bart. "I'll help Bo take care of Rick and this man."

George grabbed Bart by the arm and said, "Captain, you have to let someone else do that. You have to get the *DOVE* out of here right away. I'm going back to my boat and get the hell out of the bay as fast as I can. If no one is here when the police come, they won't know where to look for any problems. They're usually pretty slow to respond when you need them. Hopefully they'll take their time now. Maybe they'll think all the shooting was just fireworks." He handed Bart the man's gun and left.

Bart directed Thebb to take over helping the man she had shot and Bo to take care of Rick. A moment later, she felt the diesel engine crank over. Eddie and Kelsey grabbed buckets and washed the blood off the dock and the gangplank. Then they released the lines, raised the gangplank, and within minutes the *DOVE* was under way.

Bart switched off all the lights and motored out the west channel. Kelsey and Eddie were on the bow as lookouts as they steered a course southward into the open Caribbean. George followed in the darkness with *FREEDOM*. When they were out of the harbor, Bart allowed the small DC lights in the saloon to be turned on. About five miles south of St. Thomas, he cut the engine and drifted. It was a calm sea with a partial moon. George rafted up to the *DOVE*.

Rick was still shaken and woozy, but he sat up. He told Bo he was okay and to go help Bart. He could help Thebb attend to the thug on the floor. The man had regained partial consciousness and was struggling to breathe. Rick was asking him where they were taking Mrs. Pisani. He gurgled, "Abba burge." He gurgled it twice and the words, "Get money," before taking his last breath.

The man had no identification on him. His pants were ragged, and he wore an old black T-shirt. The only thing Rick could find was a pocket full of 9-mm cartridges with full metal jackets and a crumpled piece of paper with part of a phone number on it. His blood had stained most of the number. Only the first four digits were discernible.

Just as George was about to climb aboard the *DOVE*, his radio crackled. "This is *SEA NYMPH* calling *FREEDOM*. This is *SEA NYMPH* calling *FREEDOM*." George went back to his cockpit. The call was coming over the VHF radio on channel 16. George returned the call. "This is *FREEDOM*, come back, *SEA NYMPH*."

"Hey, George. Sorry I'm late. Are you in the harbor?" It was Mike, from Bermuda, calling. He had promised to meet up with George in St. Thomas but got held up waiting for an auxiliary bilge pump in Bermuda.

"*SEA NYMPH*, switch over to seven-two."

"Switching over to seven-two."

When he heard the click of the radio at channel seven-two, George asked, "Mike, where are you?"

"I'm just west of Van Dyke Island. I'm on a course of 190."

"Keep channel seven-two open. I'll call you back in a few minutes. I just left a party like the last one you and I crashed a few months ago," George exclaimed.

"Will do. Damn, you have all the fun."

CHAPTER 43

When the two men were dragging Cecilia down the dock in Charlotte Amalie, she was kicking and twisting, trying to get away. The man who had been wounded led the way to the motorboat and helped get Cecilia aboard. She tried to scream, but they had an arm lock around her neck and choked her. When the men pushed her down into the boat, she cut her legs on the rough seats and banged her head on the gunnel. She laid on the bottom of the boat in oily bilge water that stained her white shorts and green golf shirt.

As they motored out the east channel, Cecilia struggled with the man who was holding her down. She tried to jump overboard, but he hit her in the face and threw her down on to the floorboards. While she was lying dazed on the floorboards, he kneeled on her back and tied her hands behind her. Using a dirty oil-and-fuel-stained rag, he gagged her. The fumes from the rag were foul tasting and noxious. The gag didn't fit well, and Cecilia tried to scream. The man held her down and told her to shut up, or he would make her shut up for good.

As they sped around the island, Cecilia tried to pay attention to where they were going. She could occasionally see lights on the port side of the boat so she knew they were heading east. After motoring for what she thought had to be an hour, the men cut the engine, and the boat slid up on a shore. From the sound of the hull scraping against sand, she could tell they had landed on a beach. The limited light came from a partial moon and the stars in the clear sky.

The men forced Cecilia up a steep, rocky trail with thick thorny bushes on either side. In the darkness, she tripped several times, cutting and bruising her legs. After climbing for about two hundred yards, they reached level ground. Cecilia tripped and fell, aggravating her captors. One of the men hit her on the back of her head and told her they had farther to go. Again they trudged up a narrow path, through the thorny brambles to a flat area with huge structures casting dark shadows from the moonlight. The path was flat and dusty hard clay. There was a row of smaller structures to her right. In the darkness, it was difficult to tell they were old shacks.

The two men opened a door and shoved Cecilia into a shack. They pushed her down into the dirt and tied her ankles. The lower few feet of the walls of the shack were made of coral rock blocks, and the upper walls were heavily weathered boards with gaps between them. Some kind of plaster, or mortar, had once sealed the gaps, but over time a lot of it had weathered away. The shack had a corrugated metal roof and a door that didn't close properly. The men tried to close it, but it swung back partially open. One of the men found a stick and tried to latch the door closed, but it didn't hold and the door swung partly open again. They cursed at the door and ordered Cecilia to stay put and be quiet or they would kill her.

Cecilia's abductors had been quiet for a while. They were sitting on a low stone wall across the dirt path in front of the shack. One of them was trying to make a cell phone call. There was no cell service, and he cursed the phone as being worthless. He said to the other man, "They'd better be here in the morning with de money, or there gonna be trouble for them. We just gonna have to wait."

The wounded man complained, "My arm hurt. I'm gonna need a doctor right away. Dey don't say nuttin bout de woman having guns. Dey should give us mo money fo dis."

The other man tied an oily cloth around his arm and told him to lie down. "It only be a few hours before de daylight come."

It was still dark, but through the partially open door, Cecilia could see large shadows that looked like partial buildings and low walls or fences. She tried to think of someplace that had walls on an island with no cell coverage. She saw the wounded man had lain down in the rubble-strewn path in front of the shack so he could guard the door while resting. The other man walked a short distance away, sat on a rock or some sort of box, and lit a cigarette. In the darkness the cigarette lit up the man's face each time he took a puff but not enough for Cecilia to recognize him. All she could see was a man's face.

Inside, the shack was dark. Cecilia couldn't tell she had blood and dirt on her shirt and legs. She was sitting in the dirt, leaning against the coral rock wall, scared and uncomfortable. Her position was awkward, and the rough, jagged coral rocks jabbed her in the back. She was able to use the jagged rocks to loosen her nasty gag. She relished the clean air and spit out some of the taste of oil and gasoline. Being able to breathe more easily, she began to rub the rope tied around her wrists on the edge of an outcropping of coral rock. Doing it quietly was tedious work, but after a while she could feel the rope loosening.

As dawn approached and a hazy light spread over the island, Cecilia could tell the large shadows were the ruins of a sugar mill. Through the light fog, she could see lots of low walls, a large tree, and the round base of an old windmill. *This has to be an old sugar plantation. We must be on St. John.*

Between the gaps in the wood siding of the walls, she noticed a trail descending slightly to her right for several hundred feet before it turned, went sharply uphill, and disappeared into the forest of trees and bushes that covered the side of the mountain.

As the darkness faded into the eerie half light of long shadows, Cecilia sensed a movement behind her. She froze then turned slowly to see a lizard on the wall about three feet away. She almost screamed. It just stared at her and didn't move. The lizard was about seven inches long, but that didn't matter to Cecilia. She didn't like lizards or snakes or spiders. The shack probably had all kinds of horrible little things, but what could she do?

CHAPTER 44

With the partial moon and the calm sea, there was just enough light to move around on the rafted boats. George climbed aboard the *DOVE* and scrambled down to the saloon where everyone had gathered.

"Thebb, Bo, are you guys okay?" George asked. He turned and asked Rick if he was all right. Rick said he thought so.

"You don't look like it, son. You look terrible."

"Thanks, George. I have a terrible headache, but the bleeding has stopped, thanks to the butterfly bandages Bart applied."

"What about this guy on the floor?" George asked. "Is he dead?"

Bart answered angrily, "We've got some goddamn serious problems here. We have to find Mrs. Pisani, and we have to do it right now before they hurt her. And we have this dead man here. What the hell are we going to do with him?" As he asked the question, he realized it was rhetorical. Everyone already knew the answer.

Rick looked at Bart and said, "Bart, this guy muttered something just before he died. He said 'abba buggie' or 'abba burge' or something like that, and then 'get money.' It sounded like he was saying where he was going to get paid. But where the hell is abba buggie?"

"Look, guys," Bo interjected, "we know they were in a boat when they left the harbor. They went out the east channel, not the west channel. So they were probably going around the south side of the island and heading east. Are there any ports, bays, or towns called abba burge on the south side of St. Thomas?"

Kelsey jumped up, "Where are the charts? Maybe we can find abba buggie on the charts."

"Great idea, Kelsey," Bart answered as he retrieved the chart for the Virgin Islands and spread it on the galley table. It was a large chart and covered St. Thomas, St. John, Tortola, and all the islands in between. In the dim galley lights, they leaned in close and began to look for any place resembling abba burge. Thebb had to look over the shoulders of Bo and Rick. She couldn't get close enough to see the names of the bays and small towns on the south coast of St. Thomas. So she scanned the part of the chart she could see. It was the side with Tortola and St. John, and it was hanging partially off the table.

"Could it be Annaberg?" Thebb asked.

George turned to look at Thebb. "Where's Annaberg?"

"It's a town on St. John. Right here," Thebb said while pointing to the northeast coast of St. John. "It looks like it's pretty close to the coast too."

"That's it," Kelsey exclaimed excitedly. "That's it. I've been there. It would be a perfect place to hide out. Annaberg is the ruins of an old sugar mill. There are some old, partly restored shacks on the hillside near the ruins. With a powerboat, it wouldn't be too long a trip from the harbor at Charlotte Amalie."

Bart looked at the chart and exclaimed, "Annaberg is just up in the hills from Leinster Bay. We've been there a couple of times. How come we didn't know about it?"

Kelsey explained, "Sugar mill ruins are all over the Virgin Islands, and St. John has a lot of them. But the ruins at Annaberg are isolated and hard to get to on land. Even from the water! You have to climb up a steep hill, over rocks, and through some thorny bushes to get to them from the beach. It would be a great place to hole up."

George turned to Bart. "I think Kelsey is right. That's probably where they have Cecilia. It looks like it would only take about three hours to get to Leinster Bay. If we go now, we can anchor up at the mouth of the bay, on the far side, and scope out any activity before going ashore."

"I think Kelsey is right too," Bart added. "But first, we have to do something with this guy on the floor. Eddie, can you find some chain or old parts to weight him down."

Bo and Kelsey dragged the dead man topside, and Eddie brought out some old chain. Using flashlights, they checked the chain and body for any identifying marking, wrapped the chain around the body, and pushed it overboard. They were in a thousand feet of water, and the body was not likely to be found. Thebb and Rick stayed below cleaning up the saloon floor. When they came topside, everyone joined in on scrubbing and disinfecting the deck.

George went back to *FREEDOM* and called Mike who had been standing by on channel seven-two.

"Mike, come back," he called.

The speaker crackled. "Yeah, I'm here. How do you want to link up?"

"Do you have cell phone coverage where you are?"

"No. No coverage."

"Okay then. We'll stay on seven-two. I'm going to raft up with another boat on the outer edge of Leinster Bay on St. John. You can raft up with me. In the morning, we are going to a party like the last one but much bigger, and it's going to be a surprise party. Can you join us and bring all your party equipment? We really need you. You should be able to get there in three or four hours. Be sure to douse your lights before you get to the bay."

It was about three in the morning when the *DOVE* dropped anchor at the eastern outer edge of Leinster Bay. George rafted up as before. The partial moon was now lower in the sky but provided just enough light that Bart, using the ship's fifteen power binoculars, could see a powerboat at the shore. He called for Bo and asked him to take a look and see if it was the boat the abductors had used to take Mrs. Pisani away.

"I can't be totally certain, but it sure looks like it. It appears to be untethered and is sitting sideways on the shore, like they were in a hurry or were trying to get something out of the boat."

"Great, then we will go ashore just before dawn," Bart answered. "Kelsey seems to know the area so he'll take the lead. You okay with that, Kelsey?"

About a half hour after the *DOVE* dropped anchor, the *SEA NYMPH* quietly appeared out of the darkness. When he was close enough, Mike dropped his sails and drifted up to *FREEDOM*. There had been a light breeze between Tortola and St. John, and he was able to sail rather than use the small diesel engine. George helped him raft up and then took him to the saloon in the *DOVE*. The room was dimly lit by a small auxiliary light, and all the portholes had the curtains drawn. George introduced him to everyone as a close friend of his and Thebb's.

Mike whispered to George, "Who's Thebb?"

Thebb had been in her cabin retrieving the guns and ammunition. She stepped out just as Mike was learning about her new name. She went over to him and did something the crew hadn't seen before. She gave Mike a hug and then introduced him saying, "Everybody, this is my friend Mike." Bo, feeling a bit jealous and perplexed, told Thebb that George had already introduced him.

"So what's happening?" Mike asked.

George explained, "Cecilia Pisani, owner of the *DOVE*, was abducted last night. We think the kidnappers are holed up in some shacks in the Annaberg ruins on the side of the mountain. At dawn we're going up the mountain and find her. We need all the assistance we can get. With your background, you can be a great help. We had a shoot-out with them when they took Mrs. Pisani, but they got away."

Mike readily agreed and asked how much firepower they had. He had been a colonel in the Marines and served in both Vietnam and the First Gulf War. Thebb told him they had two .40-caliber semiautomatics, a 9-millimeter, George's .38, plus a shotgun. Mike said he had a .30-06 rifle, two handguns, and a shotgun. Kelsey mumbled he didn't have any guns on the *ANDROMEDA* but was damn sure going to change that.

"What about communications?" Mike asked. "Do we have enough VHF radios?"

There weren't enough portable radios so they quickly decided who would carry them.

As dawn began to break, a twenty-five-foot cabin cruiser came into the western side of the bay and headed for shore. Using the ship's binoculars, Bo said he could see two people in the boat. Mike asked Bo to wait a minute while he got his binoculars. He quickly climbed back aboard the *SEA NYMPH* and retrieved his fourteen power Techno-Stabi binoculars. Looking at the cabin cruiser through the stabilized binoculars, Mike agreed, "There are two people, a man and a woman."

They watched as the boat was beached, and the man and woman headed up the hillside.

Eddie commented, "I hope they didn't see us."

George remarked that by rafting up their boats, they probably looked like tourists and wouldn't arouse suspicion. "I think our main problem is getting discovered when we get to the shore."

Kelsey countered, "I don't think so, George. There's a short flat area about two hundred yards up the trail that blocks the view to the beach. And it's not much of a trail either. After the flat area, the trail continues, but it's not as steep as the first part. When I was there a few years ago, I couldn't see the shore from the trail. You have to be on the road at the top of the mountain to see the beach or the ruins, so I think we'll be okay all the way to the ruins. Our greatest problem will be our sudden exposure when the trail ends at the edge of the ruins. The underbrush on either side of the trail is thick and full of huge thorns that will tear you up, but it provides cover up to the edge of the ruins."

Mike recommended they use Kelsey's information and decide on a plan. He proposed they stay together until they reach the ruins and then split into three groups to flank the kidnappers. Thebb and Bo would go to the left around the ruins. Bart and Eddie would go to the right around back of the shacks. He would take the middle between the ruins and the shacks with George and Kelsey. Rick would stay aboard the *DOVE* and radio if another boat approached. They agreed. Everyone boarded the two rubber dinghies, and they paddled ashore as light was breaking.

CHAPTER 45

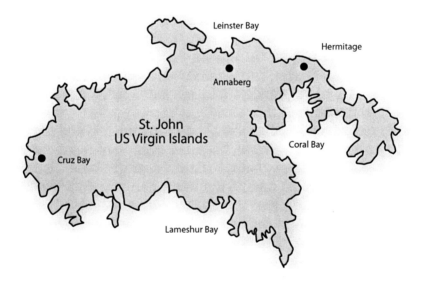

It was early morning and not yet light when Stacy and Roy were getting into the park police Jeep at Hermitage on the east end of St. John. They had an administrative meeting in St. Thomas later that morning and planned to catch the Charlotte Amalie Ferry out of Cruz Bay. They drove around Coral Bay on the East End Road. As they drove over the narrow dirt road near the top of the mountain, Stacy asked Roy to turn off and take the trail above Annaberg.

"That's out of our way, Stacy, and the trail is terrible. It's full of deep ruts and holes. Why do you want to go that way?"

"We haven't been there for over a week, and we have plenty of time."

"Yeah, we have plenty of time, but I want to get some things in St. Thomas before the meeting."

"If we take a later ferry back to St. John, you can still do some shopping. I just want to take a look at Annaberg. Last month, I noted some destructive activity near the windmill, and I want see if it's still going on. If there is, we can report on it at the meeting."

"Okay, Stacy, but it's gonna be a bumpy ride."

Annaberg was the site of what was once a major sugar plantation in the eighteenth and early nineteenth centuries. The ruins of a windmill, sugar factory building, and rum distillery sat on a hill on the north side of St. John Island facing the Sir Francis Drake Channel and the Island of Tortola. The site was surrounded by thick forest and underbrush. The windmill was constructed of coral stone, approximately thirty feet in diameter and about forty feet high. The roofless distillery walls still had window openings, and numerous low stone walls remained throughout the site. Some of the distillery walls had vines growing up and over them. The site was difficult to get to, especially from Hermitage on the East End.

From the trail above the ruins, Stacy would be able to see if there had been any activity in the area. As Roy steered around the last curve, the forest that had surrounded the narrow dirt trail opened up to expose a sharp drop-off close to the trail and a view of the beach at Leinster Bay. Roy stopped the open-topped Jeep, and Stacy climbed up on the hood to get a better view of the beach. She spied a couple of boats on the shore. One boat was not moored and was rocking sideways, back and forth, against the sand. The other was a cabin cruiser that had been hard beached. As she watched, a man darted out of sight at the Annaberg ruins. She handed Roy the binoculars and asked him to take a look. Standing on his seat in the Jeep, Roy studied the boats and scanned the ruins.

"Roy, I think that we should walk down to the ruins and see what's going on. There's something odd about the way that man darted out of sight."

"I don't see anything, Stacy. What caught your attention?"

"I'm not sure, the boats look a little suspicious. And the man running behind one of the stone walls didn't seem natural. I think we should take a look. We have time. Anyway, they can't hold the meeting until we get there. Right?"

Roy cut the engine and engaged the parking brake. He didn't try to move the Jeep out of the rutted trail, such as it was, because there was a hillside to the left and sheer drop to the right. There wasn't any place to pull over. Stacy led the way down the narrow footpath to the ruins, and Roy followed a few steps behind.

Cecilia had been quiet, and the men had not checked on her since they threw her into the shack. They must have thought she was well secured. She still had not been able to free her hands but was able to move the gag up and down. Her plan was to lean against the wall with the gag loosely in place and act like she was sleeping if the men checked on her. She overheard the men talking about someone approaching and assumed it must be whoever was paying for the abduction. She quickly shifted the gag onto her mouth.

Cecilia could only see out the partially open door in the front of the shack and through the gaps between some of the planks on the wall to her right. She sat up straight and looked out one of the gaps. To her astonishment, she saw a man and a woman dressed like policemen approaching on the trail from the mountain. They were walking unhurriedly. When they were about halfway to the shack, she started yelling for help.

"Help! Help," Cecilia screamed. "They have me tied up. Help."

Stacy and Roy stopped dead in their tracks.

Roy yelled out, "Where are you?"

Cecilia yelled back, "They have me tied up in this shack. Help me."

Stacy and Roy grabbed for their guns just as the two kidnappers started shooting. Roy ran for the doorlike opening in the old distillery building about two hundred feet away, and Stacy headed for its outside wall. Bullets were ricocheting off the stone walls. Roy made a deep guttural sound and fell to the ground in the middle of the doorway. As he tried to crawl into the interior of the building, Stacy ran to help him.

The men saw one of the policemen was wounded and started to run toward Stacy and Roy while shooting. Stacy was trying to pull Roy into the doorway for protection when she got hit in the leg and rolled into the building. Using the stone doorway for cover, she took several shots at the men. They stopped running toward her and dived behind a low stone wall about 150 feet away. Stacy used the short break to drag Roy out of the line of fire.

Cecilia scooted close to the door of the shack and could see Stacy's position through the door opening but couldn't see where the two men were hiding to her left.

The wounded man jumped up and ran for a wall farther to his left but closer to Stacy. As he started to run, Stacy shot three times and hit him with one of the shots. He went down screaming, "Shit, they hit me again," and began crawling back toward the wall where the other man was crouching. Cecilia could hear one man tell the other to stay low. "We got one of dem good, and I think I got dat woman in the leg."

Stacy looked over at the shack and could barely see Cecilia in the darkness of the shack. She motioned for Cecilia to stay down.

As Cecilia, tied hand and foot, clumsily tried to move back farther into the shack, a lizard ran across her leg. She kicked her legs desperately and jerked backward to get away. Her violent moves caused the weakened rope around her hands to break. She untied her hands and then her feet. She considered making a run for the brush but realized it was too risky with the men shooting at the police. She decided to lie low behind the door and wait for a better opportunity to escape into the woods.

Stacy cautiously peeked around the edge of the doorway and saw a man and a woman running uphill from the beach trail. She assumed they were coming to help the two men who were shooting at her. She was right. Her situation was terrible and getting worse. She moved around the rubble to another window of the distillery ruins that was farther back and offered better protection.

In her new position in the distillery ruins, Stacy was no longer in Cecilia's sight. Cecilia's heart was pounding as she suspected the police were retreating and leaving her to the abductors. She didn't know Roy might be dead. She looked out the small opening of the doorway and couldn't see any movement. Again she retreated to the darkness of the shack.

The man and woman Stacy saw running into the ruins were Maroon and Isabella. They had arrived in a rented cabin cruiser and had entered the ruins just as the shooting started. As they ran toward the two men crouching behind a low stone wall, they could hear Stacy yelling she was with the park police, and they should stop shooting and drop their guns. She yelled out several times but to no avail. Maroon took a position behind the ruins of a small building near the two men, and Isabella took cover behind a large tree near the center of the ruins.

Maroon yelled over to the two men, "What the fuck is happening here? Who is that up there?"

One of the men yelled back that it was a couple of park police. "I don't know why de fuck they here. I got de man good, but there's still de woman cop in de big building. Watch out, she shoots damn good."

Maroon yelled back. "Where's Tatianna?"

The man rose up slightly above the top of the wall to point toward the shacks. Stacy saw him. She had to shoot fast but missed him, her shot ricocheting off the top of the wall next to him. He dropped back down behind his protective cover, cursing at the "fucking police."

Maroon saw Stacy in the distillery window and took several shots at her. She moved back to the other side of the window opening.

Cecilia heard the man say, "Tatianna," and knew they were there to get her.

The man who was not wounded yelled toward Maroon, "Cover me," and ran farther to the left trying to outflank Stacy. He ducked behind another of the many low stone walls in the ruins. His new position was closer to Stacy and offered him a better view of the window she was hiding behind. Maroon and Isabella went to the right and moved in closer.

Stacy maneuvered her way back to the doorway where Roy was lying. She needed to call for help and searched his belt for his radio. It wasn't there. They hadn't expected to be on patrol and left their radios in the Jeep. She cursed her stupidity and returned to the window.

Thebb and Bo were directly behind Kelsey on the trail halfway up to the ruins when the shooting broke out.

"What the hell is happening up there?" Kelsey whispered to no one in particular

"I don't know, but Mrs. Pisani is in trouble," Bart barked back. "Let's go. Let's get up there."

Kelsey began running up the trail with everyone following close behind. Just as the trail opened up into the grounds of the sugar mill ruins, he stopped, and Mike rushed forward. They were all crouching. Mike directed Thebb and Bo to go to the left; Bart and Eddie to the right; and he, George, and Kelsey would go up the middle. He told Bart and Eddie to try to get behind the shacks. "They probably have Mrs. Pisani in one of the shacks. I'll take a position at the rear and provide cover fire with my rifle." He was about 150 yards from the distillery and took a position at the outer-perimeter stone wall.

Crouching low, Thebb ran carefully and quietly to the east and took a position near the windmill on the far east side of the ruins. Bo followed closely and ducked behind a low wall about fifty feet away from Thebb. Thebb slowly crawled up the hill toward the ruins of the windmill, using the low stone wall to give herself maximum protection.

There was a lull in the shooting, and Stacy stood up in the window. "Drop your guns and come out. This is the park police. Drop your guns."

Maroon had maneuvered to a new position to the right of Stacy. When she exposed herself to yell, he took several shots. He narrowly missed her. She dropped down below the window opening. Seeing her drop down, Maroon stood up and started to jump over the low wall to get closer to Stacy when the deafening sound of Mike's .30-06 rifle was fired, and Maroon fell on the wall. He laid motionless with his legs on one side of the wall and his arms and head on the other. His gun fell out of his hand into the weeds. A small amount of blood dripped from his nose onto his gun.

Isabella didn't see that Maroon got shot. She thought Maroon had used his shotgun to shoot at the cop in the window, but she didn't remember seeing him bring it. It didn't matter at that point because she saw Thebb coming around the south wall of the windmill. She took several shots at Thebb and ran to a short wall on the west side of the windmill. She had to jump over two low walls to get to the position she wanted. It was farther away from the windmill and gave her better cover to her north toward the bay.

Stacy peeked over the sill of the window and saw Maroon sprawled across the top of a low wall. She realized someone else was out there helping her. Then a reflection of light shimmered to her right, and she saw Isabella fully exposed. With the man who had just shot at her lying dead on the low wall, she had a clear line of fire at the woman to her right. She had to stand upright to get the best angle. The unwounded man peeked over his wall and saw her standing in the window. He took careful aim and shot Stacy in the neck. She grabbed her throat and fell backward onto the grassy interior of the distillery.

Isabella yelled, "Maroon! Cover me by the windmill," but there was no answer.

Again Isabella yelled, "Maroon, give me cover. Where are you?"

Still there was no answer.

Cecilia heard Isabella calling for Maroon and realized he must be the same Maroon wanted by the Philadelphia police. There was movement behind the shack next to her. She crouched against the stone wall behind the door to hide from anyone looking in.

Bo saw Isabella ducking behind a stone wall on the other side of the windmill and took several shots at her. It was too great a distance for accuracy. His bullets ricocheted off the top of the wall, spitting chips of coral rock across the top of Isabella's head.

With the shooting shifting more to her left, Cecilia crawled over to the partially open door to see if there was an opportunity to escape into the woods. She could barely breathe as she pushed the door open to get a better view. In the distance, she could see the ruins of the stone windmill at the top on the hill. To its left, she could see Bo crouched behind a low coral stone wall. To the right she saw a woman, Isabella, behind another stone wall. She watched in horror as Isabella moved over to a corner of the wall, about ten feet to her right, rested her arm on top of the wall and took careful aim at the spot where Bo was positioned. Isabella was waiting for Bo to pop his head up to take a killing shot. Cecilia saw a movement at the south side of the windmill, above Isabella. She watched as Thebb deftly maneuvered around the windmill to get a clear firing position as Isabella was focusing on Bo's position.

Thebb was about 150 feet away from Isabella. She braced her left hand on the wall, rested her right hand with the Glock on her left wrist, took aim, and fired twice. Isabella jerked as the first bullet hit her in the chest and then dropped suddenly as the second bullet hit her in the side of her head. She fell over onto the ground, and her Walther PPK bounced off the top of the stone wall. The shooting stopped, and there was silence.

Cecilia scampered farther back into the shack in disbelief. She had just seen Thebb kill the woman behind the wall. Her impression of Thebb was shattered. She had thought of her as a quiet, shy, and passive woman. A gourmet cook. A subjugated wife or girlfriend. Someone to be protected. Not a bold, risk-taking warrior. Not the calculating person she had just seen taking an aggressive position with a gun and methodically killing a woman to protect Bo.

After experiencing her abduction by ruthless kidnappers and the painful boat trip lying in oily bilge water, she was terrified for her life. Now in the midst of a gunfight and people dying in front of her, reality was upside down. Nothing was safe. Everything around her was dangerous.

Eddie and Bart were carefully making their way behind the row of shacks in their search for Cecilia. Eddie motioned to Bart someone was inside the shack up ahead. They crawled between the shacks to a point near the door of the shack Cecilia was in. Bart covered Eddie as he darted through the door.

He found Cecilia on the floor near the back wall. He could see that her white shorts were covered with dirt, and her legs and shirt were stained with blood. He whispered, "Are you okay, Mrs. Pisani?" and reached for her hand. In the morning light, Eddie appeared to Cecilia as a silhouette. She thought at first he was one of the kidnappers. She scampered farther back in the shack, and Eddie had to assure her he was Eddie from the *DOVE*.

After a moment of hesitation, she took his hand, and they crawled back to the doorway and quickly scanned the surroundings. It looked clear. It was quiet. Eddie held Cecilia by the hand, and they started to run out the door in an attempt to reach the safety of the woods.

The remaining kidnapper carefully peeked over his wall and saw Maroon's body sprawled on top of a wall to his left. After scanning the ruins of the refinery and the low coral rock walls in front of him for any activity, he ran for Cecilia's shack hoping to use her as a hostage. As he neared the shack, Eddie appeared in the doorway with Cecilia in hand. The man stopped briefly and started shooting at Eddie. Eddie pushed Cecilia into the shack and dropped flat on the ground in front of the door. Cecilia threw herself onto the dirt floor as splinters of wood from bullet holes in the door scattered over her.

Eddie scrambled to pick up the gun he had dropped when he dove to the ground. The man again started to run toward the shack wildly firing his gun at Eddie when another resounding shot from Mike's .30-06 exploded the silence, and the man jerked forward, fell onto the clay trail, and lay still. As he hit the ground, a small cloud of dust puffed up around his body, and the report of Mike's rifle echoed across the ruins.

Eddie picked up his gun and tumbled into the shack with Cecilia. They crouched on the ground together, looking out the door at the ruins, poised to dart into the brush behind the shack.

After a long silence, Thebb, standing next to the windmill, stepped out into the open. The windmill was positioned on the highest ground, and she had a commanding view of the area. She stood still with the morning sun, low in the eastern sky, at her back. She appeared only as a silhouette holding her Glock with both hands pointed upward and close to her head. Her left hand was bracing her gun hand. She saw no movement. "Bo! Bo! Are you okay?"

"Yeah, Thebb. Are you okay?"

She yelled back to Bo, "It looks safe. I think everyone can come out."

Bo stood up and carefully scanned the area. Then Mike, George, and Kelsey appeared at the far downhill side of the ruins, each carefully watching for any motion. Bart, Eddie, and Cecilia came out from hiding.

Everyone ran over to greet Cecilia and see if she was okay. Cecilia was shaking and crying. She was almost hysterical with tears making long marks down her dust-covered face. She began thanking everyone, over and over. She kept asking how they found her.

Mike, George, and Bo began scouting the area. The man called Maroon and the woman were dead as were the two men who had abducted Cecilia. Thebb ran to the ruins of the distillery and stopped at the door, holding her gun with both hands and stepped inside.

In the dirt, just past the opening for the door, laid the body of a male park policeman. She checked to see if he was alive. He wasn't.

She carefully maneuvered past rocks and rubble to the window where the woman cop had been shot. She too was dead. Her police shirt, pants, and hair were soaked in blood, as was the ground all around her. Stacy had been hit in the left carotid artery, one of the most critical arteries in the body, and bled to death quickly. Thebb went back to the male policeman and saw he had been shot in the chest, maybe the heart. He too had died quickly.

Cecilia left the group and ran to the distillery ruins where the two park police officers had taken cover. She stood in the doorway, looking first at the dead policeman and then at Thebb who was checking him. She saw all the blood and began crying uncontrollably. The sudden relief of fear had overcome her. She sat down in the dirt with her back against the stone ruins of the distillery, crying. The tension of the whole night and her feeling of guilt over the deaths of the two policemen were too much for her. She was sobbing and saying, "If I hadn't called out. If I hadn't screamed for help, maybe they wouldn't be dead."

Thebb sat down in the dirt next to Cecilia. She leaned back against the wall and stared at the ground in front of her. She sat quietly, without emotion, and said nothing. She didn't put her arm around Cecilia or try to console her. She just sat there, shoulder to shoulder, looking at the ground between her legs. Bart and Bo approached the two women and stopped about five feet away, not knowing what to do. Bart asked several times if they were okay but got no response.

Thebb had a distant look because her mind was indeed far away. She was thinking about Joey and asking herself, *How did I get into this mess, and how do I get out?*

She was tired of having to protect herself from bad people. She was forced into situations where it was kill or be killed. *It's surreal. I've killed a lot of people. I had no choice, but they're dead. And I'm jeopardizing the safety of people close to me. Wherever I go I cause problems.* She felt terribly guilty about Cecilia's abduction and didn't know how to express her profound regret for endangering her life.

After sitting next to Cecilia for a few minutes, Thebb leaned hard against her, shoulder against shoulder, and then looked up at Bart and Bo. They were motionless, staring at her, not saying anything. She tightened her lips and began to get up. Bo saw tears in her eyes and stepped forward to give her a hug. She crossed her arms up against her chest so her gun pointed away, and gently pushed him aside. She tucked her gun into her waistband and walked around the two men over to the trail in front of the shacks all the time looking down at the ground. The others were still gathered there, planning what to do next. Bart and Bo got on either side of Cecilia, lifted her up, and helped her walk back to where the others were standing. She was devastated and still crying.

George was excitedly admonishing everyone they didn't have much time. They had to get out of there. George said if they left quickly, no one could connect them to the fracas at the Annaberg site. Mike strongly agreed and urged them to get back to the boats. Kelsey recommended that they rendezvous at Carol Bay on the east side of Cooper Island in the British Virgin Islands. It was not a popular place for boaters sailing the Francis Drake Channel, and it would provide relatively good anchorage for all three boats. They could decide what to do next once they got there.

CHAPTER 46

The three boats rafted up in Carol Bay, and everyone gathered in the saloon of the *DOVE*. The atmosphere was at once one of joy and guilt. They were joyous they were able to save Cecilia and at the same time felt guilty about the carnage at Annaberg, but Thebb felt little joy. She was devastated over the events of the last two days and felt responsible for having caused Cecilia's abduction. She stood back from the exuberant gathering, trying to understand why no one was angry with her. She asked herself repeatedly why she hadn't stepped out of her cabin and tried to stop the abductors when they first grabbed Cecilia in the saloon of the *DOVE*.

Cecilia was grateful for Bart and the crew's unwavering effort to save her and had a new respect for Thebb. George was espousing no one should feel guilty for what was not their fault. He was saying they all did the right thing. Mike added he was proud to be accepted by such an honorable group. "You were as brave as any of the Marines I served with in Nam or the Gulf," he said several times.

Cecilia asked Thebb to join her in the master cabin. She began by telling her one of the men at Annaberg was the infamous Maroon, the head of the Philadelphia drug cartel. Since he was dead, she didn't think anyone else would be searching for her. Thebb was gracious and thanked Cecilia, telling her how terrible she felt about her abduction. Cecilia countered she didn't think it was Thebb's fault, but Thebb didn't agree.

"Obviously," Cecilia reassured her, "it isn't your fault. Hopefully, now that Maroon is dead, you can put all this behind you."

As she was listening to Cecilia's reassurances, Thebb was thinking even if this Maroon man was dead, others in the cartel could still be out to get her. Worst of all was Phillip. If he learned she was alive, he would hire someone to come after her. *I'm only safe as long as I don't get discovered.*

Cecilia called for an all-hands meeting in the saloon. She wanted everyone to totally forget what had happened the last two days. It was their secret. Bart asked, respectfully, how she was going to explain her cuts and bruises to Mr. Pisani. Cecilia told everyone she would simply stay aboard the *DOVE* until they healed. "Jack has landed a huge contract with the Air Force and is going to be very busy for the next few months. I call him every few days so I don't think he will miss me for a week or two. If any bruises remain when I finally have to leave, I'll tell him I fell while trying to get into the *LT'L DOVE* when a wake hit. I want everyone to remember that," she demanded. Everyone laughed, and Thebb gave her trademark tight-lipped smile while nodding yes.

Several times during the meeting, Bo glanced over at Thebb and saw her looking sadly off into the distance. He was sure she was listening to Cecilia, but something was seriously bothering Thebb. He could see it. Cecilia could too. Thebb worked hard at not showing her emotions, but it was taking its toll.

Bart brought up the subject of home porting. He didn't want to go back to St. Thomas for a long time to come. Mike agreed with Bart and suggested that they use St. Croix as their home port. He had a house on the northwest coast with plenty of room for guests.

"It isn't very fancy," Mike said, "but it has four bedrooms, a swimming pool, and overlooks Cane Bay beach. I try not to be there too much. I'd rather be sailing somewhere so you can use it when you are in port. After all, we're pretty much family now."

Bart turned to Cecilia to ask if she would approve using St. Croix. Without hesitation, she agreed, saying Mike had a great idea. They could have the best of land and water there. Then she turned to Mike and said if he was agreeable, she could lease part of his house and use it as an unofficial base of operations. Mike agreed. He only needed one bedroom anyhow, and it would be a good idea to have the house occupied more frequently

George suggested they should hang out in Carol Bay for a few days and listen to the radio for any news related to the Annaberg event. Kelsey asked how he was going to get back to the *ANDROMEDA*. Mike volunteered to take him over to Rhode Town in the *SEA NYMPH* where he could catch a ferry back to St. Thomas.

Following the meeting, Cecilia phoned Jack and asked if he would mind if she stayed on the *DOVE* for a while. She was having such a marvelous time. Jack reminded her it was mostly her boat. She was the one who insisted on buying it, and she should enjoy herself. His new Air Force contract required that he spend some time in Washington, DC, but if he could get away for a few days, he would fly down in their plane.

The next few days were pleasantly boring. Everyone pitched in cleaning the boats and making repairs. Bo searched the *DOVE* for bullet holes and scrapes, which he repaired. Cecilia joined Thebb in cooking, and they tightened an already-strong bond of friendship.

When not cooking, Thebb helped the men make repairs and wash the decks. She admonished George for the condition of his boat and helped him wash and polish it. She used one of the rubber dinghies to get low to the water. Everyone except Thebb went swimming and snorkeling. No amount of persuasion by Bo or Cecilia could get her to put on a bathing suit or even shorts. She preferred her baggy jeans and long-sleeved denim shirts claiming she needed protection from the sun. Even though she had slimmed down, in her mind's eye, she could only see the overweight, bruised, and scarred woman she had been. Problem was her clothes were getting baggy again, and she needed new ones.

As it approached the narrow entrance to the harbor at Christiansted, St. Croix, the *DOVE* drew a lot of attention. She was a beautiful schooner, and the sailors in the harbor admired her. Bart deftly maneuvered her to an open area and dropped anchor. When he called the *DOVE's* marine agent in Freeport, he learned that he had another charter group that could be ready to depart in two weeks. It was a six-person group out of Chicago who had learned of the *DOVE* from the Koroguru Group. They didn't want as extensive a cruise as the Koroguru Group but wanted to scuba dive and sail.

Cecilia's cuts and bruises had healed sufficiently, and she made arrangement to fly back home. Everyone was disappointed to see her go as she had become an integral member of the crew. Thebb was particularly sad to see her leave.

After Cecilia had left, Thebb made more trips into the towns in St. Croix. She felt less anxious now that she had a new identity, a new passport, and a VI driver's license. It was becoming common she and Bo went off together. She occasionally joined the crew for dinner at one of the restaurants in Christiansted. When she was out alone and men showed an interest, and it was happening more frequently, she backed away. She missed talking to Joey but firmly knew she couldn't contact him. He would be the first to tell her that. She wasn't sure what her future would be but felt certain she should stay with the *DOVE* for the time being.

CHAPTER 47

With the events in the Bahamas and Virgin Islands in their past, the crew of the *DOVE* melded into a tight familial team. The crew constantly looked out for one another, especially for Thebb. They all seemed to know down deep, in spite of her stoic attitude and calm command in emergencies, she was vulnerable. She never talked about herself or spoke about her problems. Bo had simply learned to accept her reticence and not ask about her past.

In spite of the crew's cohesion, Thebb maintained her practice of eating alone before serving the others. She argued, "I'm the ship's cook, and the ship's cook doesn't eat with the crew." Thebb diligently pursued her duties in the galley and helped with sailing whenever Bart allowed her to. Bo continued to teach her everything he could. She had come to love the manual labor of hoisting the sails and manning the sheets as they came about or jibed. Bart was pleased and told her she was developing into a fine sailor.

As the months went by, Bart was finding it difficult to book new charter cruises. When he did, they sailed to Jamaica, Puerto Rico, the Lesser Antilles, and throughout the Caribbean. Chartering the *DOVE* was not a cheap proposition. It was a large, luxurious schooner that cost a lot to operate, but for those who could afford it, the trips were wonderful. Their longest trip was to Grenada, and they sailed among the Lesser Antilles for almost a month.

Jack and Cecilia Pisani held short cruises and dinners in St. Croix, Jamaica, and other Caribbean ports. Cecilia persuaded Jack not to plan any cruises out of St. Thomas, at least for a while. No one claimed to recognize Thebb since the episode in St. Maarten.

Bo and Thebb had become very close. When in port, they were routinely seen together in various small bars and restaurants along the wharfs in St. Croix and the British Virgin Islands but never in St. Thomas. On occasion, women would take a liking to Bo, but Thebb had a way of discouraging them. Bo was tall, trim, and looked the part of a roguish sailor, so it was not infrequent that young women tried to tempt him away. It was humorous to watch Bo and Thebb when that happened. Men who thought Thebb was attractive, and with good reason, found her to be an attentive listener and pleasant to talk with but unresponsive to any advances.

The crew suspected Bo and Thebb were romantically involved, but they never saw them do anything more than bump shoulders when they agreed on something. Thebb was trying not to become romantically involved with Bo. It would simply be too complicated, but she was bending Joey's rules a little bit.

Thebb now weighed a little less than she did when she got married. Her hair was long, down to her shoulder blades, and sun bleached to a golden color. Her face had fully healed. It was tanned and much thinner.

She could not admit to herself she was attractive. What she saw in the mirror was different from what others saw. She continued to wear her baggy jeans rolled up to midcalf with a light blue long-sleeved denim shirt to protect her from the sun. She added baseball caps to her wardrobe to protect her face from the sun, and, as it turned out, they helped manage her hair as a ponytail holder.

At one point, Thebb tried wearing lightweight gloves to protect her hands from the sun, but Bart ordered her to take them off when she worked with the lines, wenches, sheets, and anchor lines. The gloves could easily get caught in the lines and pull her hands into capstans. On those rare occasions when she wore a short-sleeved shirt, blue denim of course, the muscles on her arms bulged as she worked the sails or helped haul the dinghies aboard. She was becoming much stronger. Her long delicate-looking hands were no longer as soft as they once were. The salt water had toughened them up, and they became calloused from handling the lines. She had never been in such good physical shape. Sailing was helping her regain not only her natural beauty but also her self-esteem and confidence.

Thebb had become a frequent customer at some of the grocery stores in Christiansted and Frederiksted. She felt Mike had been generous in leasing them part of his house overlooking Cane Bay so she made sure to prepare nice meals for him when he was at home. He felt he had his own private chef.

On his first visit to the *DOVE* after the Annaberg incident, Jack Pisani was surprised at Thebb's changed looks and new name. When Cecilia explained to Jack, in the privacy of their cabin, "Thebb" stood for "the Big Bitch," Jack thought it was hilarious and wanted to know what she had done to earn such a nickname. Cecilia explained it was an affectionate name the crew had given Thebb because she wouldn't let them mess up the galley. She liked it so much she adopted it as her name. In fact, Cecilia had cornered Eddie to find out why the crew nicknamed Anna as Thebb. He told her only that it stood for "the Big Bitch" and then took off to adjust something. That was all she could get from the rest of the crew.

When Jack and Cecilia were aboard the *DOVE*, Cecilia and Thebb spent hours together. They shopped at the local markets seeking various exotic foods to prepare gourmet dishes. They never brought up the past. Ever! It was a forbidden area of conversation.

On occasion, Jack and Cecilia would mischievously invite single men, almost always engineers from Wright Patterson AFB or scientists from the Department of Energy Mound Laboratories in Miamisburg, on their cruises in the hope they might strike up a relationship with Thebb. That really pissed off Bo, but there was nothing he could do. Cecilia was oblivious to just how close Thebb and Bo had become because of their extreme caution on the boat, especially when she was aboard. And when she was there, she unintentionally usurped most of Thebb's time.

Cecilia thought she was doing the right thing in trying to be a matchmaker, but it wasn't working. One guest pulled Cecilia aside and asked for help in getting to know Thebb better. He said she was not only beautiful but exceptionally bright. He had spent about an hour with her, sitting on the forward hatch cover, drinking a martini, and explaining the aerodynamics of a new aircraft he was designing. He said she showed interest and asked very insightful questions. He never had a date or girlfriend do that before, and he wanted to breech the invisible wall of separation she built around herself. Cecilia explained, "Thebb is simply a shy and private person. You have to work on your approach on your own."

CHAPTER 48

Almost a year had passed since Annaliese had died in that terrible traffic accident. Joey had been in a stupor ever since. At first, he felt guilty for being so distraught over her death. He thought he was being disloyal to his wife who had passed away just a few short years before he met Anna. Then he began to accept how much he missed Anna. His thoughts constantly drifted to the great times they had playing shooting games together. He reminisced about the wrestling matches where she had to maneuver a stronger opponent to a position so she could shoot him. Then there were the times they enacted and reenacted scenarios where she had to protect her weapon from being deflected or taken away.

Joey realized he could have been in love with Anna and she with him. But he wasn't sure. He had nothing to do with Anna's death but agonized over the thought he might have prevented it. She was in trouble when she came to him. Maybe if he had alerted the police, things would have turned out differently.

For a long time, Joey was plagued with the thought Anna's husband had orchestrated her death. She had told him many times her husband wanted to kill her and might have hired someone to do it. On several occasions, she mentioned someone was following her, and she had to take evasive routes to get to the gun shop. Apparently, Phillip had told her he would never let her get a divorce. She would die before he would let that happen.

It never occurred to Joey to ask why her husband wanted to kill her. Joey just assumed he hated her. Everything detectives Finney and Sloan had said about her husband's lack of concern about her death implicated him in some way. Joey couldn't get it out of his mind.

Over time, Joey let his business slip. Not that it was that much to start with. He hadn't promoted it with advertising, and the interior of his shop had become dusty and unkempt. He had few customers and lots of time to mope and indulge in self-pity. But he still had to eat and occasionally went into town to shop.

One day, while in the Cumberland Farms grocery in Norristown, he heard a thump, like someone getting hit in the chest, in the next aisle. It was instantly followed by the screech of a grocery cart's wheels moving sideways over the floor, followed by a woman's voice crying. It sounded like someone had grabbed a grocery cart to keep from falling. His attention aroused, Joey listened carefully and heard the muffled voice of a man threatening someone.

"Don't you interrupt me when I'm talking to one of my friends," the man said. "Just shut up and listen. Who the fuck do you think you are? Nobody gives a damn what you have to say. Just shut up and do what you're told. Understand?"

A woman's voice answered, "I'm sorry, Jim. I didn't mean to interrupt—"

Her voice was quivering, and she stopped talking mid-sentence. Joey heard the screech of the grocery cart's wheels again and the man telling the woman to just shut up, saying he was late for a meeting. Joey pushed his cart around to the next aisle to see who the man and woman were.

He was startled to see they were well dressed. The man wore a tailored suit, expensive-looking shoes, and a high-end wristwatch showing from beneath his French cuff. The woman had a stylish hairdo, expensive diamond jewelry, and also wore a tailored suit. She was slightly overweight and had a red bruise on her right cheek and a blue-black bruise close to her left ear.

Joey had a flashback to Anna and what she looked like when he first met her. Anna wore fashionable and expensive clothes, and she drove an expensive Mercedes sports car. The bruises looked all too familiar.

As Joey watched the couple, the man grabbed the woman by the arm and forcibly pushed her out of the way of the cart. As he pushed her out of the way, she cried out, "Oh, please, Jim, you're hurting me."

She had been wiping the tears from her right eye and hadn't seen him turn the cart around and head toward the checkout area.

Joey left his cart behind and followed the couple out of the store and into the parking lot. He hung back about fifty feet as they approached a bronze-colored BMW sports car with the top down. The man pushed the woman against the side of the car and hit her hard in the chest with the flat of his hand while saying something Joey couldn't hear. Joey walked up as the man was squeezing his grocery bag into the limited space behind the passenger's seat.

"Excuse me, mister," Joey called out.

The man turned around and looked at Joey, dressed in jeans, brown work boots, and a wrinkled shirt. "What can I do for you?" the man asked in a pleasant and friendly tone.

Joey was somewhat unnerved by the man's sudden change in demeanor and asked, "That's a beautiful car you're driving. What model is it?"

"It's an M-series BMW roadster. You like it?" the man asked with a smile and obvious pride in his car.

"Absolutely," Joey replied. "I've never seen that bronze color before. But the important question is, do you like it?"

"Oh yes, it's new and gets a lot of attention," the man stated.

"Well yeah, but it's a shame you're not going to able to enjoy it anymore," Joey said forcibly.

"What the hell are you talking about? What's this all about?"

With the woman staring up at him from the passenger's seat, and the man looking down at him, Joey said, "I called the police on my cell phone. They will be here in a few minutes to arrest you for assault and battery on this woman."

The man glared at Joey for a moment and started to walk around to the driver's side of the BMW while saying, "You're fucking nuts. Get the hell out of here."

As the man was opening the door to his sports car and about to get in, Joey said, "It's a felony to leave the scene of a crime. If you leave, the cops will chase you, and you'll be in a lot more trouble than just the assault charge."

The man stopped, shut the car door, walked over to Joey, and shouted, "There's no goddamn assault hero. This is my wife. I was just making a point. She's not going to say anything about it. Got that? Who the fuck do you think you are anyway?"

"It doesn't matter what she says. I saw you do it, and I'm an actual witness. I'm going to tell the cops what you did, and they are going to arrest you. You got that? And say good-bye to your car. You'll need the money for a lawyer."

Just as the man was moving closer to Joey, saying, "You dumb little son of a bitch, I am a lawyer. I ought to—," he looked up to see two police cruisers pulling into the parking lot and heading toward them.

The cops immediately separated the man and the woman, taking them over to separate police cruisers to question them. One cop took Joey's statement, and Joey promised to testify if needed.

The man was arguing with the cops and telling them he didn't hit his wife, but the cops kept asking him how she got the bruises on her face. The woman was crying and had her head down, embarrassed by the circumstances of being questioned.

Before leaving the scene, Joey walked over to the police cruiser where the cops were questioning the woman and told her, "This is your opportunity to change your life. Don't back away from your problem by trying to save him. He'll just continue to hurt you." Then he went back into the grocery store and finished shopping. He didn't need much living alone. As he got into his pickup truck, he saw that the woman was back sitting in the passenger's seat of the bronze BMW with her head down, and the man now had all the cops around him. He started up his truck and drove away.

On Joey's way home, it hit him. It was an epiphany. He should go back to the police force. Facing a woman in the same situation as Anna had been in opened his mind. He was asking himself why he hadn't done more to help Anna. He was feeling guilty and decided he had to do something to make amends with his conscience. The only thing he had ever really liked doing was being a cop, and he was good at it. The captain at his old precinct had said he understood why Joey resigned, and the department would take him back anytime. It was difficult to recruit good policemen, and Joey would require only a minimum of retraining to get up to speed. The next morning, he went to the police department to sign up.

—

After he completed his refresher training, Joey bought a small two-bedroom, one-bathroom house in a blue-collar neighborhood near his new police station. He couldn't bear to sell the gun shop so he sold as much of his inventory as he could and boarded up the building. He asked the captain if he could partner up with his old buddy, Bob Marino, who was working in a different precinct. The captain explained it wasn't an option because Bob had been promoted to the rank of detective, and Joey was a uniformed street cop. But he was willing to help Joey get on a fast track to becoming a detective if he wanted it. They needed more detectives, and Joey's previous experience would count a lot.

Joey and Bob Marino had been good friends before Joey's wife died. But after Sandy died, Joey disappeared. Bob and other friends lost track of him when he bought the gun shop and moved out of town. After he returned to the police force, Joey contacted Bob, and they began to get together frequently for beers and dinners at Bob's home. Bob's wife, Christi, who was an attorney in a firm that specialized in business law, enjoyed Joey's company and decided he needed a girlfriend. So at several of their dinners, Christi invited single friends and introduced them to Joey. She also finagled invitations for Joey to parties hosted by her friends and business associates. At one such party, Joey met Rachel, a young trial lawyer, and they began dating.

Nine months had passed since Joey had joined the police force and they had been relatively calm months in his precinct. There were the occasional robberies, domestic disturbances, and traffic violations. However, things were about to change.

For several weeks, during the routine morning briefings, the captain frequently discussed a series of violent and potentially deadly robberies in the south side of the city. The police suspected the robberies were committed by the same three or four men, possibly members of a new gang. The captain warned the gang was extremely dangerous and wanted all the officers to be on the alert.

The gang had been robbing liquor stores, and Friday nights were their preferred hit time. Two policemen had been wounded in the latest shoot-out after they challenged the criminals. Both policemen were in the hospital. One of them was wounded so seriously he was in critical condition. There were indications the gang might move to other areas because of increased police patrols on the south side.

It was late Friday afternoon when Joey and his partner, Ned, were cruising their assigned area. Ned was about twenty-two years old and very much the rookie. Joey was a twelve-year veteran of the force before he reenlisted, so although he was officially a rookie, he was in fact highly experienced.

As they approached the west end of a strip mall on a main highway, a young woman drove her car toward them, flashing her headlights, and frantically waving for them to stop. She pulled alongside the cruiser and excitedly told Joey and Ned four men had just entered the Liquor Emporium, at the other end of the mall, and were robbing it. She explained she had dropped her keys on the floor of her car and had bent down under the dashboard to search for them when she heard the men walk by talking about where the safe was and not to shoot anyone if they didn't have to. When she sat up to peek out the bottom of the windshield, she saw them drawing their guns inside the store. Joey thanked the woman and told her to get out of there.

"Ned, I know this mall," Joey said. "The liquor store sales are almost all cash transactions, and a lot of money is on hand Friday nights. The store has a rear entrance and a concrete loading platform for delivery trucks. Drive around the block on the back side of the mall and drop me off at the convenience store on the other side of the street. I'm going to go in and get something and then go to the back of the liquor store."

As they drove around the block, Ned asked, "Shouldn't we call for backup?"

"Let's get in position first. This may be that gang that shot the cops last Friday. After you drop me off, sit there until I call you on the radio. That should take only a couple of minutes."

Ned excitedly asked, "So when do I call for backup?"

"After I give you the go-ahead, radio for backup. Tell the dispatcher to have the police units approach quietly and go to both the front and back of the store. Then drive around to the front of the mall, turn on your flashing lights and siren, and drive straight toward the front doors to the liquor store. Try to block the doors with the cruiser. Get out of the car and use the bull horn to demand the robbers drop their guns and come out with their hands up. Use the car to protect yourself. Tell them police are on either side of you and they can't escape. Be authoritative."

"Geez, Joey," Ned responded, "where are you going to be? What do I do if they come out shooting, and the backup units haven't arrived yet?"

"Shoot back!"

Ned pulled up to the convenience store. Joey ran in, quickly grabbed two large bottles of liquid dish detergent, tossed a twenty-dollar bill on the counter, and ran out. He sprinted around to the back of the mall and up to the loading dock behind the liquor store. He opened the bottles of liquid detergent and poured the liquid over the concrete platform in front of the door. He jumped off the platform, crouched behind a parked pickup truck, and called Ned.

"Okay, Ned. I'm in position. Radio for backup and go around to the front."

Ned did as planned and drove up to the front of the store with his red and blue lights flashing and the siren blaring. He jumped out of the cruiser with the bull horn and demanded that the robbers come out unarmed. He could see them running behind displays and looking out the front window at the cruiser. Ned continued to demand they drop their weapons and come out with their hands up. As he spoke, he could hear sirens in the distance coming toward the mall. He thought he had told them to approach quietly. The robbers ran toward the back of the store. Ned called Joey and told him they were heading his way.

The back door swung open, and the men ran out. The first one slid forward with his arms and legs flailing, dropping his gun on the platform. He fell on his butt, twisted sideways, and tried to grab anything before falling off the loading dock. Two men followed and slid into the first, falling forward. One of the two men did a foot-swinging dance trying to get his balance and grabbed onto the other to keep from falling. But they both fell forward, over the edge of the platform, and landed on the asphalt parking lot. Their guns flew off to either side, spinning around and bouncing down the steps at the side of the platform. A fourth man saw what was happening and tried to stop but was too late. His momentum carried him onto the platform. He grabbed desperately onto the door handle to keep from falling and dropped his gun which bounced off the platform before he fell on top of the first man and rolled onto the other two.

With his Springfield XD drawn, Joey approached the pile of men squirming on the ground demanding that they not move and yelling they were under arrest. (Joey preferred the Springfield XD because the grip safety had to be squeezed before it could be fired and was safer in a scuffle than other pistols. The drawback was it had a shiny top slide.) He was alert to see if a getaway driver was nearby.

Joey radioed Ned he had four men under control and to come around quickly to help. As he lifted his thumb off the talk switch, a black SUV careened around the corner and accelerated directly toward him. Joey turned and aimed his pistol at the driver. The driver slammed on the brakes and skidded to a stop about ten feet from him. The driver sat there for a moment staring down the barrel of Joey's gun and then at the four men in a pile. He started to back up, but Ned had pulled the police cruiser up behind him, and he couldn't get out of the parking lot.

The driver jumped out and took off running at a full sprint down the side street. A moment later, a siren sounded, and another police cruiser cut him off. The two cops in the cruiser nabbed the driver, and Joey and Ned arrested the four men who were trying to rob the Liquor Emporium. The crooks were complaining that Joey had made them slip and slide and threatened to get even with him. Within minutes, three other police cars arrived and assisted Joey and Ned.

The manager of the Liquor Emporium came to the rear door. Ned warned him not to come out on the loading dock. The manager had blood running down his face from a blow delivered by one of the crooks. Joey asked him if he was okay. He said he thought so. Ned asked him if he had a hose to wash down the loading dock.

When the assisting cops learned what Joey had done with the dish detergent, they began laughing and congratulating him on his innovative capture. One cop told the crooks he liked their slick escape route. Another cop taunted them that he was pleased to see they were coming clean. Ned got the hose and washed off the platform. The other cops took the robbers to the police station to be booked.

Off to the side, a man was standing totally still with cash in his left hand watching the whole scene in amazement. One of the cops approached him and asked who he was and what he wanted. The man said he was from the convenience store across the street and wanted to give the policeman his change. Then he pointed to Joey. Joey walked over, thanked him for his concern, and told him to keep the change.

The police chief awarded Joey and Ned commendations for their arrest of the notorious liquor store gang. He also agreed to recommend that Joey take the detective exam as soon as he felt ready. He didn't expect to hear Joey say, "Next week would be great."

Within two months, Joey was a detective. He and Bob persuaded the captain to pair them up as partners. Over the next year, they worked well together and received outstanding ratings for their performance. While they had made some breakthroughs in making arrests for several murders and a couple of robberies, they had not been assigned to any high-profile, city-wide crime problems. Joey liked it that way. He had more time to adjust to being a detective and having a girlfriend.

Over time, Bob's wife, Christi, and Joey's girlfriend, Rachel, became good friends. They were in each other's company a lot because Joey and Bob were so close. Additionally, both were lawyers, albeit in different lines of work. But their personal interests diverged markedly. Christi liked tennis, reading, cooking, and generally was attracted to less-active recreational endeavors. Rachel was into sky diving, swimming, hiking, camping, and other outdoor activities.

Joey was having a difficult time keeping up with the younger and more energetic Rachel, but he tried hard. He began taking Rachel to the police pistol range and had an ongoing schedule for teaching her to shoot. Rachel was grateful for the opportunity because she was a trial lawyer and worked with some violent people. She realized the importance of being able to defend herself and began carrying the snub-nosed .38-caliber revolver Joey had bought for her.

Rachel became reasonably accomplished with the revolver, but she didn't have the instinctive feel for shooting Anna had. Joey thought Anna was the best natural shooter he had ever seen, and he had worked with a lot of policemen at the department's range. Her eye-hand coordination was flawless. That wasn't something you could learn; it was something you had to be born with. Joey had not told Rachel about his own private shooting range in the tunnel. For that matter, he hadn't told Bob either. The range had become a private remembrance of Anna.

Rachel had been trying for some time to get Christi and Bob to join her and Joey on a diving trip. She had been enthusiastic about learning to scuba dive and finally was able to talk everyone into taking lessons and getting certified. Rachel was surprised Christi agreed to take scuba lessons since she wasn't that athletic. But Christi had been a swimmer in college and had for a long time wanted to go diving in the Caribbean. She just hadn't said anything about it. The lessons went well, and they did their open-water certification dives on a shallow wreck off New Jersey. They all had a great time.

Over dinner one evening, after they were certified, Christi proposed they schedule a diving trip to the Buck Island Reef National Monument off St. Croix in the Virgin Islands. Her swimming instructor in college had mentioned the park to her class. It was one of the best places in the Caribbean for novices to snorkel and scuba dive. The park was supervised, had a plethora of reefs and fish, and was not too deep.

"Let's have dinner next Saturday night, and I'll show you the information I have on the park," Christi offered. "We can start planning for the trip then."

CHAPTER 49

Almost three years had passed since Thebb left Philadelphia. No incidents had occurred after Annaberg. Other than the Koroguru Group, Bart was able to secure only a few charters each year. He suspected the economic downturn in the United States had put a damper on bookings. Jack Pisani, because of increased business commitments, was not using the *DOVE* very much. Cecilia, on the other hand, had formed a bond with the crew, especially Thebb, and visited often, usually when the *DOVE* was in St. Croix and the crew had the run of Mike's house.

As time went by, Thebb had become less nervous about having her identity uncovered. Cecilia had continued to subscribe to the *Philadelphia Inquirer*. No additional coverage of the drug cartel appeared after the big splash that Maroon Espidito had been killed in a shoot-out with the park police in the Virgin Islands. The Philadelphia police had evidently given up on ever finding the elusive "cartel accountant" who was last known to have been in New York. With the lack of newspaper coverage, Cecilia felt Thebb was safe from the violent drug cartel. Thebb's main concern was being identified by someone she or Philip knew back in Philadelphia. As time went by, it seemed less likely. She believed she had successfully assumed a new identity, and no one was actively looking for her.

The crew particularly looked forward to the annual Koroguru Group visits. The men loved to help sail the *DOVE*, and their charters were not really work for the crew. They were more like get-togethers with old friends. Thebb and Janna Williams had forged a friendly relationship, and Janna frequently accompanied Thebb on shopping trips when they were in port. She was an attractive woman and a sharp dresser. She tried more than once to get Thebb to update her wardrobe and buy some feminine-looking clothes. But Thebb had always declined, explaining she needed protection from the sun on board the *DOVE.*

A few days before the end of the latest Koroguru charter, Bart docked in Road Town, Tortola, so the guests could do some shopping. Thebb took the opportunity to get some fresh vegetables at the market. Janna accompanied her to look for exotic foods not available in Chicago. While on their shopping excursion, Janna told Thebb the group was planning a beach party on Ginger Island the next day, and she very much wanted Thebb to go swimming and snorkeling with her. To her surprise, Thebb agreed and bought a proper bathing suit. Proper by Thebb's standards was quite conservative. Janna tried unsuccessfully to talk her into a more fashionable suit. It didn't really matter. Thebb looked great in the suit she selected.

After anchoring close to shore on the southwest beach of Ginger Island, Thebb, Janna, and the other two women spent the morning preparing for the party. The men readied the dinghies and snorkeling equipment. When Thebb appeared on the deck in her new bathing suit, Bo and Bart stopped what they were doing to comment on her finally wearing something other than her trademark jeans and denim shirt.

Bo complimented her, "Jesus, Thebb, you look great. Why the hell haven't you gone swimming with us before?"

Thebb felt self-conscious and blushed, saying, "Bo, you're embarrassing me."

Eddie started yelling to Rick who was preparing the launch, "Hey, Rick, you gotta see this. Thebb's in a bathing suit."

The good-natured teasing went on for a few minutes before Eddie looked at Bo and said, "Hey, Bo, you think we should get Kelsey on the radio and have him join us?"

Bo glared at Eddie and went back to work on the dinghy. He didn't think Eddie's remark was funny. He viewed Kelsey as a competitor for Thebb's attention. Thebb liked Kelsey and spent a lot of time with him when he was around. Bo couldn't understand why. She was obviously closer to him and he intended to make their relationship more personal very soon. *Long enough is long enough*, he had been thinking.

Bart, who was adjusting lines behind the helm, commented, "I already invited him."

"Captain, I thought this was supposed to be a private party," Bo stammered as he stood up.

When Bo addressed Bart as "captain," Bart knew he strongly disapproved of inviting Kelsey.

"What! You got some damn problem?" Bart challenged. "I was talking to him on the VHF, and he said the *ANDROMEDA* was anchored over at the Rocks. It's just across the channel so I told him to come over if he had time."

The beaches on the southwest side of Ginger Island were wide, bright, and desolate. It was an excellent place for Thebb to get used to wearing a bathing suit again. Her legs no longer had the broad bruises and scrapes she was so self-conscious about, but they were definitely not tan. Her figure had returned, and for the first time in years she felt attractive. Her only problem was the good-natured kidding she was taking from everyone. Everyone except Bo, who couldn't stop admiring her. In her new bathing suit, Thebb became the center of attention.

Janna asked Thebb to walk down the beach with her. She stopped after a short distance and told Thebb, "If I had known you were going to attract all the attention, I wouldn't have suggested that you get a bathing suit."

Thebb blushed and asked, "So you think I look okay?"

"Are you kidding? You look great. Is that why you're always wearing baggy jeans? You don't think you look good?"

"Well, yeah! But you . . ."

Thebb stopped short in her sentence as she heard Billy Moffet calling out, "Hey, there's a sharp-looking sailboat coming toward the beach. It's under full sail."

It was the *ANDROMEDA*. Kelsey anchored near the *DOVE*. He and his crew rowed their dinghy ashore waving bottles of wine and holding a basket of food.

As Kelsey came ashore, he saw Thebb and yelled out, "Holy shit, Thebb. Is that you?"

Bo walked over to Kelsey and asked, "Do you accept every invitation you get?"

"Are you kidding, Bo? You think I'd miss a beach party with you guys. You have the best food in the islands," Kelsey answered with a smirk. "Besides, look at Thebb."

Just then, Eddie saw that one of Kelsey's crew was a young woman and asked, "Who's this?"

Kelsey introduced Donnie June, his newest crew member. Donnie June was a twenty-three-year-old, blue-eyed brunette with a degree in environmental studies from Texas A&M. She spoke with a distinctly Texas drawl which became her. Kelsey took it upon himself to introduce her to everyone. With Kelsey spending most of his time with his new crew member, Bo felt him less a threat for Thebb's attention.

After two days at Ginger Island, Thebb learned the lesson of moderation in exposure to the sun and went back to her jeans and denim shirt attire. But the genie was out of the bottle, so to speak, and she began to think about buying some shorts and halter tops.

The Koroguru Group's charter was ending, and Bart needed to sail the *DOVE* back to Christiansted so they could catch their flight to Chicago. Billy Moffet and Akiya Megumi took turns at the helm until they approached the narrow channel leading into Christiansted Harbor. When the *DOVE* was just outside the channel, Billy, Akiya, and Craig lowered the sails, and Bart motored in. If the current was running or the wind was blowing from the wrong direction, the *DOVE* became difficult to maneuver in the narrow channel, requiring Bart's full attention.

As he entered the harbor, Bart found the commercial slips were fully occupied. The only space available for him to anchor was in front of Fort Christiansvaern, a yellow brick fort built by the Danes centuries ago on the east side of Christiansted. With the open waterfront and the yellow fort as a backdrop, it was a beautiful anchorage, but it required ferrying the charter guests to the city docks in the dinghies, something Bart didn't like to do.

When Bo and Rick ferried the Koroguru Group ashore, they found Cecilia and Mike waiting for them. Cecilia was down for a week's visit. Mike was having a party the next evening at his Cane Bay house and wanted everyone to attend. A lot of well-to-do folks from the island would be there, and he expected it to be a fun get-together.

CHAPTER 50

St. Croix, US Virgin Islands

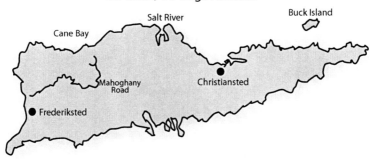

With the *DOVE* anchored in front of Fort Christiansvaern, Eddie had to ferry Thebb over to the city docks and drop her off. She needed to restock some of the supplies depleted during the Koroguru charter. Eddie had to return the Zodiac right away in case Rick had to use it to go ashore to buy parts for servicing *L'DOVE* or the engine of the other Zodiac.

Thebb took a portable VHF radio and told Eddie she would call him to get the groceries in an hour or so. She was going to stay ashore and meet with Cecilia later in the morning. They planned to do some shopping together. Cecilia was intent on convincing Thebb to buy some shorts, blouses, and a dress for the party. She was unaware Thebb had bought a bathing suit a few days earlier and might actually be amenable to upgrading her wardrobe. Several

—

single men were invited to the party, and Cecilia wanted Thebb to be in appropriate attire.

In her self-proclaimed role of relationship facilitator, Cecilia was planning to take Thebb to some of the most upscale boutiques in Christiansted and pay for Thebb's new clothes. She had assumed as a ship's cook, Thebb had a limited budget and would not be able to afford the kind of apparel she had in mind.

After gathering the needed groceries, Thebb went to the city docks to call Eddie on the portable VHF. She had two large bags, one of which she put down on the concrete finger pier next to the only empty slip on her right. She held the remaining bag with her left arm. After calling Eddie, Thebb clipped the portable VHF back on her belt. She looked up to see a man in a fourteen-foot Boston Whaler, with a small outboard motor, approaching the docks from the east.

The wind was blowing from the east, and Thebb could see that the man was uncomfortable handling the small boat with both a following wind and current. He attempted to maneuver into the empty slip, but the wind carried him past it. The current didn't help either, and he obviously didn't have a reverse gear. He hit the outer piling of the finger pier with the port bow and drifted past the dock and into the harbor proper. As he tried to gain control of the small craft, he used too much throttle and spun his Whaler in a small circle, ending up pointed away from the dock and toward the moored sailboats. He cut the throttle and sat perplexed for just a moment.

Thebb called out, "Can I help you?"

"Yes, this boat won't do what I want. It seems to be heavy in the back end, and I can't steer it."

"Come back this way, against the current at a very slow speed, and lay your starboard bow on the piling. Then use the piling to hold your boat against the current and pivot around and into the slip."

"Which side is starboard?"

"The right side."

The man followed her good-natured coaching as he maneuvered into the slip.

"Throw me a bowline, and I'll tie you down."

The man scooted forward, found the coiled bowline, and tossed it up to Thebb. She caught it in midair with her right hand without putting down the bag of groceries. Using only her right hand, while standing erect, she flipped the line around the dock cleat, making a figure eight knot. Then she continued to spin the remaining line into a loose coil next to the cleat to keep it out of the way. The man stood in his boat, watching in amazement as Thebb secured his boat in the slip using only one hand.

"Be careful standing in a small boat," Thebb admonished lightheartedly. "You don't want to slip and fall."

"Oh yeah! Thanks, miss," the man said.

"Be sure to tie off the stern and the port bow so it won't bang against the dock."

As the man was tying off his port bow, Eddie motored up to the tip of the finger pier. He threw Thebb a line, and she repeated her earlier performance, flipping the line around the dock cleat at the end of the finger pier with one hand while standing. She had practiced the technique many times while killing time on the *DOVE* and had become proficient at it. While standing, she couldn't tie a proper under curl to make the bow-tie cleat hitch, but the crisscross loops were more than adequate for temporarily docking a dinghy. The Zodiac swung around in the current and wind against the tip of the finger pier. The man in the Whaler watched intently.

Thebb reminded Eddie she was supposed to meet Cecilia in a little while, and when they had completed their shopping, she would call him. She handed Eddie the groceries and went to have a cup of coffee in the patio of the waterfront deli and wait for Cecilia. The man asked Eddie who the woman was and said he had never seen anyone so adept at boating. Eddie told him her name was Thebb, and that she was a crew member of the schooner anchored in front of the fort. The man turned to look for the schooner, and when he turned around, Eddie had untied the dinghy and was motoring away.

The street entrance to the deli was an arched narrow hallway with exposed, weather-worn brick covered with purple bougainvillea vines. The hallway wasn't very long, perhaps ten or twelve feet, but seemed longer because of the rough stone walkway. Just past the walkway, there was a rusty wire-mesh rack with small stacks of newspapers, some new and some left over from other readers. Thebb picked up an old issue of the *VI Daily News* to read while waiting for

Cecilia, who was usually stylishly late. She ordered a cup of coffee and selected a small table under the overhanging banyan tree. It was a clear morning, and the fifty-foot-high banyan, actually a giant ficus, shaded most of the patio from the tropical sun. As she tried to read the paper, which covered mostly island events, the sturdy breeze made the paper flap, and she had to fold it several times to gain control of it.

"Hi! Excuse me! Thebb? I want to thank you for helping me this morning," the man from the Whaler said as he approached Thebb. She was still wrestling with the unruly paper in the breeze and didn't see him walking up.

Thebb was surprised to have someone she didn't know call her by her name. She turned and looked.

"I'm sorry I startled you," the man apologized. "Your friend in the rubber boat told me your name. I wanted to thank you. If you hadn't coached me on how to get into the slip, I would still be out there turning circles in the harbor."

"Did you get your boat tied up safely?" Thebb said while calming down.

"Yes! But I've never seen anyone handle a rope as well as you did. Have you been boating long?"

"Sailing," Thebb corrected in a pleasant tone. "And it was a line. Not a rope," she teased.

"Sailing?"

Thebb tightened her lips in her expression of a smile and said, "Yes, sailing. I'm a sailor, not a boater."

"Oh! Ouch! How rude of me. I didn't introduce myself. I'm Jim Thornhouser, and I'm not even a boater. May I join you for coffee? I need some after my exemplary demonstration of inept boating techniques."

"Well okay, but I'm expecting someone momentarily, and I'll have to leave when she gets here," Thebb cautioned.

"That's fine. I've got to pick something up at the hardware store and get back to the ship before it leaves."

"I take it you are not very familiar with boats."

"Actually no," Jim responded. "They don't normally let me handle the boats, but this trip was inside the harbor so I guess they didn't think I could get into any trouble. Boy, what they don't know."

Jim's self-depreciating manner almost caused Thebb to laugh, something she normally didn't do. She decided that she liked this fellow. He was a bit thin, about an inch shorter than she was, and looked to be about twenty-eight or thirty years old. He was very attractive and oddly ill at ease while talking with her. The men she had been around the past few years had been aggressive, self-assured, sometimes intimidating, and completely at ease when talking to a woman. Jim seemed to be intellectual, self-conscious, and uncertain of himself.

"So how is it that you go to sea on a ship and don't know how to handle small boats?" Thebb asked.

"I don't normally go out to sea. I'm a biologist, and I study worms." Jim responded. "There is a new species—"

Thebb was just taking a sip of coffee when Jim said he studied worms. She coughed slightly, almost spitting her coffee out on the table. "Did you say . . . you study worms? In the ocean?"

Watching Thebb's reaction, Jim asked, "You don't like worms?"

Jim looked hurt, and Thebb was trying to determine if he was putting her on. She decided he was enjoying her surprise and disgust. She didn't want to be rude so she decided to go along with his ruse.

With wide eyes and the hint of a smile, she answered, "Actually NO! Whatever made you want to study worms? It sounds disgusting."

"Well," Jim explained, "worms are simple organisms that can be used to gain an understanding of more complex life forms. It just happens a new species of ice worm caught my interest, and it's in the ocean. It's a pink polychaete worm called *Hesiocaeca methanicola* and lives on methane hydrate ice on the ocean floor."

"But, Jim, there is no ice here in the Caribbean. The water temperature is over 80 degrees Fahrenheit."

Jim had captured her interest. Thebb realized he wasn't kidding when he said he studied worms.

"And besides, if I remember correctly, methane is a gas, not an ice," Thebb continued, while thinking nothing he was saying made sense.

Jim was delighted to have her attention. He continued, "Thebb, down on the ocean bottom, at depths of two to five thousand feet, the water is actually quite cold. At those depths, the water pressure is great, and the combined low temperature and high pressure provide the right conditions for methane gas and water to combine together to form an ice-like substance called methane hydrate.

"When oceanographers drop a grabbing device, like an orange peel sampler, down to the ocean floor and bring up a block of methane hydrate, it looks like a chunk of ice. It's really a wonderful substance. Sitting on the deck of a boat, methane hydrate dissociates into methane gas and water in a ratio of about 180 to 1. And the gas can be ignited with a match. It's been estimated that the worldwide reserves of methane hydrate could provide more energy than all the other fossil fuels combined many times over. That includes oil, coal, and conventional natural gas. It's really neat stuff!"

Thebb interrupted, "And the little pink worms live in the hydrate stuff?"

"Yeah," Jim continued. "And that's why I'm interested in them. They were first discovered in 1997 in the Gulf of Mexico in about two thousand feet of water. Not much is known about their life cycle yet. They live off either methane gas in the hydrate or bacteria and slime on the surface of the ice."

"So, Jim," Thebb asked while leaning a bit forward on the small table, "if they discovered the worms in the Gulf of Mexico, why are you here in St. Croix?"

"Well, it was a matter of opportunity. A group of oceanographers is going to be studying several sites south of Frederiksted. It's an unusual area for methane hydrate because of the steepness of the shelf where they found it. They have a deep submergence vehicle with robotic arms and specially designed containers for retrieving samples of the hydrate. The containers can maintain the high pressure needed to keep the hydrate from dissociating into water and gas as they retrieve it. I had some research funding from my university I could contribute for the operation, and they invited me to participate. I got a substitute to teach my classes, and here I am. I'll be diving to two or three thousand feet to study the worms."

"You're going to do the diving?" Thebb asked in amazement.

"Yeah! You might say I'd go to any depth to study worms," Jim answered with a mischievous smile.

"You're actually talking about a submarino, aron't you?" Thebb frowned. "Is it one of those little two- or three-man submarines?"

Jim was about to tell her about the submarine when Cecilia entered the deli. She was dressed in white short-shorts, her favorite teal-colored golf shirt with the white emblem of the *DOVE* embroidered above the left breast, and white canvas boating shoes. Her hair was pulled back into a French braid, and she looked much younger than her actual age. When she saw Thebb having coffee with a man in the patio, she hesitated for a moment and debated if she should interrupt them. Thebb having a conversation with a new man was a first as far as Cecilia knew. But her curiosity overcame her logic, and she barged right in and sat down across from Thebb.

Without waiting to be introduced, Cecilia announced herself, "Good morning. I'm Cecilia Pisani. And who are you?"

Jim introduced himself. Before he could continue, Thebb interrupted and explained to Cecilia that Jim was in St. Croix to study little pink worms in blocks of ice on the ocean bottom. She did it with a twinkle in her squinted eyes and her tight-lipped smile. Both Jim and Cecilia stared at Thebb. Jim was trying to decipher Thebb's facial expression to determine if she was ridiculing him or teasing.

Cecilia was thinking Thebb's statement was audacious, but she had never seen Thebb be rude. After a pause, both Cecilia and Jim started laughing. Then Cecilia asked Jim what he really did and why he was in St. Croix. Another long pause. Jim said he really did study little pink worms in ice on the ocean bottom, and he was in St. Croix aboard the research vessel *RV LAFOURCHE* out of New Orleans.

Cecilia looked at Thebb then Jim and said, "Jim, you absolutely have to come to our party tonight. No one will believe us when we tell them about your project unless you are there to explain it all."

Jim said he would be delighted to come to the party, but the chief scientist was moving the ship out of Christiansted Harbor that afternoon for an anchorage on the south side of Frederiksted. "The oceanographers will be getting ready to get on station and begin their research dives the next day."

"You must have a tender or dinghy?" Cecilia questioned. "Once your ship is anchored why not motor over to Frederiksted, and we can have someone pick you up and take you back after the party? And if you like, invite your oceanographer friends to come along. We'll have plenty of food. Our folks can meet you at the foot of the long concrete pier in Frederiksted at 1800. Here's our phone number at Cane Bay. You absolutely must come. But now, Thebb and I have to leave. We have some important shopping to do."

"But wait," Jim asked, "what's 1800?"

"It's 6 p.m.," Cecilia responded, looking at Jim with a frown.

"Are you sure you will have enough food?"

"Certainly! If need be, we'll cook more. See you tonight."

Thebb and Cecilia visited several high-end boutiques in Christiansted, and each purchased dresses, sandals, shorts, and blouses. Some of them matched. That evening, they wore their similar sun dresses, sandals, and identical French-braid hairstyles. They looked like sisters, except one was tall, blond, and reserved; and the other was shorter, brunette, and vivacious. But they were both attractive and were a hit among the mostly male guests from the island and the *LAFOURCHE*.

Bo was at first delighted to see Thebb in her new attire. After the other male guests started congregating around her, he became irritated and stood off to the side. Cecilia was a bit disappointed too. Her crowds were smaller than Thebb's, and although she was older and married, she thought she should still have been more competitive than she apparently was.

The real hit of the evening was Jim Thornhouser and the scientific crew from the *LAFOURCHE*. He brought three oceanographers with him, and they enthralled the other guests with their stories about their submarine and methane hydrate. Although Jim was somewhat shy, his self-effacing portrayal of his research gained enormous interest. He used a minimum of scientific terminology and even explained the significance of finding methane on the bottom of the ocean. Jim and his colleagues obviously enjoyed their hosts at the party and invited Mike, Thebb, Cecilia, and the crew of the *DOVE* to tour their research vessel.

Bart was late in arriving at the party. He had charter business to attend to before he could leave the *DOVE* in the hands of Rick, who had security duty. When he arrived, he apologized to Cecilia for being late. He explained he was detained because he was negotiating with their marine agent to take on a new two-week charter. It was a group of eight fashion executives from New York, and they wanted to sail and dive around the British Virgin Islands. He agreed to pick up the charter group in three days in Charlotte Amalie. Cecilia told Bart about their invitation to tour the *LAFOURCHE*, which was anchored south of Frederiksted, and asked if there was any way they could do it before picking up the new charter. She suggested in the morning they sail the *DOVE* around the west end of St. Croix and anchor next to the *LAFOURCHE*. They could tour the ship and then set sail for Charlotte Amalie.

Cecilia was impressed with the scientists from the *LAFOURCHE* and wanted to tour their ship. Although she had been around her husband's scientist friends, they were mostly into airplanes. She had never met any oceanographers. They seemed to be more hands-on with their work and quite a bit more rowdy. She also wanted to keep Thebb in the company of Jim Thornhouser.

Bart agreed the proposed schedule could work and ordered the crew to be prepared to hoist the anchor and set sail about 1000.

CHAPTER 51

As the plane approached St. Thomas, Christi nudged Bob and pointed downward out the window. "Look, Bob, you can see Culebra, Puerto Rico, and St. Thomas all at once." Rachel got out of her seat and leaned over Bob to look at the sights below.

"Wow," Rachel exclaimed. "Look at the color of the water. It's so blue. It's—"

Rachel wasn't able to complete her sentence as the flight attendant announced that everyone must be seated with seat belts fastened. In a few minutes, they would be in Charlotte Amalie.

Their plans called for them to spend two nights at the Bolongo Bay Resort on the south side of the island and then fly to St. Croix for diving on the Buck Island Reef. They toured St. Thomas and dined at several of the best restaurants. But after two days of tourist-type activities, Christi was anxious to get started diving and convinced Bob, Joey, and Rachel that they should take the early morning ferry to St. Croix instead of flying later in the day.

"It will be great," Christi enthused. "It's a catamaran hull, and you won't get seasick. Catamarans have two hulls and are a lot wider than single hull boats so they ride smoother. Besides, we'll have a beautiful view of the island from the sea."

The ferry was indeed a catamaran and was capable of speeds up to forty miles an hour. When they arrived at the terminal for the eight-thirty departure, they learned mechanical difficulties would delay their departure by about a half hour.

"Not to worry," the ticket agent announced. "It's a minor problem, and everything will be okay."

Joey could overhear another passenger complaining that the damn thing never ran on schedule. He didn't know why he made an effort to get to the terminal on time.

Joey asked the other passenger, "These mechanical problems won't affect safety will they?"

"No," the man said. "It's usually not a mechanical problem anyhow. It's mostly that they run on 'island time,' but they'll try to make up the time on the way over. Do you need to get to St. Croix in a hurry?"

"No," Joey replied. "We have plenty of time. Just curious."

"Are you a tourist or here on business?" the man inquired matter-of-factly.

"Oh, we're just diving tourists," Christi interrupted, bubbling with excitement. "We're going diving at Buck Island."

"Great choice. I go there often with the family. You'll have a good time, but be careful of the sun. It's quite intense down here you know."

The ferry was twenty minutes late in leaving, and the captain was able to make up for lost time. When St. Croix came into view, they all went forward to the port bow to see the island from the sea. The wind blew the women's hair about wildly, but the view was so awesome everyone stayed to watch the ferry enter the harbor.

As the ferry approached the channel to Christiansted Harbor, the captain slowed the vessel down only slightly and turned into the channel. To his surprise a large sailboat was entering the channel at the other end. If he hadn't been late in leaving for St. Croix, and trying to make up lost time, he would have paid more attention and waited outside the channel until the sailboat passed. But he was already in the channel and had to slow to an idle speed, or less, and try to squeeze by. The catamaran had a wide beam but a shallow draft so the captain thought he could make it past the approaching schooner without going aground. Hopefully, the captain thought, the sailboat won't be too wide. As they got closer, he realized the schooner also had a wide beam. He commented to his first mate, "This is going to be hairy."

CHAPTER 52

The morning after Mike's party at his Cane Bay home, the crew of the *DOVE* were having a tough time getting up early to prepare for their morning departure. With all the attention Thebb had received at the party, Bo had felt disenfranchised and drank too much. There was no excuse for the others who also drank too much. They were just having fun. Thebb had only one glass of wine. Cecilia had too many. Thebb anticipated everyone would be slow in the morning so she got up early and made a light breakfast for everyone except Bart, who had returned to the *DOVE* to relieve Rick on the night security watch.

After breakfast, the crew returned to the *DOVE* and went about their business preparing for departure. They had to secure the dinghies and *L'TL DOVE* and get other things shipshape. Cecilia convinced Thebb to wear her new short-shorts and canvas yacht shoes for the occasion. She gave Thebb several of her prized teal-colored golf shirts with the *DOVE* logo on them and emphasized that she wanted to make a good impression when they visited the *LAFOURCHE*. She wanted everyone to appear highly professional for the scientists.

When Thebb went topside wearing her new outfit, a white ball cap and her long blond hair in a ponytail, the crew stopped what they were doing and started making comments about who the new crew member was. She smiled a little, flipped her ponytail, and went forward to help Rick. She was on deck without her traditional jeans and denim shirt. This was a sea change in her attire. It also showed off her lithe figure which was by then, if anything, a bit on the slim side.

As she approached the bow, Rick exclaimed, "Damn, Thebb, you look great. You need to dress like this more often."

"Thanks, Rick, but I think it's causing a commotion back at the helm."

Thebb heard and felt the familiar shutter of the diesel engine cranking over and Bart giving the order to hoist the anchors. When the anchors were up, Bart slowly motored the *DOVE* into the channel. Thebb helped Rick secure the anchor locks as she had done many times before.

As they finished securing the anchors, Rick looked up and yelled, "Oh shit! This is going to be a problem. Look at what's coming."

Thebb stood up and saw the big St. Thomas ferry coming toward them. It took up most of the channel. Rick turned to warn Bart, but he had already seen the ferry entering the channel above wake speed. Thebb stood watching the ferry approach and noted the four passengers on the port bow who didn't seem to recognize the impending danger. She thought about yelling a warning for them to get back from the bow when she realized one of them looked like Joey.

It had been so long since she last saw Joey, and she had wanted to see him so desperately she couldn't believe her eyes. She stood frozen in place and watched closely as the two ships approached each other. Rick yelled at Thebb to brace herself because if they hit the ferry, she could be thrown overboard. But Thebb couldn't hear Rick. She was mesmerized with the thought of seeing Joey and stood erect, holding the bow stay line and watching the ferry approach. As the ferry drew closer, she realized that it really was Joey. She stood motionless, gaping, not believing her eyes, ignoring the danger. It was happenstance they were passing close to each other on two separate ships in the Caribbean after almost three years.

The ferry captain blew his air horns and slowed to a controlled drift. Bart shifted to neutral to slow the *DOVE* down. He was trying not to collide with the ferry and steered as far to starboard as he dared. The *DOVE* had a deep draft, and he had to be careful not to run aground. The ferry, with a shallow draft, did the same.

As the two boats approached each other, port bow to port bow, with only four or five feet of space protecting them from collision,

Thebb stood motionless staring at Joey who was now only about eight to ten feet away. She broke out into a smile, a big smile. As the ferry slid ever so slowly by, Thebb turned and walked toward the stern of the *DOVE*. She was staying directly abreast of Joey and his friends as the ferry drifted past. Her smile broadened.

Bob grabbed Joey's arm and whispered, "Who's that girl smiling at you, Joey? She's gorgeous!"

Joey, without taking his eyes off Thebb, whispered back, "I don't know, but you're right, she's unbelievably gorgeous."

Rachel, in a louder voice, demanded, "Joey, who is that woman?"

"I don't know?" Joey slowly answered in a questioning voice.

"What do you mean you don't know?" Rachel again demanded. "She seems to know you. She can't take her eyes off you, and she's smiling at you."

As Thebb approached the stern of the *DOVE* with an open smile and her teeth showing, Eddie looked up and said, "Bart! Bart! Look at Thebb. She's smiling at those people."

"Eddie, I'm trying to steer us clear of the ferry," Bart replied. "Don't bother me now." But he glanced over to see Thebb standing at the stern looking at the people on the ferry.

The two boats drew abreast of each other, stern to bow and bow to stern, with Thebb at the stern of the *DOVE* and Joey at the bow of the ferry. Thebb, in her white shorts and teal golf shirt, was standing still with her ponytail blowing across her shoulder smiling at Joey. As the ferry and the *DOVE* continued to slowly glide past each other, Joey turned and began to walk toward the stern of the ferry in order to stay abreast of the woman on the sailboat while not taking his eyes off her. They were still only eight to ten feet apart and locked in one another's gaze, Joey walking and Thebb standing still at the stern with a big smile.

Rachel turned to Christi and asked if she knew who that woman was. Christi could only say she wished she looked like that. Rachel, Bob, and Christi began walking toward the stern, following Joey.

When the boats had separated, and the distance between them was increasing, Joey watched, almost in a trance. The woman on the sailboat stuck her right hand out with her forefinger pointing at him and her thumb sticking up. She was using her hand to simulate a pistol and then clicked her thumb down to simulate firing it at Joey.

Thebb turned and literally bounced toward the entrance to the saloon with her smile seemingly locked onto her face. Cecilia was on deck, standing next to the entrance to the saloon, and Thebb almost collided with her. When she saw the huge smile on Thebb's face and the bounce in her step, she moved aside and let her pass. Bo was at the starboard gunnel and watched the whole scene unfold. He couldn't fathom what was going on. He watched Cecilia staring at Thebb as she descended the stairs into the saloon.

Cecilia bounded down into the saloon, skipping steps, following Thebb, and asking what was happening. "Who were those people, Thebb?"

Thebb nonchalantly responded, "They're just some tourists I was being friendly with. Who knows, they might be interested in chartering the *DOVE* if they see we are friendly."

"Oh no, Thebb," Cecilia challenged with a smile. "You're not getting away with that answer. I've never seen you smile like that before. Something else is going on here. That was a really happy smile. Tell me what it is. Tell me."

"It was just a case of mistaken identity," Thebb said, trying to defuse Cecilia's interest. "I thought one of the guys was someone I had known in the distant past. That's all." And with that answer, she went to her cabin; and Cecilia went topside, shaking her head all the way.

Inside her cabin, Thebb sat bouncing on her bed with excitement. She was happy to have seen Joey but dismayed he didn't recognize her. She had wanted to call out to him, but he had lectured her to never give away her identity if she wanted to disappear. And she didn't know who those other people were with him. She considered the possibility he actually did recognize her but acted like he didn't. He did, after all, walk back to the stern of the ferry to stay next to her as the two ships passed each other. But maybe he didn't. After all, her appearance had changed dramatically, and it had been a long time since he last saw her. And if he didn't recognize her, she decided, it was a good omen because others probably wouldn't recognize her either

As she sat pondering the possibilities and consequences of having seen Joey, Bo knocked on her door and told her that they were rounding the west end of St. Croix, and the *LAFOURCHE* was in sight. She came out of her cabin, and she and Bo went topside.

CHAPTER 53

As the ferry approached the dock, Joey stayed at the stern watching the sailboat leave the channel and turn to the west. He stood there with his friends watching him. He was transfixed by the sight of the woman on the big sailboat and couldn't figure out why. He was asking himself the same question his friends were. *Who was that woman?*

The cab took Joey, Rachel, Bob, and Christi to the Chenay Bay Resort on the east end of the island. Christi had chosen that resort because the individual West Indian-style cottages with red roofs were situated near the beach with close proximity to the Buck Island Reef where they were going scuba diving. After checking in, Joey and Bob immediately opted to have a beer under the umbrellas next to the pool, while the girls went for a walk on the beach. The hot, bone-white, sugar-fine sand shifted between their toes as they walked under the palm trees that arched out over the beach. They marveled at the beauty of Buck Island. It was separated from St. Croix by deep-blue water with occasional patches of reef breaking the surface near the Buck Island shore.

Rachel was upset Joey wouldn't admit to knowing the woman on the sailboat and repeatedly asked Christi if she knew who the woman was.

"I really don't know," Christi insisted. "She was very attractive though."

"Well yeah," Rachel said, showing her irritation over Christi's apparent lack of concern. "She was damn attractive, but who was she and why won't Joey admit to knowing her?"

"I don't know. Maybe she smiles at everyone to get customers for a charter or something. Maybe she's their version of a live and animated bow maiden. From what I've been reading, most of the large boats down here charter, and she certainly got our attention."

"Bow maiden? What's a bow maiden?"

"It's the carved statue of a woman the old sailing ships had attached to their bows. I'm sure you've seen pictures of them. It helped to identify the ship. And I suppose the sailors thought it brought them luck. They were pretty superstitious back then."

"Come on, Christi, she wasn't some live impression of a statue, and she didn't smile at everyone. She didn't smile at me. She didn't even smile at Bob. She smiled at Joey. Didn't you see that?"

"Rachel, are you implying there's something wrong with Bob?"

"No, Christi, dammit! I just want to know why Joey is so secretive about that woman."

"You know, Rachel, I've known Joey for a long time, and I don't think he would deliberately not tell you if he really knew who she was. Why would he deny knowing her? I'll ask Bob tonight if he knows anything about the woman. But come on, let's talk about the diving we are going to be doing in the morning. I can't wait to get into the water. Look how clear it is."

After a second round of beers, Joey and Bob were beginning to relax, taking in the whole resort scene from the pool to the bright white beach.

"Joey, that girl on the sailboat was gorgeous. Who was she?" Bob asked.

"I don't know. I really don't," Joey answered quizzically. "I've been asking myself that question ever since we saw her. As handsome as I am, I don't usually have good-looking young women smile at me for no reason."

"Yeah, you're right. You're not that good-looking."

In the morning, after breakfast, Christi led her group of novice but enthusiastic divers to meet with their dive guide and check out the scuba gear. Christi was anxious to get started and annoyed at the amount of time the guide was taking explaining sun safety. After looking his new clients over, the guide told them when they were not in the water they needed to wear long pants, long-sleeved shirts, and a full brim hat to protect them from getting sunburns. Not one of them was wearing appropriate clothing.

The dive guide refused to take them out on the boat until they had the proper apparel. Rachel was in an irritable mood and complained the sun couldn't be that dangerous. She balked at having to go back to her cottage to get additional clothing. She said she could just wear sunscreen, and that would protect her. The guide took issue with her impatience and explained the sun was not only dangerous but could ruin their holiday if they didn't take him seriously.

Rachel was having a hard time believing she could get a sunburn using sunscreen. But they all went back to their rooms and dressed according to the dive guide's requirements. On the way back to the dive shack, Joey defended the guide saying he didn't think the guide had any reason to tell them to wear more clothes other than to be helpful. Rachel was still angry about the woman on the sailboat and only responded with a "whatever."

As they motored out to the reef, there was a cool breeze. The women elected to disregard the guide's advice and stripped down to their bathing suits. The men did the same. With the sun bearing down on them from above and reflecting upward from the water, it wasn't long before they had too much sun for the day. By late morning, their dive guide insisted they put their clothes back on and return to the resort. They were already turning pink and had to cover themselves with calamine lotion. After lunch, their bodies demanded they stay out of the sun so they decided to tour St. Croix instead. Rachel desperately needed a broad-brimmed hat so they went shopping in Christiansted before proceeding on to the western part of the island.

While touring Frederiksted on the west end of the island, Christi excitedly pointed out the sailboat they had almost hit anchored near a strange-looking commercial ship a mile or two offshore.

Joey didn't sleep well that night. In the morning, his lack of sleep showed, and Rachel was worried he was badly sunburned. She complained he tossed and turned all night. But all that was forgotten when their dive guide joined them at the breakfast table with plans for the day's diving. The guide was pleased to see they had brought lightweight long-sleeved shirts and pants and were wearing wide-brim hats. He teased them about their refusal to follow his directions the previous day and suggested they would now have more faith in his admonitions. Everyone agreed they would listen more carefully.

Both Joey and Rachel fell in love with diving in the clear waters around Buck Island. Everything else was forgotten as they scrambled to get prepared for their next set of dives. Their diving guide assured them they had plenty of time to dive during their vacation. He had also convinced them not to try to get a suntan too quickly, so shopping became their next favorite activity. Rachel and Christi left the men on several occasions to do more shopping at the jewelry stores and unique boutiques in Christiansted.

While shopping, Rachel and Christi couldn't help themselves and asked various shopkeepers if they knew a young attractive blond woman on a large sailboat that left the harbor a few days earlier. They tried to give a good description of the woman, but, of course, the answer was always the same. Large sailboats were common in St. Croix, and all of them had young attractive women on them. It didn't occur to them to ask at the local grocery stores.

Several days later, while shopping in Frederiksted, Joey and Bob left the women and walked on the beach. Joey was curious to see if the large sailboat was still anchored offshore. It wasn't.

CHAPTER 54

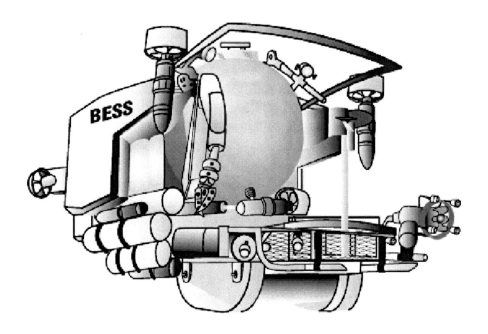

After leaving the Christiansted Harbor and the near collision with the St. Thomas ferry, Bart hoisted the sails and caught the following wind toward the west end of St. Croix. The *DOVE* rounded the western tip of the island, and they sailed southeast to join up with the *LAFOURCHE*.

The sight of the 130-foot schooner under full sail, with top sails waving, caught the attention of everyone aboard the *LAFOURCHE*. They all found places to watch as the crew of the *DOVE* dropped the sails and anchored about a half mile inshore of their research vessel.

Watching the precision of the *DOVE*'s crew engendered considerable admiration for their seamanship.

Thebb, Cecilia, and the crew took *L'TL DOVE* over to the *LAFOURCHE*. Bart opted to stay aboard the *DOVE* for security watch. He had anchored in relatively deep water and was concerned he didn't have enough scope on the rode.

Aboard the *LAFOURCHE*, the scientists delighted in explaining the function of the deep-diving submersible, and the ship's crew seemed equally happy to show off the inner workings of the ship itself.

The *LAFOURCHE* had an exceptionally high bow with all the ship's superstructure forward of amidships, leaving a long low-deck aft. It didn't have the sleekness of a sailboat or the stateliness of a cruise ship. The bridge was almost as far forward as the bow and had observation wings that extended out past the width of the hull. Some sort of smaller control center appeared to be attached to the starboard wing of the bridge that made it look out of balance with the rest of the ship.

The aft-half of the ship had a flat deck with a large, heavy-duty A-frame crane on the rear and a lighter-duty A-frame crane on the starboard side. A submersible vehicle with a large acrylic sphere sat under the large A-frame crane. The acrylic sphere was six feet in diameter and was the actual pressure hull, which housed the vessel's controls and space for two scientists. Its two large manipulator arms with claw-like pincers gave it the look of a cycloptic, crablike creature sitting on skids. Behind the acrylic sphere was a metal frame with several large yellow spheres and propellers of different sizes pointing up, back, and to the side. On each side, the submersible was emblazoned with the letters "BESS."

The *BESS* was capable of diving to the lower reaches of the mesopelagic zone, about three thousand feet deep. The scientists explained at that depth the submersible had to withstand pressure of approximately 2,900 pounds per square inch of surface area, and the spherical shape made it ideal for dispersing high pressure uniformly.

The wall of the sphere was made from six-inch-thick pentagonal pieces of acrylic plastic fused together under great pressure to form a perfect orb. The design was an excellent choice because it provided the pilot and passenger a panoramic view of the underwater world,

---

side to side and top to bottom. Their line of sight was always orthogonal to the inner surface of the sphere resulting in a view without surface reflections. They seemed to be floating free in space, except it was water, not air. Other diving submersibles had only a hemispherical window that provided a more limited view of the surroundings. Some had hemispherical domes on top that denied a downward view. And extremely deep diving submersibles had only small conical windows that could withstand the severe pressure of the abyss.

In addition to the two main manipulator arms and pincers, the front of the submersible had several large xenon lights, a camera system with lights on a smaller manipulator arm, and various sample baskets.

Under the smaller A-frame crane was a yellow boxlike vehicle with mechanical arms and pincers that folded tightly into spaces on the sides of the main body. Its front was dominated by a clear hemispherical window that housed a large camera lens. The boxlike device was a remotely operated, deep-submergence vehicle loaded with lights and cameras. It was used for research, but its most important purpose was to help retrieve the *BESS* should it ever become disabled on the bottom.

To the sailors on the *DOVE*, the *LAFOURCHE* with its submersible cargo was a uniquely unusual ship. It was very clean and well kept but lacked grace. Its form seemed to be dominated by its intended function.

Bo, an experienced diver, was thoroughly engrossed in the technical aspects of the *BESS* and the diving operations of the *LAFOURCHE*. The chief scientist invited him to sit in the pilot's seat within the sphere. He entered the pressure hull through the hatch located at the top of the sphere, and the chief scientist joined him. He showed Bo how to operate the manipulator arms and pincers and explained all the switches and gauges. Cecilia and Thebb were standing with their backs to the *BESS* listening to Jim Thornhouser explain how he hoped to use the submersible when Thebb jumped forward with a low scream and almost knocked Jim down. Bo was using the manipulators to gently nudge her. Everyone was laughing, except Thebb. She was glaring at Bo.

—

Cecilia asked Jim if the name BESS was in honor of someone special. Jim explained that research submersibles were generally named for technical capabilities. In this case, BESS stood for Benthic EcoSystem Surveyor. And the remotely operated vehicle, or ROV, under the starboard A-frame crane was called a DSRV because its main purpose was as a Deep Submergence Recovery Vehicle. Both Thebb and Cecilia began laughing, and Cecilia asked if she needed to learn a new language to converse with the crew of the research vessel.

"That's pretty much true," Jim responded. "Scientific research vessels are a lot like sailboats I suspect. Everything has a special name. I once read every line or rope on big sailboats has a specific name."

Jim wanted to get Thebb alone to talk to her. The best he could do was to have both Thebb and Cecilia together under the starboard A-frame. He explained to Thebb at the last moment his graduate-student technician had to cancel out of the cruise. The graduate student's wife was pregnant and having some medical problems. That left him without any support to help process his samples and prepare them for study back at the university. After explaining what he needed, he asked Thebb if she might be able to help him.

"Jim, it's nice you would think I might be capable of doing scientific work, but I have responsibilities on the *DOVE*. I can't leave the crew without a cook. Besides, you work with worms, and I don't know anything about them."

Cecilia interrupted, "Jim, how long would you need her?"

Thebb glared at Cecilia as Jim responded, "About two or three weeks, but it wouldn't begin for about three weeks. My research time is not scheduled to begin until the chief scientist completes his first round of bottom surveys."

"The timing is perfect," Cecilia said emphatically. "Thebb, have you forgotten? As soon as the next charter is over, in two weeks, we're putting the *DOVE* into dry dock for a month for service on the hull. It's been over three years since we did a complete bottom cleaning and maintenance on the shaft seals. While the *DOVE* is laid up, you can help Jim. It should be a lot of fun."

—

After a long silence with Thebb staring at Cecilia and then Jim, she said, "Well, Jim, I guess I can help you after all. But I've never worked in a laboratory, much less a laboratory on a boat. And I have definitely never worked with worms."

Jim explained he would teach her everything she needed to know. Then he thanked Cecilia. He was appreciative of Cecilia's support.

It was late afternoon by the time they had finished touring the research vessel. As they were departing the *LAFOURCHE*, Cecilia invited the scientific crew over to the *DOVE* for cocktails and dinner. The chief scientist accepted the invitation for the scientific crew, and Bo asked if he could stay aboard the *LAFOURCHE* for a while and learn more about the deep-diving operations. He would return with the scientists when they went over for dinner.

Cecilia noted the furtive glance of concern Thebb gave Bo as she climbed down the ladder and boarded the dinghy for the trip back to the *DOVE*. She also noted Bo's very slight nod. It was clear that Thebb was looking out for Bo. For the first time, it dawned on Cecilia a lot more was going on between Bo and Thebb than she had previously realized. *If they have a relationship, they're hiding it quite well. That would be damn hard on the DOVE.*

However, Cecilia couldn't determine the exact nature of their feelings. She realized Bo was very protective of Thebb. He seemed to always be near her if the situation seemed precarious. And they usually went ashore together and frequently visited bars in the harbor areas together. *But did they really visit bars? All evening? And Thebb didn't seem to be much of a drinker.* She also noticed that although subtle, Thebb seemed to delight in teasing Bo whenever an opportunity presented itself. On the other hand, Thebb steered clear of other personal friendships with men. The exceptions had been the continuing relationship with Kelsey Bohansen, captain of the *ANDROMEDA*, and, now maybe, Jim Thornhouser. Cecilia dismissed her thoughts and suggested to Thebb they work together in the galley and prepare a special dinner for the scientists from the *LAFOURCHE*. She felt certain the cook on the *LAFOURCHE* couldn't match their skills.

That evening at dinner, Bo offered his services to the scientific crew while the *DOVE* was dry docked. The chief scientist accepted his offer, telling him they could always use extra help, and several spare staterooms were available. An experienced diver could be a great help in deploying and retrieving the sub.

Thebb was overjoyed Bo would be helping the submersible crew. She had mixed feelings about working on the *LAFOURCHE* and lamented Cecilia had been so forceful in suggesting she could help Jim Thornhouser. She liked Jim but felt uncertain about working in a laboratory. Having Bo there would help her feel less threatened.

CHAPTER 55

Rachel, Christi, and Bob returned to Philadelphia after their diving vacation in St. Croix overly tanned, actually burnt, but relaxed and ready to go back to work. Joey, on the other hand, was tired. Very tired. He had not slept well during the entire vacation. He kept waking up in the middle of the night with a dull stuffiness in his head and felt tired during the day. Even so, he tried to make sure Rachel had a great time. Rachel knew something was wrong. When they returned home, she confronted him, asking if he was unhappy with her. She told him he seemed preoccupied during their time in St. Croix. A few days after returning, while having morning coffee in the deli next to the precinct station, Bob mentioned that Rachel had confided in Christi she was worried Joey had lost interest in her.

"No. It's not Rachel, Bob. I've got to tell you, I was having trouble sleeping and was thinking a lot about the young woman we saw on the sailboat down in St. Croix. It's like I know her from somewhere, but I don't know where. I can't get her out of my mind."

"Hey, let it go," Bob admonished. "That was a freak occurrence, and it doesn't mean anything."

"I don't know, Bob. Something was very unusual about that woman. I can't put my finger on it. It's driving me crazy. I think I know her, and it's haunting me. It's as if there's something very important about her I have to know. As weird as it sounds, I've been thinking about going back down there and see if I can find her."

"Boy! You're one sick puppy. A pretty young thing smiles at you for a few seconds, and you want to go chase her down? I shouldn't tell you this, but Rachel and Christi asked around about her when we were down there. No one knew her. If she was a local, then surely someone would have known her. How could they not? She was great looking. She was on a private yacht and probably just passing through. She could be on the other side of the world by now. Maybe it was her first trip on a sailboat, and she was just excited about being on the boat."

"Rachel and Christi were asking about the woman on the sailboat? Why were they doing that?"

"Because Rachel became very concerned when you insisted you didn't know her. She thought you were hiding something from her. Frankly, Joey, it caused all of us to suspect you really do know the woman, and you have some ulterior motive for not telling us. When they found that none of the shopkeepers knew her, Rachel calmed down. That is, until you started having trouble sleeping."

"She knew I was having trouble sleeping?"

"We all did, sport," Bob laughed. "I tried to help you out by saying I thought the woman reminded you of your wife, and you might still be having trouble letting go. She was kind of blond and thin too, right? You need to get a grip on yourself. I think you still haven't gotten over Sandy getting shot in that bank robbery."

They sat quietly for a few minutes with Joey staring at his coffee cup and Bob watching him. Then Joey broke the silence, "You know, I hadn't thought about it that way, but you're probably right. Why didn't I think of that? Subliminally, I must be remembering Sandy. She had a beautiful smile, like the woman on the sailboat."

Joey calmed down and laid his thoughts to rest. That evening, he apologized to Rachel for having been a poor companion during the vacation and started to sleep better. But after several days, he had trouble sleeping again and began waking up in the morning feeling groggy. He had a recurring dream about someone on a boat. Thinking about his dream had become an obsession. He had to take long showers in the morning to wake up and get ready for work. He seemed to always be tired.

Then it happened. While standing under the hot shower, he began to think again about the young woman on the sailboat. He analyzed the entire event, every little detail, moment by moment, piece by piece. He was remembering how the two boats had to squeeze past each other in the narrow channel, and how she walked along the deck of the sailboat to stay opposite him. He remembered her smiling directly at him. He remembered her ponytail blowing over her shoulder. It was as if she had known him in the past, and this was a reunion.

Then he remembered her standing on the stern of her boat as it got farther away and how she made a gesture to him. It was an odd gesture. It wasn't exactly a wave of hello or good-bye, but more a gesture of personal recognition. It was kind of like the gesture kids make when they are playing cops and robbers. It was the gesture of firing a gun.

Suddenly, the realization came over him like an electric shock. He stood frozen in the hot water. A chill ran up his spine. The hair on the back of his neck tingled. He started mumbling, "The gesture was that of a gun! The woman on the sailboat was Annaliese Mueller!"

"HOLY SHIT," he shouted, slamming his fist against the shower walls and stomping his foot on the floor. "Holy shit, it was Anna," he continued to shout without realizing how loud he was yelling.

When he got to work, Joey told Bob he needed his help on an old case. He suspected something was wrong with the case in which a woman, by the name of Annaliese Mueller, was killed in a traffic accident. He needed to check it out. He explained he had known the woman, and he now suspected she wasn't the one who was hit by the truck about three years ago. If it wasn't Annaliese Mueller, then something was seriously fishy.

At first, Bob resisted, telling him they didn't handle traffic accidents. They were criminal and homicide detectives. He tried to convince Joey if the victim wasn't the person listed, her relatives would have filed a missing person report, and the whole thing would have been resolved by now.

"But, Bob," Joey demanded, angrily, "if the dead woman wasn't Annaliese Mueller, then who the hell was she and where is Mrs. Mueller now? I simply want to look into the case to see if all the facts line up correctly, and I want you to help me."

Joey was determined to investigate the case. He was going to do it with or without Bob's help. Joey had been acting odd for the past few weeks so Bob gave in hoping it would put an end to Joey's funk.

Joey remembered detectives Finney and Sloan had covered the case and had questioned him about the gun permit. He used the police directory to see if they were still with the department and which precinct they were in. Fortunately, they were still around, both working in the same precinct.

Not to arouse suspicion, Joey told Finney that he was investigating another case that might have involved the woman and asked to see the file covering the traffic accident. Finney remembered the case because of the grizzly nature of the accident and because he didn't normally cover traffic fatalities. He said there wasn't much to tell other than the woman had been hit by a truck, and her body and face had been ripped apart. He remembered her husband identified the body at the site. That was kind of unusual, but the husband had heard about the accident on the radio and went to the scene right away.

"Do you have a file on the case?" Bob asked.

Finney retrieved it from one of the file cabinets that lined the hallway wall. As he opened it, he remembered the police photographer had taken a lot of pictures of the scene and the mangled body. As he flipped through the file, he saw that a few days after the accident the husband had questioned the police because the woman's wedding ring and watch had not been returned. The husband had claimed the ring was quite valuable. The report stated the jewelry was probably lost sometime between the removal of the body from the accident scene and the funeral.

"That wasn't too unusual," Finney explained. "But it was unusual the husband didn't make any further inquiries about the jewelry after the police told him it was lost. Usually people throw a fit over lost personal items. Anyhow, after the initial investigation, I wasn't involved in the case any longer."

"Do you have a place where Detective Marino and I can sit and study the case file for a while?" Joey asked.

"Sure," Finney answered. "I'll have our secretary over here show you to our conference room, such as it is."

The secretary, as Finney had described her, was actually a rookie cop in uniform. She took Joey and Bob to a small dilapidated room with a shabby table and six well-worn metal chairs with cracked plastic cushions. Most of the light for the room came from a small barred window. Otherwise, the room was bare. Only dirty walls. The rookie cop nonchalantly leaned against the door frame and asked, matter-of-factly, if she could get them some coffee. Bob replied it was kind of her to offer, and they would indeed like some coffee. When she returned with two cups, she asked that they be careful not to spill the coffee or mar the surface of the table. Looking at the table, Bob could see hundreds of rings from previous coffee spills and realized her comment was deliberately facetious. He smiled back at her.

Joey spread the contents of the file on the table. There were several investigative reports and many gruesome photos. Bob was diligently reading the reports while Joey was alternately studying the photos and looking out the window, deep in thought. Joey kept returning to two particular photos and holding them in several positions to catch the limited light from different directions.

He got up and asked the rookie cop for a magnifying glass. She gave him a round magnifying glass with a short handle. He looked at it and asked if there was a sink where he could wash the lens. After cleaning the lens, he went back into the conference room and studied the photos carefully.

Joey suddenly grabbed Bob's arm. "This woman is not Annaliese Mueller!"

"Are you sure?" Bob replied, incredulously. "How can you tell?"

"Look here in this photo. Take the magnifying glass and look carefully. Look at her arm and hand. What do you see?"

"Well, the arm and hand have a lot of blood on them. It looks like she doesn't have a wedding ring," Bob cautiously answered. "It's hard to see her ring finger because of the blood and the position of her hand. But that doesn't mean anything, Joey. She could have taken the ring off or a bystander could have stolen it before the police photographer got there. It doesn't mean anything."

"It was an expensive ring with a big diamond in it, Bob!"

"Still it doesn't mean anything, Joey! There are a lot of possible reasons for her not to be wearing her wedding ring."

"But she's not wearing it. Right?"

"Okay, I give you that. The evidence is she's not wearing a wedding ring. What else?"

"Now look at this other photo. Look at her arm and tell me what you see."

"What am I supposed to be looking for, Joey?"

"Look at the watch."

"It's hard to see. It's partially covered by her shirt and a lot of blood, but it looks like it's a gold-colored watch with a gold band."

"Look carefully, Bob," Joey demanded. "Is it a Rolex?"

"No! I don't think it is. It's a nice watch though."

"Annaliese Mueller wore an expensive gold Rolex with four diamonds in it. Someone would have had to remove her Rolex and replace it with this other watch while the crowd was milling around. I don't think that would have been possible."

"I don't know, Joey. She could have decided not to wear her Rolex that day," Bob cautioned. "My wife does that all the time. She coordinates her outfits with different jewelry. So the fact this woman is not wearing her Rolex may not mean anything."

"I doubt that," Joey argued. "Look at the watch. It's a much less-expensive gold watch. It's not the kind of jewelry she would wear. Why would a woman switch one gold-colored watch for another gold-colored watch to match her wardrobe? And besides that, all the time I was training her, she wore the Rolex. She liked it a lot and never took it off. She said it wouldn't hurt to get dirt on it."

"What do you mean 'all the time you were training her'?" Bob asked with suspicion.

"I trained Annaliese to shoot and helped her get a carry license. That's why Finney and Sloan interviewed me after the traffic accident."

"Give me the damn glass and let me see that photo again," Bob demanded. "The watch is partially covered with blood, and it's at an angle. Are you sure it isn't a Rolex?"

"Absolutely," Joey exclaimed. "Once you know what a Rolex looks like, it's hard to mistake anything else for one. Even knock-offs can be detected if you know what a real Rolex looks like. And besides, like I just said, hers had four diamonds in the face of the dial."

"But still, Joey, this doesn't prove anything. The woman could have been going somewhere and removed her ring and Rolex to dress down. Hell, Christi takes her rings off when she works in the garden. I'm not sure this means anything either."

"Okay! Now look at her arm again. What do you see?"

"Now what am I supposed to be looking for this time?"

"It's her right arm, Bob. Annaliese Mueller was right handed and wore her watch on her left arm. This woman wore her watch on her right arm. She isn't Annaliese Mueller."

"Wow! Now we have three things that don't add up. The ring, the watch, and the arm. So who the hell is this woman, and how come no one reported her missing? And where is the real Annaliese Mueller?"

"I don't know, but I think this is really strange."

"All right, Joey. Tell me who this Mueller woman really is. Did you have an affair with her? Was she a girlfriend? What?"

"I'll explain in a little while, Bob, but not here. It all fits. Mrs. Mueller was trying to get away from her husband, and somehow this accident gave her the chance. Maybe we can get some information from the autopsy report."

"There's no autopsy report in the file."

"What do you mean 'there's no autopsy report'?"

"I'm telling you, Joey, there's no autopsy report!"

Joey went into Finney's office and asked him where the autopsy report was for the victim in the traffic accident. Finney explained the coroner's office was overwhelmed during the period of the accident, and the husband didn't object to not having one. "Actually," he informed them, "it wasn't needed to determine the cause of death anyhow, so they didn't do one."

Joey and Bob returned the file, left Finney's office, and drove back to their precinct. On the way, Joey told Bob about Anna getting beaten up all the time and her fear her husband was plotting to kill her. He told him about his gun shop and his tunnel firing range. He explained how he had trained Anna for almost a year before she suddenly disappeared. Then he learned from Finney she was supposedly the victim in that traffic accident.

"So you did have an affair with her?"

"No, Bob. We were never romantic. I was still grieving over Sandy. Teaching Anna to shoot took my mind off her. Over time we became close. Very close. But we didn't have an affair."

"So where do we start?" Bob asked. "Do we try to identify the victim or try to find Anna Mueller?"

"I think I know where Anna is," Joey responded, slowly, while biting his lip and shaking his head. "She's somewhere around St. Croix."

"Why do you think that?"

"You remember the woman we saw on the sailboat when we were in the channel entering Christiansted?"

"Come on, Joey. You don't think that was the Mueller woman, do you?" Bob asked incredulously.

"Yes. I do! In fact, I'm certain of it now."

"Well, why didn't you say something then, instead of keeping it secret?"

"I didn't keep it secret. I didn't recognize her at the time. But there was something about her that kept spinning around in my head. She obviously has lost a lot of weight, let her hair grow long, bleached it or something, and I didn't recognize her. She looked a lot younger. And besides, she was dead!"

"Sounds like her husband was a nasty son of a bitch."

"Who would have expected to see her on a sailboat? Beside, Bob, she was supposed to be dead. How could she be on a sailboat if she was dead? It just didn't register. For the last month or so, I haven't had a good night's sleep. I kept waking up with headaches, and it was all wrapped around seeing that woman on the sailboat. And I didn't know it until this morning in the shower. And even then I couldn't be sure until we saw the photos of the accident victim. It all fits together. I'm certain it was Anna on the sailboat."

"Damn, Joey, this is really weird. Where do we start to unravel everything? Maybe we should go back down to the Virgin Islands and try to find her."

"No, Bob. Not so fast. She wanted to get away from her husband because she was terrified he was going to kill her. When I first met her, she was pretty badly beaten up."

Shaking his head, Joey continued, "Underneath the bruises and extra weight though, I could tell she was once an attractive woman. She was smart and obviously well-off. I couldn't understand why her husband would beat the shit out of her and then buy her a Mercedes sports car and expensive jewelry. Her husband was some kind of investment manager for a big firm in Philadelphia, and from what I

—

could tell he had a huge income. She told me they had a big house up in Bucks County."

Joey paused and took a deep breath. "If we find her, we may put her in danger again."

"You're right," Bob agreed. "It's damn near impossible to protect a woman from her husband, short of locking him up. I think we need to find out more about her husband and the dead woman before we try to find her. We need to scan all the Philadelphia newspapers starting about three years back."

"Yeah. We better not let her husband find out what we're doing."

"That sounds like a plan, Joey, but it's not going to be easy. If we're going to keep this under the radar, we're going to need help. Maybe Christi and Rachel could help us. They're both lawyers, right? If we're going to investigate Mueller's husband, and he's a big shot in the business world, Christi would be a great resource. Her practice is in business law. Rachel's a trial lawyer and may know how to quietly get information on the dead woman without bringing too much attention to what we're doing. Why don't we tell them what's happening and see if they would be willing to get involved?"

Joey agreed and called Rachel to see if they could get together for dinner at Bob's place. Over the dinner table, Joey told Rachel and Christi about Annaliese Mueller, the accident, and the now mysterious dead woman.

After hearing the story, both Christi and Rachel were intrigued and began questioning Joey about Annaliese. Christi asked, "Everything hinges on whether or not Annaliese Mueller is really alive, right?"

Bob pointed out if they could prove she was alive, they would have an official justification for determining the identity of the dead woman and why Anna disappeared.

"Joey, do you think you can say with absolute certainty the woman on the sailboat was Annaliese Mueller?" Christi questioned.

"Well no! Given the circumstances under which I saw her, I can't absolutely swear it was Anna. But I feel pretty damn sure about it. And I'm damn certain the body in the photos was not Annaliese Mueller."

"What if you had a photograph of the woman on the sailboat? Could you make a definite identification then?" Christi again questioned.

Watching the way Christi was beginning to interrogate Joey, Rachel exclaimed, "You don't just happen to have a photo of her, do you, Christi?"

"Actually, I do. When you were all gawking at her, I was standing to the side, and I took several pictures of her with my new digital camera. The one I had just bought for the trip. No one was paying any attention to me, not even the woman on the sailboat. She was smiling at Joey, and all of you were looking at her."

Rachel jumped up and demanded, "Why didn't you show the pictures to us before? Why didn't you show them to the clerks in Christiansted when we questioned them?"

"Well, you were making such a fuss over her I thought it might lead to a confrontation with Joey. So I kind of held them back," Christi apologized. "Besides, the screen on the camera is too small to see much detail, and I didn't think the pictures would be of much use."

"Well, let's see them now," Joey demanded.

Christi said she could display them on the computer. "The images will be a lot bigger and sharper."

As soon as the first photo popped up on the screen, Joey yelled, "Damn. That's definitely her! Why didn't I recognize her right away?"

Rachel looked over at Joey and saw tears welling up in his eyes. Compassionately, she said, "This Anna woman must have been something special to you, Joey?"

"Yeah," Joey replied. "Her husband was beating the hell out of her, and I spent a lot of time training her how to handle herself in dangerous situations. But that's all. She really believed her husband wanted to kill her, and I didn't do anything directly to help. I was wallowing in my own self-pity over Sandy, and I didn't try to step in and help her. I thought he might kill her in a fit of rage. I didn't think he was actually plotting to kill her, so I trained her to defend herself. And then she was dead. And now there she is, alive."

Rachel began to hug Joey, to console him in his sadness, when Rob interrupted, "So if she's on a sailboat cruising around in the ocean somewhere, how are we going to find her without an all-points bulletin?"

Rachel excitedly asked, "Christi, you didn't happen to get a shot of the back of the sailboat, did you?"

"I don't think so. Why?"

"Well, don't boats have names? And don't they paint them on the back of the boat? They usually have the name of the place they are from too. If we knew the name of the boat and where it was from, we might be able to find her," Rachel enthused. "We might be able to track down the boat through one of the maritime registries."

They all turned to the pictures and studied them again. Christie had taken only a few, but none of the stern of the boat. One photo yielded a definite clue. On the upper left side of the woman's teal-colored shirt, there was an insignia. It wasn't a shirt manufacturer's logo. It wasn't a slogan. No, it was something else, more like an emblem.

Rachel spoke out, "It looks like the outline of a dove. Could that be important?"

Christi interjected, "I don't know of any clothing line with a dove as an emblem. It could be the emblem of a club though. Perhaps a golf club or some similar place. If it's a golf shirt, maybe we should look at a registry of all the golf clubs."

Rachel continued to study the image on the computer and asked Christi if she could zoom in on various parts of the photo.

"There. Look there," Rachel exclaimed. "Look at that round life preserver in the background behind the girl. It has *OVE* on it. The girl must be obscuring the *D*. That has to be the name of the boat. The *DOVE*."

Joey turned to Rachel and said, "Damn, Rachel. You're really good."

With pride, Rachel answered, "I'm a trial lawyer. We have to pay attention to small details. But now we have to find the port where the boat is registered."

"That's great work, Rachel," Bob said in agreement. "But we can't openly search for the boat or for Mrs. Mueller without arousing a lot of suspicion. If anyone asks what we are doing, we tell them our search is for a missing person. That way, it won't get as much attention as a criminal investigation. What do you think, Joey?"

"I agree. Let's play it as low key as we can. But we have to divide up the tasks. Christi, since you're a business lawyer, how about finding out all you can about Anna's husband? I'm pretty sure his name is Phillip Mueller, and he works for an investment firm in Philadelphia. Rachel, see if anything happened around the time of the accident that might be connected to the accident itself. Bob and I will search the missing person's reports. We'll also find the registry of the sailboat. The Coast Guard might be able to give us some leads. They'll probably respond to police detectives more readily than to a lawyer, no matter how pretty she is."

CHAPTER 56

Christi Marino was an associate in a moderate-sized law firm and had enough authority to set her own agenda. After a few hours of research, Christi became fascinated with Phillip Mueller and began to spend more time on the project. When she found he was the executive vice president of Kuefer & Bach Investments, Inc., she became skeptical of Joey's information. Joey had painted a picture of Anna as the victim of a ruthless tyrant. But the man Christi was learning about was highly regarded in the exclusive circles of investment banking and a pillar of propriety. Either Anna's husband was a different Phillip Mueller, or she had totally duped Joey.

Christi invited Joey and Rachel to dinner on Saturday night to discuss the status of everyone's research. Only a week had passed and she didn't really expect anyone to have made much progress. Before dinner, Rachel got Bob and Joey to help her analyze her notes on women reported missing up to six months after the traffic accident. They were so busy helping Rachel devise various schemes for narrowing her search Christi had a hard time getting them to the dinner table.

At her first opportunity, Christi challenged Joey's perception of exactly who this Anna woman was. She explained everything she had learned about Phillip Mueller was exemplary. He was highly regarded in the business world in general and especially in Philadelphia. She went on to suggest Anna was not who Joey thought she was. Perhaps she had some other motive in learning to use guns and getting a license to carry one. Joey bristled at the suggestion and vociferously disagreed with Christi. He told her emphatically his impressions of Anna were dead-on correct. He asked her if she had found any information on Phillip's wife. When Christi admitted she had not, Joey asked if she didn't think that was odd. Usually, big shots attend various charity events with their wives and are in the newspapers a lot.

"Newspapers usually have a section covering charity events and show pictures of the people who donate money and time," Rachel offered.

"Good point," Christi agreed. "I'll look into that."

"What about marriage licenses, financial statements, and other types of documents?" Bob offered.

"That's next on my list," Christi pointed out. "I may need your help in getting the financial information though. Some of my colleagues are trying to help, but it may turn out I need official justification for seeking the information."

Rachel changed the subject and asked Bob if he and Joey had any leads on the identity of the sailboat. Bob explained they had found where the boat was registered but not its location.

"We learned the sailboat is a schooner, and its home port is Mystic, Connecticut. The boat is listed as the property of Jack and Cecilia Pisani under an LLC license that includes JP Engineering, Inc., in Kettering, Ohio. Kettering is a town just outside of Dayton. Jack Pisani is the CEO of JP Engineering. They apparently use the boat for business cruises and also accept charters. We plan to go up to Kettering next week and see if we can get some information on the crew and recent passengers. We're hoping they keep a list of all their charters."

After dinner, the group helped one another make plans for continuing their investigation into the whereabouts of Anna and the identity of the mysterious dead woman.

Not even a week had passed when Christi again called for a quick get-together to exchange information. It was Wednesday evening, and she couldn't wait to tell everyone about her success in discovering exactly who Annaliese Mueller was.

Christi explained she and a colleague had used her firm's LexisNexis account and found an eight-year-old newspaper article covering a charity event in Philadelphia. The article included photographs of the event organizers, and there, among the photographs, was a picture of the executive officers of Kuefer & Bach Investments with their wives. It included Phillip Mueller and his wife Annaliese. Christi estimated that Phillip's wife was about twenty years old in the photo. And she looked exactly like the woman on the sailboat in St. Croix.

"It's unbelievable," Christi effused. "Look at the newspaper photo and then the photo I took on the boat. The woman looks better now than she did eight years ago, and she was very attractive in the old newspaper photo. It's disgusting."

"Joey," Rachel questioned, "I thought you said this Anna woman was overweight and somewhat disfigured. She doesn't look disfigured to me!"

Joey grabbed the photos and sat looking at them long enough to alarm Rachel. She interrupted him, "Joey, let the rest of us see the photos."

As Rachel and Bob studied the photos, Christi reviewed her notes and continued telling them about her discoveries, "Hey, guys, that isn't all I found. But it was the key to finding more information. Thanks to Rachel's suggestion to search the society sections of the newspapers, which incidentally we don't do on normal business investigations, my associate found an article announcing their wedding, and it was a huge breakthrough."

Looking back at her notes, Christi continued, "The announcement listed Anna's parents as Hans and Gretta Kappelhoff who died when she was child. She was raised by her uncle and aunt, Gustav and Hanna Hadeburga from Birdsboro. It's a small town on the Schuylkill River, northeast of Lancaster. Both of them are now deceased. Using that information, I discovered that Gustav Hadeburga had owned the Reading Wire and Nail Company in Birdsboro and sold it when Anna was about twelve years old. He died when she was sixteen. Now get this, and this is interesting. He sold the company for a net of 267 million dollars, give or take a little. Can you guess who his financial management company was? Yep, Kuefer & Bach, the company that Phillip works for."

Joey, Rachel, and Bob sat mesmerized by what Christi was revealing. Joey interrupted Christi, asking, in disbelief, "So Phillip must have been the manager of Anna's uncle's money? Right? And then he married Anna? Are you sure of this information, Christi? That's just unbelievable."

"Oh yes! I am," Christi went on. "And that's not the half of it. My friend and I became really curious about that little connection, figuring that must have been how Phillip Mueller met Anna. So I called the Reading Wire and Nail Company in Birdsboro and tried to talk to the owner or plant manager to see if I was right. He was somewhere around the factory and not readily available. But his secretary was willing to talk to me. She's the executive secretary, and I learned quite a bit. It turns out Anna's uncle took 10 million dollars from the sale of the company and disbursed it among the employees at the factory as a bonus in consideration of their years of service. That was on top of their retirement plans. Needless to say, the employees really loved him."

"Are you confident the secretary knew what she was talking about?" Rachel asked.

"Yes, I am," Christi answered. "But listen to this. This is going to blow you away. The secretary, Ms. Bauer, had been Mr. Hadeburga's secretary, and she still works there. I made up a story that I was writing an article on the Kuefer & Bach Investment firm, and they touted their work for the Reading Wire and Nail Company as one of their best success stories. Then I asked if she could connect me with someone who could give me some background on their association with Kuefer & Bach. She said K&B never represented the company. I asked why K&B would say they represented the company if they really didn't. I sounded very disappointed. Ms. Bauer explained K&B represented Mr. Hadeburga personally. Not the company. She went on to say a young investment specialist did all the work. He helped negotiate the sale and counseled Mr. Hadeburga on how to invest his money. In fact, he continued to help Mr. Hadeburga up until he died."

"But . . . was Phillip the financial advisor?" Rachel asked in desperation. She wanted answers straight up, right away, without the long description. So did Joey and Bob. Christi was not giving up the opportunity to show off her research skills so she continued the overly detailed recital of her findings.

"After I asked a few more questions about the Wire and Nail Company, Ms. Bauer loosened up and began to tell me about the business and her association with Mr. Hadeburga. She said the old man was a wonderful boss and put most of his profits back into the business every year. That's how he took the business from a local manufacturing company to a national producer of wire and nails. That's also why he was able to sell the company for so much money. The new owners have a similar objective. They're trying to expand their operations internationally and need some additional funding. Ms. Bauer was effusive in explaining the company was doing very well, and it would be a good investment."

"Come on, Christi," Bob said with growing impatience. "Was Phillip the financial advisor?"

"Okay! Okay! You've just got to be patient. It gets better. It gets much better. You're just going to love this."

Rachel jumped up and said she was going to strangle Christi if she didn't get to the point.

"As I said, Ms. Bauer was effusive about the wonderful prospects for the future of the company. Then she blew me away. She suggested that perhaps Mr. Mueller would like to invest some of Anna's trust money back into the company. She thought that it would be a nice tribute to his deceased wife and a great investment."

The last comment really got Rachel's attention. "Did you say trust money? As in a trust fund?"

"Yep, I did. I commented to Ms. Bauer I had learned the Hadeburgas lived modestly in Philadelphia, and I wasn't aware of any trust fund. Ms. Bauer was surprised and said Mr. Hadeburga lived frugally putting most of the money from the sale of the company into a trust fund for his adopted niece, Annaliese. When I questioned whether Annaliese actually had such a trust fund, she became indignant and said she wasn't just a secretary, but she also managed the books for the company. She had been doing that for about forty years and had helped set up Annaliese's trust fund with the Kuefer & Bach Investment firm in Philadelphia. The trust fund was registered in Philadelphia, and my colleague found a copy of the documents. Anna was supposed to inherit the money on her twenty-first birthday, but there was no record it had happened. On Anna's death, it converted to her husband, Phillip, who—are you listening guys—had been the TRUSTEE of the fund since its inception."

Everyone was listening intently, with their mouths open. Christi was delighted she had captured their attention.

After a silent pause, Christi continued, "I don't think Anna knew about the trust fund! It looks like her husband controlled all their finances and never told her about her inheritance."

Joey jumped up and exclaimed, "Damn! I'm sure you are right. She told me she felt trapped because she wouldn't have any money if she left him. She had never had a real job and didn't think she had any skills. That bastard was keeping her trust fund secret. That's why he wanted to kill her. He wanted her inheritance for himself."

Bob added, "So, Christi, it turns out the highly respected financial guru isn't the pillar of propriety everyone thinks. He's a goddamn common crook."

Rachel started laughing and said, "So this woman is hiding out on a boat somewhere in the middle of the ocean and doesn't know she's a multimillionaire. And to think I was envying her only for her looks. It turns out she's rich too."

Christi chimed in, "Yeah. It's unbelievable."

Both women put their hands to their mouths to cover their smiles when they saw Joey was glaring at them. He stated, defiantly, "That's not funny, ladies."

Christi continued, "But the story doesn't end there. Anna's husband is actually an exceptionally good investment manager. The trust is now worth over 350 million dollars. That's a pretty good return on an investment in approximately ten years."

"But," Bob questioned, "why did he want to kill her? Why didn't he just transfer the money to her? It would still be in the family. Right?"

"I'll tell you why," Rachel answered, angrily. "As a trial lawyer, I've dealt with a few of his types in my practice. I've had to defend a couple of them. When a husband becomes violent and starts beating his wife, it's usually because he needs to control her. It's not just that he wants to manage what she does, but rather, he has a deep pathological need to be totally in charge or else. If he's a pathological controlling and violent type, and it looks like Phillip was, and she suddenly has all the money, he loses control and she has the power. If the wife is not the submissive type, and from what you've said, Joey, Anna was not, then it's an explosive situation."

Bob suggested with the information they had it was time to find Anna. "It's more urgent than we thought."

Joey explained he and Bob were scheduled to fly to Dayton, Ohio, the next day and visit the JP Engineering Company in Kettering. They were going to try to meet with the owner, Jack Pisani. They had a tough time getting authorization for the trip from their police captain. They wanted to investigate a traffic accident that happened years ago, and the captain had a hard time understanding why his detectives needed to get involved. They had to convince the captain it was likely the traffic victim, identified as Annaliese Mueller, was actually someone else, and foul play might have been involved. The captain reluctantly agreed but stipulated they would have to use their own money for the travel. The department would reimburse them only if their theory proved to be valid. He cautioned them not to stir up any problems if they were unable to get corroborating evidence.

CHAPTER 57

After departing St. Croix and the *LAFOURCHE*, Bart steered a course for Charlotte Amalie to pick up the new charter. When they reached port, Cecilia left to catch a flight back home. She was flying to San Juan and then on to the States. Before leaving she told Bart she planned to return in seven or eight weeks, after the *DOVE* came out of dry dock.

Every charter group was different and seemed to have its own personality. Some wanted to sail. Others wanted to dive. Still others wanted to party. Some wanted to do everything, but this group was mostly swimmers and loungers. They were older and seemed to be looking only for a relaxing outing. That included drinking. Because the *DOVE* was scheduled for dry dock service immediately after the cruise, Bart stayed close to St. Croix and sailed only in the British Virgin Islands. The crew became anxious whenever he sailed near Leinster Bay on St. John Island even though it had been two years since the episode at Annaberg, but Bart decided it was safe to return.

The weather was excellent, and Leinster Bay was a beautiful place to spend a few days. No one told the charter group about Annaberg and the sugar mill ruins, and no one ventured up the hillside to visit them. They spent several days swimming in the crystal blue waters of Machineel Bay on Jost Van Dyke Island. Then it was on to the Baths on Virgin Gorda and other British Virgin Islands before returning to St. Thomas to disembark the charter group. The disembarkation was professional, but Bart wasted no time in leaving St. Thomas and setting sail for St. Croix.

On returning to Christiansted Harbor for dry dock servicing, Eddie spotted *FREEDOM* anchored off the east side of Fort Christiansvaern. She was weather worn, desperately in need of cleaning, and had obviously been at sea a long time. The crew was pleased to see George might be on the island. Thebb especially looked forward to seeing him again. She had thought of him often. He and Mike had saved her life in Bermuda when they hardly knew her, and she was very grateful. And together, they all saved Cecilia.

Bart gave everyone a month of leave explaining the dry dock people would help maneuver the *DOVE* into position for servicing. He cautioned them to take everything of personal value off the boat and be back in a month. He singled out Thebb, asking her to talk to him in private. He told her she in particular had to make sure she had all her belongings off the boat. She nodded she understood and went below to pack her guns, cartridges, and personal things. She would have to store them at Mike's place.

Rick and Eddie headed back to the States. Bart stayed with the *DOVE* to supervise the maintenance work. He had no home other than the *DOVE*.

Thebb and Bo went to Mike's place to stow some of their gear before their stint on the *LAFOURCHE*. They found George and Mike on the veranda having a beer and discussing George's recent exploits in the Canary Islands. Thebb was excited to see George and gave him a big hug, an act which didn't go unnoticed by Bo. She had a unique fondness for George, almost like a grandfather, but Bo felt uncomfortable seeing Thebb hugging anyone.

"Grab a beer in the kitchen and join us," Mike suggested. "George is telling me about his escapades over the past two years."

George picked up where he had left off, telling how he ended up in the Canary Islands. "After our tumultuous get-together on St. John, I sailed from port to port in the Lesser Antilles until one day I decided to go to the Canary Islands."

"George, what possessed you to do that?" Mike asked. "You must have been fighting headwinds all the way. Sailing by yourself, that must have been really tough going."

"Yes, but I had *FREEDOM* to take me there," George said with a robust laugh. "And I had a lot of time. Actually, I had always wanted to visit the Canaries, and one day it seemed to be the right time. As

I remember it, I was in St. Lucia and had been thinking about sailing to Trinidad. But I met some sailors in a bar in Castries who had just sailed over from the Canaries, so I decided to go there instead. I spent most of my time on the big island, Tenerife. Neat place. Then I sailed around the outer islands of Palma and Hierro and finally back east to Graciosa. They're all beautiful volcanic islands with great beaches and a lot of nightlife. I picked up quite a bit of Spanish while there but not enough to get along without help."

No one mentioned Annaberg. It was a taboo subject.

Bo pulled Thebb off to the kitchen and gave her a hug. Thebb gave him a small smile and asked what that was for. "Because you smiled at me." She and Bo had agreed not to show any affection in front of the *DOVE* crew and their other friends. She flashed her eyes in a pleasing way, flipped her ponytail, turned, and went back to listen to George's stories about the Canary Islands. She knew that Bo was jealous of her attention to George, and that amused her.

When Thebb returned to the veranda, George remarked, "Mike tells me you're volunteering to work on a research vessel for a few weeks. That sounds like a fun thing to do. Tell me about it."

After Thebb related what little she knew about Jim's research, George offered to ferry Thebb and Bo out to the *LAFOURCHE.*

"George, when we anchored in the harbor, I saw *FREEDOM.* It's a mess! The *LAFOURCHE* is bright and shiny. It's spotless. We can't let you go out to the research vessel with your boat looking like it is. We have a few days before we have to be there, so Bo and I will help you clean it and polish the hull."

George admitted, sheepishly, he had the bottom cleaned only a few times in the Canary Islands by local boys looking for spending money. But he agreed, "She really does need a bit of work."

In two days, they had the hull cleaned and polished. Bo had replaced several sections of wood trim and varnished them. While they worked, George told a few more stories about his adventures in the Canaries.

After finishing the cleaning project, they met up with Jim Thornhouser and the chief scientist at the Terrace restaurant overlooking Gallows Bay on the north shore. Thebb introduced George as her close friend who had been wandering around the Atlantic Ocean for the past few years but had decided to visit them in St.

Croix. Mike showed up a little later and found them having cocktails on the patio before going in for dinner.

The chief scientist greeted Mike warmly commenting, "Some of my colleagues were at your party a few weeks ago. They spoke highly of you and your home overlooking the beach. One of them mentioned you are a sailor and spend a lot of time in the Caribbean."

George pointed out the chief scientist and Mike have a lot in common. "Besides being a great sailor, Mike became an electrical engineer after he got out of the Marines and might be of use on the *LAFOURCHE.*"

The chief scientist took the bait and invited Mike to help out maintaining their research submarine, the *BESS.* They had a lot of exciting new electronics he might enjoy seeing. And besides, they could always use an extra hand, especially a seasoned sailor. He said Bo was joining them, and he could share a cabin with Bo or take the remaining small cabin next to the chain locker. Mike thought it would be a great experience and enthusiastically agreed.

When their table was ready, Mike explained he had dined there in the past and recommended the grilled lobster cakes. "They use capers and tarragon to accent the lobster. Also, the pecan-crusted roast pork tenderloin is unique and delicious."

Thebb was listening carefully while thinking some of the menu items would be fun to experiment with on the *DOVE.* When she asked what they served with the pecan pork, Jim remembered she was a cook and suggested she might prepare something on the *LAFOURCHE.*

"I don't think that will be much of an option," the chief scientist interjected. "Ships' cooks can be testy about other people in their galleys."

"He's right about that," Thebb answered. "I totally agree. Stay out of the galley unless invited."

Thebb was feeling good. It had been several years since the Annaberg incident, and nothing more had happened. She was feeling less vulnerable. Slowly, and unwittingly, she had relaxed her high level of vigilance. Seeing Joey on the ferry and having him not recognize her, as heartbreaking as it was, gave her great relief. She began to believe she had successfully established her new identity and was in the clear.

—

Thebb had also finally accepted the fact she was no longer overweight or bruised and ugly. This, coupled with Bo's urging, led her to wearing shorts routinely. Unfortunately, Thebb was breaking several of Joey's key rules for people hiding out or in witness protection programs. "Never draw attention to yourself and never forget at any time, and at any place, unexpected circumstances can give you away. You can never let your guard down."

Thebb had not anticipated her new looks would attract more attention and make her more conspicuous. But she reasoned, she was going to be on a research vessel conducting technical operations offshore. There was little chance of being recognized. Besides, Cecilia had given her a half dozen new golf shirts, in various pastel colors, all embroidered with the *DOVE* logo. *What could be better than to wear the DOVE shirts on the research vessel?*

The next morning, George, Mike, Thebb, and Bo retrieved the two anchors mooring the *FREEDOM* and motored out the channel. Once clear, they hoisted the sails on the sloop and sailed around St. Croix to join up with the *LAFOURCHE*.

After touring the research vessel, George thanked the captain and the chief scientist for their hospitality and returned to Christiansted. He needed to catch up on some long-overdue repairs to the sails and service the small diesel engine and generator.

Jim explained to Thebb she would have to learn her role on the job, so to speak, because he was scheduled to go down on the next set of dives. He had the use of the submersible for one dive a day for two weeks, give or take, and they were starting immediately. The operations schedule, weather permitting, allowed for two dives a day. Before he began his first dive, Jim had only enough time to take Thebb to the laboratory and show her the pressure bio-canisters, microscopes, and slide preparation equipment. He cautioned some of the scientists on board had become seasick when they were looking into the microscope while the ship was under way.

The operations officer called for Jim to come to the afterdeck. The pilot was already aboard *BESS* testing all the electrical and mechanical systems. Jim climbed up the ladder and lowered himself into the acrylic sphere. A crew member followed him up the ladder and when he was situated in his seat handed him his notebooks, closed the hatch, and spun the pressure latches.

—

A crew member started the diesel engine that operated the huge A-frame crane. The operations officer called for everyone to clear the area. The crane lifted the submersible *BESS* off the deck. It swung out aft of the vessel and slowly lowered *BESS* into the water. When only the entry hatch was visible above water, a diver from a nearby launch disconnected the hoisting cable and stabilizing lines held by crew members on deck. The *BESS* began to submerge. The sea was awash in a froth of bubbles around the buoyancy tanks as the pilot released the ballast air, and *BESS* disappeared into the blue water. Jim was off in search of his prized ice worms.

Thebb was surprised at how smoothly the launch had gone. Bo had been assigned to handle one of the stabilizing lines and was coiling the line when Thebb began to ask him questions about the equipment. She had been embarrassed to ask the crew for fear of seeming ignorant.

The next four hours seemed like forever to Thebb. The submersible was 2,200 feet below. They were in a gentle sea with an almost cloudless sky. The only sound was the music from a portable radio at the operations desk amidships. Most of the research team members had disappeared. Only a small contingent stood by in case of an emergency. Thebb was becoming apprehensive waiting for the sub's return. Then she heard the operations officer announce over the intercom that the sub was surfacing.

Within a minute or two, crew members appeared on deck and took their prescribed positions. They came out of virtually every doorway and hatch. Thebb excitedly watched as the sub positioned itself under the extended A-frame and the hoisting cable was lowered. Two divers entered the water, swam over to the sub, and hooked the lifting cable to the sub's lifting ring. Crew members tossed out the guidance lines and connected them to attachment rings on the port and starboard skids. The A-frame crane smoothly returned *BESS* to its deck cradle, and Bo and other crew members tied her down securely. Bo was actively helping and needed little in the way of instructions. Being a sailor, his line handling and knot tying were superb.

Jim waved from inside the sphere. Thebb approached the sub to look at the special pressure canisters that Jim had designed to rotnovo the ice worms alive. One extra large canister had a clear, high-pressure window, and she could see several small pink worms moving about on a chunk of methane hydrate ice. A crew member scampered up a ladder and released the latches on the entry hatch of the pressure hull. Jim climbed up through the hatch and stood, half exposed above the pressure hull. He yelled he had successfully captured and brought to the surface the first-ever live samples of the methane hydrate ice worms. He was ebullient. A moment before, Thebb was standing alone inspecting the containers. Now she was being pushed aside as the crew and scientists crowded around Jim's samples trying to get a glimpse of his prize. They were as excited as he was at his success. He exited the sphere, climbed down the ladder, and told Thebb this was where their work really started. He immediately began to remove the sample canisters from the tray on the front of the submersible and explained they had to quickly get the worms into the laboratory refrigerators. The worms were highly susceptible to increased temperature and light, and it was a bright warm Caribbean day on deck.

Inside the laboratory, Jim carefully released the pressure on the large canister with the window. He wanted to observe the worms during decompression, hoping they wouldn't die. But they did. He used those specimens to show Thebb how they were going to dissect the worms and record their findings. Some of the worms would be sliced thinly and observed in the microscope. Others would be frozen for more elaborate study in his university laboratory.

While Thebb and Jim were working in the ship's laboratory, the submersible crew readied the sub for an early afternoon dive by the oceanographers. Others were playing with a sample of methane hydrate ice. One crew member held a chunk of the weird ice in his hand and lit it with a match. The spectacle of a chunk of ice burning in a man's hand caused the crew to gather and watch. Even though they had seen this before, it never ceased to amaze them. Bo, who had never seen anything like it, retrieved his camera to take photos. Except for burning the methane hydrate, the same routine was scheduled for each morning over the next two weeks.

CHAPTER 58

Jim was concerned Thebb didn't smile very much and asked Bo if she was disappointed with her work in the laboratory. Bo explained she was basically a quiet person, and that was her nature. Based on subtle comments she had made over the last year, Bo suspected she had grown up near Lancaster, Pennsylvania, in a community of serious-minded older Germans where smiling was not the norm.

Nevertheless, Jim worried Thebb was not happy working in his laboratory or being on the research ship. The makeshift laboratory was small and secluded. After working in the cramped quarters for a few hours, her clothes reeked of a chemical smell. Thebb often became lightheaded and had to go out to the aft deck to breathe fresh air. Even so, she never complained about the abominable smell and went about her work diligently but unsmilingly. Jim was keenly aware Cecilia had pushed her into volunteering. He knew he had asked a lot of her and wanted to reward her for her dedication to his project.

Jim had been thinking hard about how he could reward Thebb for helping him. After about a week and a half, he had all the samples he needed but still had a couple of dives in *BESS* reserved for his program. The oceanographers asked if they could have one of his remaining dives to scout out another area of the slope. Jim agreed and inquired if Thebb could make the dive with the pilot-scientist doing the scouting. Both the chief scientist and operations officer agreed it would be a good reward. Thebb was ecstatic. She had not anticipated she would get the opportunity to see the deep-ocean bottom from inside a research submersible.

Before Thebb's dive, the oceanographers reviewed the side-scan sonar data to select another research site. They decided to sample a location about a mile east of the current site. The side-scan sonar tracings showed a slightly steeper slope with indications of a methane hydrate outcropping. They also wanted to explore some strong anomalies in the same general area.

Curtis DeSylve would be piloting Thebb's dive. He was an oceanographic geologist as well as a highly experienced submersible pilot. He was the most skilled member of the scientific crew at finding methane hydrate outcroppings and needed a passenger only to take notes and photographs for him. His dive would be the perfect one for Thebb.

The spherical pressure hull on *BESS* seemed small to Thebb until she settled down in her seat. She was amazed at the clarity with which she could see the deck crew and how efficiently the inside of the pressure hull was organized. Curtis introduced himself, assuring her he had been on numerous deep-ocean dives in the past and had quite a bit of experience with *BESS*.

When the A-frame crane lifted the sub into the air, Thebb became apprehensive and a bit tense. But as they were being lowered into the water, she could see underwater in all directions. She was captivated by her perception of floating in space. Small fish swam around the sphere and darted back and forth with each sharp movement of the sub. She heard the clanking of the main lifting hook as the support divers untethered the sub from the ship. She saw the wash of the waves over various parts of the sub as it slowly began its descent giving her a momentary feeling of claustrophobia. That sensation quickly left, and she began to feel like she was flying through space with clear visibility but nothing to see. The water was bright blue above and black below.

As they descended deeper, the light grew dim, and Thebb noticed how much brighter the instrument panel seemed. She watched as the numbers on the depth and pressure gauges increased to larger and larger values while the temperature numbers fell. When the depth gauge registered about fifteen hundred feet, Curtis turned on the outside lights and began to explain what was happening. It was the first time he spoke since they started their descent. He had been preoccupied with monitoring the status of all the instruments.

As they slowly descended past fifteen hundred feet of depth, an iridescent red life form had fluttered into the light beam. It resembled a brightly colored washcloth with the power of locomotion. Curtis was watching Thebb's expressions with delight. He loved to watch people's reactions as they saw the creatures of the deep for the first time. He explained the beautiful apparition floating and undulating through the beams of light was a sea cucumber.

"Cucumber?" Thebb asked. "That doesn't look like a cucumber. It looks like a washcloth."

"The shallow-water sea cucumbers scuba divers are familiar with look like the kind of cucumbers you find in your salad," Curtis explained. "They live on the sandy bottom around reefs. But down here, at fifteen hundred to two thousand feet, there are a lot of strange-looking biota and swimming cucumbers are just one of them."

When the sub reached two thousand feet, the bottom came into view. Thebb's curiosity was piqued by another strange fish that appeared in the floodlights. It was long, silvery, and skinny like a snake. It appeared to be about three or four feet long and was positioned vertically in the water about six feet from the bottom. It slid slowly downward until its tail touched the sea floor and made a coil on the bottom. Then it suddenly sprang upward about eight feet and repeated the cycle of descent, coil, and springing upward again.

"What is that strange thing? It's bouncing up and down."

"I don't actually know," Curtis explained. "I've only heard it called the spring fish. Everyone likes to watch it though. It reminds me of the mythological Greek character, Sisyphus, who was condemned to roll a large stone up a hill. When he got it to the top, the gods rolled it back down the hill, and he had to start all over again."

Thebb smiled and remarked that his analogy was wonderful. "It captures the essence of what the fish is doing." Her eyes were wide with excitement, and she was scanning the bottom from side to side looking for other weird creatures.

"Look at that fish. It's the opposite of the spring fish. It's hanging upside down with its nose on the bottom."

"Oh, that's a pipefish. Lots of them down here. Keep a lookout in tho perimeter of the light path, and you may see a swordfish or some squid. One of the other pilots had a swordfish try to stab the sub."

"What happened? Was he okay?"

"We had swordfish for dinner. It got caught in the framework and came up with the sub."

"So," Thebb asked after a few minutes, "how do we find the methane mounds we are looking for?"

"They'll appear as small mounds without much growth on them. Sometimes several small streams of methane bubbles will give them away. The bubbles are kind of interesting. They're tiny here on the bottom, but they get gigantic up near the surface. It's because the high pressure down here squeezes them and makes them small."

"There's a mound about fifteen degrees to starboard. I'll pull up in front of it, and you can poke it with the mechanical arm. Just hold the handle and move it like a joystick. You can operate the claws by squeezing the stick."

Thebb grasped the concept quickly and poked the mound. To her surprise lots of bubbles escaped, and she saw several little pink worms quickly burrow out of sight. "There're some of Jim's worms," she exclaimed with delight.

"What's that?" Thebb interrupted, pointing to the port side. "It's about forty degrees off the port bow. It looks like the stern of a boat half buried in the bottom."

"Where?"

"If you turn the sub to port, the lights will shine on it. It's on the edge of the range of the lights."

"Damn, you're right. It's a wreck of some sort. That must be the source of the anomaly we saw on the side-scan. That was one of the reasons why we wanted to reconnoiter this area."

"Let's take a closer look," Curtis studiously remarked. "I think I can make out the remains of the name on the stern. I've never found a wreck before."

Curtis approached the wreck at a very slow speed. When they were about fifty feet away, the sub gave a gentle jerk and stopped moving forward.

"Whoa," Curtis exclaimed. "That's not good."

"What happened? It feels like we're caught on something!"

"Yeah. Do you see anything on your side?"

"Yes," Thebb answered in a calm, determined voice. "There's a loop of wire over the starboard skid."

Curtis leaned over to Thebb's side of the cockpit so he could see around the control stick and center console of instruments. He looked down at the skid and saw the wire. It appeared to be a simple hoop of bailing wire that stuck up out of the mushy bottom much like a croquet hoop sticking up out of the grass. As they watched, the dark silt that had provided its camouflage spilled off the wire.

"Let's see if we can back up and get untangled," Curtis told Thebb. "You're closest to it so tell me how we are doing. I'm going to descend a little and back up."

As Curtis slowly, deliberately backed the sub away from the wreck, a large coil of wire, pulled by the single simple loop around the sub's skid, began to lift out of the silt and sand starboard of the sub. A cloud of sediment lifted upward and threatened to engulf the sub but drifted away under the wash of the drive propeller's thrust. The large coil of wire had been covered with silt and bottom organisms. It originally looked like a low mound with frilly growth on top of it. Only the single loop of wire extended upward, unseen, out of the bottom sediment, and that's what caught the skid.

As the sub slowly backed up, the single loop of wire twisted downward and became wedged on the skid's structural flange. The large coil on the bottom pulled on another buried coil that began to lift out of the sediment farther starboard of the sub. The sub made a gentle jerk and stopped moving. Curtis descended to drop the skid farther away from the loop of wire, but it held tight. He sat the sub lightly on the bottom, but the wire was firmly lodged in the flange. It seemed to be spring loaded and pulled down on the skid.

Curtis turned to look at Thebb. He was afraid she might be panicking, but she was calm and looking at him with raised eyebrows. She appeared to have unlimited confidence in him. Then trying to add some levity to what she felt could become a catastrophic situation, she calmly said, "I think we have a problem."

"No, I don't think we have anything to worry about," Curtis confidently responded. "We can use the mechanical arms and pincers to lift the wire off the skid. It's not a problem!"

The starboard mechanical arm couldn't articulate backward on itself far enough to reach around the sample platform and remove the loop of wire. Curtis then used the port arm and claw. But it wasn't long enough to reach around the sample platform. Both arms were too short.

"Shit. Goddamn it!" Curtis exploded in exasperation and anger. "Now we do have a problem. We should have removed the goddamn sample platform before the dive."

He had lost his cool and that scared Thebb. But he quickly regained his calm demeanor and explained if they had a stick, he could use the port arm to hold the stick and lift the wire off the skid.

"I don't see any sticks down here, Curtis," Thebb replied lightly.

"I know. I was speaking metaphorically. Let's think if there are other alternatives."

"Can we use the mechanical arms and pincers to lift the sample platform off the sub? That would make it possible for the arms to reach the wire."

"Good idea," Curtis responded. "Trouble is the platform is bolted down."

Curtis then tried to ascend straight up to see if the sub could pull the main coil of wire loose, but the sub stopped about six feet from the bottom. As the sub lifted harder, more wire coils appeared out of the bottom muck, raising large clouds of sediment.

"They're all attached to one another," Thebb exclaimed. "There could be dozens of them. I think we're really stuck."

"Yeah, it looks that way! The sub isn't designed to lift anything heavy so I think we have to initiate emergency procedures."

Curtis turned around in his seat and unsnapped the cover of a box labeled "Emergency Radio Beacon."

"I didn't know we could communicate with a radio underwater?" Thebb stated in a questioning manner.

Curtis explained the emergency system would release a float with a flag and an antenna on a long, thin wire. When the float reached the surface, a strobe light would flash and get the attention of the crew on the LAFOURCHE. "Using the antenna, we can tell them what's happening. Then they can launch the ROV/DSRV and give us some help."

"How long should that take? Do we have enough air to be down here very long?"

"It could take the ROV a few hours or all day to rescue us, depending on our situation. I've never been involved in an emergency recovery before, but the operations officer has done one or two so there shouldn't be a problem. And the sub has enough breathing gas for four days so not to worry."

Thebb sat looking straight ahead at the hulk in the shadowy fringe of the floodlights.

"Also," Curtis continued, "we have to shut down all the power systems except the emergency radio and the life-support systems."

Then there was darkness.

CHAPTER 59

On the deck of the *LAFOURCHE*, there was near pandemonium. Crew members were running across the deck yelling, "EMERGENCY STROBE, EMERGENCY STROBE." A loud horn started sounding intermittent blasts. The operations officer and the chief scientist ran to the operations station and immediately checked to see that the radio was tuned to the emergency frequency. Then they called the *BESS*.

"*BESS*, this is *LAFOURCHE*. Come back, come back," the operations officer called calmly.

From the radio they heard crackling, several loud clicks, and then, "This is *BESS*. We read you loud and clear."

"Great," the operations officer radioed back. His voice was calm, almost indifferent. "What's the problem down there, Curtis?"

The reply was equally restrained. "There's a single loop of wire, probably about sixteen gauge, caught on our starboard skid. It appears to be part of a shipment of coils of bailing wire. We need some help in getting the loop off the skid. It seems to be spring-loaded and pushes down on the skid so we can't descend to get free. We can't reach it with the mechanical arms and pincers and haven't been able to maneuver out of it. Can you send some help down?"

The operations officer answered, "Your antenna popped up a few hundred yards away so we'll have to reposition the ship and then send the ROV down. I think we can reach you in about two hours. Just sit tight for now. How is everything else down there?"

The crew began crowding around the operations officer and chief scientist, and Bo was in front of all of them. The reply crackled

---

321

over the open speakers at the control station. "Just fine. We found another interesting mound of methane hydrate with what appears to be methane bubbles. It looks to be a good station for the next set of dives. Just inshore of our position is a half-buried commercial barge that sank with a load of industrial equipment. The wire we're hung up on is probably part of the cargo from the barge. Also the bottom begins to slope more sharply just beyond where we are sitting."

"And how is Thebb doing? Is she okay with this?" the chief scientist asked.

"Yes, sir. She's fine. She's taking notes, and before we turned the lights off, she was photographing the wreck, coils, and methane hydrate mound."

Bo asked if he could talk to Thebb. His first question was if she felt safe. She said she was okay and had every confidence in Curtis and the topside crew. She couldn't have said anything more pleasing for the crew. They were all nodding their heads in approval. They talked for only a minute more. Thebb explained they were sitting in the dark to conserve power. She said after their eyes had accommodated to the darkness, they could see numerous phosphorescent flashes from the deep water fish.

The operations officer told Curtis the crew was scrambling to prepare the ROV for deployment. They had plenty of cable, and as soon as the ship was in position, they would send it down. Then he told Thebb she and Curtis would be up on the surface in a few hours and not to worry.

After the power and control cables were connected to the ROV, the operator and electronics technician ran down the preoperations checklist. The technician detected a failure in the control system. He retested the system again, and it failed a second time. He ran back to the small electronics laboratory and returned with more testing equipment. After a half hour of testing, he identified the subsystem that was malfunctioning. He pulled the circuit board out and took it to the electronics laboratory to isolate the defective part. Unfortunately, it was an integrated chip they didn't have a spare for.

"This particular chip is highly reliable," the technician told the operations officer. "I can't believe it failed. I'll have to get a replacement before we can deploy the ROV. It isn't an unusual chip, so we should be able to get one on the island. If not, we may have to fly one in from Louisiana."

Mike offered to help the technician find the critical part. He explained he was an electrical engineer, and as they all knew, he lived in St. Croix. He was familiar with all the electronics shops on the island. They called several shops in St. Croix. Finding the right chip became a circus with the electronic shops each calling other shops in St. Thomas and Puerto Rico. They all wanted to help when the technician explained it was a life-or-death situation.

The technician finally located the elusive chip in San Juan. The distributor promised it would be on the first Prinair flight into St. Croix the next morning. There were no flights that afternoon. All the flights from San Juan to St. Croix were in the morning and from St. Croix to San Juan were in the afternoon. He promised to personally handle the package. The flight would depart at 0700 and would be in St. Croix by 0800. The technician explained to the distributor timeliness was crucial. People were trapped in a submarine two thousand feet down with a limited supply of air. The chip was critical to their emergency recovery.

The technician assured everyone they could have the ROV operational within an hour after getting the chip back to the ship. The operations officer added the weather was good, and except for their inconvenience, Curtis and Thebb were perfectly safe for the moment. But, he added, they had better get them up in the morning.

Curtis and Thebb were not happy to hear they would be spending the night on the bottom of the ocean with no lights or food. They had water and only a single energy bar Curtis found in his shirt pocket. The seat Thebb thought was so comfortable when she first got into the sub became highly restrictive, hard, and uncomfortable after the first four hours. To put Thebb at ease and pass the time, Curtis shared some of his earlier experiences with the sub and other exploits at sea. He also talked about his personal background. He quickly learned Thebb was profoundly capable of not revealing any information about herself. So their discussions began to revolve around the preparation of food, sailing, and the pelagic biota of the Caribbean.

Mike and the electronics technician arrived at the airport early and were waiting for the 0800 flight to arrive. To ensure the chip didn't get lost, the folks at the electronics distribution center packaged it in a large box. Mike and the technician raced to the commercial docks south of the airport to take the ship's launch back to the *LAFOURCHE*. As they approached the docks, they saw a deep-sea fishing boat with several people heading out of the harbor. One man had a bag with *VI Daily News* stenciled across its side.

"Damn," Mike yelled out. "How did the newspaper find out about the situation?"

"Shit," the technician answered. "One of the goddamn electronics shops must have called them. Now we're going to have to keep them out of the way."

When Mike and the electronics technician got to the *LAFOURCHE*, they found the deep-sea fishing boat already tied to the port side of the ship. Once on deck, the technician ran to the electronics lab to install the chip into the circuit board. As he ran past the operations station, he said he would have the chip installed in about fifteen or twenty minutes.

The operations officer, chief scientist, and Jim Thornhouser were talking with the news reporter who wanted to report on the recovery of the sub. The operations officer agreed to let the reporter and his cameraman stay on board only if they strictly followed directions and kept out of the way. Mike offered to shepherd them around so they could cover the story and remain safe. He explained some of the heavy equipment on board would be moving when they started the recovery operation.

Finally, the steel door of the electronics lab opened, and the technician yelled, "It's in! The circuit board's ready." He unscrewed the cover of the electronics panel on the ROV, inserted the circuit board, closed the cover, screwed it down to make a watertight pressure seal, and ran through the preoperations checklist again. Within minutes, he announced the ROV was ready for deployment.

The crew reattached the cables to the ROV, and the A-frame crane hoisted it out over the starboard gunnel. They steadied it with several lines until it was fully submerged. The ROV operator sat at a small console under a tentlike sun cover and directed the ROV toward the flag attached to the emergency antenna from the submarine. He had a monitor screen and a joystick, just like a computer game.

To ease Bo's anxiety, the ROV operator called him over and began to explain what he and the ROV would be doing.

"Bo, this will probably go smooth as silk. The *BESS* has an emergency pinger, and the ROV has a location receiver to guide it to the sub. In addition, and to help speed things up, I'm going to follow the emergency radio line down to the sub. We will establish continuous communication with Curtis so he can help guide us to him."

The communications began, and the ROV operator directed Curtis to turn on the sub's exterior floodlights to help him find it. The ROV was able to descend much faster than the sub and soon was about twenty feet off the starboard side of the sub. The operator told Curtis to sit tight until he got a good look at the wire entangling the skid.

"I see the wire," the operator radioed to Curtis. "It's remarkably thin. I don't think it will be difficult to remove. I'm going to use the ROV's mechanical arm to lift the wire. It looks like I only have to lift it about a foot or so. Did you experience much restraint in the first foot or two of vertical ascent?"

"No. The resistance wasn't noticeable until we were about three feet or so above the bottom, but it stopped *BESS* at about six or seven feet."

"Well, I don't think we'll have a problem. When I tell you to, back up without lifting up. Can you do that?"

Curtis and Thebb watched as the ROV emerged from the perimeter of lighted visibility as a square crablike creature with a central hemispherical dome in the center and two folded arms, one on either side. As it got closer, they could see the large camera lens inside the dome. Thebb was spellbound by the otherworldly appearance of the strange-looking device coming to save them. It approached slowly, and when it was only a few feet from their pressure hull, she saw the camera lens moving from side to side scanning the situation.

A voice came over the speaker. "You two look fine. We'll have you out of there in just a few minutes."

Thebb turned quickly to Curtis and asked, "Can they see us through the hull?"

The speaker crackled. "Absolutely. We can hear you too."

On the deck of the *LAFOURCHE*, the crew members had gathered around the ROV operator's console and were watching the large flat-screen monitor displaying the images from the ROV's cameras.

Mike found the *VI Daily News* cameraman a small stepladder so he could capture the events over the shoulders of the crew while staying out of the way. It was relatively easy because the camera was similar to an ordinary video camera like the ones tourists carry. Maybe a bit more expensive but similar.

The ROV moved in close, extended its port-articulating arm, and used its claw to lift the wire that had trapped the *BESS* overnight. As it began trying to lift the wire, the ROV descended slightly. The operator had to give the ROV's vertical propulsion unit a boost to compensate for the load on the manipulators. It didn't work.

"Curtis, there's a lot more spring action on the loop of wire than we thought. Other wire coils must be on the other side of the loop."

"Yeah, that's probably why I couldn't shuffle out from under it. Can you lift it?" Curtis asked with unflappable composure.

On the *LAFOURCHE*, the matter-of-factness of the communication between Curtis and the ROV operator calmed the apprehensive mood of the crew, and they backed away a little from the ROV operator's console, but not Bo.

The operator responded to Curtis saying, "Of course. It'll be a piece of cake, but I need to know how soft the bottom is. Are you in neutral buoyancy or sitting hard on the bottom?"

"Pretty much neutral."

"Okay, I'm going to settle down on the bottom to get some leverage on the wire. I probably don't need much. Then I'll try again to lift the wire."

Thebb turned to Curtis. "What does he mean by try?"

"Don't worry, Thebb. When you try to lift something up, you go down. He can probably use the vertical thrusters to offset the downward push, but they will kick up a lot of sediment and obscure his vision, so he is opting to use a technique that won't do that. He's just asking how soft the bottom is."

"And if that approach doesn't work, what then?" Thebb asked with growing alarm. "What if the bottom is too soft and the ROV sinks into it?"

"There are other options, Thebb. But let's try this one first and then worry about what else to do, if needed."

"Curtis," the operator alerted. "I'm setting the ROV down now. Tell me how far into the sediment I sink."

"Thebb," Curtis said, "you're starboard and have the best view. How about guiding him?"

"Okay," Thebb answered. "You have sunk about four inches into the sediment."

"Terrific! I'm going to try to lift the coil again. When I say to, back out from under the wire."

The ROV sank another inch into the bottom as the operator extended the mechanical arm and lifted the wire. After a slight hesitation, the wire lifted about one foot above the skid.

"Okay, Curtis, the wire is clear of the skid now. Back up straight without lifting. Keep going. Keep going. There, you're free. Don't go forward. The wire hoop is still sticking up a little."

"HALLELUJAH," Curtis yelled. "Let's go up, Thebb."

"Curtis," the ROV operator called, "just hang back a couple of minutes. Let me get out of the way first, okay! Then you can reel in the radio antenna and come on up."

"Will do! We'll see you in a little while, and thanks to everyone. Tell Thebb's people everyone down here is okay."

The crew topside began cheering at the quick success of the recovery. The reporter seemed disappointed. He asked if that was all there was to it. The chief scientist explained it might have seemed routine, but without the training and skill the operator had, the recovery could have been a disaster.

BESS appeared off the stern of the ship with only the hatch and about a foot of the acrylic pressure hull showing. The crew went into their well-practiced routine and connected the heavy hoisting hook and control lines. As the hoisting cable wound around the power drum and lifted the *BESS* upward, water cascaded out of the ballast chambers creating a bubbly froth all around it. When the sub was completely out of the water, the A-frame crane swung it over the deck and slowly lowered it to its cradle. Inside the clear sphere, Curtis and Thebb were waving to everyone. A crew member climbed the ladder to the top of the sub, unlatched the hatch, swung it open, leaned down, and welcomed them back. "Next time, don't take so long to come back up," he laughed.

Thebb was the first to climb out of the hatch. When halfway out, she stopped and waved to the crew. The newspaper cameraman was catching it all from his perch behind the cheering crew members, many of whom had cameras too. The crew was clapping and yelling, "Welcome back!" Bo was waving furiously to Thebb. The chief scientist stood in front of the sub with a big smile.

Thebb climbed down the ladder, walked over to Bo, and gave him a huge hug. She whispered, "I didn't think I was going to see you again." Bo held on to the hug whispering he had been really worried. She squeezed him once more and then turned and walked back to the sub and stood in front of the glistening crystal-like pressure sphere to wait for Curtis to climb down.

CHAPTER 60

Thebb waited for Curtis to secure the controls and power systems of the sub and climb out the top hatch. She stood with the sun glistening off the sphere and across her hair as it blew over her shoulder. With the submersible behind her and the articulating mechanical arms to either side, the scene looked as if it had been made for a magazine cover.

After he took the long last step out of the *BESS*, Curtis gave Thebb a hug, took her hand in front of the crew, and said in a voice loud enough to be heard by everyone, "Thebb, you're the nicest person I've ever been trapped on the bottom of the ocean with. But I hope we don't have to do it again anytime soon."

Curtis's comments elicited a large smile from Thebb. Everyone began hooting and clapping.

Then Thebb announced, loudly and with a heartfelt quiver in her voice, "I want to thank the emergency ROV operations team for getting us back up. It was fun, but I don't want to do it again either." The ROV team bowed to the crew, and again everyone was hooting and clapping.

Pointing toward the electronics technician and the ROV operator, Curtis yelled in agreement, "They deserve special recognition." Again everyone clapped. They were relieved and happy the mishap was over.

The operations officer walked over to shake Curtis's hand and hug Thebb. "Congratulations. You both are now members of the select group of people who have been trapped on the bottom of the ocean and survived to tell about it."

As Thebb and Curtis finished grandstanding for the crew, Thebb became aware of the cameras and realized she and Curtis were being photographed. The excitement of being rescued and then greeted with so much enthusiasm had distracted her. She didn't notice the newspaper cameraman who was dressed as casually as the crew. She hoped the crew members took the photographs only for their personal use. Nonetheless, she decided it would be best to get away from the cameras and quickly returned to her cabin.

The congratulatory gathering was cut short by the operations officer. He stepped up on a small ladder and loudly told everyone to get back to their stations. They had to prepare the sub for its next dive that afternoon. He announced the *BESS* sustained no damage, and they had only two and a half more days of diving. In three days, he would be taking the *LAFOURCHE* into Frederiksted for supplies. The attitude of the operations officer and most of the crew was the emergency recovery was simply a glitch in their schedule, and they had to get back to work. Then he approached the newspaper people and asked them to disembark.

Bo followed Thebb to her cabin and sat on the bunk listening to her explain how the sub got trapped. She felt she was responsible for convincing Curtis to veer off to look at the sunken barge. But then who could have foreseen the sub would get caught on such a small loop of wire. She told Bo the night had been exciting, boring, beautiful, and terrifying. Bo told her he had been afraid for her safety. He had felt powerless to do anything other than help the professionals on deck. He didn't tell her some of the people were from the newspaper. Somehow, in the continuing euphoria of the successful recovery, he forgot.

Thebb and Bo's discussion was cut short when Mike knocked on the door. Some people were going ashore, and he was catching a ride with them. He said he would get the house prepared for their return. "Maybe we should have a party," he suggested. "After your adventure last night, you deserve one."

For the next two days, Thebb and Bo stayed aboard to help Jim finish work on his specimens and crate up the scientific equipment. Neither Thebb nor Bo had any idea what some of the equipment was or what it did. They only knew Jim would frantically check for damage whenever they bumped one of his instruments while packing it.

Well before sunup, three days later, Thebb could feel the lurch of the *LAFOURCHE* as it turned and headed for Frederiksted. They had been on station for more than a month, and it was time to resupply the ship. The captain docked on the south side of the long concrete pier at Frederiksted so that Jim could offload his equipment and samples.

CHAPTER 61

As Joey and Bob drove up to JP Engineering in Kettering, they were surprised the building was almost a city block long. It was plain with few design features and no windows in the front, only low trees about every twenty feet with bushes in between. The lawn, trees, and bushes were well managed, obviously by a professional lawn-care company. The entrance consisted of a single door with no side panels. The name of the company was in relatively small letters above the door. The parking lot had space for only ten cars. Bob wondered what kind of company would have such a large building with no windows and so few places to park. Joey suggested perhaps all the employee parking spaces were in the rear of the building and the front was for visitors only. As they got out of the white, nondescript rental car, Bob pointed out at least four security cameras were pointed at them, and one was following them as they walked to the entrance.

On entering the building, Joey and Bob were met by four uniformed security guards sitting behind a large semicircular counter. Their uniforms were crisp, and the three men and one woman looked to be in excellent physical shape. They all carried side arms and radios with the microphones clipped to their left epaulets. Joey looked around the room and noted the photographs of military aircraft and engineering sketches of various aircraft parts. At each end of the semicircular counter was a door with a heavy digital security lock and a magnetic card swipe. Several security cameras scanned the room. On the counter, a small sign directed visitors to sign in. A digital camera system for taking photos for security badges was off to the left side of the counter.

The female guard pleasantly greeted Joey and Bob, saying, "Good morning, gentlemen. Please sign in and show me your security clearance identification."

Joey explained they didn't have security clearances but would be glad to sign in. The woman guard looked them over, obviously concerned that they had no security ID. Joey explained they were there to see Jack Pisani, at which point the woman security officer asked them to state their business with Mr. Pisani. Bob responded they wanted to talk to him about his yacht, and their visit had nothing to do with company business.

Both Joey and Bob noticed when Joey said they didn't have security clearances, one of the male security guards moved closer to the woman; and the other two walked around to the outside of the counter, guarding the doors that presumably led to the interior of the building. The woman picked up the telephone and called someone.

She spoke quietly into the phone and then listened for a moment before hanging up. All the while, the three male security guards had stopped doing anything other than watching Joey and Bob. The woman then explained Mr. Pisani was not available. She offered to give them the telephone number for JP Engineering so they could make an appointment. Joey thanked the woman, took the number, and tugged Bob's arm to leave the building. When they got in their rental car, Joey asked Bob to drive down the street and find someplace to pull over so they could talk.

"Boy, I didn't expect that," Joey exclaimed. "This guy Pisani obviously does something for the military. Lots of security. And they don't look like run-of-the-mill security guards you usually see in Philadelphia."

"Yeah," Bob replied. "That was a total bust. How the hell are we going to make an appointment with this guy without explaining why we want to see him? Maybe we should just say we are searching for a missing person and ask him to keep it quiet. It looks like he knows how to keep secrets."

"I don't know, Bob," Joey answered. "You know how hard it is to keep something out of the newspapers once people learn what

—

you are doing. I'm surprised we've been able to keep it quiet this long. In fact, I'm shocked Christi had one of her buddies at her office working on the case, and he hasn't said something to the reporters. Especially after she discovered how much money Anna has."

"Christi knows her business, Joey. She wouldn't have involved her colleague unless she was absolutely sure she could trust him. They work with a lot of secret information in the corporate world too."

"Yeah, you're right. I'm just concerned if this case gets reported in the media, all hell is going to break loose. We really have to be careful. I'm not in favor of telling Mr. Pisani anything he doesn't need to know. And if we identify ourselves as cops in order to get an appointment, his secretary, or someone else, might leak it to the press. That's all."

"Yeah, I see your point, and I agree. So what do we do now?"

Joey thought for a minute. "Let's look at the information the Coast Guard gave us again. Maybe there's something more in their notes."

"Wait. Wait, Bob," Joey exclaimed. "It says here the boat is owned by both Jack and Cecilia Pisani. It's in both their names. Let's go find Cecilia Pisani."

"Joey, didn't you just see the level of security back at Pisani's office. They probably don't have a listed phone number. How the hell are we going to get through to his wife?"

"Good question. Damn good question. Maybe we can get their address from the county's property records. That's public information."

"Wow! Excellent," Bob agreed. "We shouldn't have any trouble getting the records."

As Joey and Bob drove up to the Pisani house, they were surprised to find it was not excessively elegant. It was large, as were all the houses in the neighborhood, but not on an expansive piece of property as they had both assumed it would be. No iron gates protected a long paved driveway. No call box was posted at the entrance. Just a semicircular driveway lined with low-cut bushes leading to the main entrance.

After ringing the doorbell, Bob began looking for a security camera but didn't spot one. A woman of about fifty answered the door. Bob asked if she was Cecilia Pisani. She answered, "I'm Mrs. Pisani's housekeeper. May I ask what your business is with Mrs. Pisani?" Joey explained they were interested in her boat, the *DOVE*, and would like to speak to her briefly. She asked their names and told them to wait for a moment. She shut the door, leaving them outside. Bob turned to Joey and mumbled something about how he thought these people would be more security conscious. While they waited, for what Joey thought was an exceptionally long time, Bob kept searching for a hidden camera.

The wait was beginning to border on rudeness when the door finally opened. An exceptionally attractive brunette stood in the open doorway. She was barefooted but had on an expensive pair of white slacks and a light blue cotton sweater. She had modestly embellished her outfit with a gold bracelet and an ornamental pin on her sweater. Joey wondered if she was getting ready to go out or always dressed that nicely while at home.

"Good morning, gentlemen," Cecilia pleasantly greeted them. "I'm Cecilia Pisani. How can I help you?"

"I'm Joey Degrassi and this is Bob Marino," Joey responded. "We would appreciate it if we could talk to you about your yacht, Mrs. Pisani."

"Well, Mr. Degrassi," Cecilia answered, "if you're interested in chartering the *DOVE* you will have to contact our marine agent in Lucaya in the Bahamas. I can give you his telephone number."

"No, Mrs. Pisani. We're not actually interested in chartering it. We would like to talk about the boat itself and more specifically its crew and charter operations. Could we come in for a few minutes?" Joey asked. "We won't take long."

Cecilia looked at Joey and Bob for what seemed a long time. They were not the best dressers, but they were wearing suits. "Can you show me some identification, Mr. Degrassi?" Cecilia asked.

Joey and Bob looked at one another. Joey definitely did not want to give away who they were just yet. He didn't seem to have a choice, so he showed her his detective badge and ID with his photo on it. Bob did the same. Cecilia continued to scrutinize them even more intensely. She didn't react like most folks when shown a badge. She seemed to become increasingly suspicious, like they had done something wrong.

"So you're from Philadelphia?" she stated emphatically. Her mind was recalling the newspaper articles about the drug cartel and the crooked policemen in Philadelphia several years ago.

"Yes, unfortunately," Bob said with a smile, trying to induce some levity into what was becoming an uncomfortable standoff. That seemed to break the aura of distrust slightly, and she invited them in. She asked them to be seated in the front sitting room and inquired if they might like a cup of coffee.

"If you wouldn't mind," Joey answered, "we had to catch an early morning flight out of Philadelphia, and I could sure use a cup of coffee."

Both Bob and Joey noticed how Cecilia became more alert, with her eyes expanding, and a definite change in her voice as she asked, "So you flew in from Philadelphia just to talk to me?"

"Yes, ma'am," Joey answered.

While keeping her eyes on the two men, Cecilia said, "Marie, please get Mr. Degrassi and Mr. Marino a cup of coffee, and I'll have one too."

Hoping to break the tension, Bob offered Cecilia some perfunctory compliments on how comfortable the house felt. She showed no interest in talking about her house.

After taking a sip of her coffee, Cecilia asked, "Now, how can I help you, Mr. Degrassi?" She was being courteous but very suspicious.

Watching Cecilia's body language, Joey decided not to be evasive. He said, "Mrs. Pisani, we're looking for a woman who may have been on your boat recently. We are hoping you can help us find her."

Joey removed the photo of Anna standing on the *DOVE* from his breast pocket and showed it to Cecilia. Her reaction left no doubt she knew her. She lost color in her face and stared at the photo for an inordinately long time.

"How did you get this picture?" Cecilia demanded with an accusatory tone.

"So you do know her?" Joey stated flatly.

"Yes," Cecilia answered, feeling trapped but indignant that they had a photo of Thebb on the boat. "That's Thebb Meerschmidt, the cook on the *DOVE*. But how in the world did you get this picture, and why are you looking for her?"

Joey and Bob were caught off guard by her sudden authoritative directness and the new name for Annaliese Mueller.

Joey then showed Cecilia the picture of Anna that Christi had copied from the newspaper showing Anna and her husband when she was approximately twenty years old. He had folded the text under the photo so it wasn't visible.

"Would you say this is the same person, Mrs. Pisani?" Joey asked.

When Cecilia bit her lip and nodded yes, Joey unfolded the lower part of the picture showing the text identifying the woman as Annaliese Mueller, wife of Phillip Mueller.

Cecilia coldly asked, "Did Thebb, or this Annaliese Mueller, do something wrong, Mr. Degrassi? Why are you looking for her?"

"Annaliese Mueller was apparently killed in a traffic accident in Philadelphia about three years ago. But now, we suspect the victim was not Mrs. Mueller. She was identified as Annaliese Mueller because she had Mrs. Mueller's purse and revolver. We don't know why the victim had Mrs. Mueller's purse or who she was, but we are now pretty much certain she was not Mrs. Mueller."

As Joey explained the accident, Bob was observing Cecilia carefully. He watched her eyes grow wide. He noted she was relaxing and listening intently. Joey didn't mention the trust fund or the amount of wealth Anna had. He only told her Anna's husband was a successful financial advisor in a big investment firm in Philadelphia. In fact, he was the executive vice president of Kuefer & Bach Investments.

Cecilia stood up and called for her housekeeper. "Marie, do we have any cookies or cake we can offer these gentlemen?" Then she sat back down, crossed her legs and arms, and asked Joey, "Her husband beat her up! Right?"

"Well yes, at least we suspect he did," Joey responded in open surprise.

"How would you know that, Mrs. Pisani?" Bob asked.

"I used to be a nurse here in the Kettering area and saw a lot of abused women. That was the most common reason they wanted to get away and become anonymous. When I first met Thebb, I mean Mrs. Mueller, I suspected she had been abused for quite some time.

Probably by her boyfriend or husband. I knew she wouldn't admit it. Women who are trying to escape an abusive husband never do. She appeared to have no background, no history, and wouldn't talk about herself at all. She was highly distrustful of everyone and maintained a wall of anonymity. And she was very good at it."

Joey was listening and thinking about the lectures he had given Anna on how to disappear. *She must have been paying close attention.*

Cecilia was watching Joey and realized he was becoming uncomfortable as she talked about Anna being abused. She stopped in mid-sentence and asked, "Mr. Degrassi, before she disappeared, you knew her quite well, didn't you?"

"Well, uh, yeah, I did, Mrs. Pisani. How did you figure that out?" Joey asked incredulously.

"That's not important," Cecilia curtly responded. "What is important is what you intend to do now that you know she's not dead. If you bring her back, she could be hurt again. Her husband may even try to kill her. Have you considered that, Mr. Degrassi?"

"Yes, we have. We've thought about it a lot," Joey answered. "But her circumstances have changed considerably since then. He won't be able to hurt her anymore."

"And why is that?" Cecilia asked. "Do you intend to protect her around the clock? That won't work you know. I've seen what happens to women under the protection of the courts and the police. Their husbands or boyfriends eventually find them and kill them. And then the police arrest the husbands, but the women are dead. Maybe you should leave her alone and go about your business elsewhere. You knew her before she disappeared, didn't you? Did you protect her then? No! Of course not! So what makes you think you can do it now?"

It was becoming painfully obvious Mrs. Pisani was trying to protect Anna and didn't have much confidence in the police. Joey realized Mrs. Pisani had known from the beginning Anna, or Thebb as she was known, had been badly abused. He also began to suspect she had known that Thebb was not who she purported to be. He decided to tell her about the trust fund and how much money Anna was worth. But first he asked her if she could keep secret what he was about to tell her. At least until he had the chance to find Anna.

Cecilia agreed, and Joey began to reveal what he had learned about Anna's trust fund.

"Mrs. Pisani, we have discovered Anna was raised by her uncle and aunt. Her uncle had sold his manufacturing business and established a trust fund for her before he died. We're pretty sure she had no knowledge of the trust fund because it was set up when she was a young teenager. She thought she had no resources just before she disappeared. We know that to be true. She was supposed to inherit the trust money on her twenty-first birthday. She didn't, and we know that to be true. We also discovered her husband, Phillip Mueller, was her uncle's financial advisor and helped set up the trust fund. Her uncle designated Mr. Mueller as the trustee for the fund before he died. From what we can tell, no one told Anna about the inheritance, and her husband kept it secret.

"When she was younger, Anna must have been impressed with Phillip because she married him when she was eighteen. But still, he didn't tell her about the trust fund. As her husband, he would inherit all the money if she died. So now, if she returns, she won't have to worry about being able to support herself. We may be able to charge her husband with withholding her inheritance. Maybe even with trying to have her killed. The traffic accident in which she supposedly died may, or may not, have been an accident. We need to find Anna to figure out what really happened."

Cecilia got up and slowly walked back and forth saying, "But Thebb doesn't need money now, Mr. Degrassi. She has a job and is supporting herself by working on the *DOVE*. She's good at what she does and is happy doing it. So why change things?"

Bob had been listening carefully as Cecilia argued to protect Thebb but finally interrupted her saying, "With all due respect to you, Mrs. Pisani, I don't think her pay as the cook on your boat compares to the amount of her inheritance from the trust fund. The trust fund is now worth over 350 million dollars."

Cecilia almost spit out her coffee. "You must be kidding, Mr. Marino," she coughed. "Her inheritance is for hundreds of millions of dollars?"

Bob nodded his head and responded with a resounding, "Yes!"

Joey asked, "Can you help us find her so we can tell her about her inheritance and maybe find out who the victim of the traffic accident was?"

"Well yes," Cecilia slowly countered. "But there are certain conditions. First, I have to go with you when you meet with Thebb. Is that acceptable?"

"Certainly," Joey answered. "But that's only one condition. What are the others?"

"I don't know yet," Cecilia answered with a smile. "But I'm sure there will be more."

"So where can we find Mrs. Mueller and your boat, Mrs. Pisani?" Bob asked.

"Actually, Mr. Marino," Cecilia coldly responded with raised eyebrows, "we don't refer to a 130-foot schooner as a boat. We refer to it by its name. The *DOVE* is in dry dock in St. Croix. We're having the bottom cleaned and repainted, plus some mechanical servicing. So the *DOVE* is out of commission right now, and the crew has time off. Thebb is somewhere around St. Croix."

"Thanks for agreeing to help us, Mrs. Pisani," Joey said appreciatively. "Bob and I have to report back to Philadelphia and brief our captain about what we have found. Then we have to get authorization to travel to the Virgin Islands and that may be a problem. He won't easily authorize travel funds to go to St. Croix, so this could take some time. In the meantime, please remember the need for secrecy. If this gets out to the press, we could lose our case against Phillip Mueller. We have to be as careful and prudent as possible."

"Perhaps I can help," Cecilia responded. "I may be able to provide travel for us on my husband's private plane. And if you need to verify your findings with your boss, I'll be glad to talk to him. Now that I understand what you are trying to do, I think we ought to move quickly. Something like this will be hard to keep quiet."

"Let me give you my personal card, Mr. DeGrassi," Cecilia offered as she walked over to small table in the sitting room. "It has my telephone number here at the house and also my cell phone number. Neither are listed."

Just as Cecilia handed Joey her card, his iPhone began ringing. He apologized to Cecilia for the interruption saying it might be important. It was. It was Rachel.

"Joey, did you read the newspaper before you left this morning?" Rachel asked without saying hello or how are you.

"No! Bob and I barely had time to catch the flight to Dayton. Why? What's happening?"

"You are not going to believe this," Rachel said excitedly, "so I'm transmitting a photo of a picture in today's Inquirer."

Joey lowered his iPhone and watched the screen.

"Okay! I got it. Holy shit, Rachel. Is that Anna?"

"Unbelievable isn't it," Rachel stated. "Our girl got stuck on the bottom of the ocean in a submarine. This is a picture of her after they rescued her with some kind of robot. She has gone from sailboats to submarines. What a girl. And guess what, there's a dove on her shirt, just like in Christi's pictures."

Joey turned to Cecilia and showed her the small image on the iPhone screen. "We know where she is, Mrs. Pisani."

"Rachel, are you still there?" Joey asked.

"Yes! I thought we lost the connection," Rachel answered. "If you can get the Inquirer there, you can read about her adventure on page three. But don't worry, I bought several copies, and I'll have them here for you."

"Thanks, Rachel. I have to go. This is important news."

"Bob, a picture of Anna is in the Inquirer today. Her husband probably knows by now she's not dead. We'd better get down there right away."

Cecilia instantly agreed, "Absolutely. I'll call my husband and see if we can use his plane. We need to get there as fast as possible."

Joey placed a call to the police captain and explained what was going on. Cecilia took Joey's iPhone and validated everything Joey was saying. The captain agreed and said he would notify the police in St. Croix they were coming down and ask for their help if needed.

CHAPTER 62

It was early in the morning, and Denise Loman was sitting at her desk, sipping coffee and scanning the newspaper. It was something she had been doing for many years. It helped her stay abreast of national and local events and how they might affect the investment world. She was a financial analyst at Kuefer & Bach Investments, Inc., in Philadelphia, and knew all the top-level investment managers very well. Her husband was one of the senior partners. She was in her early forties and had been doing the same work for almost twenty years.

At the top of page three of the *Philadelphia Inquirer* that morning was a short article titled "SCIENTISTS TRAPPED 2, OOO FEET DOWN IN THE OCEAN." Denise thought that was interesting, but it wasn't something she needed to know much about. She glanced over the article and started to move on to another story when her attention was drawn back to the photograph of an attractive young woman standing in front of a complex-looking submarine. The woman was tall, thin, and had a long blond ponytail blowing across her shoulder.

The article explained the scientists had been searching for a new source of methane gas off St. Croix when their submarine became entangled in the wreckage of an ancient ship. They were trapped on the bottom until rescued by a smaller, remotely operated submarine from the research vessel that was its home base. The article went on to describe the *RV LAFOURCHE*, the ROV, and how long they had been in St. Croix. But nothing about the woman scientist except her name, which appeared under the photograph—Thebb Meerschmidt.

Denise studied the photo closely and then carried the paper to her associate's office next to hers.

"Ben, do you remember me telling you about the woman I saw in St. Maarten a couple of years ago? The one I thought looked like Mr. Mueller's wife?"

"Uh yeah. Vaguely. You thought she might be the sister or a relative of Mr. Mueller's wife. Why?"

Denise placed the paper on Ben's desk and pointed to the photograph. "I think this is that same woman. She looks just like Mr. Mueller's wife. There can't be two women in the Caribbean who look like her. Do you think?"

Ben looked briefly at the photograph. "I don't know, Denise, her cap has cast a shadow on her face. It's hard to tell."

"Look closely, Ben, and think."

Ben held the paper up close and studied the photo for a minute. "You know, Denise, I think you're right. Damn, the more I look at it, I'm sure you're right. In fact, if I didn't know better, I'd say this is Phillip's wife. She was very pretty and not easily forgettable."

"I've got to show this to Mr. Mueller."

"Hey, wait a minute," Ben cautioned as Denise began to leave his office. "Are you sure you want to do that? You know what I mean. Remember how gruesome her death was? Getting squashed by a truck and all. You may upset him."

Denise turned and stood at Ben's door, looking out his window. "No, I don't think it will upset him. It's been about three years now, hasn't it? This is rather interesting. I'll bet he will want to see it right away. Before he gets blindsided in a meeting or something."

"Denise, wait. You don't want to piss him off. You know what a temper he has."

"Somehow, Ben, I don't think this will piss him off."

With that comment, Denise turned and started for the elevator to Phillip's office. Ben called for her to wait. He wanted to go with her. "I want to see if your memory is as sharp as you think it is," he quipped. "Besides, it's damn hard to get an appointment with him. If he doesn't get pissed off, maybe I can get a few minutes to discuss this account I'm working on."

Phillip's secretary occupied an outer office with a door that separated her from his corner office with a view of downtown

Philadelphia. Compared to the other executive secretarial offices, the decor in her office was exceptional. Phillip had bought many fine pieces of art and used some of them to decorate his secretary's office as well as his. The carpet was a lush, deep rose color that perfectly complemented the mahogany and ash paneling. The paneling was exquisite as was his secretary. She was young, with long, straight, shiny dark hair, and very attractive.

Phillip's secretary explained that Mr. Mueller was working on an important project and didn't want to be disturbed. "He was here when I arrived at work, and that is usually the case when he is working on something big."

Denise wasn't about to take no for an answer and insisted on seeing him. "This will only take a minute or two. I'm sure he will want to see what I have to show him."

The secretary explained again he couldn't be disturbed. At that point, Denise asked her how long she had been Mr. Mueller's secretary. When she answered she had been working for Mr. Mueller for about four years, Denise asked if she had ever met his wife. The secretary said she had met his fiancée recently. In fact, she helped set up a party for Mr. Mueller to announce his engagement about three months ago.

"I didn't know he was planning to get remarried. We haven't heard about his engagement downstairs."

"Look, Ms. Loman," the secretary stated in exasperation, "Mr. Mueller is busy and can't see you now. You will just have to make an appointment."

"An appointment?" Denise said with growing indignation. "I do the analysis on most of his accounts. Just announce us and I'm sure he will see us."

"What's so important it can't wait?" the secretary asked.

Stung by the secretary's condescending attitude, Denise placed the newspaper, folded to show the photograph, on the desk in front of the secretary and said, "This woman looks a lot like his wife who was supposedly killed a few years ago. And here she is on a boat in the Caribbean."

The secretary looked at the photograph and haughtily responded, "Oh! So this is a personal issue. You should have said so in the first place. I'll ask if he will see you." Then she went into Phillip's office and closed the door.

Ben turned to Denise and whispered, "What are you doing? That's not his wife. Are you losing your marbles? He's going to throw us out."

"I don't know," Denise whispered back. "That young woman irritated me. Who does she think she is anyway? We ought to be able to see the boss if we want."

The door swung open, and the secretary, standing in the doorway, said pleasantly and with flourish, "Mr. Mueller will see you now."

As they entered Phillip's office, he got up from his high-backed leather chair, walked around to the front of his desk, and politely asked Denise and Ben to have a seat on the small sofa. He took a chair opposite them. Phillip was the epitome of graciousness. He knew the names of all the staff at Kuefer & Bach and started the conversation by perfunctorily asking Denise and Ben how they had been. After they both acknowledged his inquiry, Phillip told Denise he appreciated her thorough analysis of a recent account.

"So," Phillip asked, "you want to see me about a personal issue? I can only spare a moment, Denise. Are there problems downstairs?"

Denise quickly realized Phillip's secretary hadn't said anything about the photograph. *What a twit.*

"No, Mr. Mueller," Denise answered. "What we wanted to see you about doesn't have anything to do with work. You may want to know about an article in today's Inquirer. Have you seen the paper yet?"

Denise was cautious and wanted to determine if he had seen the morning paper. She didn't want to be dismissed abruptly. Phillip had a reputation for being very polite if everything was going well, but highly volatile if an employee made a mistake or took up his time with a mundane problem.

"Not yet," Phillip answered. "I've been working since early morning on a report that has to be finished by noon so I don't have much time. What's of importance in the paper? A major opportunity for investment I hope."

Cautiously, Denise answered, "There's an article about a young woman scientist who was trapped overnight in a submarine about two thousand feet underwater somewhere down in the Virgin Islands. The article includes a photograph of the woman standing in front of the submarine. We thought you would like to see the photo right away."

Denise then handed Phillip the newspaper. It was folded to show the article on Thebb. She had expected him to be surprised but was startled to see the extent of his reaction. His jaw dropped, his eyes opened wide, and his face lost all color. Phillip stared at the photo for what seemed like an eternity. Then he sat up straight, tightened his lips, and said, "This is an amazing likeness of Annaliese, my late wife. This woman appears to be about five or six years younger than Annaliese would be by now. I'm sure others may notice the resemblance and be confused by it. I appreciate your being thoughtful enough to bring it to my attention right away. Now I have to get back to work. Oh, can I keep the paper?"

With that comment, Phillip got up and returned to his desk. On the way out, Denise stopped at the secretary's desk and made a point of saying the meeting didn't take much time at all. The secretary rolled her eye and went back to typing at the large flat-screen computer. Denise and Ben returned to Denise's office feeling their meeting had been anticlimactic. It was clear Phillip thought the woman in the photo bore a close resemblance to his late wife, but Denise didn't judge his reaction to be significantly different than anyone else's would have been under the circumstances. Ben asked Denise if she actually thought the woman was Phillip's wife.

"I don't know, Ben. I only had a short glimpse of the woman in St. Maarten, but I was almost certain it was Mrs. Mueller. I knew she was dead, but I couldn't help thinking it was her. The woman looked just like her. I was at their wedding and saw her occasionally during the first year they were married. But then she gained weight and stopped coming to the office. There was something about that woman in St. Maarten I couldn't let go of. After seeing me, she turned and left the restaurant abruptly. But then we learned the woman we saw was married, had children, and lived in Chicago."

"Well, I hope this doesn't cause us any problems."

CHAPTER 63

Denise and Ben had just shut the door to Phillip Mueller's office when he reached into his pocket, retrieved his cell phone, and placed a call. There was no answer. He got up and walked to his window and looked out over the city. He redialed the same number again saying in a low voice to himself, *Goddamn it, Toro, answer the damn phone.*

A husky voice answered, "Yeah, this is Toro."

"This is Phil."

"Yeah, Phil. Haven't heard from you for a while. You have a good investment for me?"

Phillip answered in a low angry voice, "We have a problem. Do you remember the job you were supposed to have done for me about three years ago?"

"Uh, what do you mean by supposed to have done, Phil? You know how it came down."

"Have you seen this morning's paper?"

"No, not yet. What's going on?"

"Do you have today's paper?" Phillip asked assertively.

"Yeah, let me get it," Toro responded. After a moment he returned to the phone. "What do I look at?"

"Go to page three and look at the picture of a woman and a submarine."

After a long pause, Toro, in amazement, responded, "Holy fucking shit, Phil. That can't be the same person. No way!"

"Yes, it is," Phillip angrily yelled into the phone. Then quietly, he continued, "I paid you and Nicky each twenty-five goddamn thousand dollars. You assured me it was Annaliese who had been run over. Now I see in the paper she's on a goddamn submarine in the Caribbean. I have a major fucking problem, and you have to fix it."

"No, no, no! No fucking way! Nicky and I both saw her get run over. We were pretty sure she knew she was being followed that morning. She was spooked and took all kinds of weird roads trying to lose us. When she was on the sidewalk and looked up and saw us, she panicked and darted out in front of the truck. We were absolutely positive she was dead. You even went there and saw her body."

"Then who the fuck is that in the paper? She didn't have a goddamn twin!"

"I don't know, Phil," Toro angrily answered back. "But it ain't her. She's fucking dead!"

"Listen, Toro," Phillip said, lowering his voice, "it's her. I know it's Annaliese. I don't know how it happened, but I'm absolutely positive she's the woman in the paper. I want you to go fix the problem. The problem has to get fixed. You understand?"

"Okay! But this ain't going to be easy or cheap."

"Okay!" Phillip answered in a low, calm, businesslike voice. "I'll double the fee plus expenses. But I want you to fix the problem fast before it gets out of hand."

"I don't know about this week. I have obligations. If I don't meet them, they will cost me."

"Toro, this has to be done right away. You don't want me to go down on this. You don't want your other can of worms opened, do you? Find a way out of your problems. Pay them off. I'll cover your costs."

"Okay! Okay. I'll get Nicky. He won't believe this. Hey, we have another problem. They're checking all the luggage in the airports, especially the overseas flights. And they have sniffer machines to find gunpowder. How am I going to get down there right away and have the necessary equipment to complete the job. That'll take time."

Phillip sounded annoyed, "So charter a private plane. I can help you get one through the company I usually do business with. Just get the job done quickly and make sure it looks like an accident. You got that? An accident! She's in the Caribbean so have her get eaten by sharks or something. I don't care how you do it. I just don't want any questions being asked. Don't leave any loose ends."

"So, Phil, how do we find her once we get there?"

"Read the fucking newspaper, Toro. Read the paper and get down there as fast as possible."

CHAPTER 64

Cecilia had hoped to get her husband's plane for a flight to St. Croix that afternoon. It wasn't possible. The earliest they could depart for St. Croix was 1:00 p.m. the next day. Joey and Bob had to spend the night in Dayton.

Flying in from the west, in the late afternoon sun, St. Croix looked like a mountainous jewel as the JP Engineering Gulfstream-200 cruised toward the Alexander Hamilton Airport, just west of the industrial shipping channel. As they landed, Joey was observing the airport. He had learned long ago to pay close attention to his surroundings in case of an emergency. The airport was not large. Only two commercial jets were parked near the terminal building. All the other aircraft were single—and twin-engine types except for a small private jet parked off to the west side of the general aviation terminal.

Once on the ground, Cecilia went immediately into the general aviation terminal and used the pay phone to call Mike at his house at Cane Bay. She had not been able to make contact with him and thought it was irresponsible for him not to have a cell phone. But then, she mused, the cell coverage in the islands was spotty anyhow. She redialed. Again no answer, so she picked up a rental car and they drove over to Mike's place.

After returning from several errands, Mike was just entering his house as Cecilia, Joey, and Bob drove up. He was surprised but pleased to see her.

"Cecilia, we didn't expect to see you for another few weeks. I don't know the reason for your visit, but your timing is perfect. We're planning a party tomorrow night to celebrate completion of the work on the research vessel with Jim Thornhouser."

"That's wonderful, Mike, but we may not be able to make it to the party." Cecilia was anticipating Thebb would fly back to Dayton with her the next day.

"That would be a shame. It would be perfect if you could stay for the party," Mike responded. "I'm just getting ready to meet George down at the Christiansted Harbor. His boat has been serviced, and I was going to pick him up."

"Mike," Cecilia said emphatically, "before you go, I want you to meet a couple of friends of mine. Can we go inside for a few minutes? I need to talk to you right away."

Mike watched Joey and Bob suspiciously as they scanned the rooms upon entering the house.

"Mike," Cecilia said, "this is Joey Degrassi and Bob Marino."

Before she could continue, Mike shook Joey's hand, looked quizzically at him, and said, "You're a cop, right? And you too, Mr. Marino."

"Yes, we are," Joey responded, "and we are hoping you can help us."

Cecilia asked, "Mike, have you seen any newspaper articles on the recovery of the submarine from the *LAFOURCHE* with a picture of Thebb in front of it?"

"Of course," Mike answered. "There's been quite a bit of coverage on the sub. That was a big story for this little island."

Joey interjected, "The story was published all over the United States. It had a human interest slant with a beautiful young woman stranded at the bottom of the ocean, so most of the papers carried it with a photograph of Anna. And that's why we're here."

Joey could see Mike was backing away from him and becoming defensive.

"Mike," Joey asserted, "the publication of the photo has exposed Mrs. Mueller to great harm, and we're her to protect her."

Mike looked at Cecilia and asked, "Who's Mrs. Mueller?"

Cecilia answered, "Thebb."

Mike turned, found a chair, and suggested everyone have a seat. "I think I need an explanation. I know Thebb and I can't think of a

---

351

single reason why the police would be interested in her. So why are you here?"

Over the next half hour, Joey and Bob explained why they were looking for Thebb. Cecilia had to assure Mike several times what Joey was saying was correct, and they were there to protect her. She was counting on Mike not to mention anything about Annaberg and he didn't. Mike kept shaking his head in amazement as the story unfolded.

"You know, fellas," Mike finally stated, "that's the most unbelievable story I've ever heard. How could she have orchestrated such a complex accident? She's not that kind of person."

"She didn't orchestrate anything," Joey answered sharply. "It's our theory, by happenstance, she crossed paths with a woman with similar looks who snatched her bag and while trying to get away ran out in front of a truck. The accident was pretty bad. The woman's body was torn apart, and her face was unrecognizable. But she had Anna's, that is Thebb's, purse and identification. Even her husband identified the body. We think she quickly realized the accident was an opportunity to get out of an abusive marriage in which her life was in danger. She may even have thought her husband set up the accident to kill her."

"Well," Mike said, "the *LAFOURCHE* will be docking at the concrete pier in Frederiksted in the morning, probably around 0900."

"What's the *LAFOURCHE*?"

Mike explained, "The *LAFOURCHE* is the research vessel Thebb is on. If you think it would help, we can contact the vessel on the VHF."

"No," Joey answered, "if the ship is coming into port in the morning, it may be best to wait until she gets off."

"So what do we do now?" Mike asked. "George is waiting down at the harbor in Christiansted, and I have to pick him up."

"Let's just wait until morning to meet the ship and go from there. Bob and I will get a room in Frederiksted for the night."

"No," Mike countered. "We can't let you do that. Why don't you all join George and me for dinner in Christiansted and then spend the night here at the house. The dinner's on me, and there's enough room here. That way we can all stay together. You can't really do anything tonight anyhow. I'm supposed to meet George at the Rum

Runners on the harbor wharf. They have great food, and you might as well enjoy the view of the harbor."

When they arrived at the restaurant, George was sitting at a table near the boardwalk watching CNN and drinking a beer. When he saw Mike and Cecilia, he blurted out, "Boy, you guys are famous. The newspapers made it sound pretty scary, and they are still talking about that methane stuff on CNN."

"It's been on CNN?" Bob asked while turning around to find the TV.

"Oh yeah," George answered. "They've been asking all the usual experts about methane, submarines, and worms. Every time they start to have a discussion, they show a picture of Thebb in front of the sub. I wouldn't be surprised if CNN shows up down here."

Cecilia said hello to George and gave him a hug. George responded by saying that it was great to see her again. "You're one of my two most favorite women, Cecilia. Here, sit next to me."

Cecilia introduced Joey and Bob simply as friends. Over dinner, at Cecilia's insistence, Joey explained, in a brief fashion, why they were there. George sat quietly, watching Joey and Bob. Then George turned to Cecilia and questioned her confidence in the two men. He made it clear he didn't trust them, and he said it loud enough both Joey and Bob could hear.

"I'm really impressed," Joey said in defense of his position. "You are all so protective of Anna, I mean Thebb. You act like family."

"We are family," Cecilia responded emphatically. "We look out for one another. And, Mr. Degrassi, there is probably nothing we won't do to protect Thebb!"

George added, while leaning forward over the table, "If what you've said isn't true, then—"

Joey read the threat loud and clear. So did Bob. As he learned more about Thebb's friends, Joey began to think about the complex relationships he was dealing with. What was most curious was the relationship Cecilia seemed to have with these older sea salts. She was incredibly wealthy and owned a big sailboat and private jet plane. Yet she acted and was treated like one of them. At the same time, there was a subtle but definite respect for her.

After dinner, Cecilia drove back to the airport to talk with the pilots of Jack's G-2. They had been waiting at the general aviation terminal for word from her about when she wanted to depart. She told them to be prepared to leave before noon the next day. "Have a good night's sleep. But get up early, have breakfast, and then stay with the plane." She went back to Mike's hoping she, too, would have a good night's sleep. All the revelations about Thebb's true identity had her keyed up.

CHAPTER 65

"It's amazing how fast you can rent an airplane for a few days if you just have enough money," Toro commented to Nicky. "At first they questioned our ability to pay, but I had them call Phil, and he smoothed out everything. He was really pissed when he saw that picture in the newspaper, but he'll get over it."

Nicky answered, "So when do we leave?"

"First thing in the morning," Toro responded. "They have to check the plane out, fill it with gas, and do some other shit like file a flight plan. Make sure you have all our equipment. I talked to the copilot, and he's gonna help us get our special baggage off the plane after we land. That'll cost a bundle too. Phil better be ready for the bill because it's gonna be big."

As they approached the island, Toro told the pilot to make a circle and see if they could find a boat near Frederiksted that was doing some kind of work in the ocean. They didn't need to circle. As they approached the island, they could see the *LAFOURCHE* on station south of St. Croix.

After loading their baggage into a rental car, Toro told the pilots to get the plane gassed up and be ready to fly on a moment's notice. "Make sure your cell phones are on."

In their hotel room in Frederiksted, Toro studied several maps of the island. He was trying to plan an accident for Mrs. Mueller that would allow them to make a quick getaway with a minimum of complications. Phillip had suggested feeding her to the sharks, but that would mean they would have to get a boat. It might be simpler to stage a car accident. Either way, he had to learn the island quickly and watch the ship to make sure they didn't miss her.

After memorizing the roads on the map, Toro decided he and Nicky should drive around the island and learn the road system and where the towns and housing areas were. He was especially interested in desolate areas. The island wasn't very big so it wouldn't take too long. They were only a few miles outside of Frederiksted before Nicky almost had a head-on collision. Mahogany Road, also known as Highway 76, was a winding, hilly road leading into the interior of St. Croix. Many of the curves were sharp, blind, or unmarked with missing road signs. Nicky was also having trouble remembering to drive on the left side of the road. As he tried to navigate around a sharp curve, another car, obviously an islander, approached at high speed but was able to swerve out of the way at the last minute. The two cars missed each other only by inches. Toro commenced to shout expletives at Nicky, telling him to pay attention. "We're here to kill the fucking woman, not ourselves, moron."

The next morning, Toro and Nicky had breakfast at a sidewalk café overlooking the water. They could see the research vessel offshore. It appeared to be returning to port. Toro couldn't believe the good timing. He grabbed Nicky by the arm and told him they needed a good set of binoculars. Finding binoculars turned out to be easy. All the local photo shops carried them. Every brand. Every price. They returned to the café and drank coffee while using the binoculars to watch the research vessel tie up to the long concrete pier.

As the ship's crew threw out the lines and tied the ship to the large black iron bollards, Toro kicked Nicky to get his attention. "I think I see her," Toro said. "She's standing near the top of the gangplank. Let's get back to the car so we can follow her. We're gonna get her good this time."

CHAPTER 66

As the gangplank lowered into position, Thebb spotted a panel truck, followed by two cars, driving out onto the pier. She could see the first car was Mike, and the passenger was most likely George. She waved to Mike. As Thebb started down the gangplank, she saw the doors of the second car begin to open but couldn't tell who was in it until the doors fully opened. Halfway down the gangplank, she realized the driver was Cecilia, and one of the passengers was Joey. She stopped suddenly, midway down the gangplank, and was almost knocked down by Bo following her with two of Jim's boxes of samples to be loaded into the panel truck for transport to the airport. She stood frozen in place while Bo tried to maneuver around her.

Thebb couldn't take her eyes off Joey. She was excited to see him, but Cecilia was with him. Something was definitely wrong. A wave of anxiety flashed across her consciousness, but it didn't matter. She put down the box she was carrying and ran to Joey. She gave him a great big hug and began crying. Joey was crying too. Bo watched in awe. Cecilia, at first surprised, walked around the car and stood by Thebb and Joey, neither of them able to let go of the other. After watching for what seemed a long enough time, Cecilia interrupted them, "So I take it you two know each other."

Nothing happened. Her levity went unappreciated. They just kept standing there together with their arms wrapped around each other.

All the fears she had repressed over the years were coming to the surface, and her longtime wish to see Joey again was overwhelming her.

"I did everything you taught me, Joey," Thebb said. "How did you find me?"

Joey began wiping Thebb's tears away. "You did everything right," he consoled her. "Sometimes things happen that are simply unexpected, and you have no control over them. I've been looking for you ever since we passed each other in the channel into St. Croix."

"I didn't think you recognized me!"

"You're right. At first I didn't. You're were so skinny, and I thought you were dead."

Thebb smiled, took his hand, and in a low sad voice commented, "Yeah, that's a long story. But how did you find me? How did you find Cecilia?"

Joey reached into his coat pocket and showed Thebb the Philadelphia newspaper article with her picture prominently displayed. "Who would have thought it would take getting trapped in a submarine two thousand feet under the ocean to expose you?"

Joey had to grab Thebb when she saw the photo. The color drained from her face as she stepped back and stared at the newspaper article.

"Oh no! This is terrible," Thebb exclaimed. "Now Phillip must know I'm alive. He's going to be furious. He's going to kill me."

Cecilia interrupted, softly saying, "Thebb, we have to talk to you. There's a lot you don't know. Can we go to Mike's place and talk? We can have someone pick up your things from the *LAFOURCHE*. We need to talk right away, and this isn't the place to do it."

"Okay," Thebb answered weakly, "but I want Bo to come too."

Thebb's response irked Cecilia. They didn't need extraneous people with them when they were explaining what they had discovered, but Thebb insisted. Being stranded on the ocean floor overnight made her realize how important Bo really was to her.

Bo was standing next to Mike's car with Mike and George. Watching the emotional reunion of Thebb and Joey was unsettling for him. He couldn't decide if he was happy for Thebb or angry at Joey.

Cecilia decided it might be best for Thebb and Joey to drive back to the house by themselves, but Bo had walked over, and Thebb took his hand while talking with Joey. So Cecilia suggested Thebb, Joey, and Bo take her rental car, and the rest of them would follow in Mike's car. Bo offered to drive Cecilia's rental car so Thebb and Joey could sit together in the back seat and talk.

CHAPTER 67

After leaving the pier, Bo turned north onto King Street, then east on Mahogany Road. Soon after, a white sedan began to follow them. It stayed behind for several miles, along the straight portion of the road between King Street and Little La Grange Hill. Bo made a mental note of the car because he wasn't driving very fast and generally island drivers would pass at the first opportunity. Also, the road became winding with sharp curves for three or four miles after Little La Grange Hill and there would be no opportunity for the car to pass.

As Bo approached the first sharp curve south of Jolly Hill, the following car, with Nicky at the wheel, sped up and attempted to pass. When the car was alongside, it swerved sharply, hard, and unforgivingly against Bo's car and pushed him off the road. With his left wheels digging hard into the soft dirt on the shoulder of the road, Bo lost control, and his car lurched to the left. Bo yelled for Thebb to get down and hang on. Both Thebb and Joey dropped to the floor and grabbed the bottom of the front seats.

The car slid down the incline. Brakes didn't help in the soft dry dirt. The front tires dug into the dirt, and the car rolled over as it tumbled down the hill. The first flip was high. The impact on hitting the ground triggered the explosive air bag, hitting Bo in the face. The car continued into a second flip as it tumbled down the incline before landing on its wheels in a cloud of dust that engulfed the entire car. Bo sat dazed, bleeding from his forehead, nose, and cheek. His seat bolt had held him mostly in place, but during the second rollover he was thrown wildly about, hitting the dashboard. Thebb and Joey had not used their seat belts, but because of Bo's warning, and their fast reaction they were just shaken up and covered in dust.

Joey began trying to get the dust off his face and pushed the right rear door open. As he did, he saw a white car parked up the hill several hundred feet away. It was on the side of the road with both front doors open. Two men were coming down the embankment toward them. Joey was slightly disoriented, but he could plainly see the man in front was carrying a tire iron. The man behind him was walking more slowly with an automatic pistol pointing directly at them. Joey retrieved his .40-caliber XD from his rear belt holster and struggled to get out of the car.

Toro was loping down the hill toward the rolled car with a tire iron expecting to dispatch Annaliese and her friends before they could recover. Nicky followed with his gun pointing at Joey in the back seat. He had to jump over several small gullies where dirt had washed away in rain storms causing him to move more cautiously.

Nicky saw the glitter of sunlight reflecting off the bright slide on Joey's gun and opened fire. One bullet hit Joey in the left upper arm, spinning him around and backward onto the seat. A second bullet passed through the open door and hit the steering wheel in front of Bo. Bo bolted upright as the splinters from the steering wheel peppered his arms and neck, jolting him out of his stupor. He released his seat belt and rolled out the left front door and into the dirt and weeds.

Joey stretched outward, handed Thebb his gun, and yelled, "Shoot the bastard, Anna! Shoot him!"

Toro was cautiously jogging down the steep and craggy embankment when the two shots from Nicky's gun shattered the stillness and caused his ears to ring. He jolted, stopped, and turned to see what Nicky was doing. Nicky had shot over Toro's shoulder at Joey and still had his gun pointed toward Toro.

"What the fuck are you doing?" Toro yelled. "This is supposed to look like an accident."

"The son of a bitch had a gun, Toro. Look out. The woman's got a gun!"

Thebb had crawled out of the left rear door and was resting her arms on the trunk of the car. She braced Joey's gun with her left hand and took aim. When Nicky was about seventy-five feet away, running toward her, she fired. Twice! Nicky fell forward, facedown into the dirt. Arms outstretched with his gun still in his hand. Toro stopped, stunned at the reports from Thebb's shots. Instantly, he realized he was in the open, without cover, and the shooter was obviously deadly accurate. He threw the tire iron at Thebb, turned, and ran back toward his car. She ducked behind the car as the tire iron bounced off the other side of the car.

When Thebb looked up, Toro was running in a zigzag path up the embankment. He tripped and fell but got up quickly and continued to run. She had expected him to keep coming and had leveled the gun toward him. But he was getting too far away, and the immediate threat was gone. Joey crawled out of the car and stood next to Thebb. He saw the dead man in the dirt and the other man running toward his car. Bo had taken cover at the front of the car.

Joey took his gun from Thebb, saying, "I did the shooting, Anna. Understand! Bo, you hear that? I did the shooting."

As Toro was running up the hill, Mike drove up. Everyone in the car saw Toro running and Nicky on the ground. Before Toro could reach his car, Bob began yelling for Mike to cut him off. Mike sped up, honking his horn, trying to get to Toro's car before Toro could. Toro reached his car first, but there were no keys. He cursed Nicky. With Mike approaching fast and honking, Toro abandoned the car and bolted around the curve and down the hill, away from the road. Mike followed on the road above.

Toro ran toward a small pink farmhouse set back from the road. It had dark green shutters, a silvery metal roof, and a dirty green door. It was surrounded by a low stone wall, painted white as was typical on the island. As Toro approached the wall, chickens began squawking and running in all directions. Small goats bounded off to the side and scattered. Bob yelled for Mike to stop the car. He jumped out and began to chase Toro on foot. With Bob chasing him, Toro was looking from side to side, desperately trying to find an escape route. He leaped over the low white wall, almost falling but scattering more of the chickens. He ran to the front door of the house. It was locked. He slammed his body against it, but the solid wooden door wouldn't budge. It was weathered and dirty with rusty hinges, but it wouldn't give.

Toro leaped off the small concrete porch and ran toward a weathered outbuilding. A wobbly white picket fence, with more goats behind it, stood in his way. He attempted to leap over it, but his pant leg caught on the pickets, and his ankle slid down between the slats. He tried to roll over to get his gun, but Bob had reached him and was pointing a gun at him.

Bob yelled at Toro to lie still and keep his hands in sight. With his ankle trapped between the slats, dust settling over his face and eyes, and Bob standing over him, Toro had no option but to comply. Mike and George ran to help Bob while Cecilia got behind the driver's wheel and drove down to the fence. Mike retrieved some rope from his trunk, and he and George tied Toro's hands behind him. Once they had him securely bound and in the back seat of the car, they drove back to where Bo had been forced off the road.

George began grilling Toro. "Who the hell are you, you son of a bitch?" George demanded. "Why are you trying to hurt those people?"

Toro didn't answer. He sat looking at the floor mumbling something about the miserable stupid bitch.

Bob joined in on the questioning. His questions were less aggressive, but Toro refused to answer.

As Cecilia drove back to the site of the wreck, they could see smoke. Lots of smoke. Bo, Joey, and Thebb were trying to push their car away from a small fire under the car. The grass and weeds were dry and high and on fire. The catalytic converter had ignited the grass, and the fire was quickly spreading, threatening to engulf the whole car. Mike and George ran down to help. They got the car moved and began throwing sand on the fire. When the fire was finally out, they stood looking at each other. Not speaking. Just looking.

Bo seemed bewildered. He pulled Thebb to the side and hugged her. He whispered, "Thebb, I thought this was all over at Annaberg. Are these people ever going to stop?"

Thebb whispered back, "I don't know, Bo, but I can't do this anymore without you."

George came over and put his arms around both of them, saying, "Come on, guys, let's get back up the hill." Mike assisted Joey back up to his car. Bob tried to clean Joey's wound, but it was clear he needed professional medical attention. He asked if someone would call for an ambulance right away. The police also had to be notified. They needed to take Toro into custody until Joey and Bob could take him to Philadelphia. Since there was no reception where they were, Cecilia volunteered to drive back toward Frederiksted to find an area with cell coverage.

It seemed to take forever for the ambulance and police to arrive. After Joey was taken away in the ambulance, Bob explained to the police he and Joey were Philadelphia detectives. Their captain had secured approval for them to travel to St. Croix to find a woman hiding from someone trying to kill her. The police were cooperative. They agreed to withhold the release of any information about the incident until certain critical arrests were made in Philadelphia. Bob went to the police station in one of the police cars to fill out the paperwork needed to take Toro back to Philadelphia. Several other policemen were left to deal with Nicky who was still lying facedown in the dirt with his gun in his hand.

At the Juan F. Louis Hospital in Christiansted, Thebb stayed with Joey most of the afternoon. She wouldn't leave until she knew he was going to be okay. Bo stayed too. Not just for moral support but because he was concerned about another attempt on Thebb's life.

One of the emergency room doctors returned after a few hours and told them Joey was okay but would have to remain in the hospital for a few days to regain his strength. He had lost blood and needed the time to recover. They had given him sedatives and recommended everyone leave and come back in the morning. All Joey was going to do was sleep the rest of the day.

Thebb went to Mike's house, and Bo left for the *LAFOURCHE* to check on Jim Thornhouser. He felt bad they had disappeared in such a hurry and wanted to make sure Jim didn't need more help. He also needed to collect their things from the ship.

CHAPTER 68

Back at Mike's house, Cecilia and Bob agreed not to tell Thebb why they wanted to talk to her. Only Joey should do it. But they were curious why Thebb didn't ask more questions. Bob thought she must have been in shock due to the shoot-out between Joey and the two hired killers. Cecilia didn't say anything.

But Thebb wasn't in shock. She felt certain she knew why the assassins were trying to kill her. Her husband must have seen her photograph in the newspaper and discovered she was still alive.

Cecilia watched Thebb sitting, almost catatonically, deep in thought on the veranda overlooking the ice blue water at Cane Bay. Thebb seemed oblivious to the beauty of the scenery or the light breeze. She just sat staring into space. *Why doesn't Phillip just leave me alone? I'm out of his life and far away. Why does he hate me so much that he sent thugs to kill me? What did I do to him?*

Hesitantly, Cecilia stepped out onto the veranda, quietly shutting the door behind her. She took a chair next to Thebb.

"Thebb," Cecilia quietly asked, "are you okay?"

Thebb turned and looked at Cecilia. "Those men this morning were not sent by the drug dealers. It was my husband."

"That could be, Thebb, but how can you be sure? Didn't we learn at Annaberg the drug cartel would go to any length to get you? And those men were obviously professionals."

"Cecilia, listen! It's been a long time since Annaberg. I've changed my appearance and my name. The drug people wouldn't have known me from a photograph in the newspaper. Even Joey didn't recognize me when we passed in the channel. He told me in the car it took him weeks to realize it was me, but Phillip would have recognized me right away. I've been sitting here thinking about it. I'm certain Phillip sent those men to kill me."

"Thebb, I don't want to make light of your concerns over your husband, but it's important you think about the drug cartel too. A lot of the cartel members were policemen, and the newspaper reported some of them may still be at large. If any of those people learn you had something to do with the ledgers, they may try to hurt you. I'm asking you not to mention anything about the ledgers or the events at Annaberg. Not to Joey. Not to anyone. And not just for your safety but my husband's too. Jack has some very sensitive contracts with the government, and it could destroy his business. This has to be our secret."

Thebb sat still, biting her lip and listening intently to Cecilia. After a minute of silence, she responded, "Thanks, Cecilia. You're really a great friend for keeping my secret, and I promise I won't say anything about the ledgers." *The ledgers could tie me directly to the cash in Tatianna's bag. The drug dealers probably don't even know how much money she was stealing. And they certainly don't know about her account in the Cayman Islands bank.*

"But you too," she whispered to Cecilia. "You can't ever say anything about them either."

"You know I won't," Cecilia whispered back. "This is a permanent bond between us. Total secrecy about the ledgers."

"I've been sitting here thinking about how to explain what happened the morning of the traffic accident in Philadelphia. I was certain Phillip was having me followed. And it wasn't the first time. I was trying to elude the men who were after me so I ducked into a women's dress shop in an out-of-the-way part of the city. While I was in the store, a woman came in wearing an outfit similar to mine. I guess we vaguely resembled each other. As she left, she accidentally took my bag instead of hers. She was about to cross the street when I yelled she had the wrong bag. She turned her head to look at me as she was stepping off the curb. Just then, a truck came speeding down the street and hit her. It was horrible. I had distracted her, and she got run over by the truck. It was my fault."

"Hey, take it easy. How can you be responsible for the woman walking out into traffic without looking? It wasn't your fault."

"Yes, it was!" Thebb lamented. "When I yelled at her, she turned to look at me and then bolted out into traffic. I can't get it out of my head. Blood was everywhere. Her body was ripped apart so badly they couldn't recognize her."

Thebb paused momentarily. "The police announced the dead woman was me, Annaliese Mueller, and I realized it could be my opportunity to get away. To disappear. I saw the 'COOK WANTED' sign on the *DOVE*, and Bart hired me. When I finally looked in the woman's bag, I found the ledgers. The entries appeared to be a detailed accounting of drug payoffs and bribes in some type of code. I didn't know what to do with the ledgers but felt I had to get rid of them. So when you offered to help me, I decided to mail them to the DA's office. I hoped a postmark from some city other than Philadelphia would help distance me from the ledgers."

"So based on the reporting in the Inquirer, the mysterious accountant was Tatianna. The drug dealers wanted to kill her for stealing their books and turning them in to the police!" Cecilia concluded.

"Yeah," Thebb agreed. "When I realized I had the opportunity to disappear, I inadvertently took Tatianna's name. I had found her passport in the bag and used it. I'm pretty sure that's how they found me. They were looking for her. And who did they kidnap? You! I almost got you killed too. I was really scared they would kill you."

"Damn, Thebb, it's more than scary. Do you realize you had two different groups trying to kill you? Are you certain this guy Toro is working for your husband?"

"Yeah," Thebb answered wistfully, while staring off in the distance again. "I'm pretty sure it was Phillip. He's the only one who would have recognized me."

Thebb sat silent for a moment. "What a mess this turned out to be. And now I've endangered all of you. On top of it all, I have another problem. How do I explain this to Bo? He's not going to want to have anything to do with me. Everything I touch turns into a disaster."

"Thebb," cautioned Cecilia. "Don't worry about Bo. He'll be okay. It's obvious that he's in love with you. I'm sure he knows there's a lot more to your background than you let on."

"Really? You think that's true?" Thebb questioned with tears welling up in her eyes.

"Of course. We've all figured that out because you never talk about yourself. Even worse, you cut people off if they get too personal. I'm sure Bo knows it best of all, and he still loves you."

"I hope you're right. I really hope you're right," Thebb whispered as she crossed her arms and lowered her head into them.

Cecilia edged closer to Thebb. "But listen to me! There's more that you need to know. Joey is going to tell you about it. It's too complicated for anyone else to explain properly. Just remember Thebb, I mean Anna, you can't tell the story you just told me to anyone. Please! It's almost unbelievable, and it connects all of us to the ledgers and Annaberg."

CHAPTER 69

Joey had been lucky, if you can say getting shot was lucky. Nicky had used fully jacketed bullets, not hollow points. The bullet went through his upper arm and didn't hit bone. The doctors were worried about a deep infection because they weren't sure they got all the pieces of his shirt out of the wound. They couldn't be certain without doing more extensive surgery, and that could have caused more damage than the bullet hole. So they treated him with heavy doses of antibiotics and watched him for a few days.

Thebb spent most of her time visiting Joey in the hospital accompanied by Bo. On the second day in the hospital, Joey was feeling much better. Joey and Thebb were having a good time reminiscing about the past. Bo sat quietly listening in awe to their stories. He was most enthralled with Joey's shooting range and their various practice sessions. He was becoming aware of how Thebb came to be such an expert marksman. When Bo commented on her ability to handle a gun, Thebb turned her head so Joey couldn't see her face and glared at Bo. Bo realized he might have been giving away the shooting events of the Bahamas and Annaberg. He quickly stated that after the car flipped over, she was able to hit a moving target a long distance away. Thebb responded it was just luck and turned back to Joey who wouldn't have any of it. He emphatically reminded them he shot the bastard, not Thebb.

"She had nothing to do with the shooting, Bo. Remember that."

Joey knew Thebb was anxious to learn the details of how he had found her. He explained if she hadn't made the gesture of a gun with her hand as they passed each other on separate boats, he would never have figured it out.

"You were supposed to be dead. Everyone thought you were dead. I had a terrible few weeks obsessing over the woman on the sailboat in St. Croix. There was something special about her, but I couldn't put my finger on it. When I finally realized it was you, I told my partner, Bob. At first he didn't believe me. My friend Rachel and Bob's wife Christi kept asking for proof. Then Christi remembered she had taken some pictures of you when we passed in the channel. You were thinner and had longer hair, but there was no doubt it was you on the sailboat. So we teamed up, researched your background, and found Mrs. Pisani."

"I'll bet she wasn't happy about that," Thebb laughed.

"Actually, Anna, uh, Thebb, Bob and I were surprised at how ferociously she tried to protect you. She was really suspicious."

"Yeah, Joey," Bo added. "You really don't want to get crosswise with Cecilia."

Joey went on to point out that getting stuck on the bottom of the ocean and having her picture published in the Philadelphia newspaper was the coup de grace. "The newspaper article was a big help, but we were about to find you anyhow. It's odd how unexpected events can change everything. But enough of that. I have some very important news I have to tell you. Rachel and Christi researched your background and uncovered a treasure trove of information you are apparently unaware of."

"But first," Joey stated, "we have to get this name thing straightened out. As far as I'm concerned, you're Annaliese Mueller. But I don't think you should use that name until we deal with Phillip. There's a lot you don't know about him. I know he was your husband, and you think you know him, but my friends and I have learned things about him that will surprise you. So let's start at the beginning."

Thebb and Bo sat transfixed as Joey revealed facts about her history, her marriage, and the trust fund Phillip had hidden from her. Thebb expressed disbelief Joey and his friends had been able to learn so much about her. They uncovered things she didn't know. She had no response on learning that she had an inheritance or that Phillip had not told her about it. She just sat listening, matter-of-factly, without comment.

"Thebb, you don't seem to be concerned that Phillip hid your inheritance. Your trust fund."

"No. Not really," Thebb answered. "My uncle and aunt were simple people, and we lived pretty modestly. They didn't have much money so if they left me a trust fund, I'm sure it wasn't very big and doesn't compare to what Phillip was providing. I felt I was a burden on my uncle and aunt, but they never complained. They hired Phillip to help them manage their limited finances so we wouldn't starve. Then my uncle died, and Phillip spent more time helping us. He was really sweet and very generous in those days."

Joey was shaking his head in disbelief. He was thinking how naïve and vulnerable Thebb had been and how cunning Phillip was. He began to understand why she had put up with Phillip even when he was abusing her. She had a tremendous sense of debt and guilt, and she didn't know she had any alternatives.

"Thebb," Joey firmly asked, "have you ever wondered why Phillip beat you up all the time? It's because your inheritance is substantial. Why do you think he concealed it and didn't tell you? It wasn't because it was a trivial amount of money."

Still not understanding what Joey was driving at, Thebb asked, "So how much is it?"

"As far as we can tell," Joey said while smiling, "it's approximately 350 million dollars, give or take a million here or there."

Bo just about fell out of his chair with his mouth open. Thebb simply sat perfectly still, staring at Joey. Her brow was wrinkled. She sat back in her chair and crossed her arms. She sat quietly for a moment. Finally, she responded angrily, "Joey, that's not funny. There is no way my uncle could have left me that kind of money. He didn't have it. He had to have help with his finances."

Joey was enjoying himself immensely. He started laughing and shaking his head.

Bo was slapping his thighs and yelling, "Holy shit, Thebb! You're rich! Unbelievable!"

Thebb still couldn't get her head around such a possibility. She stared at Bo. He was almost dancing.

"Thebb," Joey asked while no longer laughing, "what did your uncle do before you moved to Philadelphia?"

"He had a small wire and nail company," Thebb answered. "But—"

"Yes," Joey interrupted enthusiastically. "He owned it. He inherited a small wire and nail company from his father and built it into a major enterprise with numerous national and international contracts. It wasn't just a local business."

"Actually, Joey," Thebb answered, "I don't think he actually owned it. He only managed it."

"Thebb," Joey emphasized, "he owned it. Over the years, he invested almost all his profits back into the business, upgrading the equipment and expanding his production capabilities. When he became seriously ill, he sold it for approximately 267 million dollars of profit after taxes. He must have been one hell of a special person because he distributed 10 million dollars from the sale among the employees and put almost all the remainder into a trust fund for you to inherit when you turned twenty-one. That's why he hired Phillip. It was to help him manage his assets. And Phillip did a good job. As it turns out, he has been investing the money very successfully. Your trust fund is worth about 350 million now. That's why he didn't tell you and that's why he wanted to get rid of you. As your husband, he would inherit it all. He would have full control of it. Now it's yours, and you don't have to worry about how you are going to support yourself."

Joey stopped talking, and Bo stood quietly, watching Thebb stare out the window. Slowly, very slowly, she began to smile. She turned, looked at Bo, who's eyes were popping out of his head, and smiled. It was rare she smiled that big, and Bo gave her a hug saying she deserved it.

Thebb turned back to Joey and sat on his bed. "But, Joey, if we had all that money, why would Phillip want to kill me? That's the question that torments me. If I have a huge inheritance, he should be happy. He wouldn't even have to work."

"My friend Rachel is a trial lawyer and has to defend a lot of criminals and other lowlife. She theorizes some people have a pathological need to be in charge. They have to dominate their wives or girlfriends. If they can't, they beat them into submission.

Sometimes they beat their wives even when they acquiesce, just to make sure they know who's in charge. And, Thebb, I know you didn't acquiesce easily. Am I right?"

"Well yeah! I got hurt the most when I fought back. If I didn't give in right away, he became much more violent and hit me harder. Like the time he threw me down the stairs and broke my ribs."

"That son of a bitch," Bo exclaimed. "I can't believe he did that to you."

"But, Joey, why does he want to kill me?"

"Rachel thinks it's the money. If you get the inheritance, you will have all the money and therefore all the power. In his mind, that can't happen. He would have to do something, no matter what, to have control. And in your case, it would mean getting rid of you. If he divorced you, he wouldn't get the money. His only option would be to kill you. That way, he would still be in charge and have all the money too. He wins."

"So what do we do now?" Bo asked.

"Now we deal with Phillip."

CHAPTER 70

Just as Joey said they had to deal with Phillip, Bob walked in.

"Hey, Joey, you're looking good."

"Thanks, Bob," Joey responded while falling back onto his pillow. "What's happening with the perp?"

"Quite a lot, Joey. His name is Pavel Torolovich, but he goes by Toro. He admitted he was working for Phillip Mueller. He doesn't have much loyalty. He said it was just a business deal. Nothing personal. It was just a contract."

"It was just a contract!" Thebb exclaimed.

"Unfortunately, Thebb, that's the way these guys think, but let me continue. The local police have convinced him he really doesn't want to end up in a VI jail. He seems anxious to get reduced charges. There are probably some warrants out for him, and he's looking for cover."

"That's great, Bob," Joey stated. "Have you developed a plan yet?"

"Yeah! If he does what we want, we are going to be able to nail Mr. Mueller for the attempted murder of his wife and the death of Toro's partner, Nickoli Zaturetsky. If Toro doesn't help, we'll charge him with the murder of his sidekick. He didn't show much sympathy for him either. Says it was part of the cost of doing business."

"That's great work. The quicker we get Phillip indicted the better."

"Absolutely," Bob agreed. "I called Christi yesterday and briefed her on what has been going on down here. This morning she got through to me at Mike's. She was excited. She and Rachel want to talk with us as soon as we return to Philadelphia. They will meet us at the airport. Rachel is strongly advising us to keep a lid on the fact Thebb is still alive. We need Phillip to believe Toro killed Annaliese. Rachel says it will be critical to keep her existence secret, even after Phillip is arrested, because we need to freeze his assets as fast as possible. We have to get warrants to seize his records after he is arrested but before he is arraigned. If we don't, he will have the money to pay his bond and get out of jail fairly quickly. If he discovers Thebb is still alive, he may hire someone else to kill her."

"She's right, Bob. If he gets out of jail before we can seize the documents relating to Thebb, he could destroy them. That could make it really hard to prove our case."

"Rachel volunteered to help develop the paperwork for the warrants and knows one of the assistant DAs who can help get them processed quickly. She has worked with her friend before and thinks he will help slow down Phillip's arraignment process once we have him in jail. That should give us a little more time to search for Phillip's documents."

"So how long do you think it will take to get all the documents?" Joey asked.

"I asked Christi that exact question. She's making lists of the kinds of investment documents to look for. She is especially concerned about foreign accounts and getting the bank code numbers before Phillip can hide or destroy them. We have to take control of his house and get access to any safe-deposit boxes. He may have the critical trust fund documents in them. She predicts he has a safe in his house and keeps the keys to any safe-deposit boxes in it. To answer your question directly, Joey, probably a couple of days."

"Okay then, we have to find a way to cover Thebb when we get back to Philadelphia. If the girls are going to meet us at the airport, maybe they can take her to my place. Bo, you can stay with Thebb. It isn't a big house, but there's enough room for everyone if you're not too particular about sleeping arrangements. But there's only one bathroom."

"So we have a lot of work to do when we get back," Thebb emphasized. Turning to Bob, she asked if there was anything she and Bo could do.

"Maybe! Did Phillip have a safe?"

"Of course. It's built into the wall in the study."

"And . . . you wouldn't happen to know the combination to it, would you?

"Of course not! But I might be able to help figure out where he keeps the combination. He has a safe-deposit box at a bank in Doylestown and has keys to the house hidden outside too."

Bob apologized to Thebb and Bo for not asking how they were doing. He sympathized with them about rolling over in the car and then being attacked by Toro. He thought it must have been terrifying, getting shot at and all.

"It's a good thing Joey is such a remarkable shot," Bob enthused. "He's the best marksman in the department. Being able to return fire while getting out of a wrecked car and being shot at takes exceptional skill. I'm going to mention it to our captain and recommend him for a commendation."

Joey cautioned, "Don't do anything until we get Mr. Mueller settled down in a jail cell."

Thebb and Bo nodded in agreement with Bob. Thebb went on to comment Joey was their hero. He saved their lives.

Joey started to argue with Bob that a commendation was not necessary. As he looked at Thebb, he said, "Bob, I didn't do anything that anyone else wouldn't have done."

Thebb turned her head, smiled, and rolled her eyes.

Bob was adamant. He was going to make the recommendation. He went on to tell them the good news. Joey could be released the next day.

"The nurse said you should be able to do anything you want as long as you don't stress your left arm and open the stitches," Bob said with a big grin. "They said you were really lucky. The wound will heal fairly quickly, and you shouldn't have any problems. Oh yes, I called Mike at the house and explained we have to wait another day for the VI cops to complete the paperwork to take Toro back to Philadelphia. He suggested we get together for dinner tomorrow night. He will make reservations at the Bacchus Restaurant in Christiansted. He specified lobster and steak dinners for everyone as his guests. Can't beat that."

CHAPTER 71

After leaving the hospital, Bob picked up Cecilia at Mike's place, and they drove over to the general aviation terminal at the Alexander Hamilton Airport. Cecilia needed to tell her pilots they would be departing in two days and stopping in Philadelphia before continuing on to Dayton. Bob wanted to make the pilots aware of security requirements for their new passengers.

While waiting for Cecilia's pilots to arrive, they saw two bleary-eyed private pilots, wearing wrinkled uniforms, on the far side of the terminal lounge. The copilot was lying on the couch, and the captain was sitting in a chair next to him, talking on his cell phone. On his way over to the coffee machine, Bob asked the haggard-looking pilots if they would like a cup of coffee. The copilot accepted, got up off the couch, and joined Bob and Cecilia at a small round table near the snack machines.

The general aviation terminal lounge was quite comfortable, decorated in soft drapes and carpeted, albeit in wild Caribbean colors and flaring designs. It didn't have a café as many do, but the array of vending machines made it a tolerable place to spend long hours waiting. Bob commented the pilots looked tired and asked if they had been waiting very long for their clients. The captain came over and joined them. "Yeah," he said, "we've been here for a few days on alert status and haven't been able to spend much time in our hotel. We've got to be ready for immediate departure back to Philadelphia, but we haven't been able to contact our clients."

On hearing the word "Philadelphia," Bob looked up with raised eyebrows and asked, "Did your flight originate in Philadelphia?"

The captain showed annoyance in his response. "Yeah. We're out of Philadelphia and scheduled to fly back if our clients ever show up."

Cecilia asked if the Learjet-24 parked outside was theirs. The captain answered it was and asked if they were flying in the Gulfstream-200. That's as far as the small talk got. Bob immediately identified himself as a police detective from Philadelphia and began questioning the pilots about their clients. It quickly became apparent the clients were Toro and Nicky.

Bob asked the pilots directly, "Who paid for the flight?"

The captain admitted he didn't deal with the financial end of the business. "However, I have the impression the flight was underwritten by Kuefer & Bach Investments. The clients are actually paying for the charter, but I think K&B is backing them up. Ours is a small company, and K&B is an important customer."

Bob pulled out a small notepad and began an intensive interrogation. The pilots became apprehensive. Bob assured them they had done nothing wrong and what they knew could be of extreme importance. He told them they could leave for Philadelphia immediately, but it was imperative for them, and their headquarters office, not to mention the clients hadn't returned on their plane. And it was critical they not contact anyone at K&B. He emphasized the requirement for absolute secrecy by telling them if his investigation was impeded because of a leak, they could be prosecuted. That improved the level of cooperation immensely.

As Bob completed his impromptu interrogation, Cecilia's pilots arrived. He and Cecilia briefed them on their new passengers, including Thebb and Bo. Bob identified himself as a police detective and cautioned Cecilia's pilots they were not to reveal the identity of anyone on the flight other than those on the original manifest.

Bob took Cecilia back to Mike's house and then went to the jail. In a private room in the VI police station, he conducted an intensive interrogation of Toro.

"Okay, Toro! Now is the time to start telling everything you know. Do you know Phillip Mueller?"

"Yeah. This was his gig. He paid for it. Nicky and I were just carrying out a contract."

"And you will testify to that?"

"Yeah."

Over the next half hour, Toro revealed most of the details of his association with Phillip Mueller. They had dealings other than this contract to kill Phillip's wife, but Toro held back on them. He inferred he would use the information to gain concessions once he was in Philadelphia. He also held back on his earlier contract to kill Phillip's wife, thinking there was no need to implicate himself further.

CHAPTER 72

As the Gulfstream-200 landed at the Philadelphia airport and taxied up to the general aviation terminal, two nondescript sedans pulled up to the plane. Bob and Joey's boss, the police captain, and three detectives got out of their cars and waited for the plane's stairs to be lowered. Bob escorted Toro down the stairs and delivered him to the detectives. He cautioned the captain that secrecy was critically important and promised he and Joey would meet with him back at the precinct as soon as they gathered their gear.

Everyone else waited on the plane until the police cars left. Then Joey started down the stairs with Cecilia at his side and Bob close behind. Cecilia didn't believe Joey when he said he could handle the stairs, so she stayed by his side and helped him navigate the last and highest step. As he stepped onto the tarmac, he looked up and saw Rachel running to meet him with Christi in tow. They embraced, both Joey and Rachel, and Bob and Christi.

"And who are you?" Rachel asked as she focused on Cecilia while squinting and shading her eyes from the early morning sun. She was almost rude, but it was unintentional. She didn't expect to see such a stunning brunette get off the plane with her arms around Joey. It was obvious she wasn't a stewardess.

Before Cecilia could answer, Joey introduced Mrs. Pisani.

"Oh my god," Rachel responded, "you're the owner of the big sailboat. I didn't think you would be so young or pretty."

"Yeah," Bob interjected, "and this is her airplane too."

Cecilia responded, "You must be Rachel. We've heard so much about you. Bob has briefed us on how much you are assisting in the investigation. I've been anxious to meet you. And you must be Christi."

Christi introduced herself and said she and Rachel were looking forward to meeting her. "We've been doing a lot of research to help Joey and Bob. It's a complicated situation. We're going to need all the assistance we can get."

Rachel stepped back and began scanning the aircraft windows looking for other people aboard. Just then, the pilot and copilot came down the stairs, opened the baggage hatch, and began unloading everyone's bags. They placed them in a neat row under the wing and waited for further instructions from Cecilia.

Rachel turned to Joey. "Where's Thebb? Christi and I have been waiting to meet her. We need to talk to her right away to finish fleshing out our strategy for securing Mueller's accounts and her trust money. We also have plans on how to keep her presence secret."

"Thebb and her friend, Dieter Boarman, are still on board," Bob offered. "We asked them to wait until it would be safe to get off the plane. Rachel, is your car close to the terminal entrance?"

"Yes. We parked very close, but the car is not big enough for everyone."

"That's okay. Joey and I have to get to the precinct right away. We can catch a cab over there and then get a department car to drive to Joey's. As soon as we finish briefing our boss, we will meet you there."

"Mrs. Pisani," the pilot asked, "what do you want us to do? We can wait if you like."

"No, I'm going to stay here for a few days, if it's okay with Mr. Degrassi," she replied while smiling at Joey. "But if you could help us load the luggage, it would be appreciated."

Joey was pleased. "I was hoping you would stay for a while, Cecilia. Of course, you can stay at my place."

Cecilia told the pilots they could fly back to Dayton explaining she would catch a commercial flight when she was ready to return home.

Bob walked up the plane's stairs and waved to Thebb and Bo it was safe to get off.

Thebb emerged from the plane wearing tan slacks, a long-sleeved crimson blouse with prints of Caribbean flowers, a dark blue baseball cap with the outline of a dove on it, and sunglasses. Rachel and

Christi met her at the foot of the stairs and introduced themselves. Thebb shook hands and expressed her appreciation for their help. Rachel pulled her hand back, opening and closing it as if she was in pain.

"Oh! I'm terribly sorry," Thebb whispered as she leaned close to Rachel. "I'm so nervous I didn't realize how tightly I gripped your hand." She turned and introduced her friend, Dieter Boarman.

Bo spoke up, "Please call me Bo."

"Okay! Let's go," Bob urged. "We don't have much time to make this thing happen."

CHAPTER 73

As he had warned, Joey's house was not very big. It had a large living room and a recently renovated kitchen. The yellowing white outer walls were constructed of wood siding that needed to be painted. The yard was only big enough for the small patio in the back and the awning that covered the gas grill. There was no garage so Rachel pulled up alongside the house as she usually did, and everyone entered through the back door. The large untrimmed bushes and trees in the yard gave visual protection as everyone entered the house.

Rachel suggested that Thebb, Bo, and Cecilia leave their luggage in one of the bedrooms and offered them something to drink. Thebb asked for water. Bo and Cecilia declined. They were more interested in learning what Rachel and Christi were planning.

Rachel took the lead and described what had to be done immediately after Phillip Mueller is arrested. As a trial lawyer, Rachel knew they would only have about twenty-four hours prior to Phillip's first appearance before a judge.

"If he finds out what's happening before we can secure his assets, his lawyers might be able to stop us. Also he could call his friends and business partners and have them remove important documents. Christi and I have drafted legal requests for the warrants and cleared them with one of my assistant DA friends. But we need to know as much as possible about what and where the documents are. That's where you can help, Thebb. We need some insight into Phillip's habits and record keeping. We need to know which banks he regularly uses, if he has a home safe, safe-deposit boxes, etc. Even more important, we have to have authority to ask for warrants. Joey and Bob will ask for the warrants, but we need your help too, Thebb. We have to be your personal lawyers."

"Well, of course, Rachel. You and Christi have been so generous in helping me and you don't even know me. I would really like for you to represent me."

"You need to give us a retainer, in any amount, and sign a contract with each of us so there can be no question about our authority once we start to take control of your husband's assets. We need witnesses to sign the contracts to ensure there are no glitches."

"I only have a few hundred dollars in cash. I have more in a bank in the Virgin Islands."

"Any amount will do. Now you need to sign these contracts."

Thebb gave Rachel and Christi each fifty dollars and signed the papers. Bo and Cecilia served as witnesses.

Rachel became very serious and said, "Now we have lots of work to do. If everything goes as Joey and Bob expect tomorrow, we will be very busy for the next several days. If things don't go as we hope, we will have to work even harder to sequester Phillip's assets."

Joey's dining table was small and had only four chairs. Bo found a folding chair in one of the bedrooms, and they all sat around the table while Rachel and Christi began to outline their strategy and assign roles.

When Joey and Bob arrived in the early evening, Thebb and her new lawyers were still deep in conversation. Bo and Cecilia sat quietly, amazed by the complexity of the task ahead. No one had thought about dinner so Joey ordered pizza. Over pizza, Rachel and Christi outlined what they would need from Joey and Bob.

"Tomorrow is going to be a big day," Rachel mused. "We will have to act with precision to make it work."

CHAPTER 74

Toro heard the clanking steel doors to the isolated, high-security cell block open and slam shut. Joey and Bob had come down to see him. It was early in the morning and they had a set of instructions on how they were going to get Phillip Mueller to admit, on tape, that he hired Toro to kill his wife. Toro would set up a meeting with Phillip to collect his money for completing the contract, and an undercover cop would accompany him, playing the part of Nicky.

Joey and Bob took Toro upstairs to a dingy, windowless conference room to meet the cop who would impersonate Nicky. The door opened, and a beady-eyed man with a scar down the side of his face and long, slicked-back dark hair was standing next to a metal table. He was wearing dark blue slacks, a light blue shirt, and a tan Windbreaker, the kind with flaps over the pockets. His clothes were fresh and neatly pressed, but nonetheless his appearance was menacing. He didn't seem to be the kind of person to be fooled with. Even Toro was taken aback.

The man stared at Joey and Toro and then Bob. He approached Bob and asked in a gravelly voice, "Which of these two schmucks is the perp?"

Bob took a step back and said, "And good morning to you too, Janos. This one, Pavel Torolovich, is the perp. He goes by Toro." Smiling, he continued, "The other schmuck is my partner, Joey Degrassi."

Joey frowned at Bob's attempt at humor.

The captain had picked Janos to act as Nicky because of his ethnic background and ability to project a threatening image. He had years of experience and was skilled in playing the part of a mobster. They all sat at the metal table, and Joey briefed Toro and Janos on the plan. Then Toro and Janos spent about an hour rehearsing their roles.

A police technician brought in a recording machine and attached it to the phone line.

Toro made his call to Phillip.

"Hello," Phillip answered his private cell phone. He didn't say anything more, waiting for an acknowledgment.

"Hope you're ready to meet. She's dead."

"Yeah. I have everything. And, Toro, I hope to hell you actually killed her this time. There better not be any loose ends either."

"Not to worry, Phil. We fed her to the sharks. Had to hire a boat to get it done and almost got caught by the fucking Coast Guard. That's gonna cost extra. You don't have to pay the extra today, but I'm gonna need it by next week. Any problems with that?"

"She's not going to wash up on shore somewhere, is she?"

"Not unless she can swim with a couple of anchors wrapped around her."

Phillip was irritated with Toro's somewhat-cavalier attitude but continued speaking pleasantly while trying to maintain a position of authority. "Okay! Exactly how much is the extra cost?

"Twenty-five thousand," Toro stated flatly. "We had to get a fishing boat and pay off the captain."

"I'll have the extra cash next week. I need to leave a little time between large withdrawals. Where do we meet? Same place as last time?"

"No," Toro cautioned. "I didn't like that place. We were lucky there were no complications. I found a better place. It's not too far from your office either. We'll meet at noon, at the Sardinian Bar and Grill at 324 Chestnut Street. It's on the east side near the expressway. There's a parking lot behind the place, so you don't have to walk out in public. Use the driveway next to the restaurant. Space should be available if you get there at noon. Come in the back entrance. Nicky and I will meet you inside. We'll make the transfer in the restaurant. Any problem?"

"See you in a couple of hours," Phillip replied and hung up.

"What the fuck did he mean when he said he hoped to hell you actually killed her this time?" Joey demanded.

—

Tilting his head back and acting a bit cocky, Toro explained, "About three years ago, Phillip took out a contract on his wife, but she accidentally got killed before we could complete the job. Phil was so pleased he paid me and Nicky anyhow. We didn't actually do anything."

"Goddamn it, Toro," Bob exploded, "in St. Croix you agreed to tell us everything. What else are you holding back?"

"Nothing! That's it. It was nothing so I didn't think it was important. We didn't do nothing, and we weren't involved."

Janos moved very close to Toro, almost face-to-face. He gave him an intimidating look while asking, "You want that I should take him downstairs and get some more answers out of him, Bob?"

Toro pushed back in his chair to get away from Janos. "That's all there was. Hey, we didn't do nothing. She got run over before we got there."

Police technicians and detectives from Joey's precinct had gone to the Sardinian Bar and Grill the night before, after closing, and set up wireless cameras and listening devices in the restaurant, bar, and parking lot. The owner was cooperative but demanded compensation. Certain booths and several of the more private tables were bugged with wireless, remote devices. They parked an SUV next to the rear door and wired it with listening devices so that no part of the conversation would be missed if Phillip made Toro and Janos, a.k.a. Nicky, step outside. And finally, they set up cameras on adjacent buildings with direct views of the parking lot and the SUV.

"Don't screw up," Bob warned Toro. "No more surprises. In a couple of hours it will all be over. Let's rehearse the scenario one more time. Just to be sure you've got it down."

Before he left the office, Phillip Mueller told his secretary he had an important lunch and afternoon meeting to attend. It was cover for the briefcase he was carrying. He arrived at the Sardinian Bar and Grill about ten minutes early and drove around the block twice, scouting out the area. He wasn't really worried about Toro because he had done business with him before, and he had proven to be reliable. He just wanted to make sure the place Toro selected for the transfer would be innocuous. It was.

Joey, Bob, and several other detectives were concealed in buildings around the restaurant looking at the monitors of the hidden cameras and audio feeds. Uniformed cops were stationed out of sight several blocks away, sitting in their cruisers, waiting for the signal to swarm in and make the arrest. Inside the restaurant, a pair of young male and female undercover cops sat in a corner booth acting like young lovers, but wired and relaying information to Joey and Bob.

After Phillip's second drive-by, he pulled into the lot and parked next to a black SUV. He walked around the SUV and looked at the tag. Then the inside and even under it. He entered the restaurant through the rear entrance about five minutes early, carrying a large black briefcase full of wrapped stacks of one-hundred-dollar bills. He walked the length of the short, dark hallway and stopped for a brief moment to survey the availability of tables and booths, a usual thing for customers to do.

The Sardinian Bar and Grill was a popular place for the younger business community, and about half the booths were already occupied. The noise level was high, and the waiters were taking orders at the tables and booths. The hardwood floors and old-style square metal ceiling tiles accentuated the noise, something that didn't seem to bother the younger customers. Even with the cross-pane front window mostly uncovered by the dark green curtains hanging on each side, the lighting was low, giving the place an aura of privacy.

The booths were dark and high-backed, with a post and coat hooks at the end of each set of booth benches. Several of the posts had coats hanging on them and the ubiquitous briefcases were under many of the occupied tables.

Everyone seemed to be occupied with their own conversations and menus. No one looked up when Phillip entered except Toro.

Toro motioned to Phillip to come to his booth. As Phillip walked toward the booth, Janos, a.k.a. Nicky, looked Phillip up and down and moved over to the end of the bench. Phillip slid the briefcase under the table and sat down across from Toro. The high noise level pleased Phillip. Nicky, sitting next to Phillip, took a few sips of beer and watched Phillip out of the sides of his eyes. His piercing stare was unsettling and Phillip wanted to get out of the uncomfortable situation quickly.

"Any problem finding the place?" Toro asked casually.

"No. I've been here before. Long time ago. Interesting choice for a place to meet."

"Yeah. No one pays any attention to you here," Toro observed while looking around the dining area. "It's mostly the younger crowd, involved in their own thing. You probably won't see anyone you know. Most people aren't aware of the lot out back so it's easy to find a parking place."

After a moment of silence, Toro asked, "You have the money? Is everything there?"

"Of course! I'll call you next week to complete the transfer."

Janos, a.k.a. Nicky, grabbed Phillip's arm, turned his head to face Phillip, stared directly into his eyes, and whispered, "Don't be late. Unless you want to end up with an anchor around your neck like your wife, you better have the fuckin' money on time. Clear."

"Yeah! You'll get your money next week. Now let go of my arm," Phillip said in a low, angry whisper.

"What the fuck are you doing, Nicky," Toro whispered. "Phil here is a good customer. We've done business with him before." Then he looked at Phillip and apologized for Nicky. "Sorry about that, Phil, but Nicky don't understand good business practice."

In a somewhat louder voice, Phillip asked where the men's room was. Toro pointed to the door on the side of the hallway leading to the rear entrance. Phillip slid out of the booth and went to the men's room leaving the briefcase under the table. After a few minutes, he left the men's room and exited the restaurant through the rear entrance. As he opened his car door, he was startled to see a police cruiser pulling into the parking lot and several policemen coming out of the rear door in the next building. He stood looking at them in disbelief as they approached. The police arrested him for the contract to murder Annaliese Mueller and the death of Nickoli Zaturetsky. They handcuffed him and read him his rights. Their orders were to drag the procedure out as long as possible while booking him and place him in an isolated cell away from all other prisoners. No phone calls would be allowed for twenty-four hours, the maximum legal limit.

CHAPTER 75

It was just about one o'clock when the phone rang at Joey's house. Cecilia hesitantly answered it while showing Thebb and Bo her crossed fingers. It was Joey.

"Hi, Cecilia," Joey announced. "It's done. Can I speak to Thebb?"

"They got him," Cecilia screamed with delight as she handed the phone to Thebb.

"Joey, is it really over? Did you arrest him?"

"We arrested him, but it's not over. Phillip incriminated himself on tape, and we've got video and voice recordings of him paying off Toro. One of our undercover detectives impersonated Nicky and will be a witness to validate the recordings."

"Oh, that's wonderful! Thank you, Joey. Thank you. I can't believe this is happening."

"Where are Rachel and Christi?"

"They're at the courthouse waiting for your call before they ask for the warrants. They want you and Bob to get there as quickly as possible so you can represent the police in getting the warrants. They've made all the arrangement with the prosecutor that Rachel has worked with and have an appointment with the judge in a few minutes."

"We're almost there. Let me talk to Cecilia again."

Thebb handed Cecilia the phone, sat down on the couch next to Bo, and put her head on his shoulder. She whispered to him she thought she would never see this day. Then she kissed him.

"Cecilia, please listen carefully," Joey cautioned. "It's definitely not over yet. If the press finds out we arrested a senior executive in one of the most prestigious investment firms in Philadelphia, it will be front page news. Some of the most important people in Philadelphia are his clients. The press will have a heyday. We have to make sure it doesn't leak out that Thebb is alive. The story has everything the media want to sell newspapers. It will be white hot. A beautiful young wife, battered by a wealthy husband, is identified as dead. She runs away on a sailboat, gets stranded on the ocean bottom, and turns up alive. Her husband gets caught paying off hired killers, and she inherits millions of dollars. All of you have to prepare for what's going to happen. So be careful."

"We're booking Phillip now but only for the murder of Nickoli Zaturetsky. He doesn't know that. We're holding him in isolation but can only do so for a day. His lawyers will be trying to get him out on bail so we have to work fast to freeze his assets."

There was a long silence as Cecilia stood holding the telephone receiver realizing this could seriously entangle Jack. She had been so focused on Thebb's problems she didn't think about the possible impact on her own husband. This could jeopardize his contracts with the Air Force. Her face lost color, her forehead wrinkled, and she looked vacantly at the wall. Thebb sat up as she saw the expression on Cecilia's face. From the couch, Bo could hear Joey saying, "Cecilia, are you there? Cecilia, are you there?" He jumped up and took the phone. Cecilia sat down next to Thebb, looking perplexed.

"Joey, this is Bo. What's happening? Cecilia looks like she just saw a ghost."

Joey explained to Bo what he had alluded to with Cecilia but went further in describing the possible consequences of the arrest. "The reporters will be hounding anyone who knew Thebb, especially Jack and Cecilia who own the sailboat she has been living on for the last three years." From what little Joey knew, Jack Pisani would not want any publicity about his business with the Air Force. He ended the conversation saying they should stay out of sight and wait for Christi's call.

CHAPTER 76

The light in Joey's living room began to turn a warm red-orange as the sun approached the western horizon. There had been little talk among Thebb, Cecilia, and Bo. Several times during the day, Thebb sat next to Bo and put her head on his shoulder. They didn't speak. They just sat there. Waiting. Then Thebb would get up and walk to the kitchen and back. Over and over. At one point, Cecilia asked Thebb to sit down and read something, but she couldn't. She would lay her head back on the couch and put the newspaper or a magazine over her face. The tension among them was palpable.

When the phone rang, it had the effect of an explosion. Thebb and Bo leaped to their feet, and Cecilia came running out of the kitchen where she had been preparing dinner. The phone rang twice then a third time before Cecilia answered it.

"This is the Degrassi residence," Cecilia answered softly.

"Cecilia, this is Rachel. We have the warrants. We're ready to move first thing in the morning."

"That's wonderful, Rachel. Were there any complications?"

"There could have been, but my friend in the DA's office helped. Joey and Bob presented such compelling arguments we were able to get the warrants and are ready to move. We'll be over at Joey's in a couple of hours and fill you in then."

Over dinner, Rachel and Christi presented their strategy for the next day. Timing was critical. Rachel and Christi, along with Bob and two uniformed policemen, would go to Kuefer & Bach Investments as soon as it opened in the morning and search Phillip's office for his financial records, bank accounts, investments, and other important information.

Christi added, "Thebb, you have to go to your house first thing in the morning and search for any records Phillip keeps at home. He probably has important information there. We're especially anxious to learn what he has in his home safe. We also need to find the keys to any bank safe-deposit boxes. Joey will go with you, but we can't have any Philadelphia cops help because it's out of their jurisdiction. If need be, we'll have to get assistance from the Bucks County Sheriff, out of Doylestown."

Thebb listened carefully to Christi but seemed apprehensive. "I don't have a key to the house, but we used to hide one outside in case of an emergency. If Phillip still hides the key in the same place and hasn't changed the locks, we can get in easily. Otherwise, we will have to wait for Roberta, the housekeeper, if she still works there, or break in."

Joey added, "Thebb, if we have to break in, we'll do it. We can't wait for anyone."

"There's also the code, Joey," Thebb responded. "I don't know if he kept the old code for the security system. That will cause a problem because the police will come if the alarm goes off."

Bo interjected, "If we're lucky, he may not have changed anything. Thebb was supposed to be dead so he didn't have to change anything. I'll bet he's still using the same code and has the extra key hidden in the same place."

"God, I hope you're right, Bo," Joey responded. "We'll have to wing it in the morning. Be prepared to deal with the unexpected and do it quickly."

CHAPTER 77

It was eight-thirty in the morning when Rachel, Christi, and Bob entered the Kuefer & Bach Investments building, followed by two uniformed policemen. They gambled Phillip's secretary would be in his office early preparing for the day's meetings. They were right. She was brewing coffee when they arrived. As usual, Phillip's secretary was professionally attired and very pleasant when she informed them Mr. Mueller wasn't in, and his office hours didn't start until 9:00 a.m.

"May I ask your name, please?" Bob agreeably asked the secretary.

She looked at him quizzically. "As you can see on my name plate, I'm Posie Dugger, Mr. Mueller's private secretary. Would you like to make an appointment to see Mr. Mueller?"

She was obviously proud to be the secretary of such an important officer of the firm. Her response carried a hint of haughtiness. She approached her desk to retrieve her appointment book but stopped dead as Bob presented his detective's badge.

"Ms. Dugger, I have a warrant to search Mr. Muller's office and seize his personal documents. You are required by law not to interfere and to inform us of hidden documents or safes in his possession."

Posie continued to stand motionless scanning the detective and two women in front of her. She also became aware of the two uniformed policemen guarding the entrance to Mr. Mueller's outer office. Her pleasant tone changed to one of defiance as she told them they couldn't go into Mr. Mueller's office. "Those are his private things," she announced, "and you can't just go in there and rummage through them."

"Ms. Dugger, if you interfere with us, or refuse to provide assistance when we ask, you'll quickly be wearing these," Bob aggressively stated as he showed her his set of handcuffs. "Now open the door to his office, give us the keys to his files, and unlock his safe."

"I can't do that without authorization from Mr. Kuefer," Posie protested. "I'll have to call him first."

"Ms. Dugger," Bob threatened, "if you touch that phone, I'll have one of the gentlemen at the door arrest you. And then we will have to destroy the locks to find the information we're looking for. We have the legal authority, and we want access to his personal documents now."

With tears welling up in her eyes, Posie unlocked the inner office door, walked in, unlocked Phillip's personal file cabinets, and showed them the locked file drawer in his desk. Rachel and Christi immediately went to the desk file drawer and discovered it had a combination lock. They asked Posie for the combination. She claimed she didn't have it, so Bob asked one of the uniformed policemen to bring in the tool bag. After a few minutes, every file was open, and Rachel and Christi were searching for pertinent documents.

Bob sat at Phillip's desk and laid out copies of Phillip's credit cards, insurance cards, bank cards, and other notes he had copied from Phillip's wallet back at the jail. Over the next few hours, Rachel and Christie called each of the credit card companies and other organizations and put a freeze on Phillip's assets. They used his personal fax machine to send copies of the warrants to authenticate their requests. Posie sat in one of Phillip's plush visitor chairs, not allowed to leave the office. Several well-dressed men came to the outer office for appointments, but the police gently turned them away.

CHAPTER 78

Bo's watch read 7:30 a.m. when Thebb, Cecilia, Joey, and he left for the hour-long drive to Thebb's house on the Neshaminy Creek southeast of Doylestown in Bucks County. It was Joey's car, but Bo drove. Thebb sat in the back seat with Joey and guided Bo around the country roads.

As they approached the house, they could see it was set back on a huge lot of rolling country land. There was a three-foot-high fieldstone wall running the length of the property alongside the main road. The terminal ends of the wall began with large square capped-stone pedestals. The walls extended from the ends of the property to the driveway where they curved inward to join twin high-stone pedestals with early American lighting fixtures rising out of their centers. Each twenty-foot section of the walls was enhanced with a smaller replica of the end pedestals.

The driveway was approximately three hundred feet long and curved first away from the house, and then back, ending in a large circle centered at the front door. It was laid with gray and tan granite pavers that matched the wall and a decorative fountain in the circle. Just before the circle, an extension of the driveway veered off to a three-car garage connected to the side of the house. The yard was well-kept grass with fruit trees, three very old red oak trees, and several elliptical flower gardens. The granite stone colonial style house was large and imposing. It had a slate roof and three tall chimneys protruding upward above the roofline. The first floor windows were tall and matched in height the tall round columns supporting the front porch roof.

"Holy shit, Thebb," Bo exclaimed as he slowed down while approaching the house. "Is that really your house? It's incredible!"

"It's gorgeous," Cecilia exclaimed. "I can't wait to see the inside."

"Yes," Thebb responded. "It's even more beautiful and comfortable inside. Phillip bought it after my aunt died. We had it remodeled by a professional interior designer. I helped in the upstairs rooms, but the designer did all the work downstairs."

Cecilia, who was sitting in the front passenger's seat, turned totally around to face Thebb and asked, "After your aunt died, Thebb? After?"

"I hadn't thought of it that way, Cecilia. But now that you mention it—"

Bo turned into the driveway, rounded the two curves, and parked in the circle past the front door. He parked with the back of the car facing the front door to limit the line of sight into the car. He turned to face Thebb and Joey and asked how they should handle the next step. Joey said he and Cecilia would see if anyone was home. "When the situation is clear, we'll come out and get you. Just hold tight until then."

Joey and Cecilia walked up the set of four granite stairs and onto the porch. On either side of the eight-foot-high ornamental teak doors were large colonial-style lighting fixtures that matched the sentinel fixtures at the head of the driveway. Joey used the large brass wolf's head knocker on the door rather than the clearly lighted doorbell button. He looked at Cecilia, shrugged, and told her he liked the wolf's head knocker better.

After a few moments, the door opened. "Good morning. Can I help you?" said a smiling middle-aged woman. She had dark hair with silvery streaks interspersed throughout and appeared to be of Spanish ancestry.

"You must be Roberta?" Cecilia asked.

"Yes," Roberta answered while giving them a quizzical look. "How can I help you?"

Roberta was clearly disturbed strangers knew her name, but she continued to be polite.

Deciding to be direct and official sounding, Cecilia continued, "My name is Cecilia Pisani, and this gentleman is Detective Jocy Degrassi." Joey presented the warrant and said, "This is a legal warrant that allows us to inspect the premises." Cecilia continued, "May we please come in?"

Roberta was shaken at the sight of the official-looking warrant but refused to let them in.

"No! Oh no! You can't come into Mr. Mueller's home without his permission."

Joey intervened in the conversation. He presented his badge saying, "Roberta, I'm a police detective. Mr. Mueller won't be coming home for a while. He's in jail. So may we come in and talk?"

Roberta, now looking confused, stepped back and allowed them to enter. Shaken, she watched Joey and Cecilia as they walked in, stopped, and looked around the spacious interior of the entry hall.

"Mr. Mueller can't be in jail," Roberta stated in disbelief. "He's a very important man."

"Roberta!" Cecilia stepped closer. "Is there anyone else here right now, other than you?"

"No! But why would you put Mr. Mueller in jail?" Roberta asked with tears welling up in her eyes. She was focused on the news that Phillip was in jail and didn't seem to pay attention to Cecilia's question.

"I'm sorry to tell you this," Joey answered, "but Mr. Mueller has been indicted for murder and is being held in the Philadelphia jail."

"No, no, no," Roberta cried. "Not Mr. Mueller. Sometimes he has a bad temper, but he's a good man."

Moving closer to Roberta and bending forward, Cecilia asked, "You're sure there is no one else in the house? You're sure?"

"Yes," Roberta answered in a quivering voice. "No! I mean yes. Yes, I'm sure. Ms. Rechenmacher will be here in a little while. But there's no one here now."

"And exactly who is Ms. Rechenmacher?" Joey authoritatively asked.

"Ms. Jennifer Rechenmacher. She's Mr. Mueller's fiancée. They're going to be married in a few months."

"She's coming here in a little while?" Cecilia asked. "Why?"

Shaking, Roberta explained, "She left her bridal accessories catalog here and needs to get it. She called just as I arrived and asked if it was in the living room. She said she would come over to pick it up after she leaves the gym in Doylestown."

Joey took Roberta into the living room and began to question her in a friendlier manner but maintained his direct approach. He wanted Roberta to tell him anything she knew about where Phillip kept his personal documents.

While Joey was getting information from Roberta, Cecilia went out the front door and signaled for Thebb and Bo to come in. Thebb, looking somewhat dazed, was the first to enter. Bo followed with their luggage. When they were inside, Cecilia motioned Thebb into the living room and said to Roberta, "I want you to meet an old friend."

Roberta looked at Thebb and screamed, "Oh holy spirits. God protect me," and sank to the floor. Joey caught her just before she fully collapsed. Thebb went to Roberta's side to help Joey.

"Roberta, I hoped you would still be here," Thebb said softly. "I have really missed seeing you."

Roberta kept staring at Thebb. Tears were flowing as she muttered, "Mrs. Mueller, is that really you? I can't believe my eyes. I'm so happy to see you . . . I think. No, I can't think. I thought you were dead! Is it really you? You're so thin. You look like you did when I first saw you. Oh god, help us. This is not good. Mr. Mueller is going to be furious." It was clear Roberta was terrified of Mr. Mueller but at the same time respected him.

"I'm sorry I startled you," Thebb consoled Roberta. "I had to go away, but now I'm back."

"Oh, Mrs. Mueller," Roberta said rolling her eyes upward, "Ms. Rechenmacher is coming over any minute."

Thebb's smile faded. "And . . . who is Ms. Rechenmacher?"

Roberta haltingly explained, "Oh god, Mrs. Mueller, Ms. Rechenmacher is Mr. Mueller's fiancée. They're going to get married in a few months, and she's going to live here."

"No, Roberta," Thebb said with compassion. "I don't think they will be getting married, and Ms. Rechenmacher definitely won't be living here. I'm here now. Everything's going to be okay, so please don't worry."

Joey continued his questioning that was interrupted when Thebb and Bo came in. "Roberta, do you know where Mr. Mueller keeps

—

the keys to his desk and file cabinets? And I have to warn you, you can be indicted under the law if you conceal information or try to impede this investigation in any way. If we don't have the keys, we'll break the locks and damage the desk and file cabinets. Cecilia, you go with Roberta and find anything we need to get access to information in the office. Bo, please get my tool bag out of the trunk while Thebb and I start looking through any open drawers."

Roberta had never been privy to any of the Mueller's personal information and could find no keys, so Bo used the tools to force open Phillip's desk drawers and file cabinets. He tried to do as little damage as possible, but unfortunately he had to rip off the whole front face of the desk's file drawer. The file cabinets were more difficult, and Bo had to bend the lock assemblies, but the drawers finally opened.

Joey found a hanging accordion-style file folder in the bottom drawer of one of the two file cabinets that had Thebb's old personal information. It was a bonanza.

"God bless accountants and financial managers," Joey exclaimed as he searched through the folder. "They keep all their old records."

"What did you find?" Thebb asked Joey while flipping through documents stored in the desk file drawers.

"Your birth certificate, social security card, marriage license, driver's license, lipsticks, a compact, tampons, lotion, etc. It looks like he dumped the insides of your purse in here along with all your personal papers. Some of the stuff has what appears to be blood on it. Whoa, this is your passport, and it's still valid."

Thebb spun around to look at the file. As she did, she saw a flash of sunlight reflecting off a silver blue Mercedes sports car turning into the driveway.

"Joey, that's my car driving up to the house," Thebb exclaimed with surprise. "That's 'my' car. I can't believe it."

Joey stood up from the floor where he had all of Thebb's personal documents spread out and went to the window. He put his arm around her shoulder and looked out at the Mercedes. "Yeah, that sure looks like your car all right. You would think he would have gotten rid of it."

"Damn, Thebb," Bo said excitedly, "that's one hell of a nice car. It looks like a woman driving it."

"A woman?" Thebb asked as she turned to look more closely out the window.

Joey consoled Thebb. "I'm sorry about your car. Roberta said Phillip's fiancée would be here in a little while. Apparently that's now. I hoped we could finish searching for the documents before she got here. We'll just have to deal with it."

Joey let go of Thebb and stooped over the files from the bottom file cabinet drawer. He picked up a document and showed it to Thebb. "Believe it or not, Thebb, this is the title to it. It's still in your name. Unbelievable. He didn't even bother to change the title. He just filed it away. Amazing."

"So the car is still in my name, and Phillip's soon-to-be ex-fiancée is driving it?"

"You know," Joey pondered, "I'm beginning to think Phillip wasn't quite as organized as we thought. Why would he leave the title in your name? Maybe he thought once you were dead, it didn't matter whose name the car was in until he wanted to sell it."

The car door could be heard shutting. Everyone went to watch the front door open. Roberta stood hiding behind Cecilia. A beautiful young woman stepped into the hallway. She had long, straight, raven-black hair, held back by a powder blue headband, and piercingly blue eyes. She was startling attractive in her tight light-blue workout leotards with a matching jacket. At about five feet eight inches tall, she reminded Bo of a gazelle. Even in her scrubbed white running shoes, she was taller than Joey. She stopped, with the door still open, holding a shopping bag, and scanned the four strangers looking her over. She glanced down at the two pieces of luggage on the floor and asked, in a polished but high-pitched voice, "Roberta, who are these people?"

As Jennifer closed the door, Roberta replied, hesitantly and apologetically, "Ms. Rechenmacher, this is . . . this is . . . Mrs. Mueller."

In a friendly manner, Jennifer extended her hand to Thebb saying, "Hello! Are you a relative of Phillip?"

"Well yes," Thebb started to reply, but Joey intervened. He bluntly stated, "Mrs. Mueller is Phillip's wife."

As is often the case when a person receives unexpected information, Jennifer didn't react. Looking totally mystified, Jennifer asked, "I knew Phillip had been married before, but his wife died in a traffic accident. Were you a previous wife?"

Everyone stood motionless for a moment, perceiving the internal anguish Jennifer was having. Then Thebb said bluntly, "Jennifer, I'm his current wife." Thebb viewed Jennifer as an interloper and was treating her as such.

The scene that followed was tumultuous. Jennifer started yelling she didn't know what kind of treachery was going on, but she wanted them out of the house. She demanded Roberta make them leave, or she was calling the police. Roberta ran back to the kitchen crying. Bo inserted himself between Jennifer and Thebb, fearing Jennifer might try to hurt Thebb.

He introduced himself, "Ms. Rechenmacher, I'm Dieter Boarman. This is serious business. We're not leaving. This is Mrs. Mueller's house. Now calm down and listen."

But she didn't. Jennifer was certain the strangers were up to no good. She tried to get to the phone. Bo stepped in and told her, "You can't use the phone, and if you try I'll stop you." She reached in her jacket pocket and retrieved her cell phone, but Bo tussled with her before finally taking it away.

"You can't call anyone," Bo said sternly. "Just calm down and let us explain."

Joey went to Phillip's office and retrieved Anna's passport and marriage license. He ran back and showed them to Jennifer. She stood still staring at the documents with her mouth open. She looked at the passport picture of Anna and then at Thebb. Several times. She started to say something, but all she was able to get out was, "But . . . but!" She started to cry. Stomping her foot down several times, she turned away from everyone and screamed as loud as she could, "How could Phillip do this to me?"

Jennifer started to hyperventilate while lamenting about all the people she had invited to the wedding. Cecilia helped Jennifer to the long angular couch in the living room. After she calmed down, Joey showed her his badge and the warrant and explained the house and all of its possessions were being legally seized by Mrs. Mueller.

Jennifer was about twenty-five years old, and this was hitting her hard. From her demeanor, Joey suspected she came from a well-to-do family in the Bucks County area and thought this kind of thing would disgrace her family.

Bo felt sorry for Jennifer and tried to console her. He got a glaring look from Thebb and backed off.

Jennifer stopped crying, wiped her eyes, lay back in the couch, and asked, "Does Phillip know what you're doing?"

"No," Joey answered. "He's in jail, and we've taken every precaution to make sure he doesn't find out quite yet. He will shortly though."

"In jail? Why would Phillip be in jail? What did he do?"

"He's in jail for the attempted murder of his wife and the death of one of his hired assassins."

Jennifer's mouth dropped open, and her face lost all color. Tears began to flow again, and her head began to move in a small circular motion. She was breathing very fast. Cecilia grabbed Jennifer by the shoulders. "Bo, help me. She's going into shock. Get her feet up on the arm of the couch. Roberta, get a glass of water and a blanket."

While Cecilia continued to care for Jennifer, Joey, Bo, and Thebb went back to searching the office. They didn't have time to waste. They had to call Rachel right away.

After a while, Cecilia went into the office with Jennifer who sat in one of Phillip's guest chairs. Bo and Thebb were inspecting file folders. Joey explained to Jennifer what a warrant was and cautioned her that if she interfered with their investigation, she could be prosecuted.

"I'm not going to try to call anyone! I can't believe what Phillip has done to me. He tried to kill his wife, and he lied to me. What would he eventually do to me?"

Joey watched as Jennifer's attitude changed. She became angry, and the tears stopped. Her life had just been turned upside down, and a policeman was threatening her with jail. She sat with her head down, rocking back and forth, her mind swirling.

Joey began to study the safe. It was hidden behind a fake cabinet mounted on hidden hinges. Not very original, but it at least was out of sight. He was turning the dial and listening to determine if he could hear the tumblers. Talking over his shoulder, Joey explained to Jennifer the most important thing they needed to do was gain access to the wall safe. He asked if she knew the combination, fully expecting a negative answer. To his surprise, Jennifer thought she might be able to help. She suspected Phillip had certain important passwords listed as phone numbers in the personal address book he usually kept in his locked desk drawer. She had seen him use his address book on occasion when he was working on his laptop computer.

Joey and Thebb had both scanned the address book but didn't see anything unusual. They left it sitting on Phillip's desk. Joey picked up the book and began skimming through it again but still didn't see anything out of the ordinary. Jennifer asked for the book. She studied it for a few minutes while Joey continued to listen for the almost-silent clicks when he turned the dial on the face of the safe.

Jennifer showed him a name and number she thought was the password to one of Phillip's financial computer programs. The name was listed as Fin Mgt Sys Inc. Jennifer assumed the listing was a password for access to his financial management program on the computer. She thought Phillip might be using the same system for recording the combination to his safe. Joey quickly caught on and together they searched the address book for the combination. Nothing was to be found.

Bo asked if he could see the book. The names and numbers were neatly recorded. He didn't notice anything unusual until he saw a listing for L. R. Tumbler. He stared at the name for a few seconds and looked at the safe. Everyone stopped what they were doing and watched Bo. "The safe has a tumbler, and this entry in his address book is for L. R. Tumbler. This phone number has got to be the combination for the safe."

Joey eagerly agreed, but pointed out there didn't seem to be any notation on which way to start turning the tumbler. Bo suggested that the tumbler had to be turned first to the left, otherwise, he theorized, the name in the book would have been R. L. Tumbler. He called out numbers, and Thebb slowly, sensitively, turned the dial. After a few tries, the safe opened.

In the safe, among other documents, were two small manila envelopes. Each envelope had the name and address of the First Union National Bank on Court Street in Doylestown and contained a key. Phillip had two safe-deposit boxes, and they finally had the keys!

"Jennifer, that was great work," Joey said. "How did you figure out Phillip used phone numbers to record passwords and safe combinations?"

"Well, one evening he asked me to get his address book while he was using his laptop on the back porch. He gave me the key to the desk drawer and asked that I lock it after I got the address book. He had been having a little trouble getting into some computer program. I just figured he forgot the password."

Joey immediately called Rachel and told her about their success in finding the keys to Phillip's safe-deposit boxes. He described Phillip's technique for recording passwords in his address book and suggested she study his Rolodex at the office and look for any address books. "You probably ought to check the secretary's address book too."

Rachel thought the new information could be useful. She was having success in securing a lot of investment documents, but Christi hadn't been able to access Phillip's computer files. Joey's tip might help her open the programs. Rachel told him to go to the bank immediately and retrieve the contents of the safe-deposit boxes. She needed to know if certain key documents were in Doylestown or in Philadelphia.

Joey handed Thebb her old driver's license and placed her marriage license, birth certificate, and passport in a large envelope with the two small manila envelopes. "I think we'll need these when we go to the bank."

"Bo, Cecilia," Joey announced, "Thebb and I have to go into Doylestown to get the documents out of Phillip's safe-deposit boxes. I need you to stay here with Jennifer and Roberta and make sure that nobody makes any calls or leaves the house."

Thebb turned to Jennifer. "May I have the keys to my car, please?"

Jennifer must have still been in a state of shock because she initially refused, saying, "No! Phillip gave me that car." Then she began to cry again as she remembered Thebb was Phillip's wife.

Jennifer's anguish was palpable, and Cecilia and Bo watched intently as Thebb stood still, observing Jennifer with no sense of sympathy.

"Thebb," Cecilia said softly, "she didn't do anything wrong. She's a victim here too."

In a rare display of defiance, especially toward Cecilia, Thebb snapped, "That's my car, and she shouldn't have said no when I asked for the keys."

Cecilia backed away, biting her lips. She was realizing Thebb must be under enormous stress, and this little snit was a release.

Jennifer gave Thebb the keys, and Thebb held her hand for a moment. Then she pulled Jennifer in close and hugged her tightly whispering, "I'm sorry. You must be going through hell. I know. I've done it for longer than I want to remember."

Jennifer began to cry again, uncontrollably. Cecilia took her by the arm and pulled her away, saying, "They've got to go." Then she too hugged Jennifer.

Joey interrupted, "Thebb, I think we should go in my car. It will be less conspicuous. I know you would like to drive your car again, but somebody in Doylestown would be sure to notice you in your Mercedes. We're not ready for that yet." On the way out, Thebb took a tote bag from the hallway closet for holding the contents of the safe-deposit boxes.

As soon as Thebb and Joey left, with Thebb at the wheel of Joey's car, Roberta made coffee, and the four of them sat at the breakfast table. Cecilia asked Jennifer about her involvement with Phillip. She wanted to know if their relationship had started before the traffic accident in which Anna was supposedly killed. It had not. It turned out they met at a charity ball at the Bucks County Country Club. Jennifer was volunteering as one of the models for a local designer's dresses and talked Phillip into making a significant charitable contribution.

Then it was Cecilia's turn to tell Jennifer about Thebb. She explained Thebb had been working as the ship's cook on her schooner, the *DOVE*, ever since the accident. While the *DOVE* was in dry dock for servicing the hull and mechanical equipment, Thebb and Bo had volunteered to help a friend doing research on some kind of worms found in the ocean. Thebb got stuck in a submarine on the ocean bottom, and the event made national news. Her picture was in all the newspapers. They suspected that was how Phillip learned she was still alive and why he hired two assassins to kill her.

Jennifer was astounded. She had seen the photograph in the paper but had no idea it was Phillip's wife. As they talked, Jennifer became angrier. Her comments regarding Phillip were anything but loving.

For Jennifer, the worst was yet to come. Cecilia explained that Thebb's uncle had left her a fortune in a trust fund, but she didn't know about it. The money was supposed to be transferred to her control when she turned twenty-one. Phillip was the executor of the will and the trustee of the fund. He kept the fund secret from Thebb and didn't transfer control when he was supposed to. He used the money as his own.

Jennifer was transfixed, mesmerized with each new revelation. Cecilia sat next to Jennifer, consoling her while Roberta went back to the kitchen. Bo began sifting through Phillip's documents again, looking for clues to his financial records.

As Joey and Thebb walked toward the bank entrance, Thebb commented, "I used to do business at this bank and know a few of the officers. I hope they aren't here now. It could be a problem."

"It's been about three years. Probably nothing to worry about. Besides, you're dead."

"Joey, that's not funny. This is a small town. The appearance of someone who's been missing for a long time is news. But the appearance of a dead person would really be big news. I just hope we can get out of here quickly."

"And remember, you are Annaliese Mueller now, not Thebb."

Joey opened the door to the bank. They went straight to the desk that handled the safe-deposit boxes. Luckily, the clerk behind the desk was young and had been at the bank only a few years. She didn't recognize Thebb. Thebb signed in as Annaliese Mueller. The woman asked for identification. Thebb presented her driver's license and passport. Everything was going well. The clerk asked her relationship to Phillip and Thebb showed her a copy of her marriage license and the keys to the boxes. The clerk hesitated, and Joey pulled out his badge and the warrant. He explained that Thebb had full legal authority to open the boxes. The clerk hesitated for another moment and then asked them to follow her.

In the confines of the privacy booth, Thebb opened the boxes. There were several thick manila envelopes, each containing documents relating to her uncle's will and the trust. She removed the envelopes, stuffed them in the tote bag, returned the boxes to the clerk, and left the bank with Joey.

When Thebb and Joey got back to Thebb's house, Joey called Rachel and told her the good news. She asked him to get the papers to her right away. "We need to nail this down quickly."

"Joey, you should have a sandwich," Cecilia suggested. "It's almost lunchtime, and we didn't have breakfast. Roberta has them already made."

"Okay, but it has to be quick. Cecilia, I think you should come with me to deliver the documents. I have to meet Rachel and Christi at Christi's office. We don't want people to see Thebb just yet."

"Yes, I agree, and we need to stop by your place on the way back so I can get my bag. I didn't expect to be staying in Doylestown tonight."

As they were leaving, Cecilia took Thebb aside and asked her to be kind to Jennifer. "She's distraught. None of this was her fault. She's pretty much in the same position you were in."

Joey tugged at Cecilia to leave. "We have to go. Thebb, we'll be back later this afternoon. I'll tell you over dinner what Rachel and Christi found. They may even be able to join us."

Thebb looked out the front window and watched Cecilia and Joey drive out onto the main road. She turned and told Roberta it would be okay for her to go home. But she admonished, "You cannot tell anyone about what's going on here. No one can know I'm back home. Not even your husband. Remember what Joey said about interfering with his investigation. In a few days, it will be all over, and my presence will no longer be secret. But not now. I'll let you know when it's okay."

CHAPTER 79

Two Kuefer & Bach employees rushed into Jim Kuefer's outer office and approached his secretary, asking to see Mr. Kuefer right away. They were excited and offered no pleasantries. Just a demand to see Mr. Kuefer immediately. His secretary was startled by their aggressiveness but did what her boss expected her to do. She told them they needed an appointment.

"He has a meeting starting in about fifteen minutes," she explained as she flipped through his appointment book, "and doesn't have an opening in his schedule until this afternoon." She didn't look up as she talked.

One of the employees said, "This is important!"

"But he just arrived and hasn't even had time to get his coat off," the secretary stated emphatically. "You'll simply have to wait until this afternoon."

The employees were not to be turned away. They told her two policemen were outside Mr. Mueller's office. They couldn't get in to see what was going on.

"The police said the office was sealed under a warrant, and no one was allowed to go in."

Mr. Kuefer's secretary stared at the employees, looking puzzled.

The door to Jim Kuefer's private office had been partially ajar, but suddenly it swung open, and Jim Kuefer came out.

"Did you say there are policemen in Phillip's office?" Jim asked authoritatively.

"Yes, sir," they each responded.

Without thanking the employees, Jim hurried to Phillip's outer office and tried to open the door. It was locked. He knocked on the door. No answer. He banged harder and demanded they open the door, yelling he was president of the firm. He listened carefully and could hear the opening of drawers and shuffling of paper. He banged on the door again and finally heard a metallic clank as the deadbolt lock slid back out of the door frame and the door began to open. He stepped back.

Bob Marino, flanked by two uniformed cops, stood in the doorway. He displayed his badge and stated, "I'm Detective Marino. Who are you and what do you want?"

Jim Kuefer was taken aback by Bob's authoritative manner. He replied, "I'm Jim Kuefer, president of this firm. I want to know what's going on in there."

Bob showed the warrant to Jim and explained he was searching for information related to Phillip Mueller's personal finances. He asked him to come in and shut the door to prevent employees in the hallway from looking in.

"Mr. Kuefer," Bob said politely, "we are searching for any personal records Mr. Mueller may have here in his office. We're not interested in information relative to Kuefer & Bach unless it involves Mr. Mueller's finances. Can you help us?"

"I'm afraid not, Detective," Jim responded angrily. "You'll have to talk to our financial officer, Adam Bach. He would be the one most likely to have that kind of information. But why are you searching Phillip's office? What's going on?"

Politely but firmly, Bob explained, "Mr. Kuefer, I know this investigation is unsettling, but please bear with us. Mr. Mueller has been arrested on felony charges related to his financial holdings and the death of a person involved in a criminal activity. We're sorry to cause a disturbance in your office. That's why we came so early and closed the door. If you can't help us find the documents we're looking for, you'll have to leave. We need to get back to our search."

"Look, Detective, Phil is the executive vice president of our firm, and I'm sure you've made some sort of mistake. You must have the wrong person. I've known Phil for a long time. He's highly respected in the financial community and wouldn't be involved in anything illegal. Where is he? I want to talk to him."

"I'm sure Mr. Mueller is an important officer in your firm, Mr. Kuefer," Bob said with a note of exasperation, "but I have work to do here, and if you have nothing to contribute you have to leave. Right now!"

Angrily slamming the door behind him, Jim hurried back to his office. He sternly addressed his secretary, "Get our attorney, Lance Senterfitt, on the phone immediately. I don't care what he's doing. Tell his secretary I have to talk to him right now. It's an emergency."

Kuefer & Bach Investments was a major client of the Moffitt and Senterfitt legal firm, and Jim Kuefer was pretty certain he could get Lance's attention immediately. He was right. Within minutes, Jim's secretary had Lance on the phone.

"Lance! We have a major problem here. The police have arrested Phil. I need you to find out what's going on. Something to do with his investments and somebody dying. The firm could be in serious jeopardy. I want you to get him out of jail right away. I'm going to call the mayor in a few minutes and see if we can get some answers from him. Do what it takes and stay in touch with me. This is important."

Jim immediately called his financial officer, Adam Bach, informed him of the emerging crisis, and asked him to come to his office for a telephone conference call with the mayor. Then he had his secretary rearrange his morning schedule.

Mayor Ray Rucci was a Kuefer & Bach client, and Jim Kuefer, as well as Adam and Phillip, had the mayor's private telephone number. Jim placed the call on his speaker phone.

"Good morning, Jim," the mayor pleasantly answered. "What have you got for me today? I hope it's something good."

"Hi, Ray. Adam is here with me on the speaker phone."

"Hi, Adam. With both of you on the line, it must be pretty important."

"Actually, Ray," Jim continued, "it's very important, and we need your assistance. Phil Mueller was arrested on a felony charge having something to do with his financial holdings and somebody getting killed. The police are in Phil's office right now going through his files."

"That's serious," the mayor answered. "I'll be glad to look into it immediately."

Jim explained, "I want to get Phil out of jail so we can find out why he was arrested. The police wouldn't tell me anything. I asked our attorney, Lance Senterfitt, to find where Phil is and arrange for his release. I think you met Lance at the Children's Hospital fund-raising dinner a few months ago. I'm hoping you can help us get to the bottom of this."

"Jim, I'll talk to the district attorney and see if he knows anything about Phil's arrest. Do you know if he has been arraigned yet?"

"All we know is what I have told you. I had the feeling, from the secretive way the detective was acting, that the police are trying to keep his arrest quiet and don't want to arraign him right away. They may be afraid of getting a lot of publicity, and we are too. We want to get him out of jail and keep this thing quiet. The firm doesn't need this kind of publicity. It could really hurt the local market."

"I'll do what I can," Ray assured Jim. "But if the media learns a vice president of Kuefer & Bach has been arrested, be prepared for a lot of coverage. Like I said, I'll talk to the DA and see if we can expedite the arraignment and get him out on bond. Tell Lance to stay in touch with me."

It was just past noon when the heavy bolt on the large steel door that sectioned off the high-security wing of the jail clanked twice, and the door screeched open. Two police security guards showed the duty guard their orders and asked him to open the cell holding Phillip Mueller.

Phillip immediately started demanding that he be allowed to call his lawyer. "You can't hold me here like this. It's illegal, and I want to call my lawyer."

The duty guard asked, "What's happening? I thought our orders were to hold this guy for a few days."

"I guess they changed their minds," one of the security guards answered. "We have orders from the assistant DA, Dave Kramer, to take him to his first appearance before the judge now. The judge is ready to hear his case and set the bail."

In one of the austere conference rooms down the hall from the main courtroom, Phillip was met by Robert Klinefelter, a well-known and highly successful trial lawyer.

"Mr. Muller, I'm Robert Klinefelter. Your firm has hired me to represent you, but I need you to sign this paper acknowledging I am your attorney."

In the first-appearance proceedings, Klinefelter asked the judge to release Phillip on his own recognizance. He stated Phillip was a pillar of the community and well-known for his charitable activities. Having no record, he argued, Phillip was not a flight risk. The assistant DA, Dave Kramer, stipulated there should be some level of bail to assure the defendant would appear in court. Bail was set at one hundred thousand dollars, paid by Kuefer & Bach Investments, and Phillip was released.

As soon as he exited the court room, Phillip borrowed Klinefelter's cell phone and called Jim Kuefer to thank him for his quick action. Jim warned him not to come to the office because the police had cordoned it off, and there was a cop standing guard.

"Phil, go home and get cleaned up," Jim suggested. "I'll come over later this afternoon, and we can hash this thing out. The mayor said he would try to keep your arraignment out of the newspaper for a while so we have some time to figure out how to handle the media. We have only a day or so before the story of your arrest breaks. And, Phil, I want to know what this is all about. It could do enormous damage to the firm."

"Thanks, Jim," Phillip responded. "I'm looking forward to straightening this out. I've been set up, and I think they are going to try to extort money from me. I'll see you this afternoon."

At the police station, Phillip claimed his personal items. Getting his car back required hiring a cab and driving to the police impoundment lot. His car was covered with dust, and all the interior compartments were open. He was seething over his treatment at the impoundment lot and the condition of his car.

CHAPTER 80

By the time Phillip got to his house southeast of Doylestown, it was approximately 4:00 p.m. He was surprised to see Jennifer's car parked in the circle. That wasn't where she was supposed to park when she was visiting, and she didn't get off work until 6:00 p.m. It was the kind of thing Annaliese would have done. Jennifer's job in Doylestown started at ten in the morning, and she usually didn't get home until six-thirty. He was concerned she would want to know why he didn't show up last night. Lately she had been preoccupied with wedding preparations so he hoped she wouldn't be upset. Nonetheless, he was looking forward to a happy reception. He parked in the garage and entered the house through the laundry room door. As he entered the kitchen, he saw a younger man pouring a drink from one of his bottles of Maker's Mark bourbon.

"Who the fuck are you?" Phillip demanded in a fit of growing rage. "Where's Jennifer?"

"Oh shit! You must be Phillip," Bo exclaimed as he turned to face him. "You're not supposed to be here."

Bo was caught off guard. He didn't expect Phillip to come home and burst in upon him without warning. Bo's response infuriated Phillip who immediately assumed Jennifer was having an affair with him.

Phillip ran forward and grabbed Bo by the throat, slamming him against the kitchen cabinets while shouting, "You son of a bitch! You didn't expect me to be home, did you? Where's Jennifer?"

Bo's glass of bourbon shattered as it hit the floor. He tried to use the bottle to hit Phillip, but it slipped from his hand and flew across the countertop smashing into a ceramic flowerpot before breaking on the floor. It looked odd, with the top shattered and the jagged edges of the main part of the bottle standing upright held together by the label.

Bo pulled his arms up to his chest and used his elbows to push Phillip away. Phillip came back and hit Bo hard on the side of the mouth splitting his lip. With blood dripping down his shirt, Bo spun around trying to get loose of Phillip's grasp. He used the back of his elbow to hit Phillip in the face knocking him back against the refrigerator. Bo moved in to punch Phillip, but Phillip swung upward, hitting Bo hard in the stomach and sending him back against the counter.

Bo could have been an even match for Phillip if he had been prepared. They were both in top physical condition, but Phillip had the advantage of surprise, and Bo was dazed by Phillip's sudden assault.

Phillip grabbed Bo by the throat with his left hand and began to pound his face with his right fist. Bo struggled to get away from the counter where he was boxed in. Phillip lifted him up and threw him onto the island counter under the hanging rack of pots. Bo coiled up and kicked Phillip in the chest, sending him against the other counter, causing Phillip to release a deep guttural cry. Bo was trying to get away long enough to get on his feet and gain a position to fight back. He slid off the island counter, knocking pots and pans off the overhead hanging rack. The cacophony of breaking glass and pots and pans bouncing off the countertops and tile floor echoed throughout the house.

Bo grabbed a large pot and landed a glancing blow to the side of Phillip's head. Phillip fell to the floor and lay still for a moment. Bo backed away trying to clear his head. But Phillip got up and charged him, knocking him across the kitchen and onto the floor. Phillip stood over Bo and started kicking him while yelling, "I'll teach you to fuck around with my fiancée, you dumb son of a bitch."

Thebb was in the master bathroom getting dressed after a shower and could not hear the commotion in the kitchen. It had been two days since she had the opportunity to take a shower. Joey had only one bathroom in his house, and there hadn't been time that morning to take one.

Hearing the commotion in the kitchen wasn't a problem for Jennifer who had been lying down in one of the guest bedrooms upstairs. The events of the morning were so traumatic she needed to rest and think about what she was going to do. She heard the glass breaking and the pots banging on the kitchen floor. She wondered what all the commotion was. Thebb had let Roberta go home so it couldn't be her making the noise. She heard shouting and cabinet's slamming. She ran down the stairs and into the kitchen to find Phillip stomping on Bo and yelling obscenities.

Jennifer screamed, "Stop, Phillip! You're hurting him. Stop!"

Phillip turned and pushed Jennifer away yelling, "You trashy bitch. I come home early and find your fucking boyfriend in the kitchen drinking my liquor." He turned back to Bo and gave another hard kick to Bo's chest saying, "When I'm through with you, you won't be fucking anyone for—"

Slam!

Jennifer hit Phillip hard on the back of the head with a pot. He started to go forward, yelling, "Son of a bitch." He steadied himself, grabbed her by the throat, and slapped her hard. She tried to fight back, screaming and kicking him in the crotch while trying to scratch his face. With growing rage, he grabbed her by the throat and crotch, lifted her up, and threw her across the island counter. She slid across the countertop, crashed into the corner of the opposite countertop, and fell onto the floor, landing on top of the jagged edges of the broken bourbon bottle. She lay still with blood gushing from her neck, but Phillip couldn't see her on the other side of the kitchen island.

Bo had gotten to his knees and was trying to stand when Phillip turned back. Bo hit Phillip hard in the stomach, and Phillip moaned and backed up. He tried to kick Bo, but Bo deflected the kick with his left arm and fell back on to the tile floor.

Thebb opened her bathroom door to hear banging and shouting downstairs. She ran down the stairs and stopped at the doorway to the kitchen. On one side of the kitchen, she saw Jennifer on the floor in a pool of blood. On the other side, she saw Bo deflect a kick from Phillip and fall backward onto the floor. She screamed at Bo to get up. Phillip turned, stopped, and stared at Thebb. His face turned white, and his mouth opened. He started yelling, "You're supposed to be dead. Toro said you were dead. You've tricked me. You fucking bitch!"

Bo used Phillip's surprise at seeing Thebb to crawl back away from Phillip and get his bearing. His mouth and nose were bleeding. His left eye was black and swelling, his left hand felt broken, and he was having trouble breathing. He tried to get up but fell down again.

Thebb saw Bo fall and then looked at Jennifer. Phillip followed Thebb's glance and saw Jennifer. Again he looked stunned. As Phillip stared, transfixed, at Jennifer on the floor with blood pooling around her head and hair, Thebb seized the opportunity to run back up the stairs to the bedroom. She searched her bag desperately looking for her Glock. Phillip glanced at Jennifer for only a moment before his rage returned, and he bolted upstairs to find Thebb.

Thebb found her Glock and turned to see Phillip charging toward her. She pulled the slide to chamber a round but took too long. Phillip grabbed her arm and hit her in the face, hard, spinning her around. She lost her grip on the Glock, and it bounced off the bed onto the floor. Thebb fell on the bed, hitting her face on the top rail of the footboard. She tried to roll away, but Phillip pulled her forward and hit her in the face with his knee while yelling names at her. As they scuffled, they bumped the gun and it slid away, stopping in the hallway near the head of the stairs. Phillip grabbed Thebb by the right arm and hit her full force in the face. She heard a resounding crunching sound and fell backward, bouncing off the end of the bed and landing with her chest on the footboard. He grabbed her by the legs and pulled her off the bed. She fell to the floor on her face. Using her hair, he lifted her to a sitting position with her back to the bed. Then he kneed her in the face, reached over her chest and began to choke her. She was trying to defend herself, scratching his face and hitting him any place she could.

Phillip lifted Thebb up by the throat, choking her with both hands, and yelled, "This time you're not going to get away! This is it!"

As Thebb struggled, with only her toes touching the floor, Bo grabbed Phillip by the back of his collar and yanked back hard. Phillip let go of Thebb, and he and Bo fell backward together to the floor, each of them struggling to get on top of the other. They rolled out onto the hallway floor. Phillip tried to hit Bo, but Bo flipped him over.

Phillip bumped the Glock causing it to slide out from under him. It bounced down the stairs. Twisting and somersaulting as it bounced downward, hitting a stair, skipping several stairs, and hitting a final stair before landing on the foyer floor, spinning on its side.

Bo jumped on top of Phillip and hit him in the face, but Phillip used his knees and shoved Bo off. As they struggled, each trying to gain an advantage over the other, they tumbled down the staircase with Phillip landing on top of Bo. With a decidedly loud thud, Bo's head hit the floor. He stopped fighting. He didn't move.

The gun was still slowly spinning next to Bo's head. Phillip grabbed the gun and stood up. He looked at Bo and took a deep breath.

Thebb, bleeding profusely from her nose and mouth, rolled across the bed to retrieve her bag. She found the Beretta and staggered out the bedroom door. While pulling the slide on the Beretta, she saw Phillip picking up the Glock. She slid to a prone position at the head of the stairs with the Beretta pointed at Phillip. She braced her hand and took aim.

As Phillip stood up with the Glock in his hand, the front door opened, and Cecilia walked in. She saw Bo on the floor, bloody and still, and Phillip with the gun. She turned to run, but Phillip was quick and caught her by her long hair. He dragged her back to the foot of the stairs, screaming and kicking. She lost her balance and fell. She kept screaming and trying to hit him, but he put the gun to her head and yelled for her to shut up.

Thebb was on the floor at the top of the landing aiming her Beretta at Phillip. Even with Cecilia in front of him, he made a sizable target. He looked up and saw Thebb with another gun and lifted Cecilia up in front of him as a shield. He fired the Glock three times at Thebb. One bullet hit the staircase spindle next to Thebb and peppered her with splinters. One shot hit the riser on the stair step below her, and the last shot went over her head. But she didn't flinch. She didn't move. Lying on the upper landing floor, Thebb made a small target. She lay still, bracing the Beretta and keeping her aim on Phillip.

Phillip continued pointing his gun toward Thebb and yelled for her to drop her gun. He couldn't get off an accurate shot with Cecilia squirming, screaming, and kicking. Thebb wiggled back a little to make an even smaller target but kept a deadly aim on Phillip. He yelled again for her to drop her gun or he would shoot the woman. Thebb yelled back if he hurt her she would shoot him. She demanded he drop his gun.

Joey, who was on the porch getting ready to open the front door, heard the gunshots. He had been carrying Cecilia's bag. He dropped the bag, drew his gun, pushed the door open, and leaped inside, landing on the floor with his gun pointed toward Phillip. He saw Bo on the ground and Phillip holding Cecilia while pointing a gun up the stairs. Phillip turned and shot at Joey, twice. He narrowly missed him with each shot. Instantly, two more shots rang out. Phillip dropped Cecilia and fell to the floor half on top of her. Cecilia lay still for a moment, partially in shock and partially to determine if she was hurt.

Joey continued to lay frozen, gun in hand, assessing the situation. He couldn't see where the shots had come from. He scanned the living room, got up off the floor, and cautiously looked up the stairs. Thebb was at the head of the stairs with her gun in hand, still pointed at Phillip. He quickly motioned to Thebb he was there, took Phillip's gun, and checked to see if Cecilia was okay.

Finding Cecilia to be okay but shaken, Joey ran up the stairs to Thebb. She was badly hurt. She had a gash on her left cheek, and the right side of her face was turning blue and swelling. Both eyes had blood in them. When he tried to move her, she cried out in pain. Her ribs hurt. He gently picked her up and placed her on the bed, asking if she was shot. She said she wasn't. He told her that he would be right back and ran down the stairs, three steps at a time to check on Bo. When Bo and Phillip tumbled down the stairs, Bo hit his head hard and lay unconscious on the floor. Joey tried to revive him but couldn't. Cecilia ran to get a wet towel. A long, low, terrifying scream came from the kitchen. Joey left Bo to go to Cecilia. She was bending over Jennifer who was sprawled on the floor in a massive pool of blood. Cecilia checked for a pulse. There was none!

CHAPTER 81

Late in the afternoon, Jim Kuefer picked up Lance Senterfitt, the firm's business attorney, and Robert Klinefelter, Phillip's trial lawyer, to drive out to Phillip's house in Bucks County. They needed to know exactly why Phillip was arrested and map out a strategy for both defending him and limiting damage to the firm that was sure to follow. Jim was extremely concerned about the publicity and wanted to mitigate as much of the fallout as possible.

As they approached Phillip's house, they saw red, blue, and white flashing lights from numerous sheriff's vehicles and two ambulances. Jim turned into the driveway and parked in the grass off to the side of several sheriffs' cars. When they got to the front door, a deputy sheriff stopped them and told them the area was restricted. Several deputies forced them aside as two EMTs maneuvered a gurney carrying Bo to one of the ambulances. Then two more EMTs pushed another gurney carrying Thebb toward the other ambulance. Cecilia was alongside the gurney and went in the ambulance with Thebb. With sirens blaring, the two ambulances sped off to the Doylestown Hospital.

Jim was totally shaken when he saw Thebb and called out, "Oh my god! That's Phillip's wife, Anna! This is impossible! Oh my god! This can't be."

Lance asked one of the deputies if he could talk to Phillip Mueller, the owner of the house. The deputy guarding the door refused to let them enter. He explained the house was a crime scene, and Phillip Mueller and Jennifer Rechenmacher were dead. On hearing Phillip was dead, Lance and Robert had to help Jim sit on the porch steps.

One of the deputies informed Joey someone was asking for Phillip. Joey went outside and talked with Jim and the two attorneys.

"Who are you folks, and why are you here?" Joey firmly asked Jim. Jim just looked at Joey without answering. Phillip Mueller had been Jim's protégé, and Jim had guided him to a senior position in the firm. He had a special affection for Phillip. Learning he was dead was a serious blow. He was speechless at the turn of events.

Lance interceded, "This is Jim Kuefer. He's Phillip's boss at Kuefer & Bach. I'm Lance Senterfitt, Jim's lawyer. And this is Robert Klinefelter, Phillip's attorney. Who are the people who were just taken away in the ambulances?"

Joey responded, "Dieter Boarman and Annaliese Mueller, Phillip's wife."

"But I thought Phillip's wife was dead," Lance stated in surprise. "Are you sure that was her?"

"Yes, we're sure! Mr. Kuefer, you have to leave. We have to deal with the crime scene here. We'll contact you tomorrow. Please be prepared to help us find all of Mr. Mueller's personal financial documents. And, Mr. Senterfitt, as Mr. Kuefer's attorney, you are aware any effort to hide Mr. Mueller's documents and assets is a crime punishable by law."

Lance answered, "Yes. We'll make every effort to find any relevant information your colleagues may have overlooked this morning. Mr. Kuefer has nothing to hide."

When Joey finally got to the hospital, Cecilia greeted him with good news. "Bo is awake and will be released in a couple of days. He has a concussion and a split in his scalp that the doctors sewed up. He also has a broken hand they set in a cast. Thebb has two cracked ribs and a fractured cheekbone. The facial surgeons are working on her now, and they assured me any scars would be almost unnoticeable. She will also be getting out in a few days, but she'll be wearing a head brace to hold her cheek in the proper position for a while."

"Did Thebb or Bo tell you what happened?"

"From the little Bo was able to tell us, he tried to stop Phillip from hitting Thebb, and then they fell down the stairs. He said if he hadn't stopped Phillip when he did, Phillip would have killed her."

421

Joey called Bob advising him he and Cecilia were at the hospital with Thebb and Bo. He gave Bob a brief description of what had happened. Joey said he and Cecilia would meet up with him and the girls back at his house instead of the Mueller place. He said he would give them all the details when he got home. The documents they had recovered would be more important than ever.

CHAPTER 82

Thebb and Bo were released from the Doylestown Hospital after two days. Cecilia and Joey drove them to Thebb's house. When they arrived, Thebb announced she wanted to begin using her real name, Annaliese or Anna. "Thebb's era has passed. She no longer exists."

Cecilia stayed for several weeks to help Anna until the external brace for her fractured cheekbone was removed. Roberta had initially refused to come back to work, but Anna persuaded her to return with a higher salary and assurances there would be no more violence at the house. It came as no surprise when Bo announced he would not be rejoining the crew of the *DOVE*.

As the months went by, Cecilia continued to be a frequent visitor, staying several days at a time. She divided her time between visiting Anna and Bo and the *DOVE*. Bart had hired a new cook and crew member and was training them, something he hadn't had to do for a long time.

Over the next few months, Joey and Rachel also were occasional guests. When they could get away from work, they accompanied Anna to the legal hearings required to establish her rights to her inheritance. Christi methodically managed Anna's legal affairs and suggested which investment firms she should use to manage her trust money.

Four months later, Joey and Bob got a call from the DA's office requesting they attend a meeting the next morning with Assistant DA David Kramer. The subject of the meeting was Phillip Mueller and Pavel Torolovich. Mr. Kramer's secretary asked that they not be late.

David Kramer's office was located in one corner of the third floor of city hall. The DA occupied a much larger corner office at the other end of the long corridor with many smaller offices in between.

Joey and Bob arrived promptly at 9:00 a.m. as requested and introduced themselves to Mr. Kramer's secretary. She explained he was in a meeting with the mayor and the district attorney and would be a few minutes late. She asked them to have a seat and offered them coffee. They declined. They shouldn't have. David Kramer was forty minutes late. When he returned, he pleasantly invited them into his office. David sat at the end of a large, heavy, six-person meeting table and invited Joey and Bob to sit on either side so he could be between them.

As they took their seats, Joey introduced himself, "Good morning. I'm Detective Joey Degrassi, and this is Detective Bob Marino."

"I'm the principal assistant district attorney, David Kramer, but please call me Dave."

"Degrassi? I know that name from somewhere."

"I hope it's for something good."

"About a year or so ago, a cop caught some criminals by pouring soap on a loading platform. Everyone was talking about it and making jokes about what a slick arrest it was. That was you, wasn't it?"

"Actually, yes, sir. It was," Joey admitted with a smile.

"You may not remember, but we met at the arraignment. That was excellent police work. We need more cops like you."

"Thank you, sir."

"I have an important meeting in a little while. So let me get right to the point. About three and a half years ago, several of our detectives were killed in a shoot-out with drug dealers. We penetrated the cartel's organization and captured their accounting records. My office played a major role in that operation. It was a breakthrough for our anti-drug campaign. Using information we deciphered in their coded books, we arrested most of the people involved, including a number of dirty cops and several city commissioners. The mayor and DA created a special prosecutorial team to deal with them, and I was appointed to head it up."

"Oh yes, I remember when that happened," Bob interjected. "Half the detectives in the city were involved in making the arrests. It was a huge success."

"Well, we never actually closed the case. We thought there might be a few more members of the cartel we could arrest, but nothing has happened for several years. That is, until this week."

"So what happened?" Joey asked, quizzically.

"The crime lab sent me a report on a ballistics match for the bullets from the gun Phillip Mueller used to try to kill his wife several months back. Those bullets matched the ones we recovered from two of our detectives who were killed in a shoot-out with members of the drug cartel. It occurred about the same time when we broke the case. They also matched the bullets we recovered from two drug dealers who were killed that same day."

There was silence as Joey and Bob looked at each other and then at Dave.

"Wow," Bob uttered. "That's amazing, but our investigation of Mueller didn't turn up anything related to drug dealing."

"Yeah," Joey added. "Are the lab folks sure of the match? From what we learned about Mueller, it's hard to believe he was involved in killing a couple of cops or into drugs for that matter."

"Yes. They're sure. I had my assistant review the records looking for a link between Mueller and the drug dealer shoot-out. And she found one."

"And that is?" Joey asked.

"Pavel Torolovich! We've been after him for a long time and recently uncovered evidence he was closely connected with Maroon Espidito, the man we believe was the leader of the drug cartel in Philadelphia. When we did our big sweep of the cartel, Espidito got away. That was unfortunate, but he was killed later in a shoot-out with park police in the Virgin Islands. When we learned Mueller had hired Torolovich to kill his wife, it all fit. We believe it was Torolovich who gave the gun to Mueller to kill his wife."

"Wow," Bob exclaimed. "So Torolovich may have killed the two detectives. That's a great piece of work."

"We interrogated him in jail and asked about the gun. He said he might have given it to Mueller, but then again, he might not have. He's trying to use it as a bargaining chip to get full immunity on all counts pending against him. That's simply not going to happen. We already gave him reduced charges on the death of his partner, Nickoli Zaturetsky. My assistant said during her interrogation of Torolovich it became obvious he and Espidito were the ones who shot the detectives. We're going to charge him with those deaths too. Since Mueller had a close association with Torolovich and had hired him to kill his wife, he was the likely suspect for having provided Mueller with that specific gun."

Dave went on, "So we're closing the case. That's one of the reasons I invited you here. I wanted to inform you of the results of our investigation so you can close your case too. I think we have tied up this package very neatly."

With a big smile, Bob asked, "You said that was one of the reasons you invited us here. Is there anything else you want to talk to us about?"

"Ah yes, there is. Will you please come with me to the DA's office?" David called his secretary on his intercom and asked her to notify the DA he was on his way.

When David Kramer opened the door to the DA's office, Joey saw his captain, the police commissioner, the district attorney, and the mayor standing together. The mayor called out Joey's name and asked him to come forward and receive an award for outstanding service while under fire.

Joey turned to Bob. "I thought I asked you not to do this."

"Yeah, you did, but I didn't listen! So now you get a raise, and we both get promotions."

After the mayor presented Joey with his award, he called David Kramer to come forward and receive an award for closing the drug cartel case and solving the murder of the two detectives three and a half years ago.

CHAPTER 83

David Kramer returned to his office, closed the thick office door, sat in his overstuffed chair, opened his bottom desk drawer, and took out his prized box of Oliva Master Cigars. He didn't smoke often, usually only as a self-reward when things went well. He carefully lit a cigar and leaned deep into his chair. After a few celebratory puffs, he began to think about how well things turned out. The only thing that would make his day better would be finding the bank account numbers for the millions of dollars Tatianna had stashed in foreign banks. But only Tatianna knew which banks and the account numbers. And she's dead. He sat marveling how lucky he had been in not getting caught when the bitch mailed the DA the accounting ledgers.

She was one smart bitch! By sending the goddamn ledgers to the DA, she virtually eliminated the chance that anyone could ever find her. They would all be in jail, except old Maroon. He was a cagey bastard all right. I never figured out how he escaped the dragnet the cops had out for him.

A puff on the cigar. *Goddamn Maroon. He thought he was being so damn smart by keeping Tatianna a secret and having her handle all the records. We should have had a backup for the account numbers. Maybe he was planning to run off with her and take all the money too. Wouldn't doubt it!*

More puffs on the cigar. *They were both so clever, and then they got themselves killed by park police. Not even real cops.*

Another couple of puffs on the cigar. *Yep, she was smart. But how did she screw up and get identified by a St. Thomas customs agent?*

She was too smart to do that. But then again, what if the customs agent made a mistake, and it wasn't Tatianna after all? Hmm! I didn't think about that. I was so hell-bent to find her, I didn't question it might not have been Tatianna. I should have made sure it really was her. But if it wasn't, then who was the woman who got killed with Maroon? And where is Tatianna?

As Dave sat musing about the past events, a thought crossed his mind, and he sat up straighter. *What if it wasn't Torolovich's gun used to kill the cops but was Mueller's all along? Then it could have been Mueller who killed the two cops. But that doesn't fit with what we know about him. On the other hand, his dead wife, who wasn't really dead, was in the Virgin Islands when Tatianna was supposedly there. So if she wasn't dead, then who the fuck was lying on the sidewalk, and why did Mueller identify her as his wife? Why would he have done that? Maybe the dead woman on the sidewalk was Tatianna, and he knew it.*

Naw!

But then again . . .

David got up and went to the large Palladian window on the right side of his desk. He stood looking out over the city streets thinking.

Several puffs on the cigar. *How does Mueller's wife fit into all this? Was she in cahoots with Tatianna? Could she have gotten the ledgers? Did she take off with the account numbers and that's why Mueller tried to kill her? Could this trust fund business be a cover for what they were doing?*

Hmmm!

CHAPTER 84

A month after Joey's award, Cecilia got a call from Anna inviting Jack and her to a celebration at her home in Bucks County. Her face was healing, and Bo was regaining the use of his hand. It was time to bring their close friends together for a reunion and some announcements.

Cecilia flew in early so she and Anna could plan the dinner party. Roberta brought in two relatives to help prepare the meal. Anna and Cecilia would oversee their cooking. Everyone important to Anna and Bo was invited. Bart left the *DOVE* in the care of Rick and Eddie. Unfortunately, George and Mike couldn't be located; they were probably away sailing.

The seafood dinner of red snapper was a salute to the Caribbean and Cecilia's Italian cooking. It was prepared three ways. Cecilia prepared the red snapper by baking it in grape leaves saturated in olive oil. Then she doused it with a sauce of garlic, capers, parsley, and lemon zest sautéed in sherry. Anna preferred the snapper encrusted with coconut and lime, served with jicama slaw and a dipping sauce of Dijon mustard and lime juice mixed with mayonnaise. Not to be outdone, Roberta presented the red snapper, broiled and basted with a mix of olive oil, butter, and lemon juice, and served under a covering of papaya relish. Of course, the red snapper, however prepared, was accompanied by risotto with porcini mushrooms and shrimp sautéed in pinot grigio with fresh garlic.

Dessert was Cecilia's favorite—tiramisu. She prepared it using French fromage frais and Kahlua. She uniquely prepared it in separate small individual serving bowls. And she used a lot of Kahlua.

After dessert, over Cognac, Benedictine, and other liqueurs, Anna and Bo presented each guest a small remembrance they had purchased in Doylestown. Everyone except Joey, Rachel, and Bart. It was then that Rachel asked for everyone's attention. She had an announcement. She and Joey were engaged and planned on getting married in a few months. Everyone toasted them.

After a round of congratulations, Bo stood up and announced he and Anna were also getting married. There was more toasting.

"When is the wedding?" Cecilia asked Bo.

Bo looked at Anna, smiled broadly, and answered, "After we take possession of our new boat. It's a sixty-five-foot Morgan. A center cockpit ketch. We'll pick it up in Baltimore. We've rented a house there so we can be close to the shipyard where the finishing work is being done." Anna was smiling broadly and watching Bo with pride.

"So you're moving to Baltimore?" Joey asked, showing great disappointment.

"Actually yes, we are," Anna answered. "And after the Morgan is ready, we're planning a two-year Caribbean cruise, from Grand Cayman to Grenada. We never visited the Caymans on the *DOVE*."

"But what about this house?" Cecilia asked. "Who's going to take care of it?"

"It will be well taken care of, Cecilia," Anna answered. "As some of you may know, Christi is my financial attorney and advisor. She set up a special trust fund specifically designed to take care of the house. The return on the principal will be used to pay for all the utilities, repairs, property maintenance, and taxes. Christi says the trust fund could last indefinitely if no major renovations or additions are made to the house."

"Having the funds available is one thing, Anna," Cecilia commented, "but who is going to manage the house and decide when it needs maintenance?"

With a big smile, Anna answered, "Joey!"

Joey was visibly taken back. "Anna, I don't think I'm the right person for that. I would like to help, but your house is a long way from my place and my job. Besides, I'm not sure I would know how to maintain a big house like this."

The room grew quiet with everyone looking at Joey and then Anna. That is, except for Bob and Christi who were smiling broadly.

Cecilia broke the silence, "Anna, don't you think it would be an imposition to ask Joey to take care of the house? Especially for someone who isn't living here. He would have to travel back and forth to check on it."

"No, I don't think so," Anna answered with a growing smile. "After all, when Bo and I move to Baltimore, it will be his house. It's our wedding present. Christi leaked Joey and Rachel's engagement to us about a month ago."

Neither Joey nor Rachel could speak. They just sat staring at Anna with their mouths open while everyone hooted and clapped approval. Christi hugged Rachel, and Bob hugged Joey. But they both sat motionless listening to the chatter of everyone congratulating them.

"So you're going to spend two years sailing?" Bob asked. "Will you have a base of operation somewhere?"

"We haven't decided on that yet."

"Well," Bart interrupted, "if you're going to be in the Caribbean, you can visit me on the *Dove*."

"No," Anna smiled. "You see, when we ordered the Morgan, they agreed to give us a much better price if we bought two." Bo handed Bart a large envelope. Inside, Bart found a picture of a sixty-five-foot ketch. Anna continued, "Bart, for years you've wanted your own charter company, but you needed a sailboat. Now you have one." Everyone congratulated Bart.

Cecilia, with a big smile, spoke up, "Bart, Anna and I have agreed you will have to find us a new captain for the *Dove* before you can take ownership of your new boat. And you have to agree not to hire Rick or Eddie. They stay with the *Dove*."

CHAPTER 85

Bo was in the bedroom of their newly rented house in Baltimore, unpacking boxes and storing personal items in the dresser drawers. Anna was hanging clothes in the small closet.

"Anna, where do you want me to put this jewelry box?"

"Just put it in the top drawer."

As Bo placed the box in the drawer, he opened it to make sure everything was in its place.

Among the few pieces of costume jewelry, one item caught his attention. It wasn't jewelry. He picked it up, turned to Anna, and asked, "Anna, didn't you leave the key to our safe-deposit box with Christi's legal firm for security?"

"Yes, I'm sure I did. Why?"

"Well, there's a key here that looks like a safe-deposit box key. It has the letters 'CCBCI' and a number impressed in it. What is it?"

Anna stopped hanging clothes in the closet and walked over to Bo. She held out her hand for Bo to give the key to her. She looked at it.

"Bo, I've been meaning to tell you about this key. I was waiting until we were on our way to the Cayman Islands. There's something I have to do in George Town."

CHAPTER 86

Eight months had passed since David Kramer received his award for closing the drug cartel case when the district attorney's secretary called. The DA wanted to see him right away.

As Dave entered the office, the DA looked up from his desk and excitedly greeted him, saying, "Dave, you're not going to believe this, but we just received a package, a briefcase actually, with another of the drug cartel's accounting books."

"You're kidding!" Dave responded with surprise. "Another ledger?"

"But that's not all, Dave. This is unbelievable. Totally unbelievable. Step over here and look at this briefcase."

"Wow, it's full of money!"

"Three hundred and sixty thousand dollars to be exact."

"This is unbelievable!" Dave mumbled in a halting voice while losing color in his face.

"Yeah," the DA agreed. "The ledger was in the briefcase with the money! Can you believe that?"

"It's incredible," Dave responded while staring at the money. "But . . . where's the ledger?"

"It's down in the crime lab," the DA explained. "It was kind of odd. The briefcase was locked, but the key was tied to the handle. It looked suspicious, so I sent it down to the lab to have it x-rayed. But it was okay, and we opened it this morning."

Dave backed away from the table with the briefcase and asked, "Did you got a chance to look the ledger over?"

"Yes, and although the entries in this latest ledger are in code, the lab guys say it's not as complex as the code in the earlier ledgers. They think it may help them unravel the remaining sections of the first set of ledgers. This may be the break we've been waiting for. I hope it is."

"But why did someone send us the money?" Dave haltingly asked.

"We don't know, but I bet it's drug money."

"Yeah, it probably is."

"Dave, you did such a great job heading up our special prosecutorial team after we received the first set of books that I want you to personally oversee the transcription of this latest ledger. I'm going to establish another team, and you will be in charge. This is definitely a stroke of good luck. Somebody is looking out for us."

Looking perplexed, Dave asked, "Where was the package mailed?"

"Unfortunately," the DA answered, "that's a problem. The mailroom assistant discarded the box it came in. By the time I saw the briefcase and sent it down to the lab, the trash collectors had taken the box away."

Looking distraught, Dave stated, "So we don't know where it came from!"

"The mailroom guy can only remember the box had a lot of unusual-looking stamps on it."

Dave walked over to the DA's large window and stared out at the city.

"Is there a problem, Dave?" the DA asked. "You don't look well!"